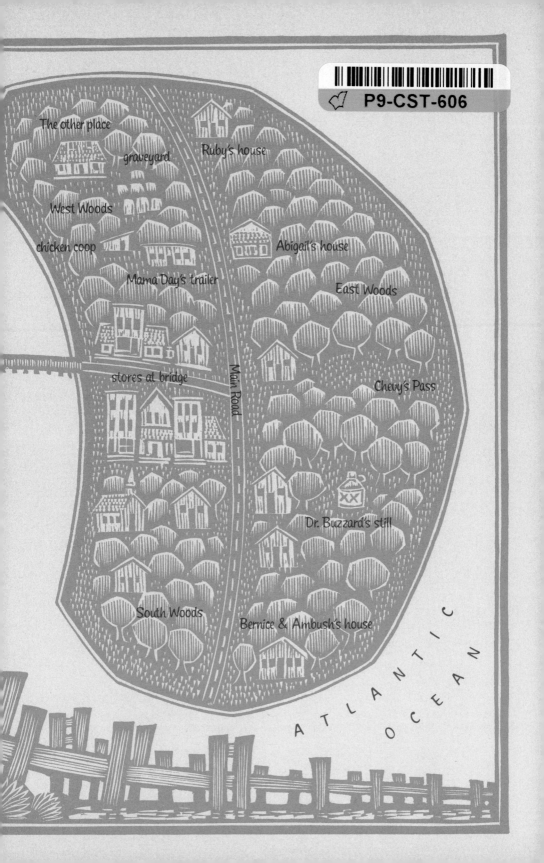

MAMA DAY

Books by Gloria Naylor

THE WOMEN OF BREWSTER PLACE

LINDEN HILLS

MAMA DAY

MAMA DAY

GLORIA NAYLOR

NEW YORK

TICKNOR & FIELDS

1 9 8 8

THE AUTHOR
WISHES TO THANK
THE NATIONAL ENDOWMENT FOR THE ARTS
FOR ITS GENEROUS SUPPORT DURING THE WRITING
OF THIS NOVEL.

For information about permission to reproduce selections from this book,
write to Permissions, Ticknor & Fields, 52 Vanderbilt Avenue, New York,
New York 10017.

Library of Congress Cataloging-in-Publication Data

Naylor, Gloria.
Mama Day.

I. Title.
PS3564.A895M3 1988   813'.54   87-18157
ISBN 0-89919-716-7

Printed in the United States of America
Q 10 9 8 7 6 5 4 3 2 1

"Take My Hand Precious Lord" by Thomas A. Dorsey. Copyright ©
1938 by Hill & Range Songs, Inc. Copyright renewed and assigned to
Unichappell Music, Inc. International copyright secured. All rights re-
served. Used by permission.

Endpaper map by David Frampton.

For Corlies Morgan Smith

MAMA
DAY

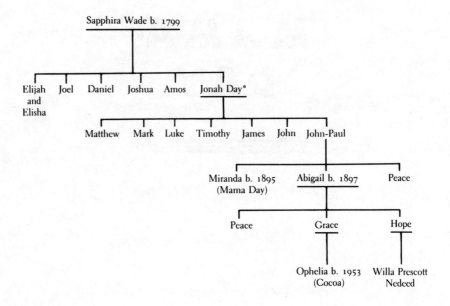

*"God rested on the seventh day and so would she." Hence, the family's last name.

Tuesday, 3rd Day August, 1819

Sold to Mister Bascombe Wade of Willow Springs, one negress answering to the name Sapphira. Age 20. Pure African stock. Limbs and teeth sound. All warranty against the vices and maladies prescribed by law do not hold forth; purchaser being in full knowledge—and affixing signature in witness thereof—that said Sapphira is half prime, inflicted with sullenness and entertains a bilious nature, having resisted under reasonable chastisement the performance of field or domestic labour. Has served on occasion in the capacity of midwife and nurse, not without extreme mischief and suspicions of delving in witchcraft.

Conditions of Sale
one-half gold tender, one-half goods in kind.
Final.

WILLOW SPRINGS. Everybody knows but nobody talks about the legend of Sapphira Wade. A true conjure woman: satin black, biscuit cream, red as Georgia clay: depending upon which of us takes a mind to her. She could walk through a lightning storm without being touched; grab a bolt of lightning in the palm of her hand; use the heat of lightning to start the kindling going under her medicine pot: depending upon which of us takes a mind to her. She turned the moon into salve, the stars into a swaddling cloth, and healed the wounds of every creature walking up on two or down on four. It ain't about right or wrong, truth or lies; it's about a slave woman who brought a whole new meaning to both them words, soon as you cross over here from beyond the bridge. And somehow, some way, it happened in 1823: she smothered Bascombe Wade in his very bed and lived to tell the story for a thousand days. 1823: married Bascombe Wade, bore him seven sons in just a thousand days, to put a dagger through his kidney and escape the hangman's noose, laughing in a burst of flames. 1823: persuaded Bascombe Wade in a thousand days to deed all his slaves every inch of land in Willow Springs, poisoned him for his trouble, to go on and bear seven sons — by person or persons unknown. Mixing it all together and keeping everything that done shifted down through the holes of time, you end up with the death of Bascombe Wade (there's his tombstone right out by Chevy's Pass), the deeds to our land (all marked back to the very year), and seven sons (ain't Miss Abigail and Mama Day the granddaughters of that seventh boy?). The wild card in all this is the thousand days, and we guess if we put our heads together we'd come up with something — which ain't possible since Sapphira Wade don't live in the part of our memory we can use to form words.

But ain't a soul in Willow Springs don't know that little dark girls, hair all braided up with colored twine, got their "18 & 23's coming down" when they lean too long over them back yard fences, laughing at the antics of little dark boys who got the nerve to be "breathing 18 & 23" with mother's milk still on their tongues. And if she leans there just a mite too long or grins a bit too wide, it's gonna bring a holler straight through the dusty screen door. "Get your bow-legged self 'way from my fence, Johnny Blue. Won't be no 'early 18 & 23's' coming here for me to rock. I'm still raising her." Yes, the *name* Sapphira Wade is never breathed out of a single mouth in Willow Springs. But who don't know that old twisted-lip manager at the Sheraton Hotel beyond the bridge, offering Winky Browne only twelve dollars for his whole boatload of crawdaddies — "tried to 18 & 23 him," if he tried to do a thing? We all sitting here, a hop, skip, and one Christmas left before the year 2000, and ain't nobody told him niggers can read now? Like the menus in his restaurant don't say a handful of crawdaddies sprinkled over a little bowl of crushed ice is almost twelve dollars? Call it shrimp cocktail, or whatever he want — we can count, too. And the price of everything that swims, crawls, or lays at the bottom of The Sound went up in 1985, during the season we had that "18 & 23 summer" and the bridge blew down. Folks didn't take their lives in their hands out there in that treacherous water just to be doing it — ain't that much 18 & 23 in the world.

But that old hotel manager don't make no never mind. He's the least of what we done had to deal with here in Willow Springs. Malaria. Union soldiers. Sandy soil. Two big depressions. Hurricanes. Not to mention these new real estate developers who think we gonna sell our shore land just because we ain't fool enough to live there. Started coming over here in the early '90s, talking "vacation paradise," talking "pic-ture-ess." Like Winky said, we'd have to pick their ass out the bottom of the marsh first hurricane blow through here again. See, they just thinking about building where they ain't got no state taxes — never been and never will be, 'cause Willow Springs ain't in no state. Georgia and South Carolina done tried, though — been trying since right after the Civil War to prove that Willow Springs belong to one or the other of them. Look on any of them old maps they hurried and drew up soon as the Union soldiers pulled out and you can see that the only thing connects us to the mainland is a bridge — and even that gotta be rebuilt after every big storm. (They was talking about steel and concrete way back, but since Georgia and South Carolina couldn't claim the taxes, nobody wanted to shell out for the work. So we rebuild it ourselves when need be, and build it how we need it — strong enough to last till the next big wind. Only need a steel and concrete bridge once every seventy years or so. Wood and pitch is a tenth of the cost and serves us a good sixty-nine years — matter of simple arithmetic.) But anyways, all forty-nine square miles curves like a bow, stretching toward Georgia on the south end and South Carolina on the north, and right smack in the middle where each foot of our bridge sits is the dividing line between them two states.

So who it belong to? It belongs to us — clean and simple. And it belonged to our daddies, and our daddies before them, and them too — who at one time all belonged to Bascombe Wade. And when they tried to trace him and how he got it, found out he wasn't even American. Was Norway-born or something, and the land had been sitting in his family over there in Europe since it got explored and claimed by the Vikings — imagine that. So thanks to the conjuring of Sapphira Wade we got it from Norway or theres about, and if taxes owed, it's owed to them. But ain't no Vikings or anybody else from over in Europe come to us with the foolishness that them folks out of Columbia and Atlanta come with — we was being un-American. And the way we saw it, America ain't entered the question at all when it come to our land: Sapphira was African-born, Bascombe Wade was from Norway, and it was the 18 & 23'ing that went down between them two put deeds in our hands. And we wasn't even Americans when we got it — was slaves. And the laws about slaves not owning nothing in Georgia and South Carolina don't apply, 'cause the land wasn't then — and isn't now — in either of them places. When there was lots of cotton here, and we baled it up and sold it beyond the bridge, we paid our taxes to the U.S. of A. And we keeps account of all the fishing that's done and sold beyond the bridge, all the little truck farming. And later when we had to go over there to work or our children went, we paid taxes out of them earnings. We pays taxes on the telephone lines and electrical wires run over The Sound. Ain't nobody here about breaking the law. But Georgia and South Carolina ain't seeing the shine off a penny for our land, our homes, our roads, or our bridge. Well, they fought each other up to the Supreme Court about the whole matter, and it came to a draw. We guess they got so tired out from that, they decided to leave us be — until them developers started swarming over here like sand flies at a Sunday picnic.

Sure, we coulda used the money and weren't using the land. But like Mama Day told 'em (we knew to send 'em straight over there to her and Miss Abigail), they didn't come huffing and sweating all this way in them dark gaberdine suits if they didn't think our land could make them a bundle of money, and the way we saw it, there was enough land — shoreline, that is — to make us all pretty comfortable. And calculating on the basis of all them fancy plans they had in mind, a million an acre wasn't asking too much. Flap, flap, flap — Lord, didn't them jaws and silk ties move in the wind. The land wouldn't be worth that if they couldn't *build* on it. Yes, suh, she told 'em, and they couldn't build on it unless we *sold* it. So we get ours now, and they get theirs later. You shoulda seen them coattails flapping back across The Sound with all their lies about "community uplift" and "better jobs." 'Cause it weren't about no them now and us later — was them now and us never. Hadn't we seen it happen back in the '80s on St. Helena, Daufuskie, and St. John's? And before that in the '60s on Hilton Head? Got them folks' land, built fences around it first thing, and then brought in all the builders and high-paid managers from mainside — ain't nobody on them islands benefited. And the only dark faces you see now in them "vacation paradises" is the ones cleaning the toilets and cutting the grass. On their own land, mind you, their own land. Weren't gonna happen in Willow Springs. 'Cause if Mama Day say no, everybody say no. There's 18 & 23, and there's 18 & 23 — and nobody was gonna trifle with Mama Day's, 'cause she know how to use it — her being a direct descendant of Sapphira Wade, piled on the fact of springing from the seventh son of a seventh son — uh, uh. Mama Day say no, everybody say no. No point in making a pile of money to be guaranteed the new moon will see you scratching at fleas you don't have, or rolling in the marsh like a mud turtle. And if some was waiting for her to die, they had a long wait. She says she ain't gonna. And when you think about it, to show up in one century, make it all the way through the next, and have a toe inching over into the one approaching *is* about as close to eternity anybody can come.

Well, them developers upped the price and changed the plans, changed the plans and upped the price, till it got to be a game with us. Winky bought a motorboat with what they offered him back in 1987, turned it in for a cabin cruiser two years later, and says he expects to be able to afford a yacht with the news that's waiting in the mail this year. Parris went from a new shingle roof to a split-level ranch and is making his way toward adding a swimming pool and greenhouse. But when all the laughing's done, it's the principle that remains. And we done learned that anything coming from beyond the bridge gotta be viewed real, real careful. Look what happened when Reema's boy — the one with the pear-shaped head — came hauling himself back from one of those fancy colleges mainside, dragging his notebooks and tape recorder and a funny way of curling up his lip and clicking his teeth, all excited and determined to put Willow Springs on the map.

We was polite enough — Reema always was a little addle-brained — so you couldn't blame the boy for not remembering that part of Willow Springs's problems was that it got put on some maps right after the War Between the States. And then when he went around asking us about 18 & 23, there weren't nothing to do but take pity on him as he rattled on about "ethnography," "unique speech patterns," "cultural preservation," and whatever else he seemed to be getting so much pleasure out of while talking into his little gray machine. He was all over the place — What 18 & 23 mean? What 18 & 23 mean? And we all told him the God-honest truth: it was just our way of saying something. Winky was awful, though, he even spit tobacco juice for him. Sat on his porch all day, chewing up the boy's Red Devil premium and spitting so the machine could pick it up. There was enough fun in that to take us through the fall and winter when he had hauled himself back over The Sound to wherever he was getting what was supposed to be passing for an education. And he sent everybody he'd talked to copies of the book he wrote, bound all nice with our name and his signed on the first page. We couldn't hold Reema down, she was so proud. It's a good thing she didn't read it. None of us made it much through the introduction, but that said it all: you see, he had come to the conclusion after "extensive field work" (ain't never picked a boll of cotton or head of lettuce in his life — Reema spoiled him silly), but he done still made it to the conclusion that 18 & 23 wasn't

18 & 23 at all — was really 81 & 32, which just so happened to be the lines of longitude and latitude marking off where Willow Springs sits on the map. And we were just so damned dumb that we turned the whole thing around.

Not that he called it being dumb, mind you, called it "asserting our cultural identity," "inverting hostile social and political parameters." 'Cause, see, being we was brought here as slaves, we had no choice but to look at everything upside-down. And then being that we was isolated off here on this island, everybody else in the country went on learning good English and calling things what they really was — in the dictionary and all that — while we kept on calling things ass-backwards. And he thought that was just so wonderful and marvelous, etcetera, etcetera . . . Well, after that crate of books came here, if anybody had any doubts about what them developers was up to, if there was just a tinge of seriousness behind them jokes about the motorboats and swimming pools that could be gotten from selling a piece of land, them books squashed it. The people who ran the type of schools that could turn our children into raving lunatics — and then put his picture on the back of the book so we couldn't even deny it was him — didn't mean us a speck of good.

If the boy wanted to know what 18 & 23 meant, why didn't he just ask? When he was running around sticking that machine in everybody's face, we was sitting right here — every one of us — and him being one of Reema's, we woulda obliged him. He coulda asked Cloris about the curve in her spine that came from the planting season when their mule broke its leg, and she took up the reins and kept pulling the plow with her own back. Winky woulda told him about the hot tar that took out the corner of his right eye the summer we had only seven days to rebuild the bridge so the few crops we had left after the storm could be gotten over before rot sat in. Anybody woulda carried him through the fields we had to stop farming back in the '80s to take outside jobs — washing cars, carrying groceries, cleaning house — anything — 'cause it was leave the land or lose it during the Silent Depression. Had more folks sleeping in city streets and banks fore-closing on farms than in the Great Depression before that.

Naw, he didn't really want to know what 18 & 23 meant, or he woulda asked. He woulda asked right off where Miss Abigail Day was staying, so we coulda sent him down the main road to that little yellow

house where she used to live. And she woulda given him a tall glass
of ice water or some cinnamon tea as he heard about Peace dying
young, then Hope and Peace again. But there was the child of Grace —
the grandchild, a girl who went mainside, like him, and did real well.
Was living outside of Charleston now with her husband and two boys.
So she visits a lot more often than she did when she was up in New
York. And she probably woulda pulled out that old photo album, so
he coulda seen some pictures of her grandchild, Cocoa, and then Cocoa's mama, Grace. And Miss Abigail flips right through to the beautiful one of Grace resting in her satin-lined coffin. And as she walks
him back out to the front porch and points him across the road to a
silver trailer where her sister, Miranda, lives, she tells him to grab up
and chew a few sprigs of mint growing at the foot of the steps — it'll
help kill his thirst in the hot sun. And if he'd known enough to do
just that, thirsty or not, he'd know when he got to that silver trailer
to stand back a distance calling *Mama, Mama Day*, to wait for her to
come out and beckon him near.

He'da told her he been sent by Miss Abigail and so, more likely
than not, she lets him in. And he hears again about the child of Grace,
her grandniece, who went mainside, like him, and did real well. Was
living outside of Charleston now with her husband and two boys. So
she visits a lot more often than she did when she was up in New York.
Cocoa is like her very own, Mama Day tells him, since she never had
no children.

And with him carrying that whiff of mint on his breath, she surely
woulda walked him out to the side yard, facing that patch of dogwood,
to say she has to end the visit a little short 'cause she has some gardening
to do in the other place. And if he'd had the sense to offer to follow
her just a bit of the way — then and only then — he hears about that
summer fourteen years ago when Cocoa came visiting from New York
with her first husband. Yes, she tells him, there was a first husband —
a stone city boy. How his name was George. But how Cocoa left, and
he stayed. How it was the year of the last big storm that blew her
pecan trees down and even caved in the roof of the other place. And
she woulda stopped him from walking just by a patch of oak: she
reaches up, takes a bit of moss for him to put in them closed leather
shoes — they're probably sweating his feet something terrible, she tells
him. And he's to sit on the ground, right there, to untie his shoes and

stick in the moss. And then he'd see through the low bush that old graveyard just down the slope. And when he looks back up, she woulda disappeared through the trees; but he's to keep pushing the moss in them shoes and go on down to that graveyard where he'll find buried Grace, Hope, Peace, and Peace again. Then a little ways off a grouping of seven old graves, and a little ways off seven older again. All circled by them live oaks and hanging moss, over a rise from the tip of The Sound.

Everything he needed to know coulda been heard from that yellow house to that silver trailer to that graveyard. Be too late for him to go that route now, since Miss Abigail's been dead for over nine years. Still, there's an easier way. He could just watch Cocoa any one of these times she comes in from Charleston. She goes straight to Miss Abigail's to air out the rooms and unpack her bags, then she's across the road to call out at Mama Day, who's gonna come to the door of the trailer and wave as Cocoa heads on through the patch of dogwoods to that oak grove. She stops and puts a bit of moss in her open-toe sandals, then goes on past those graves to a spot just down the rise toward The Sound, a little bit south of that circle of oaks. And if he was patient and stayed off a little ways, he'd realize she was there to meet up with her first husband so they could talk about that summer fourteen years ago when she left, but he stayed. And as her and George are there together for a good two hours or so — neither one saying a word — Reema's boy coulda heard from them everything there was to tell about 18 & 23.

But on second thought, someone who didn't know how to ask wouldn't know how to listen. And he coulda listened to them the way you been listening to us right now. Think about it: ain't nobody really talking to you. We're sitting here in Willow Springs, and you're God-knows-where. It's August 1999 — ain't but a slim chance it's the same season where you are. Uh, huh, listen. Really listen this time: the only voice is your own. But you done just heard about the legend of Sapphira Wade, though nobody here breathes her name. You done heard it the way we know it, sitting on our porches and shelling June peas, quieting the midnight cough of a baby, taking apart the engine of a car — you done heard it without a single living soul really saying a word. Pity, though, Reema's boy couldn't listen, like you, to Cocoa and George down by them oaks — or he woulda left here with quite a story.

You were picking your teeth with a plastic straw — I know, I know, it wasn't really a straw, it was a coffee stirrer. But, George, let's be fair, there are two little openings in those things that you could possibly suck liquid through if you were desperate enough, so I think I'm justified in calling it a straw since dumps like that Third Avenue coffee shop had no shame in calling it a coffee stirrer, when the stuff they poured into your cup certainly didn't qualify as coffee. Everything about those types of places was a little more or less than they should have been. I was always thrown off balance: the stainless steel display cases were too clean, and did you ever notice that the cakes and pies inside of them never made crumbs when they were cut, and no juice ever dripped from the cantaloupes and honeydews? The Formica tabletops were a bit too slippery for your elbows, and the smell of those red vinyl seats — always red vinyl — seeped into the taste of your food, which came warm if it was a hot dish and warm if it was a cold dish. I swear to you, once I got warm pistachio ice cream and it was solid as a rock. Those places in New York were designed for assembly-line nutrition, and it worked — there was nothing in there to encourage you to linger. Especially when the bill came glued to the bottom of your dessert plate — who would want to ask for a second cup of coffee and have to sit there watching a big greasy thumbprint spread slowly over the Thank You printed on the back?

I suppose you had picked up the stirrer for your coffee because you'd already used the teaspoon for your soup. I saw the waitress bring you the Wednesday special, and that meant pea soup, which had to be attacked quickly before it lumped up. So not risking another twenty-minute wait for a soup spoon, you used your teaspoon, which left you without anything to use in your coffee when it came with the bill. And obviously you knew that our pleasant waitress's "Catch ya in a men-it, Babe," doomed you to either your finger, a plastic stirrer, or coffee straight up. And you used plenty of sugar and milk. That guy knows the art of dining successfully on Third Avenue, I thought. When the lunch menu has nothing priced above six dollars, it's make do if you're gonna make it back to work without ulcers.

And there wasn't a doubt in my mind that you were going back to some office or somewhere definite after that meal. It wasn't just the short-sleeved blue shirt and tie; you ate with a certain ease and deci-siveness that spelled *employed* with each forkful of their stringy roast beef. Six months of looking for a job had made me an expert at picking out the people who, like me, were hurrying up to wait — in some-body's outer anything for a chance to make it through their inner doors to prove that you could type two words a minute, or not drool on your blouse while answering difficult questions about your middle initial and date of birth.

By that August I had it down to a science, although the folks here would say that I was gifted with a bit of Mama Day's second sight. Second sight had nothing to do with it: in March of that year coats started coming off, and it was the kind of April that already had you dodging spit from the air conditioners along the side streets, so by midsummer I saw it all hanging out — those crisp butterflies along the avenues, their dresses still holding the sharp edges of cloth that had been under cool air all morning in some temperature-controlled box. Or the briefcases that hung near some guy's thigh with a balance that said there was more in them than empty partitions and his gym shorts. And I guess being a woman, I could always tell hair: heads are held differently when they've been pampered every week, the necks massaged to relax tense muscles "so the layers will fall right, dear." The blondes in their Dutch-Boy cuts, my counterparts in Jerri curls, those Asian women who had to do practically nothing to be gorgeous with theirs so they frizzed it or chopped it off, because then everybody knew they had the thirty-five dollars a week to keep it looking that way. Yeah, that group all had jobs. And it was definitely first sight on any evening rush-hour train: all those open-neck cotton shirts — always plaid or colored — with the dried sweat marks under the arms of riders who had the privilege of a seat before the north-bound IRT hit midtown because those men had done their stint in the factories, warehouses, and loading docks farther down on Delancey or in East New York or Brooklyn.

But it took a little extra attention for the in-betweens: figuring out which briefcases that swung with the right weight held only pounds of résumés, or which Gucci appointment books had the classifieds neatly clipped out and taped onto the pages so you'd think she was expected wherever she was heading instead of just expected to wait. I have to admit, the appointment-book scam took a bit of originality and class. That type knew that a newspaper folded to the last section was a dead giveaway. And I don't know who the others were trying to fool by pretending to scan the headlines and editorial page before going to the classifieds and there finally creasing the paper and shifting it an inch or two closer to their faces. When all else failed, I was left with watching the way they walked — either too determined or too hesitantly through some revolving door on Sixth Avenue. Misery loves company, and that's exactly what I was searching for on the streets during that crushing August in New York. I out-and-out resented the phonies, and when I could pick one out I felt a little better about myself. At least I was being real: I didn't have a job, and I wanted one — badly. When your unemployment checks have a remaining life span that's shorter than a tsetse fly's, and you know that temp agencies are barely going to pay your rent, and all the doorways around Times Square are already taken by very determined-looking ladies, masquerades go right out the window. It's begging your friends for a new lead every other day, a newspaper folded straight to the classifieds, and a cup of herb tea and the house salad anywhere the bill will come in under two bucks with a table near the air conditioner.

While you finished your lunch and were trying to discreetly get the roast beef from between your teeth, I had twenty minutes before the next cattle call. I was to be in the herd slotted between one and three at the Andrews & Stein Engineering Company. And if my feet hadn't swollen because I'd slipped off my high heels under the table, I might have gone over and offered you one of the mint-flavored toothpicks I always carried around with me. I'd met quite a few guys in restaurants with my box of toothpicks: it was a foolproof way to start up a conversation once I'd checked out what they ordered and how they ate it. The way a man chews can tell you loads about the kind of lover he'll turn out to be. Don't laugh — meat is meat. And you had given those three slabs of roast beef a consideration they didn't deserve, so I actually played with the idea that you might be worth the pain of forcing on my shoes. You had nice teeth and strong, blunt fingers, and your nails were clean but, thank God, not manicured. I had been trying to figure out what you did for a living. The combination of a short-sleeved colored shirt and knit tie could mean anything from security guard to eccentric V.P. Regardless, anyone who preferred a plastic stirrer over that open saucer of toothpicks near the cash register, collecting flecks of ear wax and grease from a hundred rummaging fingernails, at least had common sense if not a high regard for the finer points of etiquette.

But when you walked past me, I let you and the idea go. My toothpicks had already gotten me two dates in the last month: one whole creep and a half creep. I could have gambled that my luck was getting progressively better and you'd only be a quarter creep. But even so, meeting a quarter creep in a Third Avenue coffee shop usually meant he'd figure that I would consider a free lecture on the mating habits of African violets at the Botanical Gardens and dinner at a Greek restaurant — red vinyl *booths* — a step up. That much this southern girl had learned: there was a definite relationship between where you met some guy in New York and where he asked you out. Now, getting picked up in one of those booths at a Greek restaurant meant dinner at a mid-drawer ethnic: Mexican, Chinese, southern Italian, with real tablecloths but under glass shields, and probably Off-Broadway tickets. And if you hooked into someone at one of *those* restaurants, then it was out to top-drawer ethnic: northern Italian, French, Russian, or Continental, with waiters, not waitresses, and balcony seats on Broadway. East Side restaurants, Village jazz clubs, and orchestra seats at Lincoln Center were nights out with the pool you found available at Maxwell's Plum or any singles bar *above* Fifty-ninth Street on the East Side, and *below* Ninety-sixth on the West.

I'd never graduated to the bar scene because I didn't drink and refused to pay three-fifty for a club soda until the evening bore returns. Some of my friends said that you could run up an eighteen-dollar tab in no time that way, only to luck out with a pink quarter creep who figured that because you were a black woman it was down to mid-drawer ethnic for dinner the next week. And if he was a brown quarter creep, he had waited just before closing time to pick up the tab for your last drink. And if you didn't show the proper amount of gratitude for a hand on your thigh and an invitation to his third-floor walkup into paradise, you got told in so many words that your bad attitude was the exact reason why he had come there looking for white girls in the first place.

I sound awful, don't I? Well, those were awful times for a single woman in that city of yours. There was something so desperate and sad about it all — especially for my friends. You know, Selma kept going to those fancy singles bars, insisting that was the only way to meet "certain" black men. And she did meet them, those who certainly weren't looking for her. Then it was in Central Park, of all places, that she snagged this doctor. Not just any doctor, a Park Avenue neurosurgeon. After only three months he was hinting marriage, and she was shouting to us about a future of douching with Chanel No. 5, using laminated dollar bills for shower curtains — the whole bit. And the sad thing wasn't really how it turned out — I mean, as weird as it was when he finally told her that he was going to have a sex-change operation, but he was waiting for the right woman who was also willing to get one along with him, because he'd never dream of sleeping with another man — even after the operation; weirder — and much sadder — than all of that, George, was the fact that she debated seriously about following him to Denmark and doing it. So let me tell you, my toothpicks, as small a gesture as they were, helped me to stay on top of all that madness.

I finally left the coffee shop and felt whatever life that might have been revived in my linen suit and hair wilting away. How could it get so hot along Third Avenue when the buildings blocked out the sun-light? When I had come to New York seven years before that, I wondered about the need for such huge buildings. No one ever seemed to be in them for very long; everyone was out on the sidewalks, moving, moving, moving — and to where? My first month I was determined to find out. I followed a woman once: she had a beehive hairdo with rhinestone bobby pins along the side of her head that matched the rhinestones on her tinted cat-eyed glasses. Her thumbnails were the only ones polished, in a glossy lacquer on both hands, and they were so long they had curled under like hooks. I figured that she was so strange no one would ever notice me trailing her. We began on Fifty-third Street and Sixth Avenue near the Sheraton, moved west to Eighth Avenue before turning right, where she stopped at a Korean fruit stand, bought a kiwi, and walked along peeling the skin with her thumbnails. I lost her at Columbus Circle; she threw the peeled fruit uneaten into a trash can and took the escalator down into the subway. As she was going down, another woman was coming up the escalator with two bulging plastic bags. This one took me along Broadway up to where it meets Columbus Avenue at Sixty-third, and she sat down on one of those benches in the traffic median with her bags between her knees. She kept beating her heels against the sides and it sounded as if she had loose pots and pans in them. A really distinguished-looking guy with a tweed jacket and gray sideburns got up from the bench the moment she sat down, went into a flower shop across Columbus Avenue, came out empty-handed, and I followed him back downtown toward the Circle until we got to the entrance to Central Park. He slowed up, turned around, looked me straight in the face, and smiled. That's when I noticed that he had diaper pins holding his fly front together — you know, the kind they used to have with pink rabbit heads on them. I never thought anyone could beat my Central Park story until Selma met her neurosurgeon there. After that guy I gave up — I was exhausted by that time anyway. I hated to walk, almost as much as I hated the subways. There's something hypocritical about a city that keeps half of its population underground half of the time; you can start believing that there's much more space than there really is — to live, to work. And I had trouble doing both in spite of those endless classifieds in the Sunday *Times*. You know, there are more pages in just their Help Wanted section than in the telephone book here in Willow Springs. But it took me a while to figure out that New York racism moved underground like most of the people did.

Mama Day and Grandma had told me that there was a time when

the want ads and housing listings in newspapers — even up north — were clearly marked colored or white. It must have been wonderfully easy to go job hunting then. You were spared a lot of legwork and headwork. And how I longed for those times, when I was busting my butt up and down the streets. I said as much at one of those parties Selma was always giving for her certain people. You would've thought I had announced that they were really drinking domestic wine, the place got that quiet. One of her certain people was so upset his voice shook: "You mean, you want to bring back segregation?" I looked at him like he was a fool — Where had it gone? I just wanted to bring the clarity about it back — it would save me a whole lot of subway tokens. What I was left to deal with were the ads labeled *Equal Opportunity Employer*, or nothing — which might as well have been labeled *Colored apply* or *Take your chances*. And if I wanted to limit myself to the sure bets, then it was an equal opportunity to be what, or earn what? That's where the headwork came in.

It's like the ad I was running down that afternoon: a one-incher in Monday's paper for an office manager. A long job description so there wasn't enough room to print Equal Opportunity Employer even if they were. They hadn't advertised Sunday, because I'd double-checked. They didn't want to get lost among the full and half columns the agencies ran. Obviously, a small operation. *Andrews & Stein Engineering Company:* It was half Jewish at least, so that said liberal — maybe. Or maybe they only wanted their own. I had never seen any Jewish people except on television until I arrived in New York. I had heard that they were clannish, and coming from Willow Springs I could identify with that. *Salary competitive:* that could mean anything, depending upon whether they were competing with Burger King or IBM. *Position begins September 1st:* that was the clincher, with all of the other questions hanging in the balance. If I got the job, I could still go home for mid-August. Even if I didn't get it, I was going home. Mama Day and Grandma could forgive me for leaving Willow Springs, but not for staying away.

I got to the address and found exactly what I had feared. A six-floor office building — low-rent district, if you could call anything low in New York. Andrews & Stein was suite 511. The elevator, like the ancient marble foyer and maroon print carpeting on the fifth floor, was worn but carefully maintained. Dimly lit hallways to save on overhead, and painted walls that looked just a month short of needing a fresh coat. I could see that the whole building was being held together by some dedicated janitor who was probably near retirement. Oh, no, if these folks were going to hire me, it would be for peanuts. Operations renting space in a place like this shelled out decent salaries only for Mr. Stein's brainless niece, or Mr. Andrews's current lay. Well, you're here, Cocoa, I thought, go through the motions.

The cherry vanilla who buzzed me in the door was predictable, but there might still be reason for hope. When small, liberal establishments put a fudge cream behind their glass reception cages, there were rarely any more back in the offices. Sticking you out front let them sleep pretty good at night, thinking they'd put the ghost of Martin Luther King to rest. There were three other women there ahead of me, and one very very gay Oriental. God, those were rare — at least in my circles. The four of them already had clipboards and were filling out one-page applications — mimeographed. Cherry Vanilla was pleasant enough. She apologized for there being no more seats, and told me I had to wait until one of the clipboards was free unless I had something to write on. A small, small operation. But she wasn't pouring out that oily politeness that's normally used to slide you quietly out of any chance of getting the job. One of the women sitting there filling out an application was actually licorice. Her hair was in deep body waves with the sheen of patent leather, and close as I was, I couldn't tell where her hair ended and her skin began. And she had the body and courage to wear a Danskin top as tight as it was red. I guess that lady said, You're going to see me coming from a mile away, like it or not. I bet a lot of men did like it. If they were replacing Mr. Andrews's bimbo, she'd get the job. And the way she looked me up and down — dismissing my washed-out complexion and wilted linen suit — made me want to push out my pathetic chest, but that meant bringing in my nonexistent hips. Forget it, I thought, you're standing here with no tits, no ass, and no color. So console yourself with the fantasy that she's mixed up her addresses and is applying for the wrong job. Why else come to an interview in an outfit that would look better the wetter it got, unless you wanted to be a lifeguard? I could dismiss the other two women right away — milkshakes. One had her résumés typed on different shades of pastel paper and she was shifting through them, I guess trying to figure out which one matched the decor of the office. The other had forgotten her social security card and wanted to know if she should call home for the number. To be stupid enough not to memorize it was one thing, but not to know enough to sit there and shut up about it was beyond witless. I didn't care if Andrews & Stein was a front for the American Nazi party, she didn't have a chance. So the only serious contenders in that bunch were me, Patent Leather Hair, and the kumquat.

I inherited the clipboard from the one who'd forgotten her social security card, and she was in and out still babbling about that damn number before I had gotten down to Educational Background. Beyond high school there was just two years in business school in Atlanta — but I'd graduated at the top of my class. It was work experience that really counted for a job like this. This wasn't the type of place where you'd worry about moving up — all of those boxes and file cabinets crowded behind the receptionist's shoulder — it was simply a matter of moving around.

One job in seven years looked very good — with a fifty percent increase in salary. Duties: diverse, and more complex as I went along. The insurance company simply folded, that's all. If I'd stayed, I probably would have gone on to be an underwriter — but I was truly managing that office. Twelve secretaries, thirty-five salesmen, six adjusters, and one greedy president who didn't have the sense to avoid insuring half of the buildings in the south Bronx — even at triple premiums for fire and water damage. Those crooked landlords made a bundle, and every time I saw someone with a cigarette lighter, I cringed. I was down to Hobbies — which always annoyed me; what does your free time have to do with them? — when Patent Leather Hair was called in. She stood up the way women do knowing they look better when all of them is at last in view. I wondered what she had put down for extracurricular activities. I sighed and crossed my legs. It was going to be a long wait. After twenty minutes, Kumquat smiled over at me sympathetically — at least we both knew that he didn't have a possible ace in the hole anymore.

The intercom button on the receptionist's phone lit up, and when she got off she beckoned to the Oriental guy.

"Mr. Andrews is still interviewing, so Mr. Stein will have to see you. Just take your application to the second door on the left, Mr. Weisman."

He grinned at me again as I felt my linen suit losing its final bit of crispness under the low-voltage air conditioner. God, I wanted to go home — and I meant, home home. With all of Willow Springs's problems, you knew when you saw a catfish, you called it a catfish.

Well, Weisman was in and out pretty fast. I told myself for the thousandth time, Nothing about New York is ever going to surprise me anymore. Stein was probably anti-Semitic. It was another ten minutes and I was still sitting there and really starting to get ticked off. Couldn't Mr. Stein see me as well? No, she'd just put through a long-distance call from a client, but Mr. Andrews would be ready for me soon. I seriously doubted it. He was in there trying to convince Patent Leather that even though she thought she was applying for a position as a lifeguard, they could find room for someone with her potential. I didn't give her the satisfaction of my half-hour wait when she came flaming out — I was busily reading the wrapper on my pack of Trident, having ditched my newspaper before I came in. The thing was irreversibly creased at the classifieds, my bag was too small to hide it, and you never wanted to look that desperate at an interview. And there weren't even any old issues of *Popular Mechanics* or something in the waiting area — bottom drawer all the way.

I was finally buzzed into the inner sanctum, and without a shred of hope walked past the clutter of file cabinets through another door that opened into a deceptively large network of smaller offices. I entered the third on the left as I'd been instructed and there you were: blue shirt, knitted tie, nice teeth, and all. Feeling the box of mint toothpicks press against my thigh through the mesh bag as I sat down and crossed my legs, I smiled sincerely for the first time that day.

UNTIL YOU WALKED into my office that afternoon, I would have never called myself a superstitious man. Far from it. To believe in fate or predestination means you have to believe there's a future, and I grew up without one. It was either that or not grow up at all. Our guardians at the Wallace P. Andrews Shelter for Boys were adamant about the fact that we learned to invest in ourselves alone. "Keep it in the now, fellas," Chip would say, chewing on his bottom right jaw and spitting as if he still had the plug of tobacco in there Mrs. Jackson refused to let him use in front of us. And I knew I'd hear her until the day I died. "Only the present has potential, *sir*." I could see her even then, the way she'd jerk up the face, gripping the chin of some kid who was crying because his last foster home hadn't worked out, or because he was teased at school about not having a mother. She'd even reach up and clamp on to some muscled teenager who was trying to excuse a bad report card. I could still feel the ache in my bottom lip from the relentless grip of her thumb and forefinger pressed into the bone of my chin — "Only the present has potential, *sir*."

They may not have been loving people, she and Chip — or when you think about it, even lovable. But they were devoted to their job if not to us individually. And Mrs. Jackson saw part of her job as making sure that that scraggly bunch of misfits — misfitted into some-body's game plan so we were thrown away — would at least hear themselves addressed with respect. There were so many boys and the faces kept changing, she was getting old and never remembered our individual names and didn't try to hide it. All of us were beneath poor, most of us were black or Puerto Rican, so it was very likely that this would be the first and last time in our lives anyone would call us sir. And if talking to you and pinching the skin off your chin didn't work, she was not beneath enforcing those same words with a brown leather strap — a man's belt with the buckle removed. We always wondered where she'd gotten a man's belt. You could look at Mrs. Jackson and tell she'd never been a Mrs., the older boys would say. Or if she had snagged some poor slob a thousand years ago, he never could have gotten it up over her to need to undo his pants. But that was said only well out of her earshot after she had lashed one of them across the back or arms. She'd bring that belt down with a cold precision that was more frightening than the pain she was causing, and she'd bring it down for exactly ten strokes — one for each syllable: "Only the present has potential, *sir*."

No boy was touched above the neck or below his waist in front. And she never, ever hit the ones — regardless of their behavior — who had come to Wallace P. Andrews with fractured arms or cigarette burns on their groins. For those she'd take away dinner plus breakfast the next morning, and even lunch if she felt they warranted it. Bernie Sinclair passed out that way once, and when he woke up in the infirmary she was standing over him explaining that he had remained unconscious past the dinner he *still* would have been deprived of if he hadn't fainted.

Cruel? No, I would call it controlled. Bernie had spit in her face. And she never altered her expression, either when it happened during hygiene check or when she stood over him in the infirmary. Bernie had come to us with half of his teeth busted out, and he hated brushing the other half. She was going down the usual morning line-up for the boys under twelve, checking fingernails, behind ears, calling for the morning stretch (hands above head, legs spread, knees bent, and bounce) to detect unwashed armpits and crotches. Bernie wouldn't open his mouth for her and was getting his daily list of facts (she never lectured, she called it listing simple facts): If the remainder of his teeth rotted out from lack of personal care, then the dentist would have to fit him for a full plate instead of a partial plate. And it would take her twice as long to requisition twice the money that would then be needed from the state. That would lead to him spending twice as long being teased at school and restricted to a soft diet in the cafeteria. She said this like she did everything — slowly, clearly, and without emotion. For the second time she bent over and told him to open his mouth. He did, and sent a wad of spit against her right cheek. Even Joey Santiago cringed — all six feet and almost two hundred pounds of him. But Mrs. Jackson never blinked. She took out the embroidered handkerchief she kept in her rolled-up blouse sleeve and wiped her face as she listed another set of facts: she had asked him twice, she never asked any child to do anything more than twice — those were the rules at Wallace P. Andrews. No lunch, no dinner, and he still had his full share of duties. I guess that's why he passed out, no food under the hot sun and weeding our garden — that and fear of what she was really going to do to him for spitting on her. He was still new and didn't understand that she was going to do nothing at all.

Our rage didn't matter to her, our hurts or disappointments over what life had done to us. None of that was going to matter a damn in the outside world, so we might as well start learning it at Wallace P. Andrews. There were only rules and facts. Mrs. Jackson's world out there on Staten Island had rules that you could argue might not be fair, but they were consistent. And when they were broken we were guaranteed that, however she had to do it, we would be made to *feel* responsibility for our present actions — and our actions alone. And oddly enough, we understood that those punishments were an improvement upon our situations: before coming there, we had been beaten and starved just for being born.

And she was the only person on the staff allowed to touch us. Even Chip, who had the role of "good cop" to her "bad cop" — you needed a shoulder to cry on sometimes — could only recommend discipline. It must have been difficult with sixty boys, and I'd seen some kids really provoke a dorm director or workshop leader, and the guy would never lay a hand on them. They all knew her rules, and it was clear those men were afraid of her. And I could never figure it out, even with the rumor that was going around, which Joey Santiago swore by. Joey was a notorious liar, but he was the oldest guy there when I was growing up. And he said that some years back there was a dorm director who used to sneak into the rooms where we had the "rubber sheet jockeys" — kids under eight — and take them into the bathroom. After he was finished with them, they'd fall asleep on the toilet, where he'd make them sit until their rectums stopped bleeding. Mrs. Jackson and Chip came over one night, caught him at it, and she told the boys she was going to call the police. They took him back to the old stucco house she lived in on the grounds. The police car never came, but her basement lights stayed on. And Joey swore you could hear that man screaming throughout the entire night, although all of her windows were bolted down. It was loud enough to even wake up the older ones in the other dorms. That man was never seen again, and they knew better than to question Mrs. Jackson when she came over to pack up his things herself. And Chip had absolutely nothing to say about what had happened but "Keep it in the now, fellas" as he dug Mrs. Jackson a new rose garden the following morning. Every staff member and boy who came to Wallace P. Andrews heard that rumor and, one way or another, went over to see those roses in the corner of her garden. I can only tell you this, they were incredibly large and beautiful. And in the summer, when the evening breeze came from the east, their fragrance was strong enough to blanket your sleep.

Some thought that I was her favorite. I was one of the few who had grown up there through the nursery, and she couldn't punish me the way she did them, because I had a congenital heart condition. So she took away my books, knowing that I'd rather give up food or even have her use her strap. And once pleaded with her to do so, because I said I'd die if I had to wait a full week to find out how the Count of Monte Cristo escaped from prison. She said that was a fitting death for little boys who were caught cheating on their math exams. But fractions are hard, and I wanted a good grade at the end of the term. Ah, so I was worried about the *end* of the term? Well, she would now keep my books for two weeks. "Only the present has potential, *sir*."

And the discipline she tailor-made for all of us said, like it or not, the present is *you*. And what else did we have but ourselves? We had a more than forgettable past and no future that was guaranteed. And she never let us pretend that anything else was the case as she'd often listed the facts of life: I am not your mother. I am paid to run this place. You have no mothers or fathers. This is not your home. And it is not a prison — it is a state shelter for boys. And it is not a dumping ground for delinquents, rejects, or somebody's garbage, because you are not delinquents, rejects, or garbage — you are boys. It is not a place to be tortured, exploited, or raped. It is a state shelter for boys. Here you have a clean room, decent food, and clothing for each season because it is a shelter. There is a library in which you study for three hours after school — and you *will* go to school, because you are boys. When you are eighteen, the state says you are men. And when you are men you leave here to go where and do what you want. But you stay here until you are men.

Yes, those were the facts of life at Wallace P. Andrews. And those were her methods. And if any of the boys complained to the state inspectors about being punished, nothing was ever done. I guess at the bottom line, she saved them money. We grew and canned a lot of our own food, painted our own dorms, made most of the furniture, and even sewed curtains and bedspreads. And the ones she turned out weren't a burden on the state, either. I don't know of anyone who became a drug addict, petty thief, or a derelict. I guess it's because you grew up with absolutely no illusions about yourself or the world. Most of us went from there either to college or into a trade. No, it wasn't the kind of place that turned out many poets or artists — those who could draw became draftsmen, and the musicians were taught to tune pianos. If she erred in directing our careers, she erred on the side of caution. Sure, the arts were waiting for poor black kids who were encouraged to dream big, and so was death row.

Looking back, I can see how easy it would have been for her to let us just sit there and reach the right age to get out. It only takes time for a man to grow older, but how many of them grow up? And I couldn't have grown up if I had wasted my time crying about a family I wasn't given or believing in a future that I didn't have. When I left Wallace P. Andrews I had what I could see: my head and my two hands, and I had each day to do something with them. Each day, that's how I took it — each moment, sometimes, when the going got really rough. I may have knocked my head against the walls, figuring out how to buy food, supplies, and books, but I never knocked on wood. No rabbit's foot, no crucifixes — not even a lottery ticket. I couldn't afford the dollar or the dreams while I was working my way through Columbia. So until you walked into my office, everything I was — all the odds I had beat — was owed to my living fully in the now. How was I to reconcile the *fact* of seeing you the second time that day with the *feeling* I had had the first time? Not the feeling I told myself I had, but the one I really had.

You see, there was no way for me to deny that you were there in front of me and I couldn't deny any longer that I knew it would happen — you would be in my future. What had been captured — and dismissed — in a space too quickly for recorded time was now like a bizarre photograph that was developing in front of my face. I am passing you in the coffee shop, your head is bent over your folded newspaper, and small strands of your reddish-brown hair have come undone from the bobby pins and lie against the curve of your neck. The feeling is so strong, it almost physically stops me: *I will see that neck again.* Not her, not the woman but the skin that's tinted from amber to cream as it stretches over the lean bone underneath. That is the feeling I actually had, while the feeling I quickly exchanged it with was: *I've seen this woman before.* That can be recorded; it took a split second. But a glance at the side of your high cheekbones, pointed chin, slender profile, and I knew I was mistaken. I hadn't even seen you sitting those three tables away during lunch. But I remembered your waitress well. The dark brown arms, full breasts threatening to tear open the front of her uniform, the crease of her apron strings around a nonexistent waist that swung against a hip line that could only be called a promise of heaven on earth — her I had seen. And you had to have been there when she took your order and brought you whatever you were eating, and the fact is I never saw you. Not when I stood up, reached into my pocket for change, passed the two tables between us, and didn't see you then — until the neck bent over the newspaper. And it all could have been such a wonderful coincidence when you first walked into my office, a natural ice-breaker for the interview, which I always hated, being forced to judge someone else. I could have brought up the final image of the weary slump, the open class-ifieds, and the shoes pulled off beneath the table. A woman looking for a job; we were looking for an office manager five blocks away. Afternoon interviews began at one o'clock and it was twelve-forty-five. *And just imagine, Miss Day, when I passed you I said to myself, Wouldn't it be funny if I saw her again?* Except that it was terrifying when you sat down, and then ran your hand up the curve of your neck in a nervous mannerism, pushing up a few loose hairs and pushing me smack into a confrontation with fate. When you unconsciously did that, I must have looked as if someone had stuck a knife into my gut, because that's the way it felt.

YOU SAID, Call me George. And I thought, Oh God, this is going to be one of those let's-get-chummy-fast masquerades. Nine times out of ten, some clown giving you his first name is a sure bet he's not giving you the job. And they can comfort themselves because, after all, they went out of their way to be "nice." And in this case, you were stealing my thunder when the moment came for pulling out my toothpicks and reminding *Mr. Andrews* where I'd seen him before. But if we were George and Ophelia — chat, chat, chat — my mint tooth-picks would just be added fuel to the fire that was sending this job up in smoke. These fudge-on-fudge interviews were always tricky any-way. You have the power freaks who wanted you to grovel at their importance. They figure if they don't get it from the other bonbons, it's sure not coming from anywhere else. Or there were the disciples of a free market with a Christ complex: they went to the Cross and rose without affirmative action, so you can too. But our interview wasn't anything I could put my finger on. You just seemed downright scared of me and anxious to get me out of that office. And I knew the fastest way was this call-me-George business. I decided to fight fire with fire.

"And I'm used to answering to Cocoa. I guess we might as well start now because if I get the position and anyone here calls me Ophelia, I'll be so busy concentrating on my work, it won't register. I truly doubt I could have moved up as fast as I did at my last job — with a fifty percent increase in salary — if those twelve secretaries, thirty-five salesmen, and six adjusters in the office I was managing almost single-handedly had called me Ophelia. The way I see it, over half of the overtime I put in would have been spent trying to figure out who they were talking to."

There, I stuck that one to you. And you knew it, too, because you were finally smiling. And this time you took a real good look at my application.

"So you picked up this nickname at your last job — Omega Home Insurance?"

"No, I've had it from a child — in the South it's called a pet name. My grandmother and great-aunt gave it to me, the same women who put me through business school in Atlanta where I ended up graduating at the top of my class — A's in statistics, typing, bookkeeping. B plusses in —"

"That's fascinating. How do they decide on the pet name?"

"They just try to figure out what fits."

"So a child with skin the color of buttered cream gets called Cocoa. I can see how that fits."

I wanted to slap that smirk off your face. "It does if you understood my family and where I come from."

"Willow Springs, is it? That's in Georgia?"

"No, it's actually in no state. But that's a long story. And not to be rude, Mr. Andrews, but I really would like to talk about my credentials for working here. Where I was born and what name I was given were both beyond my control. But what *I* could do about my life, I've done well. And I'd like to spend the few minutes I have left of your time being judged on that."

Something happened to your face then. I had hit a raw nerve somewhere, and I cursed myself because I was sure I had succeeded in destroying the whole thing. It was little consolation knowing that I was going to be on your mind long after you kicked me out of your office.

"That's the only way I'd ever dream of judging anyone, Miss Day. And I meant it when I said call me George."

Great, I'd been demoted *up* to Miss Day. This man was really angry, and that George business again just clinched it, I guess. But then he did say *I meant it*, which means he knows about the whole charade and he's trying to reassure me that he's not angry about what I said. Ah, who can figure this shit out.

"And you can call me . . ." I was suddenly very tired — of you, of the whole game. "Just call me when you decide. I do need this job, and if you check out my references, you'll find that I'll be more than able to perform well."

"Fine. And this is the number where you can be reached?"

"Yes, but I'll be away for the next two weeks. If you don't mind, you could drop me a card, or I'll call when I get back since the job doesn't start until the first."

You frowned, but it came out the way it came out. Sure, he's thinking, how badly does someone need a job who's taking a vacation?

"But we'll be making our final decision after tomorrow. The person starts Monday."

"Your ad said the first."

"It did, but our current office manager told us this morning that she has to leave earlier than she had planned. And she'll have to break in her successor. This is a deceptively busy place and to have someone come in here cold — well, it wouldn't be fair to the new employee or to us. And we thought whoever got the position would probably appreciate starting work before September. I know how tight things are out there right now — most people have been looking for a long time."

Jesus, all we needed was the organ music and a slow fade to my receding back as the swirling sand of the rocky coastline began to spell out The End. Oh, yeah, if you aren't ready to start yesterday, there are a dozen who will be.

"I understand, and I wouldn't have wasted your time if I knew it was necessary to begin right away. I have to go home every August.

It's never been a problem before because I had the same job for seven years. You see, my grandmother is eighty-three and since we lost my cousin and her family last year, I'm the only grandchild left."

If you thought it was a cheap shot, sorry. At that point I was beyond caring.

"The whole family? That's really terrible — what happened?"

"Did you read about the fire in Linden Hills this past Christmas? Well, that was my cousin Willa and her husband and son. It upset us all a lot."

"I did read about it. It was an awful, awful thing — and on Christmas of all days."

My God, the look in your eyes. You actually meant that. This would go down in Guinness as the strangest interview I'd ever been on.

"So you understand why I'm going back to Willow Springs."

"Of course I do. And you must understand why any qualified applicant would need to start Monday."

"Yes, I do."

We had sure become one understanding pair of folks by the time the lights in the theater came up and they pulled the curtain across the screen. We got up out of our seats and shook hands. Was it my imagination — did his fingers linger just a bit? Was it possible that since I was more than qualified, no one else would come along and they'd save . . . My heart sank when I got back to the reception area. I had to wade through a whole Baskin-Robbins on my way to the outside hall.

YOU HAD SPUNK, Ophelia, and that's what I admired in a woman. You were justified to come right out and tell me I was prying, and I hated myself all the while I was doing it. I had always valued my own privacy, and just because you were in a position where you had to answer questions that bordered on an invasion on yours made what I did all the more unfair. If it's any consolation, I didn't enjoy the sour aftertaste of abused power. But I was searching for some connection, some rational explanation. The only way I could sit through that interview was by lying to myself about what had really happened in that coffee shop: when I passed your bent neck, I stopped because I had seen you somewhere before, and I couldn't remember — that's all.

I had definitely seen your type before, and had even slept with some of them — those too bright, too jaded colored girls. There were a few at Columbia, but many more would come across the street from Barnard. They made no bones about their plans to hook into a man who — what was the expression then? — who was going somewhere. Well, after classes I went to work as a room-service waiter in the Hilton. It wasn't as glamorous as the work-study jobs in the library or dean's office, but it paid a lot better when you counted tips. During the slack periods my boss let me read, and I had Sundays off. But you see, that wasn't the right day. All the guys who were going somewhere had been able to take girls to the fraternity dances on Friday and Saturday nights where they could show off their brand-name clothes. They only needed a pair of jeans to go to the park with me, or to sit in my room and study. I was too serious, too dull. George doesn't know how to have fun, they'd say, he's so quiet. I suppose I was, but what could I honestly talk to them about? They would have thought I was crazy if I had told them that seeing them flow around me like dark jewels on campus was one of the most beautiful sights on earth.

Yes, I was one of the quiet ones who thought them beautiful, even with the polished iron webbing around their hearts. I understood exactly what they were protecting themselves against, and I was willing to help them shine that armor all the more, to be the shoulder they could cry on when it got too heavy — if they had only let me in. But they didn't want me then. And I was to meet them years later, at parties and dinners, when the iron had served them a bit too well. They were successful and they were alone: those guys who were going somewhere had by either inclination or lack of numbers left a good deal of them behind. They had stopped being frivolous, but they were hurt and suspicious. And maturity made me much more hesitant to take a chance on finding an opening into hearts like those. Often, I had wanted to go over and shake some silk-clad shoulder who thought she was righteously justified in spreading the tired old gospel about not being able to meet good black men. She had met *me*. But I would have been too proud to remind her where.

Yeah, I knew your type well. And you sat there with your mind racing, trying to double-think me, so sure you had me and the game down pat. Give him what he wants. I fooled you, didn't I. All I wanted was for you to be yourself. And I wondered if it was too late, if seven years in New York had been just enough for you to lose that, like you were trying to lose your southern accent. It amused me the way your tongue and lips were determined to clip along and then your accent would find you in the spaces between two words — "talking about," "graduating at." In spite of yourself, the music would squeeze through at the ending of those verbs to tilt the following vowels up just half a key. That's why I wanted you to call me George. There isn't a southerner alive who could bring that name in under two syllables. And for those brief seconds it allowed me to imagine you as you must have been: softer, slower — open. It conjured up images of jasmine-scented nights, warm biscuits and honey being brought to me on flowered china plates as you sat at my feet and rubbed your cheek against my knee. Go ahead and laugh, you have a perfect right. I had never been south, and you couldn't count the times I had spent in Miami at the Super Bowl — that city was a humid and pastel New York. So I had the same myths about southern women that you did about northern men. But it was a fact that when you said my name, you became yourself.

And it was also a fact that there was no way I was going to give you that job. And your firm plans about returning to Willow Springs helped to alleviate my guilt about that. We were going to turn other qualified people down — and it's never a matter of the most qualified, there's no such animal. It's either do they or don't they "fit." And where could I possibly place you? My life was already made at thirty-one. My engineering degree, the accelerating success of Andrews & Stein, proved beyond a shadow of a doubt that you got nothing from believing in crossed fingers, broken mirrors, spilled salt — a twist in your gut in the middle of a Third Avenue coffee shop. You either do or you don't. And you, Ophelia, were the don't. Don't get near a woman who has the power to turn your existence upside-down by simply running a hand up the back of her neck.

◈◈◈

MIRANDA'S TEA KETTLE jets out boiling steam with a low rumble; that old whistle's been lost for years. She reaches for the handle and suddenly stops. Bringing her tongue up over her toothless gums, pushing out her top lip, she concentrates awful hard as the column of steam disappears along the back of the gas range into the bottom of her pine wood cabinets. Her daddy had made those with his very hands, using nothing but a flat chisel and mallet. John-Paul worked each apricot cluster and trailing vine into them panels so lifelike you'd think they was still growing. A little drop of vapor beads up on the tip of an apricot leaf and shines there in the morning sun. Miranda smiles as the bead of water turns golden in color — my, what a pleasant surprise. She must ring up Abigail and tell her Baby Girl is coming in today, a little earlier than expected — and on the airplane to boot.

She pours the hot water over a handful of loose tea leaves and allows 'em to steep as she pushes open the back door of that silver trailer and takes a lungful of fresh air. Dew comes splattering from the top of the screen, landing on her forearm. Her arthritis had told her it was gonna be a dampish kind of day long before she shades her eyes and spots the camel-backed clouds forming on the horizon. The chickens she leaves out to scratch around the yard hear the screen door creak open and come scattering over, setting up a racket. An old black hen, the boldest of the lot, hops up on the brick steps.

"Miserable beggars." She picks up her broom and shoos them off. "And you, Clarissa, oughta know better — nobody eats before me." The hen flies out the way of the swinging broom to land and start pecking on the doorsill again. "Keep it up, hear? A little stewed fricassee with my grits wouldn't taste half bad this morning." Miranda throws them a handful of fresh bread crumbs she keeps in the bag that hangs on a peg just inside her door. "Now, that's all the charity you getting today — go grub up some worms. And mess on my doorstep, there'll be the devil to pay."

She returns to the kitchen to strain her tea. Searching through the cabinets, she finds that her last bit of honey done formed white crystals at the bottom of its Mason jar. "I told Buzzard to bring me six new jars of honey — now, where they at, huh? Miserable, miserable." She puts a little hot tea into the jar and swirls it around to dissolve the crystals before pouring it back into her favorite cup. It's a chipped ceramic mug with a blond woman's smiling face over the red lettering: #1 AUNT. Baby Girl brought that to her from Atlanta, her first summer vacation from business school. She'd told the silly yellow thing that she wasn't a number one Aunt, but a great-aunt, and the only great-aunt at that.

"But they don't make them with 'Great-Aunt' and I knew better than to even start looking for one that said 'Mama Day.' Next time I'll get one made up special for you."

"Why they ain't got no Great-Aunt cups? There is great-aunts, ya know — even in Atlanta."

"Look, now don't start blaming those folks in Atlanta just because you're living longer than you should."

"Getting kinda quick at the mouth, Miss C, since you come back from the city smelling like gasoline fumes."

"I do not. I smell like the lavender water you sent me — by the boxloads."

"Use more of it, then. And when you get my cup made up special, have it say Great-Great-Aunt. I plan to keep on living till I can rock one of yours on my knee."

"We're talking the turn of the century, Mama Day?"

"We're talking as long as it takes."

And it *is* taking a long time, Miranda thinks as she carries her tea into the living room and picks up the phone. It was another year at that school in Atlanta, and near seven up in New York — and no man worth speaking of. Why, Baby Girl must be . . . She concentrates. . . . three years lacking thirty. They were gonna have a good talk when she brought her tail in this afternoon. And she could sit there with her fresh self and pout all she want. Ain't no kinda sense, you living in a place with more men than the whole of Georgia and South Carolina combined, and can't take care of business. There are ways, and there are ways — and she'd just have to explain a few of 'em to her. The phone rings only twice before Miranda hears that melting hello which can only be Abigail's.

"You there, Sister?" Miranda says.

"Uh, huh."

There ain't no other way for Miranda to greet her, or for Abigail to respond — not after eighty years. It don't matter when and it don't matter where: Abigail bringing a fresh bunch of collards from across the main road, Miranda sliding into the pew beside her at church, them running into each other at the post office.

"You there, Sister?"

"Uh, huh."

The five-year-old moves quiet-like away from the darkened room where the bundle of soft flannel lays amidst flowers and the smell of melted candle wax. Moonlight floods in through the window, making bars across the tiny casket that is carved with rosebuds and the trailing circles of water lilies. The wavery shadows of the horsehair divan and the marble fireplace against the hardwood floors are a betrayal: Peace was not supposed to die in their home. Her mama's wail and the angry thud of her daddy's hobnail boots spiral above her head, louder and louder. The sound will fill the house while one and then the other grows mad, mad. There was Miranda, Abigail, and now there is no Peace. Creeping into the bedroom, she sees the three-year-old curled up tight with her thumb in her mouth. The counterpane rises steadily with each breath, but that ain't to be trusted. She will see Peace breathing too, at the bottom of the open well, long after her daddy carves the box and they wrap her in white flannel. Long after her mama will spend her days rocking and twisting thread, twisting thread, while her daddy spends his nights digging, digging into blocks of wood. But there will be no Peace. She begins to learn even at this age: there is more to be known behind what the eyes can see. So climbing up on the bed, she shakes the younger child awake. "You there, Sister?" The answer is coated with phlegm, on the edge of tears. "Uh, huh." Miranda's small fingers place themselves around the rhythm of Abigail's breathing. Nested under the quilt, they are four arms and legs, two heads, one heartbeat.

"Baby Girl is coming in today."

"Well, Lord. It's gonna be good to see my child. I better get her room dusted out and ready. And she thought she was catching the train up there tomorrow night — even wrote and said to meet her at the station Tuesday morning."

"It's the airplane though, at that field beyond the bridge."

"Oh, no. Now what put it in her mind to do that? I never did trust them things — they ain't natural. If I can get my hands on Buzzard, I'll have him go pick her up."

"If I get *my* hands on him, I'm gonna wring his scrawny neck. Ain't seen a speck of that honey he's supposed to bring me. Having the last in my tea this minute."

"Sister, waiting on Buzzard is like waiting on Judgment Day. How Old Arthur doing you this morning?"

"Now, he's dependable as ever. Only man I been able to roll out of bed with since I passed my seventies."

"Stop your badness. I got another poultice for you, found some black cohosh growing down by Ruby's. Soon as it's dry good, I'll make you up a nice plaster."

"Hope it ain't like that other mess that burns so."

"Miranda, you gotta feel it if it's gonna help."

"Felt Old Arthur this morning, and he sure don't help. Just a poking me in my back, poking in my left hip. You think he gonna get it right one day and start poking in my — "

"Uh, uh — let me get off this line before I lose my religion. Listen, bring me over a batch of that dried rosemary you got out at the other place to season this pork shoulder — Baby Girl loves herself some roast pork. And a good half-dozen eggs — I'll do up one jelly and one coconut cake. We only got two weeks to fatten her up — know she gonna come dragging in here puny as the law allows — 'less you wanna make the jelly and I'll do two coconuts. Your jelly cakes always turn out better than mine."

"I ain't making her nothing, 'cause she's too fresh. You go spend all day over a hot stove in this heat — and all my eggs is for setting now."

"A *good* half dozen now, Miranda. And did you know it's almost nine o'clock?"

"Dear Lord, let me get off this phone. See you in the by-and-by."

"The by-and-by."

She hurries real quick to turn on that ancient Motorola of hers with aluminum foil balled on each antenna. She finds channel six, and seeing that the commercials are still playing before her favorite program comes on, she turns down the volume and goes into the kitchen to warm up the stove. By the time she's checked the levels of her sugar and flour cans and found two jars of apple jelly in the back of her pantry, the television camera has swept over the back of the audience to a close-up of Phil Donahue's thick gray hair and dark-rimmed glasses. She turns up the volume just as he's about to introduce the people sitting up on the stage. He's brung somebody in from Kansas, Oregon, and Secaucus, New Jersey, all of who got photographs and claim they spotted UFOs. The fourth fellow is an astronomer from Palo Alto, and the fifth is an official from NASA.

"Is there intelligent life in outer space?" Phil looks dead serious, staring right into the cameras. "*And* are they trying to get in touch with us? If so, for what purpose? We'll be right back after this message to explore this fascinating topic."

Miranda's never been much on television, but she started watching this show religiously once she found out it was based in Chicago. It gave her an idea of the kind of people Cocoa was living around since she'd moved north. Even the folks in Atlanta were different from the folks in Willow Springs, and when you started talking Chicago, Philadelphia, New York, they were way different again. And this show gave the audience a chance to speak, and what they had to say was always of more interest to her than the people on the stage who were running off at the mouth about being male strippers, lesbian nuns, or talking about some new book they just wrote, showing folks who lived in apartments how to turn their bathrooms into fallout shelters. On all of these "fascinating topics" she had one opinion and that could be summed up in two words: white folks. And when they found a colored somebody to act the fool — like the man from New Jersey, holding up a snapshot of his cousin posing with a family of Martians — she expanded it to three words: honorary white folks.

But at least the faces out in the audience keep changing with each new program, and she wants them faces. Sometimes, she'll keep the volume turned off for the entire hour, knowing well that what's being said by the audience don't matter a whit to how it's being said. Laughter before or after a mouth opens to speak, the number of times a throat swallows, the curve of the lips, the thrust of the neck, the slump of the shoulders. And always, always the eyes. She can pick out which ladies in the audience have secretly given up their babies for adoption, which fathers have daughters making pornographic movies, exactly which homes been shattered by Vietnam, drugs, or "the alarming rise of divorce." What she finally settled on about Chicago — and, by guilt of association, New York — was that it's no worse or better than other places Baby Girl could have chosen to live in.

Those big cities ain't changed in the years since she'd visited her folks up there, so there weren't no need to go again. She'd been north a few times when Hope was alive and her girl, Willa, was small. Hope had been her favorite niece — always something funny to say. Married a nice man, too, that Benjamin Prescott, though he never made too much of himself — gambling took a lot of it away. Still, no reason for little Willa to carry on like she did, setting herself off from the family and breaking her mama's heart. She knew that high-society marriage was all bound to come to no good. Just before Hope passed, she'd sent them little Willa's wedding picture. Miranda remembers the face on Willa's husband — like a bottomless pit — and shudders. There's more to that Christmas Eve fire than meets the eye — much more. Miranda frowns and refuses to think into the flames that dance at the back of her head. Little Willa didn't deserve that kind of end; she was a good enough child if not a whit of courage. So unlike Grace's child. That Ophelia came into the world kicking and screaming — kicked her right in the eye as she brought her up to her lips to suck the blood and mucous out of her nose. A little raw demon from the start. Miranda smiles. Under five pounds and being kept alive on nothing but sugar tits and will. It was touch-and-go many a day with that one.

We ain't had much luck with the girls in this family, Miranda thinks, and I begged Abigail not to name her first baby Peace. She didn't live long enough to get a crib name. No, not much luck at all. It was peculiar when she thought on it, and she didn't think on it much. Most all of the boys had thrived: her own daddy being the youngest of seven boys, and his daddy the youngest of seven. But coming on down to them, it was just her, Abigail, and Peace. And out of them just another three girls, and out of them, two. Three generations of nothing but girls, and only one left alive in this last generation to keep the Days going — the child of Grace.

At least Abigail had the presence of mind to give Grace's baby a proper crib name. Miranda would have done it herself and had fixed it in her mind to crib name her No — this was one girl they would *not* let get away. But it had to be the mama's mama, and Miranda was so afraid with the baby failing as she was, and Grace carrying on so after the daddy, drying up her milk with hate, that Abigail, nervous as she gets, would do it wrong. But that little ball of pale fire, spitting up practically every ounce of goat's milk she could finally take, pulling Mother's china knickknacks off the curio before she could barely crawl, running before she could walk — she was *the* baby girl. They dropped the "the" when they were sure she was gonna stay, and after Ophelia got to be five years old, she refused to answer to Baby Girl, thinking it meant just that. So they gave her the pet name Cocoa. "It'll put color on her somewhere," Miranda had said, but she and Abigail kept calling her exactly what she was between themselves, and where it counted most of all — in their minds. She'll answer to Baby Girl again when she's a mama in her own right — there'll be no need to explain to the silly thing what she's been knowing all along.

Just as a woman on the TV gets up to ask why is it that all the visitations from outer space have been friendly, carrying warnings and advice for the planet Earth — ain't it possible that if there's other intelligent life, some of it must be warlike, hoping to conquer us? — Miranda decides to turn the program off. The man from Oregon had just bent over to respond, but he did not really answer that woman's need. Her husband beats her, Miranda thinks, having seen the slight twitch around her mouth, and that's what she wants explained. She fears her dreams. Pain comes hurling down from the space outside her pillow, and she wakes to find a stranger has left her with a twisted arm or a split lip. Tell me how to sleep at night, she's asking. Now the NASA person was holding up a chart as the woman sat back down, clutching her handbag beneath her breast.

Miranda shakes her head as the audience and all of Chicago disappears into a dot of flashing light. She pushes down the television's antennas and goes into the kitchen. All she needs is to get herself a little shame weed and bake it up in something sweet. The bowls come out, the flour, the butter — she'd sleep tonight, sure enough. She sets the square of butter into the bowl to soften, takes an old shoe box and candle from beneath her cabinets, and goes out her back door. She was gonna need at least six fresh eggs for her two cakes, and then six for Abigail's — a good dozen, and Baby Girl ain't worth a one. The chickens that run loose around her trailer flock to her feet as she nears the wired-in coop.

"You missed being breakfast this morning, Clarissa, but don't get too sure of yourself. There's worms and bugs out here aplenty — go find 'em."

The old black hen fixes Miranda with an unblinking bright eye as she enters the wire fence gate and fastens it securely behind her. Placing her shoe box and candle on a post, she runs fresh water into the trough, clearing out the loose feathers and dust. Calling the chickens to her, she spreads their mash. This yard needs cleaning and so does the inside of that coop, but she has no time for that today. Baby Girl would have a way to make herself useful in the next two weeks. While the chickens eat, she goes into their coop. Having to bend to get through the door, she can stand upright once inside. The rafters are a good two feet above her head, and the cloudy sunlight that's filtering in through the windows shows the little specks of fluff that's swirling among the beams in the musty air. Two setting hens, having refused food and water, are wedged into a corner nest and she knows not to go anywhere near them. Rummaging through abandoned nests, she holds each egg she finds up to her lighted candle. She moves them around in her fingers gently, tip down, and can see straight through the shells as she searches for clear, firm yolks. The candlelight flickers across her face, the flesh stretched like tight leather against her cheeks and temple bones, and the light gives a kinda mellow edge to skin the color of brown parchment. She pushes her lips up in concentration as she squints at a tiny blood spot — but this one is good. If life is being formed, breaking the shell means a double loss: it can't be eaten and the chick won't be made. Her fingers curl gently around a warm egg that shows a deepening spot with tiny veins running out from it.

"Well, well, well." Candlelight makes the shadowy life within her wrinkled hand seem to breathe as she rotates it real careful. The setting hens in the corner flutter and let out sounds like muted groans.

"Uh, huh." She places the egg back into the pile of straw. "You know, don't you."

Outside, she blinks her eyes rapidly in the strong light and flexes her back. The scent of pine and grass burst out as the sun moves for a minute from behind a group of clouds.

"Peek is all you gonna be doing today." Miranda looks up at the sky.

When she's unfastening the gate to her hen yard, a young rooster tries to sneak in and she pushes him back with her foot as she juggles the full box of eggs.

"Now, Cicero, you ain't got no business in there and you know it. Stay out here and earn your keep. Clarissa, what good are you if you can't keep this boy of yours in line? He woulda gone into the pot long along if he weren't one of yours."

She was sorry that she had kept Cicero. Two roosters were a problem she didn't need. And this one couldn't get it into his head that those hens inside weren't for him.

Bernice Duvall's dark green Chevrolet pulls into her front yard just as she's ready to step into her trailer, and Miranda sighs. Here was another problem she didn't need right now.

"Morning, Mama Day." Bernice leaps out the car as if she's been pushed.

"How you keeping, Bernice?"

"Fair to middling."

Bernice has been the same way from a child: thin as a stick and always in motion. It's nerve-racking sometimes just to watch her. Her hands play with the buttons on her blouse, the ends of her sleeves, run across her collarbone. When she's sitting, the muscles in her calf and knees move with a will of their own, and the moment she stands up, she'll start shifting from one foot to the next. She was always good to run an errand: it seems she was at the store before finding out why she was sent. She stands by the car, her hands making little fluttering motions from the door handle to the hollow under her breasts, waiting for Miranda's next question to find out if she's welcome.

"You on your way to work now?"

Bernice nods and moves a step closer.

"And Ambush, he doing well?"

"Well as can be expected. He got up early to take a load of tomatoes beyond the bridge. He takes care of most of the fresh produce for the big supermarket now. So we're doing real well — on that end. He wants me to give up cashiering at the drug store. Says it tires me out too much, and that's why we can't —"

"You only go in half a day, don't you? That little bit ain't doing nothing to you — it's not like you lifting or something."

"But ain't nothing happening, Mama Day!" Bernice shrinks back at the sound of her own outburst.

"These things take time, Bernice. All in good time."

"It's been a long time." Her voice gets real low, hesitant. "And I've done everything you've told me — everything everybody's told me and —"

"What I told you first of all is to wait — and you ain't doing that, Bernice."

"There's a new fertility drug they carry over at the store. It's supposed to work miracles."

"The only miracle is life itself. And when it comes, it comes."

"Two of our customers already got pregnant from it."

Miranda sighs. "Then go to the clinic and see if Dr. Smithfield will get it for you."

"I tried, but he said he don't believe in them things."

"Well, I agree with him — it ain't natural. And your constitution can't handle them strong drugs. *I* told you that long ago. Ain't you better be getting on to work? And I got cakes to bake — Cocoa is coming in today."

"That's right, it's mid-August already. I bet Miss Abigail is real happy. Tell Cocoa I'll be over to see her — hear what's happening up in the city. She got any babies yet?"

"She better get herself a husband first, and she's been slow as molasses about that. You done beat her out long ago on that score."

"To what end, if I can't keep him." Her hands start fluttering again. Miranda puts down her egg box, takes Bernice's hands in her own, and forces them to be still.

"Any man — and I say, any man — who would leave you just because of something like that is well worth the going. And I've known Ambush before he knew himself — I brought his *mama* into the world — and he ain't that kind of man. So if that's what's on your mind, lay it to rest."

The fingers that grip Miranda's feel like ice and the fine bones tremble under the skin.

"Maybe we could go to the other place, Mama Day?"

Miranda pretends that she don't hear her. "You still got plenty of star grass? You taking them teas?"

"Morning and night."

"Then just give it time. And next week, I'll make you up some ground raspberry to take along with it — and a little something for your nerves."

"At the other place, Mama —"

"No." She pats Bernice's hand and turns to go into her trailer.

"But there's a new moon tonight."

"I know," Miranda says without turning around. She hears the car's engine start up and the wheels bite into the grass, flinging gravel as Bernice backs out of her yard.

In the kitchen she creams the sugar into the softened butter until no grains are felt beneath her spoon. Real careful, she breaks a fresh egg so that the yolk stays whole. Cupping the shell in her hand, she watches for a while as the bloated yellow swims in the thick mucous — not this month. She breaks another egg — nor the next. The third yolk is slipped into the sugar and butter — nor the next. She shakes her head. But she would still make up the ground raspberry for Bernice — tones the insides, strengthens the blood.

Abigail is sweeping her front porch when Miranda crosses the main road between their places, loaded down with two foil-wrapped cakes and a paper bag of eggs. Abigail's full head of silvery hair is pinned up with those mother-of-pearl combs she usually wears only to church, their rosy tints matching the fine pink lines in her new sundress. She is still a beautiful woman, and able to turn a few heads yet in front of the barbershop when she's done up right. Her body's grown plump but not loose like some. Age done only softened the olive brown flesh of her upper arms, neck, and jaw line, giving the sense that one day it'll all just melt away into the surrounding air. Her false teeth gleam when she sees Miranda, who's wearing the same old house dress she put on that morning, with flour powdering her stomach.

"You there, Sister?" Miranda calls.

"Uh, huh."

Miranda stops at the foot of the porch. "Somebody sure don't want me and my cakes in their house today if they sweeping straight toward me."

"Not you I don't want, it's this here dust." Abigail laughs. "And I ain't sweeping salt, am I?"

She puts the broom aside so Miranda can climb the porch steps and takes one of the cakes from her. "Ummm, I can smell that jelly right through this foil."

"Let 'em sit for a few days to let the flavor soak in and they may be worth eating. We can have one of your coconuts for supper."

"You gonna help me grate?"

"Woman, ain't I worked enough today for that no-'count grand-daughter of yours? Why didn't you send by the store for some Bakers?"

"That old packaged stuff don't taste the same — and where's my rosemary?"

"Lord, Abigail, and I had plenty drying out at the other place. But Bernice came by this morning and it slipped my mind."

"I thought that was her car over in your yard. Then she musta come straight here after leaving you — looking for Buzzard."

"Now, what she want him for?"

"You know what she want him for." Abigail frowns. "I told her I done sent him beyond the bridge to pick up Baby Girl. I don't know what we gonna do about Bernice."

"Bernice is gonna have to do about Bernice, herself. But it's a bad sign if she starts messing with Buzzard."

Inside, Abigail's living room gleams with lemon oil and a light breeze moves her freshly starched curtains. A bunch of wildflowers — daisies, periwinkles, marsh fern — sits in their mama's cut-glass vase on the mantelpiece. Off to the right, the spare bedroom has a new rag run on its polished floor which matches the ruffled bedcover and throw pillows. More wildflowers are arranged on the night table and dresser.

"You'd think the preacher was coming," Miranda says on their way into the kitchen.

"Baby Girl probably thought she was gonna sneak up on us," Abigail says. "But we got a surprise for her."

The carved wooden cabinets in Abigail's kitchen are identical to Miranda's, but there are three sets that run along the wall to end at the window, where basil, thyme, and sage are growing in clay pots. A fresh pork shoulder is marinating on the counter next to her sink, which is filled with string beans and potatoes.

"Your sage is holding up fine." Miranda feels the feathery leaves and sniffs. "Fresh sage tastes good in pork."

"Don't try to get out of forgetting my rosemary."

Miranda finally sees the coconuts. "No, Abigail — two of 'em?"

Abigail ties on an apron, picks up a small hammer, and cracks the shell with a dull thud.

"Don't waste the juice. Add it to your cake batter."

"Naw, it makes my layers too moist and they falls apart."

" 'Cause you too heavy-handed with it. Just a little gives it a nice flavor."

"I just ain't got your touch, Miranda."

"That ain't working twice in one day, Abigail. I'm not making up no more cake batter."

"Who asked you to?"

"Well, good then. Where's the grater?"

Their cake pans are cooling on the side counter when a car horn begins playing "The Battle Hymn of the Republic" from the front yard.

"My baby's here!" Abigail smooths her hair and dress as she rushes toward the front porch.

Dr. Buzzard's pickup truck is missing both fenders and the wheels wobble inward on loose axles; there are so many dents along its side, it's hard to tell that it was blue at one time. He's sitting alone behind the wheel, but he's wearing his beyond-the-bridge clothes: a clean T-shirt under the denim overalls that he usually wears by itself, and a rooster feather stuck in the band of his felt hat. He jumps down out of the truck, and they see that he's even changed into his good Nike sneakers, but he still ain't bothered to put any strings into them. He reaches into the back and brings out a cardboard box with six Mason jars of honey.

Abigail wilts pitifully. "Buzzard, where's Cocoa?"

"Cocoa — your grandbaby, Cocoa?"

"Yes, you addle-brained, slew-footed son-of-a-crow, Cocoa!" Miranda comes to the edge of the steps, and he backs up toward his truck.

"Now, Mama Day, why you carrying on so? Miss Abigail asked me this very morning would I go beyond the bridge to the airport and pick up her honey. Now, none of that didn't make too much sense to me, since I had these here jars waiting for y'all out by my hives — ya know I keeps my hives over near Chevy's Pass, which ain't no place near the airport — ain't even beyond the bridge. But I did it just the way she asks — went home, changed my clothes and everything — 'cause after all, y'all are Days, and your daddy, John-Paul, was a big man in these parts. Why, your daddy was practically a legend, and so —"

"Fool!" Miranda's voice makes both Dr. Buzzard and Abigail jump. "Don't be standing there talking about no daddys. You ain't got a daddy — nothing human could have put you on this earth. You mean, you went all the way out to the airport and didn't wait for the plane?"

"Oh, the plane come in all right, but —"

Abigail turns to Miranda. "Maybe, you were wrong — she wasn't on that plane."

"Yes, she was." Miranda picks up the broom laying against the house and whacks it down on the porch railing with each word. "But this out-and-out miserable excuse for something that should be living and breathing ain't had enough sense to —"

"But Miss Abigail said to bring back *her honey*," Dr. Buzzard wails. "And that's just what I did. And you oughta be glad, Mama Day, 'cause you been after me for two weeks to fetch you some too. Now" — he places the box gingerly near the porch steps — "if that ain't the honey you meant, maybe you meant *this* honey." He yanks the canvas off the truck bed, and Cocoa sits up laughing.

"We did it, Dr. Buzzard."

As Abigail runs toward the truck, Miranda shakes her head, showing all her gums.

"I ain't did a bit of vaudeville in my time for nothing." Dr. Buzzard takes out a handkerchief and wipes his grizzled head. "But things was getting mighty tight here."

"Buzzard, I oughta kill you." Abigail hugs her granddaughter. "My heart almost stopped."

"And I still oughta take this broom to you." Miranda grins as he carries the suitcases from the back of the truck.

"Now, don't you all go blaming Dr. Buzzard. I was determined to get my surprise in — one way or the other."

Miranda watches Cocoa approach with her grandmother's arms tightly around her waist. She thinks for a moment that the sun musta come from beneath the clouds again and actually glances up. When did it happen — this kind of blooming from pale to gold? She remembers the little girl running home crying and almost taking off her middle finger with a butcher knife, fearing she really had the white blood she was teased about at school — she wanted red blood like everybody else. And now she strides so proud, a sunflower against the brown arms over hers, the sweat flowing from the reddish gold hair and absorbing every bit of available light to fling it back against those high cheekbones, down the collarbone, on to the line of the pelvis, pressing against the thin summer cotton. The lean thighs, tight hips, the long strides flashing light between the blur of strong legs — pure black. Me and Abigail, we take after the sons, Miranda thinks. The earth men who formed the line of Days, hard and dark brown. But *the* Baby Girl brings back the great, grand Mother. We ain't seen 18 & 23 black from that time till now. The black that can soak up all the light in the universe, can even swallow the sun. Them silly children didn't know that it's the white in us that reflects all these shades of brown running around Willow Springs. But pure black woulda sucked it all in — and it's only an ancient mother of pure black that one day spits out this kinda gold.

"I knowed you were coming," Miranda says, hands on hips.

"You know too much, Mama Day." Cocoa mimics her stand and winks. "That's why I took you down a peg this afternoon."

"Bring your fresh self here." She draws the girl's body into her own. "I'm sure glad you're home."

Home. Folks call it different things, think of it in different ways. For Cocoa it's being around living mirrors with the power to show a woman that she's still carrying scarred knees, a runny nose, and socks that get walked down into the heels of her shoes.

"Your resistance is always been low."

"I told you, I never intend to put another spoonful of that horrible stuff into my mouth."

"You wanna go back up there and catch pneumonia? This agueweed will clean you out and get your system right."

"Grandma, it gives me the runs."

"How else them nasty city germs coming out your body?"

"I'm tired of spending my first two days here sitting on the toilet."

"Have it your way."

"You gave up pretty easy."

"Well, you grown — and you can't tell grown folks what to do."

"Give it here. If I don't take it, you'll just mix it in my food."

"Since when?"

"Since the last two times I've been home."

"It weren't me, it was them raw sweet potatoes you insist on eating."

"Sure, sure."

*

Home. It's being new and old all rolled into one. Measuring your new against old friends, old ways, old places. Knowing that as long as the old survives, you can keep changing as much as you want without the nightmare of waking up to a total stranger.

"You going by to visit Miss Ruby?"

"Don't I always?"

"But she said she ain't seen you any last week. You know Ruby can't get around so well."

"If she lost some of that weight, she could."

"Nasty, nasty."

"It's true, Mama Day, she's humongous. And all she wants to do is fool with my hair."

"You didn't mind, you fresh heifer, when she got them cockleburs out your scalp."

"I was ten years old! And we've both gotten too big for me to still be sitting between her knees."

"Well, it'll break her heart, you don't get by there."

"I said, I will — I just haven't found the time."

"You found the time to be gallivanting all over the place with Bernice — to them juke joints beyond the bridge. Spending money you ain't got."

"They're called clubs."

"I don't care what they're called. Bernice is a married woman now, and instead of that rubbing off on you, she acts up something terrible when you come home. Ambush oughta take a stick to both of you."

"But he's with us most of the time."

"Then for the times he's not."

"Mama Day, did you know Bernice is talking about seeing Dr. Buzzard?"

"I know."

"She wants children very badly."

"That ain't the way to get 'em. All Buzzard's gonna do is take her money."

"But she needs help, Mama Day, and you really could . . . I mean . . ."

"You best leave Bernice and that business alone. You got plenty to worry about your own self. At least she done found herself a husband."

"I don't need a man right now, I need a job."

"A place like New York got plenty of men — and jobs — for the taking."

"I've been trying, but that's easier said than done."

"Not if you know how to do it."

"Well, then you tell me how to do it. I interviewed for a job I could do with my eyes closed just before I came, and the guy was *this close* to giving it to me — I could see it in his face. But they needed someone right away and I had to come home."

"No, you didn't have to, but it speaks right well of you that you did. You the only one Abigail's got left now, with Hope's child gone."

"I told him all that."

"So how you know they didn't hold the job for you?"

"Because there were a dozen people who could do it if I didn't."

"That don't mean nothing. You should write and ask."

"I can just call when I get back to New York, but . . ."

"No, I think you should get in touch with them from right here — in your own handwriting. You remember the man's name?"

"Andrews. George Andrews, but he . . ."

"Yeah, go on in the house now and use some of Abigail's yellow writing paper, the one with the little flowers at the bottom. Tell him that you really are looking forward to that job, and you hope it's waiting for ya — things like that."

"Mama Day, that won't help."

"Can it hurt?"

"Well, no."

"And Miss C . . ."

"What?"

"When you done — make sure you let me mail it."

Home. You can move away from it, but you never leave it. Not as long as it holds something to be missed.

"All right, Buzzard, you drive carefully with my baby, now."

Abigail holds a young woman on her front porch who moves different now. It only took a little while for her body to remember how to flow in time with the warm air and the swaying limbs of the oaks.

She is deeper in color and rounder in her face and hips. Cocoa's got to carry back twice what she brought: a hand-stitched counterpane, jars of canned preserves, a basket of potpourri, and a boxful of paper bags marked chest cold, fever, headache, and monthly. Miranda follows Dr. Buzzard to his truck, carrying the counterpane folded up in a plastic bag.

"Buzzard, I hear that Bernice is planning to come round your way."

"Bernice Duvall? Now what she want?"

"You know what she wants, and make sure she don't find it."

"Now, Mama Day, when folks come to me seeking help, my conscience don't allow me to turn 'em away."

"Your conscience ain't got nothing to do with it, Buzzard — it's the money. And if you really had a conscience, you wouldn't be selling them hoodoo bits of rags and sticks — and that watered-down moonshine as medicine, passing yourself off as a —"

"I am just what I say I am. You do things your way and I do 'em mine. And it hurts my feelings no end that you won't call me *Doctor* Buzzard — I gives you respect."

"There ain't but one Dr. Buzzard, and he ain't you. That man is up in Beaufort County, South Carolina, and he's *real*. You may fool these folks in Willow Springs, but ain't nobody here older than me, and I remember when your name was Rainbow Simpson. And you can change that all you want, but you can't change the fact that you still nothing but an out-and-out bootlegger and con man. But what you do ain't none of my business . . ."

"If Bernice comes to me for help, I'm helping her." He throws the suitcases into the back of the truck real hard. "And in all due respects, like you said, it ain't none of your business."

"It ain't, Buzzard, it really ain't. And that's why it would cause me no end of sorrow to make it so. 'Cause the way I see it, you been walking round on this earth a long time and got just as much right as the next fella to keep walking around, healthy and all — living out your natural life."

"I believe you're threatening me, Mama Day."

"Now, how could I do something like that? What could a tired old woman like me do to a powerful hoodoo doctor? Why, that little mess I got out at the other place wouldn't hold a candle to —"

"Ain't nobody talking about the other place. Ain't nobody mentioned —"

"That's right, we ain't said a word about nothing — but Bernice."

It's one happy man who sees Abigail and Cocoa finally coming toward the truck. "I do believe Cocoa is ready now, ain't you, honey?"

"As ready as I'll ever be. But I sure hate to go."

"Now why?" Miranda says. "All them good things waiting for you up in New York — jobs and husbands and what-all."

Cocoa laughs. "They sure weren't waiting when I left."

"A lot can happen between your leaving and getting back to a place."

"It did — seven pounds on me, and about seventy pounds in overweight baggage."

They're gonna stand and watch until the tail lights of the truck disappear over the horizon. It's a pretty evening, the kind that comes with a blending of reds and purples with the mist rising off The Sound. The parting ain't easy. But we are old, old women, Miranda thinks, and if we let you go now, we can see the road you set out on before it gets to be too late for us.

◇◇◇

I HAD, TO BE TRUTHFUL, almost forgotten about you until the letter came. A new office manager was hired the day after your interview, and my partner went on vacation, having promised to wait only until the moment we got someone. I couldn't protest being left with a new manager *and* the groundwork for implementing Ray Hopewell's new piping system — Bruce had done more than his share that year for our first big account. Andrews & Stein was a production and design company — Stein thought up the impossible and Andrews made it work. So Bruce reminded me that he had given up the opening of the trout season that spring, dumped his lousy blueprints on my desk, said, Now it's your turn, and left for the Catskills.

There wasn't much I could say, knowing that if the tables were turned, nothing short of an account from God to mechanize the Pearly Gates would have gotten me to give up my winter vacations. If I didn't get two weeks during the playoff season, we were guaranteed a miserable year together. Just that January I had been sprinting between Tampa, Pittsburgh, and Pasadena while he handled the moving and painting of our new offices with only his wife's niece for a stand-in receptionist, who couldn't spell her own name without chewing a wad of Juicy Fruit, which inevitably landed between our files. He was good-natured enough to say her gum helped somewhat, because that way he was certain of having the B's follow the A's. Hopewell got one look at her, realized that we didn't squander money on receptionists with the smarts to demand more than minimum wage, and gave us a chance with his apartment complex. And Bruce, who wouldn't know a football from a nymph fly at the end of his reel, actually congratulated me that the AFC — if not my beloved Patriots — stormed Pasadena that year. It would have taken a lesser man than I was to complain about his desertion, with our quarterly taxes due in mid-September, the inherent tension of two projects nearing completion and Hopewell's to get going, as well as an overzealous office manager whose motto was, Ask before you do (even in ordering paper clips) so the blame won't be laid on your doorstep. Dwight was terrific at his job, but hardly what you'd call an original thinker.

With all of that, and no time for lunch and sometimes dinner unless I had it after ten-thirty, there was definitely no time for Shawn. And we probably could have saved five good years with something as simple as a few quiet evenings together. Our relationship had reached the pouting stage earlier that year, a winter and spring of stony silences that replaced the rational debates or even battles over small bones of contentions we had tried to work out once before. Now, those small irritations just sat between us as each tried to figure out if *this* silence should actually be a conversation or screaming match — we'd had them all — about what ultimately couldn't bring me to marry her when the obvious differences no longer applied. She had stopped being a redhead with freckles a long time ago and had become just Shawn. But we had come to the point where I was afraid to touch her, not knowing if I'd be unrightly accused through her silence of using her — or worse, be accepted into her body with a plaintive sadness that made me question silently whether I was or not. It was a relief not to have to worry about that for those hectic three weeks and bitter to realize that she took my apologies for canceled dinners and needing the space to sleep alone just a bit too quickly — the parting "miss you" and "miss you too"s ringing hollow between us after we put the receivers down.

But it would have taken a bigger man than I would ever be not to curse Bruce that particular morning: the phone literally never stopped ringing, giving me no time to decide how I was going to be in two places at once during lunchtime and still have only half a Saturday to myself. It wasn't fair, the trout ran up in the damn Catskills all year round, but the Patriots only had sixteen lousy weeks to get a shot at the Super Bowl. The small envelope was stuck between a batch of project proposals and I split it open without a glance at the return address. Too bad, lady, the job is taken, but you'll survive — we all will. And it would have stayed in my trash basket if I hadn't noticed the film of yellow powder on my hands. It was the consistency of talc and very sparse — as if I'd touched a goldenrod.

I frowned and retrieved the crumpled letter and envelope — it had been mailed from Willow Springs. Now, where had she said that place was again? South Carolina? Georgia? No, she had said it was in no state, and there were no state initials on the postmark, just Willow Springs and a zip code. Strange. Had she put sachet on the letter? I brought it to my nose, but there was no scent. And the only trace of extra powder was on my fingers. It didn't rub off easily, and for some reason I felt uncomfortable about brushing it off on my pants. I left the phone ringing and went to wash my hands in the bathroom. As the water ran and the powder finally dissolved from my fingers, it all came back, a movie being played in reverse frame to frame: the defiant set of your back and my overwhelming relief when you walked out of my office, your spunk, the story of your cousin's death, your grandmother, Willow Springs, the suppressed accent, the hand rising to move stray hairs from your neck. Your neck. There was now the faintest scent of lavender on my wet fingers although I had washed with the rough Oxydol soap that we used to remove blueprint ink. Had she smelled of lavender that day? I couldn't depend upon my senses to remember something like that about a woman I had already forgotten, could I? And it would have been the end of it, Ophelia, truly the end, if Hopewell hadn't insisted upon eating in a Chinese restaurant.

I had never trusted foods that are mixed together — soups, stews, fancy sauces. I wanted a potato to be a potato, a slice of meat just that. So in those places I'm confined to clear soup, boiled rice, and barbecued spareribs, which worked hell on the cholesterol level I was forced to watch like a hawk. Having to sit there and pick at food that I hated for a totally unnecessary meeting didn't help my disposition that day. I felt put upon by Hopewell's wealth and doubly resentful of Bruce's vacation, although even if he were in town, he wouldn't have gone. Besides being the production end of the company, I was also public relations. On my better days I wouldn't have minded, because we'd both still be glorified draftsmen at the city's Building Department if we had to depend upon Bruce to communicate our ideas to clients. Ten minutes into the meal he would have called Hopewell an overbearing asshole for wasting half an afternoon having a design explained to him that was as simple as it was brilliant. But I knew that an account like Hopewell's would move us toward that elevated stage where we would be dealing with companies that send their staff engineers to work out details with contractors.

But for now it was businessmen who had to be sold on cost efficiency because their millions were too recent and personal to be relinquished without our holding their hands every step of the way. Without Bruce's artistic temperament, I had the patience to explain that nothing saved him more money than the extra money we wanted for copper piping. You buy the material at 1980 prices and waiver 1990 plumbing bills — and there weren't even any joints in the system for potential leakage. But with all those right angles in this diagram, wouldn't the thing simply break? Of course, it would break, it had to break. All moving parts or parts with motion flowing through them — in his case, water — wore out even if the pipes were straight as an arrow. But the point was that his great-grandson or -daughter would have to worry about it, not him. I had to draw the line at why we insisted that a pipe angling right would send the water flowing left. There's a point when you say trust us or give the job to someone else. But, yes, we could guarantee that the dame's dishwasher on the tenth floor could run at the same time as the fag's Jacuzzi on the first. Dame. Fag. That's how the man talked. He *was* an overbearing asshole, and if he had jabbed me in the side once more with his "Ya know what I mean, soul brother," I was going to tell him what he should have read in my eyes — he didn't have much of a soul and he was hardly my brother. Sure, like him, I felt that the private sector held the solutions to our current recession, not more government spending. But why did he think I'd appreciate the sentiment that he was going to help vote out Jimmy

Carter because he had ruined the economy and no self-respecting black man would let a southern cracker cut his profit margins for the sake of those welfare cheats? Meeting his type always made me ashamed to be a Republican.

Thank God, the fortune cookies came. You always pick the one with the ends pointing toward you, he told me. And incredible as it might seem, my refusal could have affected the three-million-dollar contract I'd reassured him into leaving with us. His strip of paper said, "You always rise to the occasion," and we spent another few minutes on his tasteless jokes before he actually ate that concoction of cardboard, sugar, and water. Mine crumbled in my hand and the powdery slip of paper read, "All chickens come home to roost." Total nonsense, but after dusting the yellowish powder off my fingers, I looked up and told him I had the perfect person to replace his accounts manager. There was no need to pay an agency to do a search next week — there was someone we had wanted badly to hire ourselves, but she had walked in the moment after we had made a commitment to someone else. Her work experience and references were impeccable. Yeah, but how were her legs? he wanted to know. Not bad, I lied again. And if she didn't work out — fire her. He hadn't lost a thing, not even a finder's fee. So what was in it for me — or better, what was in her for me? A gargoyle, that's what he looked like when he leered. Not a thing, but if she worked out, then he owed me — his promise that she'd never know where the recommendation came from.

I went back to the office, got your filed application, and had it messengered over to him. I was throwing a lamb to the wolves — but Hopewell would survive. I worked especially late that night, never allowing myself to think about the rationale for any of this. There wasn't any. I hadn't done you a favor. I hadn't felt sorry for a black woman out there up against it looking for a job. I hadn't thought you the best person for the position. I hadn't thought at all, not even two weeks later when I sent the roses.

My FIRST WEEK on the new job wasn't bad. From our first meeting I had Hopewell figured out as a rump roast. I had come highly recommended by a guy he knew who worked at my old company, so just show him my stuff. And sure, he'd call me Cocoa, because he loved hot chocolate. Your class-A sleaze, but I knew just how to handle that. A couple of coffee breaks with the office gossip and then everyone knew about my breaking up with a man who I found out had been committed twice for homicidal rages and who now took to slinking around my apartment building. Then the second week I come in without make-up except for a little maroon blush under my eyes and ask Hopewell to have a drink after work, because he looked like the kind of man to help me with a personal problem I was having. You would have thought I had invited him to sip a glass of cholera. You're doing fine so far, Miss Day, but your personal problems should be left entirely out of this office. Cowardly bastard. I went to the bathroom and howled. I didn't even have to worry about him using my first name, no less using the front of my blouse to shine his wedding ring on. You see, when you can get that crap out of the way good and early, you can get on with your job.

And you don't know the satisfaction when I found out that Andrews & Stein was one of our engineering contractors. Well, so much for you, buddy, and your call-me-George. Now, I'm managing the accounts of the man you're working for. Life goes 'round, doesn't it? I couldn't wait to tell Grandma and Mama Day that I was finally working again, so I called them both up. One would have been sufficient — those two didn't breathe without telling the other what it felt like. But I wanted to let Mama Day know how wrong she was about my sending you the note — they did give the position to someone else. I know these big cities, while her whole impression of what's happening up here comes from the Phil Donahue Show.

"You're working, ain't you? So now you can stop calling collect."

And she actually hung up on me. Sitting down there on a good five thousand acres of prime land, a lot of it waterfront and timber, a lousy call off hours wouldn't have dented her. But the great-aunt — God love her — hated to be wrong about anything. She always had a way of seeing right through people and their motives, but sometimes it wasn't quite the whole picture. She and I fought a lot about my boyfriends and the way I wanted to spend my time. And she always seemed to know when I was planning something behind their backs. As a kid, I often wondered if it was just the dope grown-ups had on you because they'd pulled the same tricks themselves, or if it was because Mama Day was special. And it wasn't good to run up against her too much. Unlike Grandma, she'd take a peach switch to me. Mama Day just didn't believe in cuddling. But if Grandma had raised me alone, I would have been ruined for any fit company. It seemed I could do no wrong with her, while with Mama Day I could do no right. I guess, in a funny kind of a way, together they were the perfect mother. But they had each taught me that living without manners in this world is not living at all. And so when the flowers came, I owed it to myself to thank you. I admit a simple note would have done it, but I called.

I'd been warned that gifts were the norm with my job — silver-plated bolts for paperweights, crates of Indian River grapefruit, mon-ogramed address books from contractors who wanted to stay on the good side of the accounts manager. I might forget a late budget, over-look an inflated estimate. So seeing the yellow roses I thought, Trying to suck up to me already — he remembers what a bastard he was. And the note really bowled me over. "There are only eleven yellow roses here. The twelfth is waiting on a table at Il Ponte Vecchio if you'd like to retrieve it one evening." Now, what kind of fudge stick asked a woman out like this — who's this guy used to dating, Mary Tyler Moore? My call was to say thank you but no to dinner. I had plenty of legitimate reasons, mind you. Professional ties are best left professional — objectivity and all that. Conflict of interest, mixing business with pleasure, etcetera, etcetera. Although, at the bottom line I couldn't imagine how an evening alone with you and that twelfth rose could be anything but a total downer. I was never in that camp of a night out with someone is better than a night alone. I was someone, and there was always something to do with *me*. I actually enjoyed polishing my nails or washing my hair and sitting in front of the mirror to admire the effect — for myself. Anything that gave me pleasure wasn't a waste of time. You were going to be a two-minute debt paid to my upbringing and a two-second dismissal with a "No, *I'll* call *you* for a rain check."

The damn phone rang eight times before I got your cherry-vanilla receptionist, another few minutes waiting while she read her instruc-tion manual on switching a call, and then four times before you picked up. In all the delay I could hear my heart pounding through the cupped space on the receiver. I was getting angry at myself for being nervous and even angrier at you for putting me in that position in the first place. And then finally hoping that my rejection would cut you to the quick and even things up. The point is that when I finally heard your voice I had started caring about the effect of what I was going to say to you and I couldn't have cared less when I began dialing.

And after we had gone through the thank you for the flowers, blah, blah, blah . . . It was nothing and glad you got the job, blah, blah, blah . . . "And about dinner, George . . ." It was just half a breath: my lungs had simply to bring up enough wind from the diaphragm to push out the "I" of "I can't do it any time soon, but . . ." In just that half a breath, the caring in your silence stunned me. And it wasn't directed toward me personally. It was like when a kid labors over a package — the wrapping paper is poorly glued, the ribbon is half tied — and all of his attention is directed toward that space between the hands that offer and the hands poised to receive. It's the gesture that holds the heart of the child. And you cared deeply about what I thought of the gesture — not you. So I couldn't have scored any points for myself by refusing, and I certainly couldn't have hurt you. The only damage would have been done to a kindness. And God knows, there was little enough of that in New York to kill it off with cheap shots. And so there I was, trying to keep that alive in my bumbling way. And I ended up trapped at a corner table, staring over your shoulder at a potted fern, having one of the most boring evenings in recent memory.

I HAD READ about other disasters — the sinking of the Titanic, the last days of Pompeii — and just that evening I had left King Lear naked and wandering on a stormy heath before coming to meet you and finding myself longing to be in any of the above situations. We had absolutely nothing to say to each other, and it was partly my fault. I knew beforehand that any conversation about your job with Hopewell had to be ruled out because I didn't want you to think that I was there to pump you for information or to curry favors. And since I had never been good with small talk, we got the weather, the menu, and the restaurant's decor taken care of before we'd ordered the antipasto. The wine list could have taken up a few more minutes but neither of us drank. I was left with my silver tie clip, which I'd worn purposely for the inevitable "Tell me, what exactly does a mechanical engineer do?" I took off the tie clip and showed you that it was actually a miniature butter knife with circular indentations along the blade. Do you remember the nursery rhyme, I eat my peas with honey. I've done it all my life. It may make them taste funny, but it keeps them on my knife? Well, my job is to redesign the structures that take care of our basic needs: water supply, heating, air conditioning, transportation. So if that poor man had only come to Bruce and me, we would have shown him how to use what tools he had on hand to get those peas into his mouth without risking diabetes from all that honey. This little knife was our logo — we each had a letter opener shaped like it, and we had created an actual model that worked at the table.

And here it becomes your fault: instead of laughing or even smiling, you raised an eyebrow and said, Oh, and they make you go to college for that? I snatched my tie clip from you and put it back on. And to think that I had actually changed shirts twice before leaving the house. I wasn't expecting total appreciation from a layman for the brilliance of that design, but a simple murmur of admiration could have saved the evening. I would have gone into the planning it took to gauge the size and curve of those indentations: allowance for the natural horizontal- and vertical-degree swings of the wrist — right- or left-handed — the arc involved from the forearm to the mouth, compensation for variance in the shape of the peas — someone actually could eat peas from our knife gracefully. And then that could have brought us to the type of person who would commission such a design, because I had loads of entertaining stories about clients and what my job had taught me about human nature. And since we were both human, at least, we could have sailed through the meal exchanging ideas and observations about that.

But your indifference to my tie clip and my bruised ego closed the door to that avenue of commonality, and as we made our way through an incredibly large antipasto, it was becoming increasingly clear that being human beings was about the only thing we had in common. You were Harold Robbins in general and James Michener when you wanted to get deep. I hadn't read any fiction more recent than Ernest Hemingway and Ralph Ellison, remembering with a sinking heart the worn copy of *King Lear* I could have been spending my evening with.

I told you about the old movies at the Regency and you countered with surprise that anyone would pay to see things they could watch on television after midnight. It would have been too much to hope that you were a football fan — and it was. You hated all sports except for aerobics, which I silently dismissed as middle-class female hysteria about their appearance. You don't have to jog and stomp yourself to death in order to stay healthy. I should know — I'd had a heart condition from a child, and taking long walks was all that was necessary to keep the cardiovascular system fit.

But since you enjoyed aerobics, I made the mistake of asking you if you liked to walk. For God's sake, no — it was too boring. And besides, no one walked in New York, you said with such smug certainty. And you could easily understand that — it was after all one of the most exciting places in the world. And as you went on and on, telling me all about *my* city, I could see that you understood nothing. You and those just like you who had gone there following a myth: you've got to be fast, and you've got to be fierce, because isn't everybody running? You all made the same mistake. We were running — but toward home or toward jobs, rushing *through* the streets, because we knew what you couldn't possibly, with your cloistered arrogance: New York wasn't on those Manhattan sidewalks, just the New Yorkers.

My city was a network of small towns, some even smaller than here in Willow Springs. It could be one apartment building, a handful of blocks, a single square mile hidden off with its own language, newspapers, and magazines — its own laws and codes of behavior, and sometimes even its own judge and juries. You'd never realize that because you went there and lived on our fringes. To live *in* New York you'd have to know about the florist on Jamaica Avenue who carried yellow roses even though they didn't move well, but it was his dead wife's favorite color. The candy store in Harlem that wouldn't sell cigarettes to twelve-year-olds without notes from their mothers. That they killed live chickens below Houston, prayed to Santa Barbara by the East River, and in Bensonhurst girls were still virgins when they married. Your crowd would never know about the sweetness that bit at the back of your throat from the baklava at those dark bakeries in Astoria or from walking past a synagogue on Fort Washington Avenue and hearing a cantor sing.

You often arrived young and sometimes grew old, making your own small town among us. And it was so easy to see where you'd settled. No development planning for schools, hospitals, or funeral homes. You weren't about having children or aging. You'd pour your polyester bodies into natural fibers and litter the sidewalks on wrought iron chairs, so you could be seen sitting outside eating whatever food was currently "in." You mated to the rhythm of sterile music that came from the bars and clubs spread from the Village to the Upper West and East sides before dragging yourselves home to spend Sunday mornings alone reading the Gospel according to the *New York Times*. So you'd rarely meet a native New Yorker: we gave you, the tourists, and our riff-raff the streets at night. We'd windowshop in amusement at the stores you'd gutted and redecorated in pastel and chrome to sell something as simple as a hammer and nails or as exotic as smoked seaweed that went for half the price in our communities.

And there you were, offering me your projections about the future of my city. Your opinions of our political system were only a bit less horrifying than your attitude on race relations. You were one of the youngest — and most evenhanded — bigots I had ever met. The bagels were definitely in power, which was fine with you, but given the population breakdown it was only a matter of time before the spareribs took over — either us or the olés would be calling the shots in Gracie Mansion pretty soon. And didn't I think so?

"Ophelia, why are people food to you?"

"What?"

I put down my fork. There was no point in pretending any more, I had lost my appetite half an hour ago.

"Food. Stuff you chew up in your mouth until it's slimy and then leave behind as shit the next day."

"That's a disgusting thing to say."

"But that's what you've been saying most of the evening — fudge sticks, kumquats, bagels, zucchinis. You just called Herman Badillo a taco. Number one, it's ignorant because tacos aren't from Puerto Rico, and number two, your whole litany has turned the people in this city into material for a garbage disposal. And I'm just wondering why you do that?"

"Look, I don't have to sit here and be insulted."

"I'm not insulting you, I'm just questioning."

"Well, it's a question that implies you think I'm shallow and a bigot."

"That's true."

There was no sarcasm in my voice, because I felt none. I was just curious about why you thought the way you did, and still you kept looking at me thoroughly confused. You just hadn't met a man who wanted absolutely nothing from you but honesty. It was working everywhere under your skin — a frantic search for the dusty file you had put away long ago after labeling it "response useless." And when you finally unearthed it you spoke hesitantly, your voice so clouded with its dust that you took a sip of water to clear your throat.

"You know, I was scared when I came to this city. Really scared. There were more people living on my one block than on the whole island where I grew up. And instead of getting better in seven years, it's gotten worse. Because just when you think you've gotten a handle on it, there's a new next-door neighbor or the Laundromat at the corner becomes a hole in the ground and the next year it's a high rise with even more people for you not to know. A whole kaleidoscope of people — nothing's just black and white here like in Willow Springs. Nothing stays put. So I guess the way I talk is my way of coming to terms with never knowing what to expect from anything or anybody. I'm not a bigot, but if I sound like one, I guess its because deep down I'm as frightened of change and difference as they are."

"What did you call me after that interview in my office?"

"A bonbon."

For the first time that evening we laughed together, and it felt good.

"Oh, I see, dark on the outside and white on the inside."

"Not necessarily, there are other varieties."

"Well, Ophelia, I guess your way is a bit more flexible than thinking of me as an Oreo. And I won't ask you what flavor of bonbon you had in mind. But I'm wondering, what do you call yourself?"

"If you remember, I answer to Cocoa."

It was a pity you didn't like being called Ophelia. It was a lyrical name, pleasant to say because my tongue had to caress the roof of my mouth to get it out. Not that I'd have the opportunity to use it much. The evening was almost over, and we were both thankful for that — we had gotten through it with a great deal of difficulty. And yet, I couldn't say why I felt a sense of incompletion when the check came.

I didn't have any set agenda at the start, but it seemed as if something important had not been accomplished.

SURELY, HE JESTS. I swear, that's the first thing that popped into my head when you asked me out again. I don't know where that phrase came from — had to be something from my high school Shakespeare and you had been going on and on about him earlier in the evening. Just proves that Shakespeare didn't have a bit of soul — I don't care if he did write about Othello, Cleopatra, and some slave on a Caribbean island. If he had been in touch with our culture, he would have written somewhere, "Nigger, are you out of your mind?"

Because that's what I really meant to think. You must have seen that I couldn't get out of there soon enough, and had gotten up so quickly from the table I forgot that my napkin was still on my lap. I had been trying to figure out whether to dump you at the door of the restaurant or at the corner while I tried to get a cab. But it takes a century to get a cab in the Village so that would mean your hanging around longer than either of us wanted. I had decided my best bet was to head straight for the subway after showing you my can of mace and Jiffy bag of black pepper, so you wouldn't feel guilty about not wanting to offer to ride part of the way with me when — BAM — that came up. But you weren't joking and that only left the alternative that you were psychotic. A guy like you couldn't have been desperate for company. You weren't bad looking, had a fairly decent personality, a damn good job. As a matter of fact, taking two steps backward, that made you prime stuff in an arena where anything over eighteen, toilet trained, and not interested in meeting your brother was considered a good catch. A masochist — had to be that. You were laboring under some *extreme* inferiority complex, thinking yourself such a total piece of junk that you would only date women who wanted absolutely nothing to do with you. The end to all this was clear: a black-lacquered bedroom, hardwood floors, black semigloss walls, and an antique set of razor straps and silk handcuffs. I'd read all about your type in *Cosmo:* ambivalent about your mothers, distant and uncaring fathers, should really be gay but thought other men were too good for you. I kicked myself because I should have known — the yellow roses, the top-drawer restaurant, the open and sensitive attempts at conversation, the gentle manipulation so that I spilled my guts and actually felt good about it. Oh, God, I should have known. Now it was a matter of finding a tactful way to turn you down so you wouldn't start sobbing and pleading in the middle of the street. If I remembered right, *Cosmo* said that your type wasn't given to open violence, but would sink to degrading displays in public. I tried to keep my voice as low and even as possible.

"Why would you want to see me again, George?"

"I don't believe that's what I said."

"But you just —"

"I said, I'd like you to see New York."

"Oh, well, then, there's no need for you to worry about that. I do see New York — too much of it — every day."

"No, you ride the subway from your apartment to your job, and then you ride back. And I'll lay even odds that if I took my compass and drew lines that radiated from your home and made a circle, you haven't moved beyond an area much larger than Willow Springs for your shopping, entertainment, or friends. Am I right?"

"So?"

"So that's why you still feel like a stranger to this city after seven years. And you can die here and feel that way if you confine yourself to the tourist ghettos that are being set up for you."

"I'm not a —"

"No, you're not a vacationing tourist. You live and play in the ghettos for our permanent tourists. And like any ghetto resident, you pay more for cramped, shoddy housing and the local support services than the rest of us. The mortgage on my house is less than the studio you're renting on the Upper West Side. But you thought it was a find at six hundred dollars a month, and you know why? Because you've bought the illusion that this is where you *have* to live — midtown is New York, and you try to stay as close to it as possible. And if they stick you in Brooklyn or Queens, it's downtown Brooklyn or Long Island City — the closer to a bridge, the better, right? Always facing midtown and so your back is turned to the rest of us. Most people are confined in ghettos by economic circumstances, so there's no chance for them to grow and explore, to be enriched by the life of a city. And I just think it's a little sad that here, of all places, the young and talented confine themselves by choice."

"So I should get out and see more of New York?"

"You really should, Ophelia."

"With you as the tour guide?"

"No. When you're willing to open up your home to someone, aren't you called a host?"

Weird, weird, weird — weird weird. You for offering or me for accepting, I wasn't sure. But we had one hell of a time that summer.

◇◇◇

IT'S WHAT WE CALL in these parts a slow fall. The weather's slow about changing, the leaves on the hickories and oaks are hanging on for dear life, the water millet's still green, but with the wind blowing warm and steady from the east the fish won't bite for spit, while the night air can bring a chill without a hint of frost in the morning. So it's too early to dig the sweet potatoes and too late to chance a fresh crop of tomatoes. Miranda and Abigail are sitting out on the front porch, answering a letter they just got from Cocoa. It's really Abigail doing the writing — she owns the box of good writing paper and her script is the prettiest — but Miranda looks over her shoulder as the referee. Although they gonna fight about what to tell or not to tell, Abigail shoving the paper and pen over to Miranda and saying, "You do it if you know so much," Miranda saying she would if Abigail had bought decent paper with lines on it so her words don't slant, and then Abigail saying that you can't send a letter to a place as important as New York City on some no-class, plain, ruled paper — although it's the same fight every letter they answer, it never occurs to either of them to write back to Cocoa separately.

A letter comes once a month, addressed only to their joint box number — and it's answered the very next day. It's usually in there mixed up with the seed catalogues, the electric and phone bills, or an invoice from something Miranda or Abigail ordered from Sears or Montgomery Ward's. But since Cocoa is smarter than them big companies, she don't waste the time writing "Miss Abigail Day" or "Miss Miranda Day" on the front of her envelope. Both of them ladies done outlived two mail clerks already, so everybody knows Box #7 been belonging to the Days for over fifty years. It don't matter who's there first to pick it up, who opens the envelope. Cocoa's letters always begin, "My Dears."

"We are so glad you are having a lovely time seeing New York." Abigail says each sentence out loud before writing it down, giving Miranda a chance to nod approval, or in this case —

"That don't make no sense, Abigail. She been seeing New York for seven years."

"But her letter said that she was having a lovely time seeing New York, and I'm just telling her how glad we are."

"I know what her letter says, I got it right here. But it still don't make no sense. What she been doing up there all this time, then?"

"I don't know, Miranda. She didn't say what she *been* doing, she says, 'I am *now* having a lovely time seeing New York.' "

"Sounds fishy to me. You think Baby Girl is into them mind-altering drugs or something? The folks were just talking about that on my program this morning. It is just messing up them young people in Chicago."

"She ain't in Chicago."

"Same difference. Ask her if she's on them drugs."

"I ain't putting down no such thing — make her think we don't trust her."

"Well, then put it this way: 'We are so glad that you are having a lovely time seeing New York, but exactly what is it that you *see*.' "

"All right, that's a little bit better."

"More than one way to skin a cat. We wouldn't have to be trying to figure all this out if you'd let her call more often."

"Daddy always said no news is good news. My heart would be pounding every time that phone rang, so I'd rather have her write, if nothing important's happening." Abigail continues her letter. "As for us, we are in good health."

"Good as can be expected." Miranda nods.

"How is your weather? We are having a slow fall."

"That's for sure." Miranda looks up and down the main road. "I hate this old tricky weather. Throws everything off. Ain't got but a handful of leaves falling on my compost pile and it's already November. And like a fool I already seeded my new lavender and rosemary out at the other place. Late frost gonna kill 'em sure enough. Miserable, miserable."

" 'Cause you don't listen. I told you there was a red ring around the moon Easter Sunday. If that don't mean a slow fall, nothing does."

"Red, purple, or pink, a spring moon can't tell you nothing about fall weather. I don't know where you picked that mess up, Abigail."

"I guess I picked it up the same place where I'm picking up my *second* planting of late tomatoes, while some folks is only getting one in before the frost hits."

"Well, I hope some folks is gonna get that letter finished to Baby Girl before the light fades. Where we at now?"

"She wanna know what news we got."

"They got a new principal at her high school — old Feeling Sam done retired."

"Your principal, Mr. Samson Wilbright, has left Willow Springs High after thirty years of dedicated service."

"Good thing, too. Wonder somebody ain't shot him over their daughter before now."

"He calmed down in later years, Miranda."

"He calmed down plenty after I got after him about patting on Baby Girl. Told him we weren't raising no public toilet for him to be doing his business into — told him loud. What we ain't touched since she was in diapers, he don't touch."

"Lord, Miranda, I remember that day — in front of the whole auditorium. I was planning to go about it softer."

"Yeah, I know, that's why I put on my hat and went with you. But I told him something soft too. Leaned over and whispered that I could fix it so the only thing he'd be able to whip out of his pants for the rest of his life would be pocket change."

"You didn't."

"As God is my judge. And I had it all ready at the other place. I can't stand a dirty, old —"

"Think we should tell her about Junior Lee and Miss Frances?"

"Oh, yeah — now that's some juicy news. And you know what I hear, Abigail? He's taken to hanging around Ruby's."

"Ruby's got more sense than that."

"Don't seem so. Hear she's baking peach pies and frying up drumfish every night to beat the band. And that's the last thing Ruby need to be doing. I was right there when Dr. Smithfield told her to take off some of that weight. Talking about she can't count calories. And I told her she ain't gotta count 'em. Just take her fishing pole down to The Sound and steam everything she catch, and everything she pull up out her garden, eat raw. But now Buzzard tells me him and Junior Lee is eating *royal* at Ruby's — she ain't had the nerve to tell me. And you know Buzzard's gonna follow anyone to where there's a greasy pot."

"Miranda, Junior Lee's got to be fifteen years younger than Ruby."

"More than that, 'cause she lies about her age. Ruby could talk when I delivered her baby brother, Woody — the one got killed in the Second World War. And Irene named him after Woodrow Wilson, who was president then. So what that make Ruby?"

"Too old for Junior Lee, that's for sure."

"But Frances ain't no girl, either. She must be going on sixty herself."

"Wonder why Junior Lee likes to take up with women so much older than him?"

" 'Cause he can use 'em. Don't have to work and spends their money. But he's barking up the wrong tree with Ruby — she can fix his butt in more ways than one."

Abigail goes back to her letter. "And besides Mr. Wilbright's retirement, there is some sad news about Junior Lee and Miss Frances. They are having a few problems in their home . . ."

"His whoring, his gambling, his drinking."

"And if they get divorced . . ."

"Can't divorce someone you never married."

". . . the rumor is that the widow Ruby will be his next wife."

"I guess you qualify as a widow, even though you murdered your first husband."

"Ruby did no such thing."

"She did."

"The man drowned, Miranda."

"You would, too, if someone hit you in the head with a two-by-four and pushed you off your boat. She told him she was gonna kill him if he kept messing with that little loose gal of Reema's. I guess all them roots she had working on him wasn't doing the job fast enough for her."

"I ain't gonna believe that."

"Believe what you want. But no point in sugar-coating that letter —

Baby Girl can read between the lines. She grew up around these folks."

"Are you writing this or me?"

"If I was writing it, I'd just come right out and call a spade a —"

Yup, it is just about nearing the point for Abigail to shove the paper and pen over to Miranda when a horn starts sounding long and frantic down by the bend onto the main road. They look toward the left from where they're sitting, but all they could see way off is a cloud of dust and gravel. Something is coming, and coming fast. A dull throbbing begins in Miranda's head.

"Lord, it's Ambush," Miranda says.

"Ambush?" Going to the porch railing and leaning over, Abigail squints down the road at the approaching dust cloud and soon Ambush's flat-bed truck comes heading over the horizon. He's going so fast that he almost passes the house before jamming on his brakes, sending the smell of burning rubber into Abigail's yard.

There ain't a politer boy in all of Willow Springs than Ambush Duvall. Church-going since he was a tit, without being overly sanctimonious like his mama, Pearl. He'd take a little drink or tap his toe to music at times, enjoyed his Saturday nights. But it was early morning service on Sunday, and what he promised you on Monday still stood on Friday, with a good word for most folks in between. So they know something is terribly wrong when he walks right past Miss Abigail without a how-do and heads straight for Miranda.

"Mama Day, I'd appreciate it if you'd come on over to the house with me right now. Bernice is awful sick — she thinks she's gonna lose the baby."

"Baby?" Abigail can't hide the shock on her face. "Since when Bernice . . ."

Miranda takes the bowl of beans off her lap and gets up right away. Ambush ain't hardly what you call the excitable type, it's hard to tell anything by his tone of voice. But Miranda sees the trouble in his eyes, and whatever is going on over there, now ain't the time to piece it all together. She knows Bernice Duvall is about as pregnant as she is, but this is one scared boy in front of her.

"I better head on over there, Abigail."

"But, Miranda . . ."

"I'll talk to you later."

Ambush is already in the truck and gunning the motor. Miranda gets in beside him and tells him to stop by her trailer so she can pick up a few things.

"Is she bleeding, Ambush?"

"No, m'am. But she's curled over clutching her stomach, and she's got an awful high fever."

"How long she been like that?"

"Since morning."

"Since morning? And you wait till now!"

"But it wasn't that bad at breakfast."

"She ate breakfast?"

"No, 'cause she talked about a little queasiness in her stomach. And we just thought it was morning sickness — she been going on for a while about that."

Dear God, Miranda thinks, Bernice, what have you done?

"Is it dry or wet?"

"M'am?"

"The fever, Ambush — is she sweating or is she just hot? I gotta know what to get out the house."

Ambush's hands are trembling. "I can't remember, Mama Day. I guess she's sweating if she's burning up like that . . . But then, maybe I just thought she was because . . ."

"It's okay, boy. Let's just go on to your place. You got lard in the house, right? And some baking soda? Well, I can bring down the fever with that." If fever's all it is, Miranda thinks.

As they fly on out toward the south end of the island, past the cluster of stores on the branch of the road leading to the bridge, Miranda is so distracted she doesn't wave back to the few folks who can make out that she's up in the truck with Ambush.

"She won't lose the baby, will she, Mama Day?"

"I can't say, Ambush. I can't even say there is a baby. Why ain't nobody known Bernice is pregnant?"

" 'Cause we wanted to be good and sure before we told folks — we've been disappointed before. Bernice didn't even wanna tell my mama, since she'd carried on so about us not having kids after all this time. You know how upset Bernice can get, and Mama always going on about a judgment from God. But I don't see how God can punish us for liking to go out and dance on the weekends. Why, I never even touched Bernice before we —"

Your mama is a Bible-thumping idiot, Miranda almost says aloud. But instead, "If Pearl thinks all God got to worry about is two young people hearing some of that silly boogie-woogie music y'all like, then He ain't worth serving. But now how long Bernice say she been pregnant?"

"Her monthly is six weeks overdue."

"And she always been regular, ain't she?"

"Yes, m'am. And then when the morning sickness started, we were so happy. I told Bernice she could stop taking them pills now, but she said she'd keep on just in case."

"Pills? What pills, Ambush?"

"The ones she got from Dr. Smithfield. No offense, Mama Day, but I told her since she got the pills from Dr. Smithfield we oughta call him, but she said no — go get you."

"Were you with her when she got the pills?"

"No, m'am. She said she was going to see Dr. Smithfield about something, and the next week she had 'em."

They make it the rest of the way in silence. Ambush and Bernice live in one the prettiest parts of Willow Springs. Counting all the Duvalls, they have near a thousand acres, over half of it turned to truck farming, and the rest woods and bluff land that slope down to the water. And Ambush built Bernice a house that lets her look out over The Sound from her front window, and that's shaded by the woods in the back. When they pull up to the brick house, Miranda is so angry with Bernice that she could strangle her. Dr. Smithfield never gave her no fertility pills — he told her long ago her system couldn't handle 'em. So if that's what she taking, she's stole 'em from where she works. She's risked losing her good name — and for what? For lack of a little patience. She softens a bit when she sees how sick Bernice really is. Just walking into the bedroom, she can smell the fever — a dry burning. She's laying on top of the covers, still in her paisley nightgown, and has dozed off into a fitful sleep.

"Bernice, I got Mama Day for you." Ambush touches her shoulder gently.

Bernice blinks her eyes open on a stone-faced Miranda. Her lips are cracked, her tongue is thick, and her thin body shudders with each dry swallow.

"Mama Day, my baby — I don't want to lose . . ."

"Hush now, you just hush." With the back of her hand, Miranda feels Bernice's forehead and the side of her neck. She lifts Bernice's wrist and feels for the rhythm of the blood while pressing her ear against her chest. Then she pulls back her eyelids and makes her roll her eyes around.

"Now, where is the pain, Bernice?"

"In my stomach."

"You sure it's your stomach?" She turns Bernice on her back and makes her fold her hands gently on her belly. "Close your eyes and try to concentrate on the pain. Is it coming from your stomach for true?"

"No, Mama Day, it's my sides." Bernice winces.

Miranda nods. "And what kind of pain is it, Bernice?"

"It hurts."

"I know it hurts, honey, but is it like little needles all in one spot or does it kinda radiate out and down?"

"It's like it's happening in my stomach and side all at one time."

"Okay, lay still now." Real gentle, she presses her fingers along the bone under Bernice's stomach, and then starts to move up along her sides. "Now, you just nod when I touch a place more tender than the rest." She ain't but a little ways up when Bernice presses her lips and eyes together and nods.

"Good girl. That's what I thought."

"Can we save the baby?" Ambush asks her.

"She ain't pregnant."

"Then you gonna try to bring down her fever?" Ambush is the kind of man to ask that question next without missing a beat.

"If it's what I think it is, we can't break this fever from the outside. Ambush, go get me a plastic bucket — spotless now — and a warm wash rag. And do you know where she keeps them pills?"

Bernice cries out and doubles over in the bed. Ambush stands stock still as if the pain happened to him.

"Go on, and get me what I asked, Ambush." When she finally gets him out the room, she bends back over Bernice.

"Now, Bernice, you listen to me good. You ain't gonna die, though you probably feel like you are. And if you weren't so sick, I'd give you a good horsewhipping this minute. Now, them fertility pills you stole done inflamed your female parts, and I won't be able to tell what part it is till I go inside of you. But even then, since I don't know much about them chemical drugs, we gonna have to get Dr. Smithfield over here to see if he knows. And if he don't, then we got to find out through them folks at the drug store. And you know what that means — you done lost your job if they're kindly, and you'll end up in jail if they ain't."

"I'm so sorry, Mama Day, so . . ."

"Now, don't take on to crying. The first order of business is to get you well. Think you can get out the bed and squat, Bernice? You gonna have to pee for me. And when Smithfield gets here, he's gonna want some to take back with him."

Ambush comes in lugging a huge, four-gallon bucket.

"Lord, Ambush, what did you think — I wanted her to swim in it? Now, take off her gown, help her squat on over it, and then wash her parts good down there with the rag."

Ambush stands there kinda bashful, and Miranda's gotta smile.

"Boy, there ain't nothing there new for you to look at. And since I brought you both into the world, neither of you got any surprises for me. If I recollect, you pissed right in my hand when you got here. And let me see them pills."

While he's helping Bernice, Miranda turns her back on them and uncaps the old vitamin bottle to shake out some flat, oval-shaped tablets. Silently, she spells out the name printed on 'em: Perganol. Miranda shakes her head. God only knows what she done did to herself. She gets Ambush to lay Bernice back on the bed and prop up her knees.

"Since we being so proper, you can throw a little sheet on her, just below the waist," Miranda says as she takes the bucket toward the window. She puts her head in and sniffs and then tilts it toward the light.

"You say she ain't had no breakfast?"

"No, m'am."

"What about supper last night?"

"A little Campbell's soup."

Miranda sniffs again. There's pus in her, all right, and it's in the upper parts.

"All right, Ambush, show me where to wash my hands. And then pour a little of this in a clean Mason jar and cap it up tight before you call Smithfield."

"We gotta get Dr. Smithfield?"

"Yeah, tell him it's serious. But don't tell him I'm here, or he'll take his own sweet time."

In the bathroom, Miranda turns on the water hot as she can stand it and lathers her hands good with Ivory soap. Finding a box of Q-Tips in the medicine cabinet, she cleans under her fingernails and then splashes a little alcohol over her right hand.

"You hanging in there, Bernice?" Miranda touches the top of her forehead.

"Yes, m'am. But it hurts so bad."

"I know, and it's gonna be a bit more uncomfortable but you gotta work with me, okay? Now, you keep them legs propped up and relax as much as you can. See these two fingers?" She holds up her middle finger and pointer. "I'm gonna dab a little Vaseline on 'em, go up in you with this hand, and press below your belly with the other hand — it'll help me to figure out what's wrong. You won't tense up on me, will you?"

"I'll try, Mama Day."

"Good. And pretend it's something pleasant — like the first time you was with Ambush."

"He was awful clumsy the first time." Bernice manages to smile.

"Well, that grin tells me he musta gotten a heap better, so think about the last time, then."

Miranda slides her fingers up into Bernice real gentle. Them wrinkled fingers had gone that way so many times for so many different reasons. A path she knew so well that the slightest change of moisture, the amount of give along the walls, or the scent left on her hands could fix a woman's cycle within less than a day of what was happening with the moon. When she gets up to the beginning of Bernice's womb, she pushes up against it and cups her left hand — heel at the private hair, fingers near the navel — and presses down. Good thing she's nothing but a bone, Miranda thinks. I could just about feel this womb if I had put my right hand behind her spine. It's warmer than it should be, but that's from the infection, and it's gotta be spreading down from her tubes, 'cause it ain't here. This womb is good and strong — all my star grass and red raspberry tea — sized right, shaped right, moves about like it should. She could hold triplets in here. Lord, girl, why didn't you just wait? You done undone months of care. When she moves her left hand a fraction to the side and bears down a bit harder, a spot the size of a dime sends off blazing heat. Bernice cries out and tenses her legs.

"Uh, huh. Uh, huh," Miranda whispers, and kneads her fingers along the spot, twice the size it should be. And I'll lay my life, the other one's the same way. But no point in putting her through no more torture. She draws her fingers out of Bernice.

"It's all right, child. It's over." She covers Bernice up with the sheet. "You know, the little sack where a woman makes her eggs — the ovaries? Well, you got something growing on them. And it can't be no tumor, 'cause it's not large enough to give you this kind of pain, so it must be one of them boils. It's done pussed up, that's for sure, and blocked your tubes. That's why you ain't had no monthly, and you ain't about to have one till it gets cleared up — if it can get cleared up."

"Mama Day, you mean, I done taken them pills and sterilized myself? I ain't never gonna have a baby?" The way she says it, all quiet, frightens Miranda some. It woulda been better if she had cried or argued, called her a know-nothing old woman — fought back in some way.

"Now, I ain't saying that, Bernice — I'm not God. But we gotta find out exactly what them pills do. And when Smithfield gets here, you can tell him how long you been taking 'em, and how many. You done moved yourself out of my hands with that."

Bernice just curls herself up in the bed, holding her sides, and shivers. It's too much for her, Miranda thinks, the body pain and now the head pain — where in the blazes is Ambush?

She finds him in the living room, having heated words on the phone with that little fish-eyed gal in Dr. Smithfield's office. Next to putting folks on hold, she loves telling 'em that the *doctor* is out, the *doctor* is busy, the *doctor* can be reached only at such-and-such a time of day if it's an emergency. Guess it makes her feel powerful, knowing that what she does or doesn't do is only important to folks when they in need of help. And since they know all about Mama Day beyond the bridge, any call she gets from Willow Springs she figures gotta be mighty pressing. Ambush is trying to tell her that he can't give his wife some aspirin or Tylenol and wait till tomorrow — she can't keep nothing on her stomach, so how she gonna keep the aspirin down? But since fish eyes only got three sets of answers — Yes, he's on his way; No, he can't make it; and, He'll come out tomorrow, take aspirins — she's at a total loss about what to do with Ambush's problem. Miranda asks Ambush if he'd mind if she gave it a try.

"Sue Henry? Sue Henry, this is Miranda Day. I'm fine, thank you, and you? That's good, glad to hear it. Now, I got somebody here *I'm* nursing who ain't doing so good. And I want you to get on that little beeper you got, call Brian Smithfield, and tell him I need him out at the Duvalls — he knows where it is, the south end of the island — and I need him tonight. Not tomorrow, tonight. You been knowing me a long time, ain't you, sugar? So if you don't do that, you know I ain't phoning back to find out why. You know I'm coming over the bridge tomorrow to stand in front of your face to ask you. Why, of course, there won't be no call for that. We'll see him here soon as he can make it. You take care now. And my best to your mama."

"She's a snippy little thing," Ambush says.

"That's what happens when you send 'em off to fancy schools and they settle beyond the bridge — they start forgetting how to talk to folks. Sue Henry was the runt of Reema's litter, and I'd take a peach switch to her now as fast as I did when she was running around here, picking snot out her nose."

"I better go on back in to Bernice," Ambush says. "But I wish we could give her something for her pain."

"Just try to keep her comfortable. I found out the problem's with what them pills done to her female parts, but he's gonna have to tell us where to go from there."

"Mama Day, forgive my manners, you can rest on in this room. Or would you like a little something to eat?"

"No, thank you, Ambush. I could use a little fresh air, so I may take a stroll in your woods. Lend me your pocketknife, would you?"

"You ain't gonna run across nothing worse than a gray fox or an ornery water rat," Ambush teases her. "The few copperheads down by the stream been run off since Dr. Buzzard built his still. Not that my knife woulda helped you against them."

"You know what an old collector I am." Miranda smiles. "Always like to be prepared if I come up on a little useful bit of something in the bush. But my daddy told me that one time he and his brothers hunted wolves out here — imagine. Even said his daddy saw a panther once. Now all we got is a few coon, some possum — and one buzzard in our woods."

Miranda kinda blooms when the evening air hits her skin. She stands for a moment watching what the last of the sunlight does to the sky down by The Sound. They say every blessing hides a curse, and every curse a blessing. And with all of the aggravation belonging to a slow fall, it'll give you a sunset to stop your breath, no matter how long you been on the island. It seems like God reached way down into his box of paints, found the purest reds, the deepest purples, and a dab of midnight blue, then just kinda trailed His fingers along the curve of the horizon and let 'em all bleed down. And when them streaks of color hit the hush-a-by green of the marsh grass with the blue of The Sound behind 'em, you ain't never had to set foot in a church to know you looking at a living prayer.

Miranda makes her way to the back yard toward the woods, trying to beat the failing light. It's a little tricky finding the tree she wants even in midday. And she weren't as familiar with these woods near the Duvalls' as she was with her own. Passing the bedroom window, she can hear Ambush's low murmuring and Bernice crying out every now and then. Pity she can't keep nothing on her stomach, 'cause there was plenty of stuff she had right at the trailer to let her sip for the pain. In the woods, Miranda follows the ground that's sloping down, stopping once in a while to place her palm against the earth to see if she is nearing the stream. If there was a choke-cherry tree anyplace in here, it'd have to be there. A bramble scratches her on the face, and a few feet on she trips over a creeper from a sweet bay. *No point in cussing*, she hears her daddy's voice. *Little Mama, these woods been here before you and me, so why should they get out your way — learn to move around 'em*. And in her own part of the woods she could, even now in her eighties when it was pitch black. But younger, the whole island was her playground: she'd walk through in a dry winter without snapping a single twig, disappear into the shadow of a summer cottonwood, flatten herself so close to the ground under a moss-covered rock shelf, folks started believing John-Paul's little girl became a spirit in the woods.

She hears Dr. Buzzard singing before she hears the flow of water. Miranda stays upstream from him; she's too put out to be bothered with Buzzard this evening. Peering through the oaks and cypress, she can see the glow from the fire in his still. He's making a second run-through, and from the looks of him he done drunk up half his profits from the first run. He'd made camp there for the night, which shows how addle-brained he is, Miranda thinks — the weather's gonna turn chill. Same old overalls and sneakers, no shirt. And laying up against a tree with his hat pulled over his eyes while his liquor's collecting in an oak barrel, he's going through the second chorus of "The Battle Hymn of the Republic." I oughta sneak over there and pour some potash in that devil's brew, but he'd probably sell it anyway.

An outsider might figure this strange behavior for a moonshiner. And Dr. Buzzard done built his reputation as a hoodoo man on the fact that he can make liquor with no secret of his whereabouts, never worrying about the law. I got my mojo to thank, he tells them silly young pups who hang around him. He got Willow Springs to thank. The folks tolerate him 'cause he don't do no real harm — anybody who's inclined to buy from him would just buy it someplace else. And there ain't no sheriff to watch out for, and no jail to put him in if there was. The nearest courthouse is fifty miles beyond the bridge on the South Carolina side, and over a hundred on Georgia's. The folks here take care of their own, if there is a rare crime, there's a speedy judgment. And it ain't like the law beyond the bridge that's dished out according to likes and dislikes, and can change with the times.

There ain't been no trouble with the sheriff beyond the bridge since the '60s, and even that wasn't old Russell Hart. Was some hotshot new deputy he had, bringing himself over uninvited to look for "northern agitators." If he had asked old Russ he woulda told him what everybody told them college kids when they came around here knocking on doors, getting people to register to vote. Them that was inclined had been registered to vote in Willow Springs since 1868, after they passed that Sixteenth Amendment. None never went over for local elections, 'cause there was no place to go, us being neither in Georgia or South Carolina. And them local politicians couldn't do nothing for Willow Springs that it wasn't doing for itself. But we've had a say in every national election since President Grant.

But guess that new deputy wanted to show off his badge while it was still shiny. Come on up to the general store and stumbled across a jar of Dr. Buzzard's moonshine and figured he was on to bigger game. Asked Parris right out who was making it. Parris hesitated, not 'cause he was forming a lie, he was just stunned that some white boy would think that there was any possible way he could get an answer to something like that. It was clear that the boy was an out-and-out fool, and Parris, taking pity on him, was about to say something tactful, when he stuck his face all ugly up into Parris's talking about, Nigger, didn't you hear me? And nigger this and nigger that. The folks on the porch of the general store got real quiet. So he had no problem hearing Miranda. "You'll address him proper before the night is over." Guess he only saw an old colored lady with a bag of groceries and a red straw hat cocked on her head. Snapped right at her. Granny, ain't nobody talking to you. Yeah, he was a fool, all right — and a fool who had to be taught a lesson. I'll do better than telling you where that still is, Parris said, I'll show you.

The rest is history. How that boy got left alone wandering down in the cypress swamp. Took him half a night to find the road again, and his patrol car sitting on three flat tires. Still could have radioed for help, except Willow Springs saw one of its worst lightning storms in a decade. Not a drop of rain or a bit of wind — just a sky lit up so with them lightning bolts that you could smell the air burning. A bad night to be stirring about, but it seemed nobody was home when he staggered up and down the road begging to be let in somewhere. Being young and strong, he made it to the bridge, but even he wasn't stupid enough to try to walk over water on metal-studded planks with lightning singeing all around him. It was either sweat in his eyes or tears that kept him from making out the driver of an old Studebaker that was turning down the road to cross over the bridge. Started running along, waving his hands over his head — Hold up there, sir!

Please, sir, hold up there! Musta said it half a dozen times before Parris stopped and rolled down his window. Don't know what surprised him more: when Parris leaned out and grinned, a flash of lightning turning his teeth into glowing pearls before he sped off; or the tongue-lashing he got from old Sheriff Hart for abandoning county property in a place where he had no business anyway. Russ Hart didn't have to go on to tell him that moonshine or no, Willow Springs was one place that's best left alone. With a little planning, some things you can even show a fool.

Course now, Dr. Buzzard takes that story and turns it to his own ends. How he uses a mojo hand to make him and his still invisible to the sheriff. It is sorta easy to be invisible to someone who ain't nearer than fifty miles to you. He's into the third chorus of "The Battle Hymn" when Miranda finds the choke-cherry tree she's been hunting for. She runs her fingers up along the smooth trunk and pulls off a small piece of branch so she can peer a little closer at the shape of the leaves and measure out the cluster of fruit. Even in broad daylight, if she ain't careful, she can mix it up with a rum-cherry tree, and the bark from that won't do a bit of good tonight. Satisfied that it's the right one, she takes Ambush's pocketknife and removes a small patch of outer bark. Then she strips the green layer underneath, making sure to scrape up. She gets herself a piece about long as half a hand. Much more than she needs, but she could take the rest back home — you never know when it might be useful.

Miranda starts to head on back, but looking downstream at Dr. Buzzard, it's just too good a chance to pass up. She breaks off a heavy, long branch from a palmetto. Then she creeps over, stands behind the oak tree, and reaching around swats him on the side of the face.

"*Oooo, oooo,*" Miranda calls, throwing her voice off into the bush. She can still stand so quiet, she becomes part of a tree.

Dr. Buzzard jumps up groggy, wiping at his face.

"*Oooo, oooo.*" Miranda throws her voice off again.

"Who's out there? What you want?"

"*Oooo, oooo, youuu, youuu . . .*"

"Lord have mercy — it's haints. But I got something here for ya — yes, I do." Dr. Buzzard grabs up his shotgun and points it toward the bushes. "Now, you just come on now — you come on."

Miranda slips on off out of the woods. Better leave before that addle-brain shoots her. But bet he won't be drinking no more tonight. Gotta keep his wits about him to ward off them haints.

She's limping a little when she finally clears the woods. Lord, don't tell me I'm gonna need a walking stick for that little bit of exercise. There's still no sign of Dr. Smithfield's car.

"He called and said he's on his way," Ambush tells her.

"How long ago was that?"

"About an hour."

"You can drive halfway from Charleston in that amount of time."

"I believe that's where he was, Mama Day. And he didn't seem none too pleased."

"Well, if we broke up his good-timing, too bad. Nobody's having a good time here."

Bernice's skin done turned an ashy shade; her breathing is low and shallow. She seems too weak now to even take her head up from the pillow. Her body ain't gonna let her take much more of this — she'll pass out soon from that pain.

Miranda washes off the choke-cherry bark and then cuts a piece about the size of the last joint on her little finger. She has to be careful with this stuff — awful careful. It could kill as easy as cure. And there weren't no time to dry it out and make a syrup. She props Bernice up in her arms and first makes her suck on a piece of peppermint candy she had Ambush bring her. When Bernice has worked up a good spit, Miranda takes the candy from her.

"Now, Bernice, I want you to put this here piece of bark in your mouth and chew good. I'm warning you that it's bitter, but try not to gag. Keep moving it around in there, 'cause if it stay in one spot, it's gonna burn the lining of your mouth."

When Bernice has chewed for a while, Miranda makes her spit the bark out in her hand and then gives her the peppermint candy. Miranda strokes her throat to help the sweet juices go down, and then makes her chew on the bark again. They keep doing this till it's nothing but a pulp, and the muscles in Bernice's body start to relax with her breath coming in a little deeper.

"All right, now, lay on down, the pain's gonna lessen even more. And you'll probably go to sleep."

Bernice does close her eyes and doze off. Miranda puts her ear to Bernice's chest and brings her hands up under her throat to feel for her pulse again. Good. It's a little slow, but that's to be expected. Ain't near slow enough to worry about. She tells Ambush he can leave her, but he insists on sitting in the room.

Miranda says she's gonna go stretch the kink out of her legs. She'd love herself a cup of tea, but if she started rattling around in the kitchen, Ambush would feel obliged to come in and help her. They're good kids, Miranda thinks. Some folks just don't deserve the trouble they bring on themselves. Bernice's kitchen is all tile, Formica, and stainless steel. Walled-in oven and other fancy gadgets these young people cotton to. She gets herself a few saltines from the box on the table. There's a plate of cold chicken in the icebox and she nibbles on a wing — Bernice sure ain't much of a cook. And look at the mess up in this freezer — frozen pizzas, Sara Lees. And a cabinet full of canned soup, pork and beans, Jiffy cornbread mix. That's why she finds it hard to be patient with all this time on her hands. Don't she know that baby she want so bad is gonna run her ragged? They give 'em throwaway diapers to buy now, packaged formulas, but ain't no such thing as instant love. After quietly running herself a cold glass of water, Miranda decides to wait for Smithfield out on the front steps.

As she passes down the hall to the living room there's a door ajar to her left, and from the corner of her eye she catches a small flash of light. Miranda pushes open the door and hears the faint tinkling of music. Turning on the switch, she sees it's one of them glass chimes hung up near the window. Little green and yellow rectangles strung together with silver twine. Them colors are repeated throughout the room: there's a maple crib, matching chest, and a little tiny rocker with a stuffed yellow teddy bear in it. The crib's been made up fresh — pale green toy prints on the sheet and a green hand-knitted blanket. Seeing that the carpet is beige, she takes off her muddy shoes and her toes almost disappear in the soft pile. One of them little mobiles is hanging over the head of the crib, and when she touches it lightly the tiny pigs, chickens, and cows start going round and round to the tune of "The Farmer in the Dell." Each drawer of the maple chest is stuffed to bursting with hand-stitched jumpers, crocheted blankets, sweaters, and booties — all yellow and green. Miranda's gotta swallow a little hard when she remembers Bernice's voice. "Ya know, Mama Day, folks always carrying on about wanting a boy or girl. But I done told God and I'm telling you, just give me anything." How long ago was that? Miranda frowns. Too long for me not to have listened. And if I had really listened to that child, I woulda known this day was coming.

Headlights are turning just off the road when Miranda gets out on the front steps. She cocks a hand on her hip — it took him long enough. For years Miranda and Brian Smithfield have had what you'd call a working relationship — some seasons it worked better than others. But each knew their limitations and where to draw the line. Since he married a gal from Willow Springs and Miranda was his age now when he was born, he had a measure of respect for the way things was done here. It just saved him a lot of aggravation. No point in prescribing treatment for gout, bone inflammation, diabetes, or even heart trouble when the person's going straight to Miranda after seeing him for her yea or nay. And if it was nay, she'd send 'em right back to him with a list of reasons. Better to ask straight out how she been treating 'em and work around that. Although it hurt his pride at times, he'd admit inside it was usually no different than what he had to say himself — just plainer words and a slower cure than them concentrated drugs. And unless there was just no other choice, she'd never cut on nobody. Only twice in recollection, she'd picked up a knife: once when Parris got bit by a water moccasin, and the time when Reema's oldest boy was about to kill 'em both by coming out hind parts first. Brian Smithfield looked at Miranda a little different after that birth. Them stitches on Reema's stomach was neat as a pin and she never set up a fever. Being an outsider, he couldn't be expected to believe the other things Miranda could do. But being a good doctor, he knew another one when he saw her.

"You stealing my patients again, Miss Miranda?" He gives her that slow grin when he gets out the car. "A poor country doctor like me can't keep body and soul together that way."

"Well, if they paying you a dime, it's ten cents more than I get. And thank you for hurrying."

"I had a breech birth almost halfway to Charleston."

"Do tell? They both make out all right?"

"Yeah, but it was touch-and-go for a while. You know, they waited till the last minute to call me. Had an old midwife over there who had put a butcher knife under the bed and told the mother it was gonna cut her pain." He shakes his head sadly. "Some people. So what's the story here?"

"From what I see, Bernice got some kinda boil up on her female parts — feels like the ovaries to me. She's been taking these pills, trying to have a baby." She hands him the vitamin bottle.

He shakes 'em out and squints at the name printed on 'em.

"Good God — Perganol. How in the high holy hell did she get her hands on these? Excuse my mouth, Miss Miranda. But of all the things she coulda done, this is about the worst. I wouldn't even give Bernice Clomid — and that's a lot less potent. How long has she been taking this?"

"I'd guess about two months."

"But how did she get it?"

"Would you believe me if I told you I got my hands on some and gave 'em to her?"

"No." He gets real snippy. "I wouldn't believe that at all."

"Or maybe you'd believe that since they in a vitamin bottle, she thought she was taking vitamins and was taking that instead?"

He gives her a long, hard stare. "What's the point, Miss Miranda?"

"The point, Dr. Smithfield, is that it don't matter how she got 'em — she got 'em. And we needed you here to find out exactly what kind of damage they done to her system."

He gives her that slow grin again. "You give her anything for the pain?"

"A smidge of choke-cherry bark."

"I'm not familiar with that one."

"The way I gave it to her, it knocked her out. Slows down the pulse. Sorta acts like dope."

"Okay, about how long ago?"

"No more than half an hour."

"I appreciate it. Guess she did, too. I have a feeling I'm going to find myself a sweet little case of ovarian cysts in there. Just hope there's no liver damage."

"There ain't — I checked her eyes."

Miranda sits out on the front steps while Smithfield goes in to see

Bernice. The night's turned chill, but there was something out there in the air. Something the air was telling her. She gets up, stretches, and moves around to the back of the house. It'd be a good place for a vegetable garden — even enough space for corn between here and the woods. But with Ambush truck farming, there'd be no need for that. Still, there were no flowers. With them dogwoods and wild camellias just on the edge of the woods, guess she don't need to bother. She turns and goes a bit to the edge of the bluff, and Pearl's house is sitting down there, closer to The Sound. Her lights are off, but her car is parked out front. Pearl can see everything happening up here, Miranda thinks. She must be at that window peeping, since it ain't prayer meeting night. And never came up or called to see what she could do for her son and his wife. Everybody knows she hated to see Ambush marry Bernice. Naw, she'll wait till everybody's gone, then come up tomorrow and get Bernice alone. It won't take much to make that girl feel ashamed. Something the air was telling her. She sighs, and circles the house again. I'll walk home from the bridge road. I'll walk and think this through on my own ground.

A shotgun blast echoes in the woods. Another follows soon behind. Well, I guess Buzzard got himself a haint. Just then Ambush lets Dr. Smithfield out the front door.

"Somebody coon hunting?" Dr. Smithfield asks.

"You might say that." Miranda nods.

"Mama Day, you been out here all this time? I feel awful bad."

"Naw, Ambush, I wanted to. Let me just go on in and say goodbye to Bernice, and then if Dr. Smithfield don't mind, he can drop me home."

"I'll do that," says Ambush.

"No, boy, you've had yourself a day."

"I think we all have." Dr. Smithfield touches her arm. "And it would be my pleasure, Miss Miranda."

Bernice's color is a little better and she's propped up on the pillows. She kinda bows her head when Miranda comes into the bedroom. Miranda sits on the edge of the bed and lifts her chin.

"I told him, Mama Day. I told him what I did."

"Well, it was for you to tell. What he say to you?"

"He said I got them cysts on my ovaries, just like you said. He don't think nothing's wrong with my liver, but he's gonna take that urine to the lab. And he gave me these here pain killers."

Miranda looks at the box and nods.

"That's all?"

"Yeah, 'cause he says the cysts will probably just go away since I won't be taking them pills anymore, and . . ." Bernice's eyes fill up with tears.

"And?" Miranda's heart starts pounding.

"And there ain't no reason for me not to conceive after them cysts clear up, because my womb is sound as a drum. And when I told him about them teas, he said I had you to thank for that."

"So what you sitting here crying for?" Miranda wipes the tears from Bernice's face.

"I don't know, I just . . ."

"I saw the room you got ready for the baby, Bernice, and it's awful pretty. Musta taken you a lot of work. Folks say I can do things most can't do. Whether that's true or not, I can help you if you willing to work with me as hard as you worked on that room. I'm gonna need you and Ambush both in the beginning."

"Anything, Mama Day, any — "

"Hush, now, and let me finish. The hard work is just the beginning. And I ain't sure yet exactly how it will all end. But if it turns out that we gotta go to the other place together in the end, what happens there we gotta keep a secret. Not a secret for now or a secret for then — but a secret forever. Even from Ambush. You understand that, Bernice? You were willing to give up your life to have a baby, but strange as it seems, it might be harder for you to keep your silence."

The room is so quiet they can hear the little glass prisms in the other room tinkle.

"I told you, I'd do anything."

Time will tell, Miranda thinks. Time will tell. "But now it's time to get your insides healed," she says aloud. "Get yourself a good rest tonight. And tomorrow afternoon I'll come on back to check up on you. And next week sometime, I'll tell you how we can begin all this."

"There ain't never gonna be no way to thank you, Mama Day."

Miranda pats her shoulder. "So you ain't got nothing to worry about, do you?"

When they reach the branch to the bridge road, Dr. Smithfield argues hard with Miranda about leaving her off there. He shoulda learned after all these years he was wasting his time. If he weren't willing to forcibly hold her round the neck with one arm and speed off, steering the car with the other hand, when she said she'd made up her mind to walk home from there, she was gonna get out and walk. She waits until she sees his tail lights way off in the distance, approaching the head of the bridge, before she goes back and picks up a stout stick she'd seen lying at the edge of the road. She leans her weight on it and makes her way slowly north toward home. The night is so thick she can tell she is there only by the scraping of her feet and the tap, tapping of the stick in the loose gravel. A moonless night with only the call of the katydids and marsh frogs. A night to swallow you up, the stars hid by clouds, and memory guiding her tired feet home. The tap, tapping of the stick in the loose gravel. Daddy, you said *live on*, didn't you? *Just live on*. Her and Abigail teasing John-Paul about the cane he needed in later years. Grabbing it and running a ways off from him on this very road. Her tossing John-Paul's stick to Abigail — Abby, do it look like a sugar cane? No, Little Mama, too crooked for a sugar cane — Abigail tossing it back. Then, Abby, do it look like a candy cane? No, Little Mama, too big for a candy cane. You'll find out what kinda cane it is, heifers — John-Paul taking his stick and giving them a gentle swat on the behind — just live on.

Miranda smiles into the darkness. My, that was a beautiful walking stick. Hickory. Studded with brass nails on the curved handle, polished so they shone like gold. And the long, sleek bodies of them snakes carved so finely down its length that when he turned it they seemed to come alive. The tap, tapping of the stick. So few times like those. No time to be young. Little Mama. The cooking, the cleaning, the mending, the gardening for the woman who sat in the porch rocker, twisting, twisting on pieces of thread. Peace was gone. *But I was your child, too*. The cry won't die after all these years, just echoes from a place lower and lower with the passing of time. Being there for mama and child. For sister and child. Being there to catch so many babies that dropped into her hands. Gifted hands, folks said. You have a gift,

Little Mama. John-Paul's eyes so sad. It ain't fair that it came with a high price, but it did. I can't hold this home together by myself. And Abby, she ain't strong like you. We need you, Little Mama. Gifted hands, folks said. Gave to everybody but myself. Caught babies till it was too late to have my own. Saw so much heartbreak, maybe I never wanted my own. Maybe I never thought about it. Except that once. That one summer of the boy with the carnival smile. Lean as an ear of Silver Queen corn and lips just as sweet. The tap, tapping of the stick on up the gravel road. Make no kinda sense, them memories. Ain't even had airplanes that summer — or automobiles. Just the bathing, clothing, and feeding of the woman who sat in the porch rocker twisting, twisting on pieces of thread. How could she have gone, with Abigail terrified to go near that rocker, trembling and choking for air when the woman rises up to scream, Peace, Peace? How can I go with you? she asked him. One foot before the other, he told her. A voice dancing on the fading night wind. Mama and child. Mama and sister. Too heavy a load to take away. Why, even Abigail called me Little Mama till she knew what it was to be one in her own right. Abigail's had three and I've had — Lord, can't count 'em — into the hundreds. Everybody's mama now.

The old Buick comes creeping down the road toward her, nothing but the parking lights on. It stops and the window on the driver's side rolls down.

"I thought that was you, Mama Day. I been sitting up by your trailer, waiting."

"Frances?" She peers at the woman through the darkness. "What you doing out this time of night?" And she coulda added, "looking that way," 'cause Frances is a mess. Hair all tangled and pushed up on the side of her head. Eyes all red and sunk in. A house dress dirty as it is wrinkled, and missing two buttons. You wouldn't know the woman who strutted out to church on Sundays, creases so pressed she wouldn't let nobody sit near her in the pew.

"He's up at Ruby's, Mama Day. I followed him there, the lying dog. Said she was only fixing him supper. But supper's been over, they done turned out the lights, and Junior Lee's still in there. I ain't letting Ruby take my man."

She'd be doing you a favor, Miranda thinks, but she's too tired to be getting into all this nonsense tonight with Frances.

"Well, if you wanted him so bad, why didn't you just go in there and get him? Then y'all can try to work this out."

"I done tried talking to him, but Ruby got something on him, sure as I'm sitting here. What would he want with that fat, ugly woman? 'Cause she's feeding him something in his food — everybody knows she trucks with that stuff. And that's why I was coming to you. You gotta give me something to get him back."

"The only thing I can give you is some good advice — and by the looks of you, you ain't willing to take that tonight."

"Mama Day, you just gotta help me. I know Junior Lee's not much, but I ain't young no more."

"Neither is Ruby. And if she found a way to take him, you can find a way to get him back."

"I told you how she did it."

"And I'm telling you — if she did or not, *I* don't truck with that stuff. A man don't leave you unless he wants to go, Frances. And if he's made up his mind to go, there ain't nothing you, me, or anybody else can do about that."

"But she's messing with his mind!"

"Then you mess with it too."

"That's just what I'm planning," Frances says before she cuts on her headlights and speeds on down the road.

She ain't understood a word I said. Miranda sighs and makes the last little slope toward home. The mind is everything. She can dig all the holes she wants around Ruby's door. Put in all the bits of glass and black pepper, every silver pin and lodestone she'll find some fool to sell her. Make as many trips to the graveyard she wants with his hair, her hair, his pee, her pee. Walk naked in the moonlight stinking with Van-Van oil — and it won't do a bit of good. 'Cause the mind is everything. When she passes the patch of burnt pines just around the bend from Abigail's house, she throws away her stick. If she can't make it from here to home without that thing, she might as well curl up and die.

Abigail had gone to bed, but she'd left their candle burning. Miranda mounts the porch steps, removes the hurricane lamp cover, and blows it out. It's about half gone. That'll let Abigail know in the morning what time she came back. Many a night that candle burned itself out, and the new one placed there half gone too. But weren't no slow babies keeping me this time, Abigail — no, weren't no babies at all. She stands on the porch for a minute, frowning over at her trailer. Then she looks back up the road and nods. So that's what the air was telling her. She knew now for certain that her and Bernice would end up at the other place, and she knew what had to be done there. It was gonna be tricky though, real tricky.

Them last few feet across the road to her trailer seemed the hardest to make this night. There's a plate on her kitchen table, double wrapped in foil and next to it the letter they were writing to Cocoa. Miranda lifts up the foil and sniffs at the aroma of shrimp fried in onions and tomatoes over a pile of seasoned rice. Bless you, Abigail, but I'm too tired to swallow my own spit. Sitting down and stretching out her aching legs, she lets her hand drop over the letter tucked into the flap of the envelope. It's for her to add the last line in her own writing, fold up, and seal. Usually, all she's got is a P.S. — Find yourself a husband. But now as she glances back over it . . . We are so glad that you are having a lovely time seeing New York . . . She wonders why it hadn't hit her earlier. Baby Girl was seeing New York with someone. Special enough that she wrote about him, but not enough to call him by name. The night air will do that, Miranda thinks, it'll make so many things clear.

She opens the back door of her trailer and stands behind the screen, listening to the soft flutter of her loose chickens roosting among the low tree branches. She was still finding eggs out there among the bush. And one or two even setting. This slow fall had fooled even them. Good thing, though. She'd need to bring a few of them chicks in here for the winter. Fix them up a box, get 'em used to her touch and smell. Then she'd take the box out to the other place. Miranda counts on her fingers. Yeah, the little pullets would be laying easy by March. But the rest was gonna be tricky, real tricky. Well, she'd worry about that come spring. She heaves a heavy sigh and closes the door. Going back to the table, she licks the envelope and seals it, pressing her thumb along the edge, without adding her usual postscript. Naw, this time she'll send no reminders. This time just let things ride.

A week later Dr. Buzzard done drawn himself twice the crowd in front of Parris's barbershop and tripled the number of haints he fought off in the south woods. Started out selling his mojo hands for a dollar-fifty — genuine graveyard dust and three-penny nails in a red flannel bag — when he'd used it to scatter two of them demons out of his sight. But now it's three dollars 'cause there was six of them suckers: two hanging off an oak tree, changing from monkeys to black cats and back again, two growing big as cows with gleaming yellow teeth and trying to stomp his still to pieces, and the other two raising general hell. He stood his ground, he did. 'Cause he had him some powerful stuff working. He ain't never seen a haint yet who could come up against his mojo hand.

"Sure you ain't used no silver bullets?" Miranda says, coming by on her way from the grocery store. The crowd parts to let her move toward the front, and gets real still to listen.

"What's that, Mama Day?" Dr. Buzzard kinda squints his eyes.

"Silver bullets. See, I was over at the Duvalls' the night you talking about, and I heard gunshots coming from them woods and an awful lot of yelling. So I'm just figuring that maybe you put some silver bullets in your shotgun to use on them haints — everybody knows regular bullets won't do no good."

"No, I never bothered to use that remedy myself." Dr. Buzzard starts sweating, and it ain't a bit hot. "But if you heard a gun go off, could be somebody was shooting at coons."

"Or a coon shooting."

Miranda leaves the crowd laughing and stamping its feet. Dr. Buzzard's sales was certain to fall off a little this afternoon. Ambush's mama is on her way into the beauty parlor: it being Saturday, she's to get her hair pressed and curled for services tomorrow. Folks often wondered why Pearl bothered; she was just gonna mess it all up, hollering and rolling in the middle of the church aisle. If getting into heaven meant being heard by the Lord, Pearl had herself a guaranteed ticket.

"Ain't it awful," she says to Miranda, nodding toward Dr. Buzzard's crowd. "It makes you downright embarrassed being part of the Negro race, with all them ignorant superstitions. Reverend Hooper says we all should get together and run Dr. Buzzard out of Willow Springs — this is a Christian place and he's doing the devil's work."

Miranda shifts her heavy bag and stares into Pearl's buck eyes. She ain't been over to see her son's wife but once this week, and that was to tell Bernice what a burden her getting sick all the time was to Ambush. Never a kindly how-do or may I help you.

"Well, Pearl, the devil — like the Lord — works in mysterious ways. And maybe he's using Buzzard to let folks see the *big* difference between the way he's living his life and the way you're living yours."

"Why would the devil do that? It would only bring disciples to the Lord."

"Maybe the devil don't see it that way."

Pearl stands there kinda puzzled; she ain't got the reputation of being the quickest mind on the island. Finally, she shrugs. "But anyway, speaking of devilment, Mama Day" — she leans a little closer to whisper — "the deacon board met this week, and they gonna read Frances out of the church."

"Why would they do that?"

"All kinds of reasons — it breaks my heart to tell you. You know she's been driving up there to the widow Ruby's house at night . . . You musta seen that Buick pass your way on the main road."

"I ain't seen nothing."

"Sure enough? Even I've seen her in that old Buick."

"Well, I don't make it out to prayer meeting as much as you, so I miss the chance to find out what folks is doing in the evening."

"But anyway, seems that she's been harassing Ruby something terrible, talking about Ruby's stealing her husband — and she and Junior Lee weren't even married to begin with."

"Do tell?"

"Uh, huh. Just living common law. And to top it all, she's been up there at Ruby's sprinkling salt on her doorstep, throwing eggs up against the porch, and Lord knows what other kinda advice she got from that fool over there. But the last straw was when Ruby came out one morning and found a *hog's* head swinging from the limb of her peach tree — had a red onion stuffed in its mouth and nine little bits of paper with Ruby's name written on 'em. Well, Ruby took her before the deacon board. Said here she was a proper widow woman, trying to make ends meet by renting out the extra room in her house to Junior Lee — and besides that, for appearances and all, her and Junior Lee was gonna get married, right there in church come spring — and she didn't see why she had to be subject to such hoodoo going-ons from Frances."

"What Frances say to that?"

"Frances told 'em all to go to hell — stood right there in Reverend Hooper's office, called *him* and the deacon board a bunch of hypocrites. Said they all knew Ruby was working roots, and them that ain't slept with her themselves was just scared of her. So that's why they even bothered to call a meeting on something weren't none of their business in the first place. Lord, these are some evil days — bring Your judgment on."

"Well, I gotta be moving along, Pearl."

"But what you think about all this, Mama Day?"

"I think the Lord sits high and He looks low, Pearl. And sometimes He's gotta look a little lower than other times."

"I know what you mean. Why, just the other day —"

"I really gotta go, Pearl. See, I done promised to get these groceries over to *Bernice* since she ain't keeping so well."

Pearl tries to peer over into the bag, and Miranda shields it from her. She lets out a deep sigh. "Yeah, I know, it's such a trial and tribulation on my poor boy. A trial and tribulation — that gal staying sick and nervous so much. Sometimes, I do believe she's putting on 'cause soon as a little music starts playing, she's off shaking her hips somewhere. And you don't hear nothing about her nerves then. Some of these young girls will do anything to hold a man — and my boy is so patient about it all. Bears up, he does, and never breathes a word about the miserable life he's leading. I'm so proud of Ambush — of all my boys. I raised me some decent, Christian children."

"Miracles do happen," Miranda says, turning her back. She walks off before Pearl has the chance to take another deep breath; she can keep talking half an hour on just three lungfuls.

Abigail has washed and scaled all the things Miranda had brought over from the other place by the time Miranda returns from the store. Little beads of sweat are dotting her upper lip as she pours the boiling water out of the butter churn into the back yard.

"You there, Sister?"

"Uh, huh." Abigail takes the edge of her apron to wipe her face. "I see you timed it so the last of the work was done before you got back."

Miranda runs her hands over the old coffee grinder, the cast iron skillets, wire whips — all clean and gleaming. She picks up the ceramic mortar and pestle — amazing, them blue periwinkles look painted fresh after all these years.

"Woulda been back long ago, but I ran into motor-mouth in front of the beauty parlor."

"I know Pearl had plenty of news."

"Plenty of bad news — it's the only kind she carries. But she ain't talked about what a disgrace she is, not going over to see about Bernice one bit."

"You tell her what we trying to do?"

"I'm old, but I ain't lost my senses."

"Miranda, you sure this is gonna work?"

"Why, look at this — Mother's old sewing basket."

"It was in the bottom of the churn." Abigail presses her lips real tight. "Don't know how it got there."

Miranda runs her fingers along the weaving of dried sweet grass and lifts up the lid to look at the faded silk lining. Naw, too much to ask that it still carried a whiff of lemon verbena. "I think I'm gonna keep this. Put my needles and threads in it."

"It's better burnt." Abigail's soft voice takes on a sharp edge that's so unusual it startles Miranda.

She's thinking of the child she gave to Mother. But I begged her not to do it. She couldn't put her own guilt to rest by naming her first baby Peace. Peace was gone, I told her. And now Peace is gone again. She only lost one of her babies to Mother, I lost them all. She's got much less to forgive than me.

"We can get rid of the basket. But you can't burn away memories."

"You can let 'em lay be. And I don't see how giving these old things to Bernice is gonna help her — all of it's better left be."

"We're giving her *time*, Abigail." Miranda picks up a wooden butter mold. "Remember how much it took just to get a pint of butter? The milking of the cow, the hauling, the churning down of the cream — the washing, the salting, the pressing in this here thing. A simple pint of butter. And don't talk about it going into cornbread — the grinding of the corn, gathering of the eggs, chopping the wood, firing up the stove. Took half a day for a pan of bread, not to mention the other things you needed to put on the table. Looked like soon as the sun set, it was day again."

"Lord, don't I remember. These young people talk about tired. They don't know tired."

"Yes." Miranda nods. "They can't dream what it's like to live that way. Not that I'm wishing it on 'em — them days were rough. But if we can bring a little bit of that back for Bernice, just give her so much time to use that she won't have any left over at the end of the day to think about anything but a good night's sleep, nature's gonna do the rest."

"She's gonna have to do a bit more than sleep at night if she's having this baby."

"Nature'll take care of that too. Daddy's mama had seven boys, and her times were even rougher than ours."

"Guess that's why they had such big families back then — kept the woman too worn out to say no."

"Or if she said no, she was too damn tired to stop him."

Abigail laughs. "Now, there you go, getting fresh."

"Well, let's get all this packed. Ambush is coming by to pick me up. Oh, yeah — did my seeds dry?"

That morning Miranda had taken a handful of pumpkin seeds and shook 'em up in a bottle of saffron water, then another handful of crook-neck squash and mixed them into a little dewberry juice. They were all laying out drying on Abigail's back porch in colorful rows of yellow and black. Miranda scoops 'em up and puts them in the pocket of her sweater.

"She got something to keep her busy, and now she got something to hope for."

"Bernice gonna know they're nothing but pumpkin seeds."

"The mind is a funny thing, Abigail — and a powerful thing at that. Bernice is gonna believe they are what I tell her they are — magic seeds. And the only magic is that what she believes they are, they're gonna become."

"So churning milk and planting pumpkin seeds — that's gonna do it?"

"That should do it till spring."

"And then we hope for a miracle."

No, Miranda thinks, then we go to the other place. But that she couldn't share even with Abigail. There weren't no danger of her sister stumbling across the box of chicks in that front parlor — she never went into them back woods and out to the old house. She'd feed and nurture them there till spring, then pick out the best one. Bernice had said she'd do anything. Well, come the end of March, she'd see. All this gadding about now was to help get her ready; Miranda could do only so much. She could march in that kitchen, tell her for the first time in her life she was gonna learn how to really cook. Oh, she'd keep her exercising. And she'd keep Pearl off her back, giving her them seeds and saying, Every time she comes to visit you plant a black one to carry everything negative she says to you into the ground. And she could even give her hope, saying, Every time you get your monthly, plant a gold one — let the life blood flow out of you into this seed. And come spring, she could tell Bernice, When you take the vines from them gold seeds out into the garden, you're really taking the life line between you and the baby. And the way you watch that grow — round and full — the life will sure to be growing inside of you. Yeah, she could disguise a little dose of nothing but mother-wit with a lot of hocus-pocus. But it was all leading up to the other place. Nothing would be real until the end. And in the end, Bernice would have to step over the last line all by herself.

◇◇◇

I DIDN'T TELL my friends about the way I spent the weekends with you, because they wouldn't have believed that I could be having fun simply riding the subways with some guy out to the godforsaken reaches of the Bronx, Brooklyn, and Queens. And from a little girl I had been taught that you don't waste your time telling people things you know they won't believe. I had seen Mama Day do a lot of things out at the other place, and when I told the kids at school they called me a liar. I got into some awful fights that way, coming home crying with my pinafore torn at the waist. But if I could just bring them here and let them *see*, I'd say. Folks see what they want to see, she told me. And for them to see what's really happening here, they gotta be ready to believe. So it's not that I was hiding you from them. None of my crowd was ready to believe that, one, I'd waste a Saturday morning on the D train to end up in Flatbush, strolling past those old

Victorian houses, and, two, I could really like it. Selma could have been following us right in the next subway car and all she would see behind her Dior sunglasses was a couple getting off the A train at Hoyt and Schermerhorn to grab some hot dogs at an underground stand and then washing them down with cherry colas on a windy boardwalk at Rockaway Park. I can hear her now — "A cheap date."

I would have thought that myself, except they weren't dates at all. I was out with you practically every weekend from the late summer until the end of October, but I wasn't "going out" with you. You had said you wanted me to see New York, and you did your damnedest. Every inch. Any schoolkid knows that Manhattan is an island, but you have to stand in the middle of the George Washington Bridge on a clear day to really understand: the low sweeping coastline from the south, creeping up into the rocky Palisades on the north end with the Hudson glimmering along its side — the sailboats, the rowers, the gulls. My first reaction was where in the hell did all this water come from? Water that changed from a muddy brown into fingertips of real blue as it wound its way past the north Bronx into upstate. Standing there under and over all that incredible space, I saw how small and cramped my life had been. I actually lived on this island — somewhere down there on Ninety-sixth Street, among all the clutter of those buildings looking as if any minute they would push themselves into the river. And I had told Mama Day I knew New York — God, what a fool I had been. I never admitted that to you, I'd just say thank you when I got off the Broadway line and you were heading on down to South Ferry. We'll do it again next weekend? you'd ask, just before the doors closed. Yes, I said, I'd like that a lot. I'd leave the subway smiling until I hit Broadway — and then I'd begin to wonder.

What was this guy up to? Slowly, the exact same answer began to disappoint more than relieve me — absolutely nothing. He'd only taken up my Saturday or Sunday morning, time I would have spent sleeping late or doing something really exciting like watching my clothes spin around in the dryer at the Laundromat. I had all the rest of the afternoon and the night to see who I wanted or do what I wanted, and he never asked me who or what. And come to think of it, he never told me about his whos or whats during the weekend. The clown was probably married. So why should that bother me? We couldn't be doing anything more innocent — he never touched me except a light tap on the shoulder when it was time to get off at some subway stop. As a matter of fact, he never held my hand or indicated any desire to — an arm would brush now and again in some crowded spot like Chinatown or the market in east Harlem. I would have had no idea how soft and agile his hands were if I hadn't dropped that knish in Williamsburg, and he caught it midair and gave it back to me, showing me how to fold the wrapping paper so the steamy potato filling wouldn't burn my fingers. Pretend it's a baked yam, he'd said, with those strong teeth of his showing. I know you southerners all eat baked yams. No, he wasn't married — the clown was probably gay. But then why should *that* bother me? I'd climb the three flights to my dark studio apartment and usually kick my pile of dirty laundry viciously into the corner.

What did I want — a sleazy morning where he's throwing out comments about the way my narrow hips move freely through the turnstiles? Or having to tense up when a crowded train jerked to a stop because it's an easy opening for him to accidently grab the side of my breast or get in a quick groin rub? The guy is acting like a gentleman, damn it. Is that so complicated to understand? He doesn't have to be some married wimp, out to spice up his mornings by teasing himself with forbidden fruit, or some closet gay who's into "straight illusions." Why is it so hard to believe that what I see is what I see: an ordinary man who only wants you to be comfortable and enjoy yourself?

George, it's not that it was hard to believe, I wasn't ready to believe. Nothing I had met in that world had prepared me for your possibility. So it only stands to reason that I felt what I saw was impossible. I'd end up thinking about you until I dressed to go out that night. One of Selma's parties or the usual round of dinner dates singing the life's-tough-on-fifty-grand-a-year-and-you-can't-find-a-decent-black-woman-anyway blues. And in the middle of all Selma's high-tech music or his melancholy sigh as he pulled out the gold American Express, I'd hear the sound of hummingbirds in the gardens at the Cloisters. And I'd try to remember if I'd said thank you when I left you that day. I made a promise to myself to speak a bit louder the next time.

I DON'T KNOW exactly when it changed for me — my wanting you to see New York, and then my just wanting to see you. Not being able to pinpoint the time or reason of that transformation made me uncomfortable. But one Saturday morning you were a little late at the meeting place we'd picked out, and the thought of your not coming bothered me. It's not that I was wasting my time; I usually spent my weekend mornings alone doing what I had been doing with you. The doctors had told me regular exercise was important for my heart, and I'd get bored walking in the same old places. And since I'd been over much of the city many times, it was fun showing it to someone new, seeing it all over again through their eyes. And it had been loads of fun, watching you change. You weren't becoming different, you were going back to the way you were. The heavy accent of a Greek pastry shop owner, flirting and offering you a taste of something special he'd just baked, would bring out your own accent with a, Why, it's just as good as Mama makes it, and the two of you would laugh. You'd catch a ball some child had sent rolling into the streets, take their hand, and then stand there chatting with the mother about the dangers of city traffic. And best of all, you'd stopped calling people food. You were learning the difference between a Chinese, a Korean, a Vietnamese, and a Filipino, that Dominicans and Mexicans weren't all Puerto Ricans. You could finally pick out German Jews, Russian Jews, Hasidics, and Israelis. And when the old Bajan woman took a flower from her cart and pinned it in your hair — " 'Cause de child, she pretty some" — your eyes got a little misty, and if you still thought of Jamaicans, Trinidadians, or Antiguans as "monkey chasers," you never said it aloud again.

I was so busy enjoying the change in you, I didn't notice it in myself. Sure, I'd wear any old pair of jeans stomping around the streets alone and the ones I met you in were freshly pressed. I'd gone into taking a moment over deciding which aftershave from two days of not shaving at all. But that had been done without thinking. I did give up one Sunday afternoon game with some thought, but it was only the Bears against the Oilers — both turkeys. Houston may have gone to the playoffs the year before — a fluke as far as I was concerned — but they were doomed for 1980, and I wanted to show you the willow trees in Flushing Meadow Park before they lost their leaves. You had told me that there were no willows in Willow Springs, which was the least of the odd things about the place. Although I never asked, I wanted to know more about where you'd come from, and what it was like growing up there. It should have been a warning sign — my increasing curiosity about the way you spent your life before and after you got off the train at Ninety-sixth Street. If it was a warning, I didn't listen. Or maybe, I didn't want to listen.

But now I heard what was happening loud and clear. When you finally rounded the corner after my half-hour wait, my heart started to beat just a tiny bit faster. It was second nature for me to monitor every change that took place with the rhythm in my chest, so there was no disputing what the sight of you did to me from a distance — flushed and out of breath, a red silk scarf flying over your slender shoulders, those long arms swinging a yellow and black paper bag. This I did not need. Shawn and I had been doing a lot of talking lately — serious talking — about making a go of it, once again. About this time, picking up enough speed to push ourselves on over the line, the stupid, senseless color line that was threatening to keep us away from what five years had built. We didn't know if we had the energy, but it was worth talking about. And it was comfortable being around her again, thinking of holding a body that you didn't have to prove anything to. No old ground to go over about who and what you were, no new moods or tics to learn, none to explain. Shawn was a safe haven. And coming around that corner was trouble. Beautiful trouble — the full lips, butternut skin, the tight wavy hair catching the sunlight in its brownish red tint. The high-behind, sway-backed walk that moved in sync with something buried deep in my gut.

This would have to be the last morning I'd spend with you — I couldn't control what my heart was doing, but I'd made up my mind about that. I could tell you, mission accomplished, you'd seen enough to go out on your own. I could tell you I'd be busy with extra work. Or since I owed you nothing, I could simply tell you nothing at all. Then you came up to me, smelling like a stranded summer day, apologizing profusely for being late, but you'd been to the Coliseum book store, got turned around because it was a section you're rarely in, pulled out a copy of *King Lear* — and took my breath away. But I had enough left to take you walking by Riverside Park and to tell you about Shawn.

THERE ARE SOME TIMES in your life when you have to call upon the best of all God gave you — and the best of what He didn't. I've had a few of those times over the years, and that first walk with you by Riverside Park was one of those very times. A crisp fall day when the trees, the sky, and the streets are standing out in colors too solid and unblemished to be real. The air is more than fresh, it makes your senses come alive — so you'll remember something as unimportant as a crushed Pepsi can lying in a patch of weeds, a loose awning hitting the front of a building, the sun reflecting off the edge of a Gothic stone in Riverside Church. Yeah, it was one of those days for poetry. One of those days Mama said there'd be . . .

I'd tripped on a curbstone crossing the street to the river promenade, and you caught my hand to steady my balance and never let it go. Maybe I was concentrating on how our palms cupped so easily into each other, or maybe I was still thinking about the flip my stomach took from the way you looked at me when I met you earlier — whatever it was, it took me a hell of a lot longer than it should have to realize who the woman was in this "special relationship" that you were telling me about. Now, I'm gonna tell you about *cool*. It comes with the cultural territory: the beating of the bush drum, the rocking of the slave ship, the rhythm of the hand going from cotton sack to cotton row and back again. It went on to settle into the belly of the blues, the arms of Jackie Robinson, and the head of every ghetto kid who lives to a ripe old age. You can keep it, you can hide it, you can blow it — but even when your ass is in the tightest crack, you must never, ever, LOSE it.

And I didn't, did I? I dug back to wherever in our history I had to get it, and let it put my body on remote control. I never missed a beat — my steps didn't falter, my voice stayed even, I nodded where I should have, stuck in a question now and then, my hands didn't even sweat — cool. And when you got to that business about "she'd stopped being a redhead with freckles and had just become Shawn," I thought about how lucky you were that you weren't walking there with my friend Selma. Because you were really a nice guy. And Selma wouldn't have heard the pain in your voice — you just weren't the type to turn your back on five years of a woman's life with a collect phone call. You brought more than an open zipper into a relationship, and Selma just couldn't have heard that it was all that *work* you regretted going down the drain. No, not Selma, hailing from Selma, Alabama. Selma who at twenty-one had come to New York with a bad accent and a bad attitude, knowing she had to lose one and keep the other if those bastards weren't going to get the best of her. And fourteen years later she had the best — and not one of you to share it with her, or likely to. Because after all, Lord knows, there's nothing worse than a colored woman with a bad attitude.

Oh, Selma would have let you begin, but what you had to say would not compute. And by the time you got to that redhead-with-freckles shit, circuits would be popping, wires shooting fire all over the place. And you'd have found that copy of *King Lear* stuffed into a hole so small, Blue Cross wouldn't cover its removal. That is, after she had cut you up with some down-home truths: I bet you had to go sniveling around two dozen before you "chanced into" this special one. Did she meet you in her anthropology course? I hear y'all are a lot easier for them to housebreak than chimpanzees. Or did her shrink tell her that the only way to get you out of her nightmares was to screw you? Maybe she's one of those affirmative action nymphomaniacs — running through you like water, looking for that ever elusive nine-inch thrill? She musta been awful disappointed, huh? But don't despair, baby, she'll go on trying, thinking that you and the last two hundred were only the *small* exception to the rule. No doubt about it, Selma would have lost her cool.

But, see, I was from Willow Springs and brought up by some very shrewd old women. And as Selma's spirit was tearing up trees and smashing benches in Riverside Park, I heard my grandmother's gentle voice: Cocoa, a real lady never has to get mad — if she knows how to get even. And I was already a little more than even. The man was walking with me, holding my hand, telling me about his problems with *her*. I didn't care if she was Helen of Troy or the reincarnation of Venus de Milo, she wasn't there — and she was losing him. I knew the quickest way for me to drop him back into her lap would be to force him to defend their relationship. Because if he had to do that, wasn't she his closest ally?

"I'm sure she's a wonderful woman, George."

"She is. And so are you, especially for listening."

"Anytime — and I mean that. I wouldn't wish what you're going through now on a dog."

"You know, you're being very understanding."

"Hey, look, who's the guy that's been dragging me all over this city when there must have been other things you could've been doing with your mornings."

"No, I've enjoyed every minute of it, Ophelia. It's just that . . ."

"It's just that you're a little confused. And I'm really flattered that I mean enough to you to be part of that confusion. And you were afraid that I might misunderstand — it's not an issue of black and white, although the crazy, sick world we live in makes it so important. You're not out to hurt me — still, you owe her an awful lot. So what you need right now is space, to work things over in your head. Well, you've got it from me. We can end these meetings, your mission has been more than accomplished."

While you were still stunned from relief that I'd spared you from having to say all that, I went in for the kill — planted both feet on the ground, a hand to your shoulder to steady the target before focusing my baby browns and aiming right between your eyes — "I don't have to see you again. You've already turned me into a better woman." No, I hadn't misfired, your mind was blown so far up in the air, it was going to take a while for the dust to settle. Selma, honey, calm yourself — this one is a goner.

THE GAMES PEOPLE PLAY. I wasn't coming to your apartment the following Tuesday night to talk about *King Lear*. You knew it, I knew it, and why we couldn't just come out and say it, God knows. I hated tiptoeing around the facts of life, probably because of the way I'd been trained. Mrs. Jackson never catered to the romantic side of the birds and the bees. There were no cutesy posters hanging up in the rec room where we all had to meet once a week for hygiene hour; two ugly blowups of the skinned male and female anatomy were taped on the blackboard. And if anybody dozed off during one of her dry lectures about "procreative responsibility," they'd wake up fast enough in the end when she whacked our half of the blowups with her pointer. You had to cringe for that poor headless guy, getting it straight across the balls — "A final word, gentlemen: keep it in your pants or you'll pay through your pocket."

But I found out most women just didn't have Mrs. Jackson's pragmatism about the whole thing. Come right out and tell her what you were both thinking half an hour after meeting someone you've clicked with, and you're a pig. No, you had to join her in fantasy land, and each one had a different threshold for you to cross over: she wanted to be pretty, to be intellectual, to be engrossing, to be adored, needed — special. She wanted to be anything but a skinned-down poster on Mrs. Jackson's blackboard. And they're all waiting with some form of that inevitable question, "What is it about me personally that turns you on?" So depending upon the woman, you pick one of the above. And if you lucked into the right answer, it could take anywhere from an hour to a couple of weeks to finally get down to the business at hand. But you're getting absolutely nowhere if you give them the truth: How can there be anything personal about you to turn me on? At this stage of the game, it's my own hormones. See, then you're a smart ass, and even one of those "liberated" ladies will swivel around on her bar stool and find someone else to tell her what she wants to hear.

And when you have an inkling that someone could be special, even though she's one of a hundred who happens to be pretty, or smart, etcetera — that takes time to find out. And if you wait for that to develop naturally before asking them to go to bed, they start wondering if something's wrong with you. You're a fag or a wimp. So what's a guy to do? When women run around screaming that men lie to them, it's because we've learned that they want — or even need — to be lied to. They aren't programmed to accept the fact that in the beginning, sex is sex.

So there we were with *King Lear* on our laps, and no, I didn't want to unravel the symbolism in Act Three, I wanted to jump on your bones. I had wanted to from the moment I walked in the door and saw that you weren't wearing a bra under that red silk halter. You didn't need one, you were small up top. And the matching floor-length lounging skirt — now what was that supposed to prove? But you looked fantastic in red. Black women of any shade should live in bright colors — it deepens their skin, and the deeper, the better. Still, I kept imagining how you were going to look soon without any of that stuff on. The question for the evening was how soon. We'd gotten through the preliminaries: I had admired the skillful arrangement of your furniture in that cramped space, and those woven baskets hanging around with dried flowers were actually very lovely. Gifts from home, you

said, and your great-aunt even made the cologne you were wearing.
God bless her, because you filled the air with lavender every time you
moved. I then sat down and had my obligatory glass of mint tea — it
was nice that neither of us drank or smoked. I'd never tasted mint that
sweet and strong. Also from home, you said. It was amazing what
your great-aunt could do with herbs and plants. But didn't I want to
get into the play now? Yes, that's exactly what I wanted to do, but
instead we opened our copies of *King Lear*.

I guess my well-worn edition helped to prolong your nonsense. I'd
gone through *Lear* uncountable times. It had a special poignancy for
me, reading about the rage of a bastard son, my own father having
disappeared long before I was born. Even if he was the type of man
to care, he didn't — and couldn't — know that I had been conceived.
Under my mother's circumstances there was no way for him to dream
of such a thing. It came as a shock when you opened up and told me
that you cried when you first read through the play. It seemed that
although your parents were married, your father had taken off before
you were born, too. And you were so glad I'd turned you on to this.
It showed you how hard the playwright tried to convey that men had
the same feelings as women. No, that was not true. No way. Along
with *The Taming of the Shrew*, this had to be Shakespeare's most sexist
treatment of women — but far be it from me to contradict anything
you had to say. I didn't want to waste any more time than necessary
for you to work yourself up to untying the strings on that red halter.
I had to admit I was touched by your sharing that part of your life
with me — more than I had been willing to do — and filed it away
for a later date. But I was starting to get a little impatient when we
reached Act Three and you had settled yourself into the other end of
the couch for a long discussion on symbolism.

"You know," I said, "I can identify with this line: 'None but the
fool who labors to outjest his heart-struck injuries.' I have an injured
heart."

"I can imagine — you're such a nice guy, a lot of women must have
run over you."

"No, I mean a *real* injured heart. I caught rheumatic fever when I
was a kid, and now I have a murmur."

"Oh, my God, is that dangerous?"

"Not if I'm careful. I don't get overtired, watch what I eat, get plenty of moderate exercise."

"But it's so frightening, thinking of something going wrong with that part of your body."

"That's because people don't understand. The heart's a muscle, that's all. And we go around fine with other weak muscles — in an ankle or a thigh."

"Yes, but you're talking about —"

"I'm talking about nothing but a slight inconvenience, which stops being even that with a small adjustment in your life. Two pills a day, and I've learned to listen for any irregularities. Come here, Ophelia, I'll show you."

You moved over from your cushion and shared mine. I placed my hand flat on the left side of your chest. "Now, a normal heart would sound and beat like yours: lub-dub, lub-dub, lub-dub. But listen to mine . . ."

I put your ear to my chest, cradling your neck gently with my right hand. "Can you hear it? Lub-dub-*swish*, lub-dub-*swish* . . ."

"Oh, George, that's so awful." You raised your face, a breath away as I kept my hand on your neck. I moved my thumb gently up and down, collarbone to chin, to erase that worried pout.

"Nooo, it's not." A light touch of lips. "Imagine a pipeline with a tiny leak. The blood flows in, it leaks out a little. Flows in, and leaks out a little. As long as too much blood isn't pressured in, the hole gets no larger, and the leak stays small."

"But that means you can't get too excited or anything."

"Oh, you mean like now?" This kiss was long, moist, and deep. "Yes, that's true," I whispered as my thumb slid down to encircle the nipple straining to burst through the red silk. "But it also means that from here on in, we take it slow and easy."

◇◇◇

MIRANDA'S KITCHEN FLOOR is strewn with pots and pans. There's only so much space in them little trailers, and she's gotta clear her pantry 'cause it's only three weeks till Candle Walk — there'll be so much stuff she'll have no place to put it.

"I think I'm gonna have to start storing my gifts out at the other place," she tells Abigail, who's sitting at her table with a large bowl in her lap. Abigail is making sweet orange rocks; she plans taking them out on Candle Walk. She buys a large sack of fresh oranges around the first of December, punches holes in the fruit, and studs them all over with cloves. Sprinkling a few tablespoons of powdered orris root into her bowl, she rolls her orange all around in it before dropping it in a paper bag that'll sit in her cedar chest for the next few weeks to dry. She's gotta make a good three dozen, 'cause folks been greeting her all week. "Come my way, Candle Walk." They love them sweet orange rocks. One will keep a room or closet smelling good all year. Hear they're called pomanders in other parts, but that don't stop the folks in Willow Springs from calling them what they want, just like old Reverend Hooper couldn't stop Candle Walk night. He ain't been the first to try — that's what happens when you get them outside preachers who think they know more than they do. When you open up your mouth too much, something stupid's bound to come out, talking about folks should call it Christmas. Any fool knows Christmas is December twenty-fifth — that ain't never caught on too much here. And Candle Walk is always the night of the twenty-second. Been that way since before Reverend Hooper and it'll be that way after him.

"I guess I could clear out the shed over there, but I'd hate to start on that." Miranda sighs.

For years Miranda ain't had to greet, "Come my way, Candle Walk." Folks use that night to thank her. Bushels of cabbage, tomatoes, onions, and beets. A mountain of jams, jellies, and pickled everything. Sides of beef, barrels of fish, and enough elderberry wine to swim in. The ginger cakes ain't worth mentioning — the ginger cookies, pudding, and drops. And from the younger folks who don't quite understand, new hats, bolts of cloth, even electric toasters.

"Hope I don't get another automobile." Miranda laughs. "Remember that little Tatum boy, fixing up that old Ford? Now, how he figure that to come out of the earth — guess folks don't explain to their children like they used to. He was a cute thing, though. And his leg healed so good — can't imagine him over six feet tall and a daddy now. They gave that new one a funny name — what was it, Keisha or something?"

She don't get an answer and looks over at the table. "Abigail, you ain't heard a word I said. And you done rolled that orange twenty times."

Abigail glances down at her lap. "Lord have mercy, I was a million miles away." She drops the orange in a bag and goes to wash her hands at the sink. "I was worried about the new letter we got from Baby Girl. What we supposed to make of that?"

"I told you it was just some of her foolishness."

Abigail takes the letter out of her pocket. Reads it again and frowns. "But I still don't know how we gonna answer this part: 'I met a man. He's no good. And it's over.' Now, we can say, 'We are very glad you met a man. We are sorry he's no good.' But, then, should we be glad or sorry it's over?"

"Abigail, Abigail, Abigail." Miranda shakes her head. "Don't you know Baby Girl by now? That don't sound to me like nothing but a temper tantrum. This is probably the same man who in the last letter she was having such a *lovely* time seeing New York with. And in one single month — he's no good, and it's over. She's hard-headed and she's spoiled, and this is one who won't let her have her way. I'm starting to like him already."

"Well, it seems he ain't around no more for you to like or dislike."

"Uh, huh. You think about it. In seven years, we get a letter a month — not counting September, 'cause she's just been home. That makes in my calculation . . . seventy-seven letters. Now, in all them letters, how many times did she mention who she was seeing — named or unnamed? How many, Abigail?"

"I can't recollect."

"You can't recollect 'cause there ain't been *a one* — excepting this one. And she's always going out, 'cause she'll come here and talk about 'em if you press her. And you know me, I press. But this is the first time she's written us about one. And whoever the boy is, God bless him, 'cause he's shaking her up — and she needs a good shaking. Baby Girl's got a strong will, Abigail, strong as mine. And it's gonna take a strong man to do her. Sure sparks are flying up there — that's what happens when like meets like. But I'll lay you even money on one thing, when we hear about him again, he'll have a name."

"So what we gonna tell her in the letter?"

"We'll tell her . . ." Miranda studies for a moment. "You know, we're gonna play us a little game. Tell her that we are *extremely* happy that this is over. Because the last thing she needs is a no-good man. Yeah" — Miranda nods — "let's tell her that."

Candle Walk night. Looking over here from beyond the bridge, you might believe some of the more far-fetched stories about Willow Springs: The island got spit out from the mouth of God, and when it fell to the earth it brought along an army of stars. He tried to reach down and scoop them back up, and found Himself shaking hands with the greatest conjure woman on earth. "Leave 'em here, Lord," she said. "I ain't got nothing but these poor black hands to guide my people, but I can lead on with light." Nothing but a story, and if there's an ounce of truth in it, it can't weigh even that much. Over here nobody knows why every December twenty-second folks take to the road — strolling, laughing, and talking — holding some kind of light in their hands. It's been going on since before they were born, and the ones born before them.

This year is gonna be a good one, 'cause the weather's held and there ain't no rain. A lot of the older heads can bring out their real candles, insisting that's the way it was done in the beginning. They often take exception to the younger folks who will use kerosene lamps or sparklers, rain or no rain. They say it's a lot more pleasant than worrying about hot wax dropping on your hands. The younger ones done brought a few other changes that don't sit too well with some. Used to be when Willow Springs was mostly cotton and farming, by the end of the year it was common knowledge who done turned a profit and who didn't. And with a whole heap of children to feed and clothe, winter could be mighty tight for some. And them being short on cash and long on pride, Candle Walk was a way of getting help without feeling obliged. Since everybody said, "Come my way, Candle Walk," sort of as a season's greeting and expected a little something, them that needed a little more got it quiet-like from their neighbors. And it weren't no hardship giving something back — only had to be any bit of something, as long as it came from the earth and the work of your own hands. A bushel of potatoes and a cured side of meat could be exchanged for a plate of ginger cookies, or even a cup of ginger toddy. It all got accepted with the same grace, a lift of the candle and a parting whisper, "Lead on with light."

Things took a little different turn with the young folks having more money and working beyond the bridge. They started buying each other fancy gadgets from the catalogues, and you'd hear ignorant things like, "They ain't gave me nothing last Candle Walk, so they getting the same from me this year." Or you stop by their place, and taking no time to bake nothing they got a bowl of them hard gingersnaps come straight from a cookie box. A few in this latest bunch will even drive their cars instead of walking, flashing the headlights at folks they passed, yelling out the window, drunk sometimes, "Lead on, lead on!"

There's a disagreement every winter about whether these young people spell the death of Candle Walk. You can't keep 'em from going beyond the bridge, and like them candles out on the main road, time does march on. But Miranda, who is known to be far more wise than wicked, says there's nothing to worry about. In her young days Candle Walk was different still. After going around and leaving what was needed, folks met in the main road and linked arms. They'd hum some lost and ancient song, and then there'd be a string of lights moving through the east woods out to the bluff over the ocean. They'd all raise them candles, facing east, and say, "Lead on with light, Great Mother. Lead on with light." Say you'd hear talk then of a slave woman who came to Willow Springs, and when she left, she left in a ball of fire to journey back home east over the ocean. And Miranda says that her daddy, John-Paul, said that in his time Candle Walk was different still. Said people kinda worshipped his grandmother, a slave woman who *took* her freedom in 1823. Left behind seven sons and a dead master as she walked down the main road, candle held high to light her way to the east bluff over the ocean. Folks in John-Paul's time would line the main road with candles, food, and slivers of ginger to help her spirit along. And Miranda says that her daddy said *his* daddy said Candle Walk was different still. But that's where the recollections end — at least, in the front part of the mind. And even the youngsters who've begun complaining about having no Christmas instead of this "old 18 & 23 night" don't upset Miranda. It'll take generations, she says, for Willow Springs to stop doing it at all. And more generations again to stop talking about the time "when there used to be some kinda 18 & 23 going-on near December twenty-second." By then, she figures, it won't be the world as we know it no way — and so no need for the memory.

But looking at Willow Springs tonight, it's impossible to imagine such a day coming. The roads are all aglow, filled with young and old, laughter ringing out into the chill evening air. Even them sanctimonious folks like Pearl got their candles and shopping bags of gifts and food. Pearl wouldn't miss Candle Walk no matter what Reverend Hooper preached. With everybody out on the road, she's sure to overhear something. She ain't too pleased with some of the talk, folks marveling about the cakes that Bernice Duvall brought 'em: I'm gonna have to tell that daughter-in-law of yours to come my way again. Ain't tasted gingerbread like that since Mama used to churn butter. Pearl, you teach her to do all that? Coulda sworn there was fresh ground nutmeg in it, and real blackstrap molasses. Kinda gives you hope for this new generation, don't it?

She'd move on away from that crowd quick. The ones over by the pine stumps is more to her liking: they'd just been up past Ruby's and she wasn't gonna let Junior Lee come out for Candle Walk. Ruby hadn't been doing it much herself since she'd gotten so big, but she'd manage a coupla steps across the road to a neighbor and she always brought something to Miranda. This year she's sitting up there on her porch, a candle stuck between her knees, talking about Junior Lee don't need to be traipsing up and down the roads with all them little fast gals waiting out there in the dark. A peculiar sort of behavior for a *landlady*, ain't it? And Junior Lee's most peculiar of all, 'cause since when he let a woman tell him what to do? And you didn't hear a peep from him. Might be something to that rumor going around — and now they start to whisper — that Ruby's working roots on him. She's got stuff that can dance rings around Dr. Buzzard's mess; some say she's even as powerful as Mama Day. And it ain't no secret what she done to Frances, no, ain't no secret at all. Frances went clear out of her mind, wouldn't wash or comb her hair. Her city folks had to come shut down her house and take her to one of them mental hospitals beyond the bridge. But Ruby had warned her — and Pearl was there when Ruby warned her — deacons or no deacons, come the next full moon she'd stop her from hanging them hogs' heads on her peach tree. But ain't it nice about Bernice, though, filling out and looking so good? Why, I do believe . . . Pearl wasn't there for the tail end of that conversation.

Abigail bangs on the door of Miranda's trailer. Lights are flickering all up and down the main road. Miranda sticks her head out the door, red straw hat cocked on the side.

"You there, Sister?" Miranda says.

"Uh, huh." Abigail's bag of sweet orange rocks is bulging full. "Miranda, what's keeping you so? Folks been out for ages."

"Candle Walk ain't going no place. They gonna be out there till dawn. Just let me get my Thermos of ginger toddy."

"What? All you giving folks is a sip of toddy?"

"They better be glad for that this year. Three babies born in the last month alone, and everybody with a bad spell of the croup — I'm wore out. Had no time for baking and sewing."

"Come on, then, but I'm ashamed to be seen with you. Lord, Miranda, it's a *little* Thermos at that."

"I ain't being out here long — save my legs for better things."

"We gotta get at least to the bridge road." Abigail looks around, candlelight taking twenty years off her face. "How I love this night. Remember when Baby Girl could barely tip, she was out here with herself two candles. And we had to hold her by the scruff of the neck to keep her from falling over."

"I do kinda miss her this time of year." Miranda smiles. "But since she's so far away. I guess it's best she does make it back for mid-August."

It takes them a good two hours to make it halfway to the bridge road. So many folks to exchange a word with, a new toddler to admire or hug. Off in the distance a round, bright spot is zigzagging along the road. When it gets a little closer, they see it's Dr. Buzzard with a huge flashlight.

"Now, ain't that nothing." Miranda shakes her head.

Dr. Buzzard is dressed to kill for Candle Walk. He's got a new pair of overalls, red flannel shirt, and even put strings in his sneakers. He's surrounded by a horde of children, 'cause they know he keeps his pockets filled for them tonight with his special honey ginger drops.

"Lead on with light! Lead on with light!" Dr. Buzzard, face flushed, waves his Duracell at them.

"You're lit up enough already." Miranda sniffs.

"Lead on with light, Buzzard." Abigail smiles and gives him one of her sweet orange rocks. "And you look right nice, too."

"Why, thank you, Miss Abigail. So do you. And Mama Day, you is always beautiful."

"You musta been Candle Walking since yesterday." Miranda narrows her eyes.

"Naw, I ain't. Just feeling good." He reaches in his pocket and pulls out a handful of candy. "Here, give these to little Cocoa. She loves my ginger candy."

"She ain't little no more, Buzzard," Abigail says. "Cocoa turned twenty-seven this year. And come April, she'll —"

"Abigail, don't bother. Buzzard's so out of his head, he don't —"

"I know what I'm saying, Mama Day." He drops some candy into the tiny hands outstretched around him. "Don't they always stay our babies?"

He starts on past them down the road. Miranda looks back for a minute and calls out to him. "Buzzard."

"Yeah, Mama Day?"

"Lead on with light."

When they're making the turn to come back after reaching the cluster of stores at the junction to the bridge road, a truck's headlights start flashing at them, coming from the south.

"It gets worse and worse each year," Abigail says. "And if it's some of them crazy teenagers, they gonna get a piece of my mind."

They're surprised to see it's Bernice and Ambush, their truck all decorated with sprigs of winterberry and ginger cookies on red ribbons.

"Now, don't be looking that way," Ambush says. "We was out walking proper earlier. But we had a little something too heavy to carry we was bringing by your house. Bernice got your present, Miss Abigail. And I got one for Mama Day."

Bernice had made Abigail a Sunday dress: lace that was tatted fine as spider webs over a silk chemise.

"I know you like pink," Bernice says. "I hope it's all right. Miss Pearl was saying it might not be proper for church service."

"Don't worry about that. Honey, this is so pretty, I wanna be buried in it. How did you get the time?"

"It's so strange, Miss Abigail, with all that I been doing, I just seem to find it now."

Miranda and Abigail ain't gotta look at each other to exchange a smile.

"And this is for you, Mama Day." Ambush brings her to the back of the truck and pulls up the canvas. Miranda stands stock still for a minute and Abigail gasps when they see the rocking chair. Bernice and Ambush think they're reacting that way from pleasure — and the chair is a beautiful thing. Handmade. Seasoned oak treated and rubbed with linseed oil so that the finish under candlelight almost hurts the eyes. The domed headpiece and slats have matching designs, carefully carved petals and vines of intertwined water lilies. The spindles on the seat back curved so well to fit the body, a pillow wouldn't be needed. A comfortable chair. You could be content to sit all day and night in a rocker like that, doing nothing but twisting, twisting on pieces of thread.

"I did every bit of it myself." Ambush beams.

"Mama Day, he worked so hard," Bernice says, "getting it ready for Candle Walk."

"I'm sure he did," Miranda whispers.

The young people begin to sense something.

"Don't you like it?" Ambush says.

"Of course she does." Abigail takes his arm. He don't notice her hands are trembling. "She's just speechless, that's all."

"It's not that I'm saying you're old or nothing . . ." Ambush begins.

"If you did, you'd be telling the truth." Miranda manages to laugh. "If eighty-five ain't old, what is?" She strokes the chair. "And if this ain't beautiful, child, nothing is."

"Ambush, what made you decide on water lilies?" Abigail tries, but can't bring herself to touch the design.

"I don't know — just thought it'd look nice. And you really do like it, Mama Day?"

"Very much so. Here, let me give you a little sip of this so we can finish up Candle Walk."

While Ambush is covering up the chair, Bernice takes Miranda off a bit to whisper, "My seeds are doing well, Mama Day. They already starting to make vines in the kitchen window. And I knew Miss Abigail would like my dress, 'cause when Miss Pearl said she wouldn't, I stuck a black seed right in the dirt."

"Good for you, child. Come spring, we'll take 'em outside."

Come spring, Miranda thinks. Spring seems so far away. A lifetime away. Now, what was she gonna do with that chair? So much work, so much caring — could she bear to sit in it? It belonged in the other place, no use lying about that. She looks into Bernice's eager and hopeful eyes. What kinda destiny is happening here, between you and me? I asked you to churn butter and you did it. Walk two miles a day, you walked four. Never thinking that something might be asked of me before we meet this spring. Now, I'm not so sure about myself, but I ain't gotta worry about you. You're gonna make it over that line. And maybe, you'll just have to drag this tired old lady with you.

The rocking chair is waiting outside her trailer when Miranda and Abigail make it back from the junction. Some folks have thinned out, but the diehards will keep strolling till dawn. They stand there for a good while, just looking at it resting under the canvas.

Abigail sighs. "Water lilies, of all things."

"You know, Abigail, we say it over and over again — life is strange. Still, something like this happens and it kinda knocks you for a loop."

"You think he coulda heard . . ."

"From who? Mother died before his *grandfather* was out of diapers. And we ain't even told Baby Girl about . . . And we should, you know, Abigail. It ain't nothing to be ashamed of, it's her family and her history. And she'll have children one day."

"There's time before you saddle her with all that mess. Let the child live her life without having to think on them things. Baby Girl —"

"That's just it, Abigail — she ain't a baby. She's a grown woman and her *real* name is Ophelia. We don't like to think on it, but that's her name. Not Baby Girl, not Cocoa — Ophelia."

"I regret the day she got it."

"No, Sister, please. Don't ever say that. She fought to stay here — remember, Abigail?"

"I could forget to breathe, easier than I could forget those months. Sitting up with her night after night, trembling every time she choked. Oh, that child . . ."

"And she's the child of Grace, Abigail."

"Ophelia." Angry tears are in Abigail's eyes as she looks at the rocking chair.

"I'm gonna take that thing out to the other place. It's where it belongs."

"Tonight?"

"No, not tonight. But I might take a last Candle Walk over that way." Miranda continues gently, "Is it too much to ask for you to go with me?"

"It's too much, Sister."

Miranda lifts her candle in parting. "Then, lead on with light, Abby."

"Lead on with light, Little Mama."

Miranda watches the slump in her sister's back as she crosses the road to her house. For some reason, in many a month, she feels like she wants to cry.

There's three sets of big woods in Willow Springs. The ones on the south end near the Duvalls' where Dr. Buzzard keeps his still. The set running east toward the high ocean bluff, through Chevy's Pass where you can find the gravestone of Bascombe Wade. And there's the west woods, where Miranda's walking now, that's part of the forty-nine-hundred acres belonging to the Days. These start right out back Miranda's trailer and move on toward the smaller bluff over The Sound. About midways in is the family plot, a lovely stretch of land within a circle of live oaks. Got Miranda's daddy and his six brothers buried there. Got her daddy's daddy and his six brothers. Got Peace, Grace, Hope, and Peace again. They never found her mama's body, although John-Paul and three of his brothers dragged the bottom of The Sound for a week. Mother flew off that bluff screaming Peace. And she coulda been put to rest with Peace — and later on, Peace again.

Ophelia. No comfort in that graveyard for Miranda tonight. She heads on toward the other place, but her steps are slow and halting. Miranda could walk those west woods stone blind. She knows every crook and bend, every tree that falls and those that are about to sprout. But the light from her candle is playing tricks with the dark, making branches seem longer and bringing up shadows to look like rocks. She'll go to step over and find she's only stepping on air. Ophelia. Miranda stops and leans her back against an oak. She wasn't meant to get to the other place tonight. A twig snaps near her right side, but she ain't gotta turn around. A squirrel, maybe, or a gray fox. Nobody, drunk or sober, would come this far into the west woods at night. It's too near the other place. And even in broad daylight, they not gonna make it much past the graveyard. Where do folks get things in their head? It's an old house with a big garden, that's all. Me and Abigail and Peace was born there. My daddy and his brothers as well. And it's where my mama sat, rocking herself to death. Folks can get the craziest things in their head. But then again there *was* the other place, where she was gonna bring Bernice in the spring. Will she see just an old house with a big garden? She remembers the hope shining in Bernice's eyes. No, she won't. But the important thing is, will I? Let me finish this Candle Walk, thinks Miranda, 'cause there's something waiting for me to know.

Suddenly, she's afraid. An icy ball cramps the middle of her gut. Ophelia. "I'm gonna finish this Candle Walk." Her voice echoes through the empty woods, bouncing off the naked tree branches. And when it bounces back it carries a light breeze, and her candle flickers out. There's a book of matches in her coat pocket, but she leans back against a tree in the comforting darkness as the woods she knows begin to take shape. The old pine stump around the bend from the other place, the Mayapple bushes near the clump of dogwoods, the rock pile under the scarred and bare hickory. The chill breeze picks up, coming around the bend from the other place. A wet breeze that's rolling in from The Sound. It don't take long to turn to a wind that starts whipping the dry weeds and bushes.

She tries to listen under the wind. The sound of a long wool skirt passing. Then the tread of heavy leather boots, heading straight for the main road, heading on toward the east bluff over the ocean. It couldn't be Mother, she died in The Sound. Miranda's head feels like it's gonna burst. The candles, food, and slivers of ginger, lining the main road. A long wool skirt passing. Heavy leather boots. And the humming — humming of some lost and ancient song. Quiet tears start rolling down Miranda's face. Oh, precious Jesus, the light wasn't for her — it was for him. The tombstone out by Chevy's Pass. How long did he search for her? Up and down this path. What had daddy said *his* daddy said about Candle Walk? She was trying too hard, she couldn't remember. But she'd bring out the rocking chair. Maybe move back here herself after spring. Lord knows, she'd be back in that garden enough come then. And summer, it'd be real pleasant. Listen to the wind from The Sound. Maybe it would come to her. Yes — it just might come to her. Up and down this path, somehow, a man dies from a broken heart.

◇◇◇

GEORGE, I WAS FRIGHTENED. Can you understand that? Things were going so well between us that I dreaded the day when it would be over. Grown women aren't supposed to believe in Prince Charmings and happily-ever-afters. Real life isn't about that — so bring on the clouds. And each day that it was exhilarating and wonderful; each time you'd call unexpectedly just to say, I was thinking about you; each little funny card in the mail or moment in a restaurant when you'd reach over for no reason and squeeze my hand — each of those times, George, I'd feel this underlying panic: when will it end? And it was worse when we were in bed. You'd take me in your arms with such a hunger and tenderness, demanding only that I be pleased, that I'd feel a melting away of places in my body I hadn't realized were frozen voids. Your touch was slowly making new and alive openings within me and I would lie there warm and weak, listening to you sleep, thinking, What will I do when he's not here? How will I handle all this space he's creating without him to fill it?

And you — you would be so cheerful the mornings after you slept over. Running down to the deli to get us fresh rolls and orange juice. Circling some announcement in the paper for a show we could catch that weekend. Never understanding that it was three whole days until the weekend and my seeing you again. Three days was time enough to settle into what my girlfriends were saying: "He sounds too good to be true." I'd look around that empty apartment and yes, it had to be that — untrue. You were only part of some vision, or at best a temporary visitor in my life. Too good to be true. Too good to last. I found enough courage to ask you that one night, do you remember? No, men don't remember those things. You thought I was teasing you to prolong the moment when I brought your head up from between my thighs and stroked your lips with my fingers. What will I do when you're not here? I said. It stung me that you took it so lightly: I'm not going anywhere for the next fifteen minutes, I plan to be coming.

The more you began to mean to me, the more I was losing control — and I hated it. I wasn't angry at you for phoning later than you said you would, for ending an evening early because you were genuinely tired — I was angry at myself for allowing it to matter that much. And when I was brooding or sarcastic after you finally called, it never seemed to bother you. You'd laugh it off, and that would make me angrier. It was horrible feeling that I needed you more than I was needed. And so I would push you, making petty demands. If you cared, you'd do X. If you cared, you'd do Y. I was tearing my hair out, and all you had to say was, I'll call you when you're in a better mood. Giving in to me so effortlessly made you all the more unreal. He just wants to glide on through this, he doesn't care. If he cared, he'd . . . What? Fear is unreasonable, and that's what I was being. And it seemed as if I couldn't stop myself from picking up the phone and instead of telling you how I really felt —

"So you're not coming over Monday night *again?*"

"I don't come over any Monday night. You know that's for football."

"And I'm supposed to believe that?"

"I don't see why you shouldn't, I've never lied to you."

"Or I've never caught you."

"Ophelia, if you want to take the train down to South Ferry, get on the boat, and come over to Staten Island tomorrow, you're welcome. But on Monday, I watch the games."

"And you watch them for *six hours* on Sundays, too."

"That's right. And I even have my satellite dish so I can follow the Pats when they're not on network."

"So where is that supposed to leave me? If I want us to go somewhere Sunday afternoons or Monday nights, it's tough shit, right? I take second place to some overgrown clowns running around in —"

"Is there something you wanted to do Monday?"

"That's not the point."

"Then I don't know what the point is."

"Well, then clearly there's no point in my trying to explain it to you. When someone doesn't care, they just don't care. Obviously, there are things in your life that matter more than me."

"Of course there are. My health, my work — to start off the list — *and* the New England Patriots. It's a short season, you'll just have to live with it."

"And if I don't want to?"

"Then you don't."

"You know, George, if you really cared . . ."

"I don't care that much, damn it!"

After making you hang up on me, for a brief moment I'd be satisfied. Just imagine if I'd been a fool enough to tell this man how I really felt about him — see the way he treats me. He's insensitive and selfish. No doubt about it, he'd walk right over me if I ever opened up. Yes, for a brief moment I was comfortable feeling that I was insulating myself from all the damage you were capable of. And then it didn't seem so awful that one day it would be over. Good riddance to bad rubbish, I could handle that version of you. Sounds crazy, doesn't it? Here was a relationship I needed to turn into a catastrophe, out of fear of losing a perfect one. And when I was in that state of mind, I found plenty of support:

What are you so upset about? The truth had to come to light.

A leopard can't hide his spots but for so long.

It's easier to get run over by a flying saucer than to find a decent man in New York.

If he's not married by now, you shoulda figured something was wrong.

I couldn't sleep well those nights. Why should I call you when you had hung up on me? Slammed down the phone, as a matter of fact. Maybe I had gone a little too far, but there was no reason for you to act like that.

"But I do care."

"Huh?"

You had the most disconcerting habit of calling me back and picking up a conversation where we may have left off two hours or even two days before.

"I said, I do care."

"You should tell me that more often."

"Maybe you aren't listening."

I don't think I was. Because I kept picking fights about your football games. It was the only thing that seemed to tick you off — that and being called a son-of-a-bitch. I had a pretty dirty mouth and it often amused you. Southerners can't swear, you'd say with a laugh, you make *bastard* sound like it should be a woodwind instrument. November and December gave me plenty of opportunities to complain; important games were played during the holidays. And it's not as if I cared about Thanksgiving or Christmas, I hadn't grown up celebrating either of those. I was eighteen years old and going to school in Atlanta before I even saw a live Christmas tree. And all of the forced gaiety and noise about the holiday I found unsettling. But Selma was having a huge Thanksgiving dinner party and I wanted to show you off, but you were going out of town for a game. And no, I didn't want to come along. Outside Detroit — where it was probably a million degrees below zero? Besides, I was determined that you were going with me to that dinner.

"I am serious about this, George. Dead serious."

"I'm going to the game."

"Then don't call me when you get back."

"I've heard that one before."

"No, I really mean it — don't call me."

"You mean that — over a stupid party?"

"Yes, I really mean it."

"Okay, Ophelia. I won't call you."

"You mean that?"

"Yes, I really mean it. You mean it, don't you?"

"*Yes.*"

So why didn't he call? This was the end, the absolute end. That dinner party was a total disaster. Selma had gotten drunk and put too much wine in the stuffing, so it looked like her turkey was having diarrhea. And after another half bottle of Johnny Walker, she got onto one of her favorite subjects — black men dating white women. Later that night I caught a twenty-second news clip about the game, saw a red-headed blur in the crowd, and swore it was Shawn. The bitch. Some women have no pride — they'll go to any lengths to run after a man who doesn't want them. Not me. What did Grandma used to say? She was short on money but long on pride.

My pride had to stretch a long way. November left, December came — no call. I was utterly depressed when I wrote home, and even more depressed when I got my Candle Walk package the next week. What in the hell was I doing in this city? It was cold and unfriendly. I took out the sweet orange rock Grandma had sent me and Mama Day's eternal lavender water. Seven years away from that place and December twenty-second still didn't feel right without my seeing a lighted candle. The same old news from home, but if those letters had ever stopped coming, I don't know what I'd do. I got to the line "The last thing you need is a no-good man," and started to cry. They were so right. Your phone rang twelve times — twelve.

"You know I didn't mean it."

"I didn't know, Ophelia. But I was hoping."

I WOKE UP ONE MORNING, sometime in early November, and realized I wanted to be with you for the rest of my life. Whether I could or not was seriously open to question, but the desire was certainly there. From a child I had to accept that some things you may want aren't meant for you — or worse, not even good for you. I had wanted to know my parents, I had wanted to be able to take part in sports. But none of that was to happen because of reasons beyond my control, and being carefully trained not to let that upset me, I made the best of it. The life I had, I had, and what I could do, that was that. So the revelation about you that day wasn't earth shattering — I had my usual shave and shower, fixed a bowl of oatmeal, and went on to work — it was simply another item in a long list of things I had wanted. But was it possible, could we live around each other? The rest of your life seems like a long time when you're only thirty-one. We had to look at each other and see if we could accept what was there — because that's exactly what we were getting.

That was when I decided *not* to go out and buy the video cassette recorder. I had been toying with the idea because the relationship was fairly new and most women are so insecure in the beginning. They think it proves something if they call on the spur of the moment — Could you come over? — and you do. It only means that you came over, and if the weather's bad, you're wet. But I enjoyed pampering them — a little time and silly little attentions, and they would purr. Add some sort of personal gift to that now and then, and they'd walk on water for you. They were happy, and I was happy because I couldn't tolerate pouting. When a woman was screaming about the big things, I found out she just wanted something small. That "you don't care" crap could be nipped in the bud by randomly checking off days in your appointment calendar to have your secretary mail out a Hallmark card. That way you're "thinking" about her — whether you are or not.

Unfortunately, you and I were in the middle of the football season. A VCR could have solved that. But if it was going to be possible to spend the rest of my life with you, I might as well find out if you could accept me totally — and that meant football. It wasn't a pastime, it was a passion. I didn't talk, I didn't cuddle, I didn't want your hand on my crotch when the games were on — and television was a poor second best to a live stadium. I was always fascinated with the mechanics of the game, the mixture of science, raw strength, and a touch of human unpredictability. It challenged me more than other sports, with its infinite possibility of moves. Baseball and basketball were a linear display of skill and strength: if you thought fast and were strong and flexible, you could endure. But football took that extra ounce from a man: when your physical frame is being beaten and slammed, you can simply become too tired to think, to move. And sometimes your guts can even give out. So you keep going because you keep going. It produces a high that's possible only when a man has glimpsed the substance of immortality.

Since I couldn't be out on the fields in high school, I would help the coach design plays, and he often listened to my suggestions because he said I had a very rational mind. But there was nothing rational about what happened when I became part of the crowd — and the bigger, the better. Unless you've been there, you can't understand what it's like. Yet, even being there for someone like you wasn't enough — you'd only see twenty-two men on a field and seventy-odd thousand screaming people. So why tell you what you couldn't believe? The crowd became a single living organism — one pulse, one heartbeat, one throat. I've seen it bend down and breathe life into disheartened players. I've seen it crush men with its hate. And I'm not talking in metaphors — it could create miracles. It did at the Super Bowl in 1976. First quarter and the Steelers were down seven-nothing to the Cowboys after only five minutes of play. That can wreak havoc on a team's morale and throw a whole game off. But my half of the crowd's body leaned forward as Terry Bradshaw dropped back at the Cowboys' forty-eight and missiled the ball, too high and heading out of bounds, on the right side. But there was the wide receiver, Lynn Swann, his dark, lean body defying gravity as he leaped up — caught it — and twisted midair to ram it down in bounds. A thirty-two-yard gain. No, being there wasn't enough. You'd have to feel the force that suspended almost two hundred pounds of flesh above the ground to believe that we had willed him those wings.

I had gone to my first big game in 1968, the Jets against the Raiders in the AFC championship, and I had been hooked on live games ever since. I had made every AFC playoff and most of the NFCs even if they were on different coasts. But if there was a conflict, or I couldn't get a flight to make both, the AFC was my league, just like the Pats were my team — I guess I had a special affinity for underdogs. I took a lot of kidding from Bruce about them. What do you know about football? I'd say. I know a lot about losers, he'd answer, and the New England Patriots are definitely that. But he shut up in '78 when they took the Eastern division championship on a tie breaker over Miami. He had no choice — I wouldn't let him get a word in edge-wise for weeks. Of course, they didn't make the final round of playoffs. But I still believed that I would live to see them get to the Super Bowl. Maybe, as Bruce said, that was a bit too much to ask. He and I had a good working relationship: we broke our butts together and knew when it was time to go our separate ways — he in April for the start of the trout season, and me in January for the end of the games.

That was the way it was, but more important, the way it was going to be. And sure, I could give in to you that first year, get a VCR and maybe only do the Super Bowl on my vacation. But what about the next year and the next? You were obsessed with the idea of my behavior spelling the ending of us, and I was laying the groundwork for the beginning. So why didn't I just come right out and tell you? Because I had my own insecurities as well. It was frightening, wanting you as much as I did. I couldn't imagine your being able to equal that inten-sity, and I didn't even hope for that. Just some sign that I was beginning to matter, that I was special from the other men you'd known. And if there were no signs of that, why give you carte blanche to hurt me — or worse, despise me for my vulnerability? The more you were beginning to mean to me, the more close-mouthed I became, waiting. And waiting for what? Something more than temper tantrums about whether it was a Monday or Tuesday night I was free to see you — those weren't about me, they were about you. Even something more than the conditioned responses I knew I would receive by being thoughtful — that was about human nature. I guess I was waiting for some action — words would not suffice — that said, Yes, I'm doing this because he makes the difference.

*

YOU WOULDN'T TALK to me. I don't mean when I was being irrational and demanding — I deserved having the phone hung up on me then. But by the time the new year came, it was more than apparent that you were football. And I started trying to read the sports section although it confused the hell out of me. I even tried watching a game one night, but where's the fun in all of it when you can't see the ball? They line up, bend down, and all of a sudden they're in a pile, smelling each other's behinds. Okay, this was a part of your life I couldn't share and you seemed to prefer not talking about it. I could handle that, since I was bored by the whole subject anyway. But, George, there were too many other things we didn't talk about.

I had told you about where I grew up. I painted the picture of a small rural community and my life with Grandma and Mama Day, so it seemed like any other small southern town and they two old ladies doting over the last grandchild. Of course, some things about Willow Springs you could never believe, but I showed you Candle Walk, we exchanged gifts that night instead of Christmas Eve. You thought it quaint and charming, and it was fun, undressing each other on the floor with all that soft light around us. But I did open up fully to share my feelings about my father running off and my mother dying so young. I talked to you about loneliness — all kinds. About my day-to-day frustrations with the job, the plans I had for my future — going back to college and getting a history degree. Not a marketable skill, but something I'd wanted to do. Coming from a place as rich in legend and history as the South, I'd always been intrigued by the subject. I talked and talked, but getting you to say anything about yourself was like pulling teeth. Oh, you'd hold a conversation — and you could make me laugh with the stories about some of your clients, about your partner's offbeat relatives and the niece who put chewing gum in the filing cabinet.

And when I pressed you for *your* life, you'd say that you grew up in a boy's shelter, that it was hard, working your way through Columbia and getting set up in your own business. You'd mention a woman named Mrs. Jackson sometimes. The world lost a lot when she died, you said. But you'd never talk about your *feelings* surrounding any of that. "Only the present has potential" is how you'd brush me off. Deal with the man in front of you. I was trying, George. But what you didn't understand is that I thought you didn't trust me enough to share those feelings. A person is made up of much more than the "now." I had opened up to you about the frightened little girl inside of me because I'd finally come to believe that you would never hurt her. And the more I did that, the more you shut yourself off. I wasn't going to beg you to trust me. And since I refused to think of my life anymore without you in it, this was just the way it would have to be. But it was a bitter pill to swallow. I have to admit, sometimes it went down better than others. And the day I dropped by your office was not one of those better days.

It was so weird, walking back into that lobby, thinking about how it felt the first time. It seemed as if I'd changed so much since then and it was only five months later. The next day you were going to Philadelphia for the playoffs and from there to San Diego, so you were working late to tie up loose ends. I was bringing you the T-shirt as a going-away present. I forgot who you said was playing who, or whose side you were on, so I just had printed up: HE'S MY FOOTBALL BABY. The broken elevator should have told me to turn around and go home. No need to meet you after work, you were coming over anyway. And your guilt about not spending a single day of your vacation with me would make you extremely nice. When I thought about how nice, I figured I'd meet you halfway and climb those steps.

I was out of breath by the fifth floor, and that's when I got my second warning: the exit door was locked, and I was trying to decide if it was worth it to go down one flight and try the other end of the building when a woman with curly red hair opened the door from the hall. Short and pretty. Blue-green eyes. And fine sprays of freckles over her nose and forehead. She said I was lucky she had worked overtime because the janitor always locked this stairwell door after a certain hour. I thanked her and stood there, looking at the stairway where she had disappeared, for a long, long time. When I finally made it into your office, the bag holding your T-shirt was small enough to fit between my fists.

"Why didn't you tell me Shawn worked in this building?"

"I didn't think it was relevant. How did you find out?"

"It's not *relevant*. But I'm sure that's the least of what you've been keeping from me."

"I'm not going to start with you, Ophelia, okay? That part of my life is over — she knows it, I know it, and you know it."

"I don't know anything, George. Not one goddamned thing. You see, nothing about your life is relevant to me. I'm just someone you fuck when you have a mind to — I should start charging."

"You've got a dirty mouth, and I don't like that."

"I don't care what you like. Since when do you care about me — you sneak around and hide things from me, you —"

"Ophelia, what difference did it make where she worked? If I still wanted to see her, I could see her."

"I'm not talking about *her*."

"Then what are you talking about, or is this some new kind of tantrum to take up my time because I'm going to the games?"

"Forget it, George. Just forget it. Here, I brought you —"

You ignored the bag on your desk. "No, I don't want to forget it. What do I hide from you? You know as much about me as anyone."

"Then that's pathetic — because I don't know anything."

"This is getting us nowhere."

"That's where we've been for a while."

"Okay, Ophelia, what could you possibly need to know about me that I haven't told you — my age, my background, you're standing in the place where I work. The only thing left is my social security number and shoe size. So come on — ask me a question. Any question. You've got my undivided attention. Ah, I see we have silence. That just shows you how ridiculous you can be with absolutely no effort."

"And you can be one sarcastic son-of-a-bitch."

"You know I hate that word."

"Yeah, that I do know. And here's a question for you — why, George? Why do you hate being called a son-of-a-bitch? A pompous, snide, uptight son-of-a-bitch?"

Your face was unreadable as you put on your coat, picked up your briefcase, and walked out. You had left my T-shirt on your desk. I walked out without it as well. You were nowhere in sight when I got to the outer hall. You didn't call me that night, and you didn't answer your phone. I knew not to try the next day, you were in Philadelphia. And from Philadelphia to San Diego. Come hell or high water, you were going to the games. And when you got back I would have to make the first call anyway. I suppose I owed you an apology, but there was something that you owed me.

The third warning was my crushing disappointment when the phone rang the next evening and it wasn't you. An old boyfriend. No, I wasn't doing a thing. And sure, I'd like to have dinner. His place? Why not. Yes, I remembered where it was. Those seven blocks were long ones: four over to Riverside Drive, and a left turn to go north. I pushed all of those warnings out of my mind as I was passing Riverside Park. So when I reached his building, I didn't hesitate before going in.

I CAME BACK from Philadelphia that night to answer your question. And to ask you to marry me. Enough was enough. If we kept on like this, there wasn't much hope for us. Somebody had to take the first chance. I had understood what you were saying in my office perfectly, but I didn't want to deal with it. I wasn't going to let you manipulate me into opening up my guts before I was ready. But the point was, when would I ever be ready? How frustrated would you have to get before I had this elusive guarantee from you that I was seeking? It's funny, I was losing you because of my fear of losing you. Star-crossed. Yeah, that's what we were. Always missing each other. That weekend was a total bust. I didn't have the spirit to be racing to a plane out to California — it was hard enough concentrating on the game in front of me. It didn't matter that the Eagles had won. They were coming up against either Oakland or San Diego in the Super Bowl, and either of those teams could beat them with their hands behind their backs. Yeah, in two weeks it was going to be an AFC victory in New Orleans. I was charmed by that city, and maybe I could enjoy it again, once I got all of this straightened out with you.

New Orleans. Tampa. Miami. None of those cities seemed like the real South. Nothing like the place you came from. I was always in awe of the stories you told so easily about Willow Springs. To be born in a grandmother's house, to be able to walk and see where a great-grandfather and even great-great-grandfather was born. You had more than a family, you had a history. And I didn't even have a real last name. I'm sure my father and mother lied to each other about even their first names. How would he know years later that I might especially wonder about his? When the arrangement is to drop twenty bucks on a dresser for a woman, you figure that's all you've left behind. I had no choice but to emphasize my nows, while in back of all that stubbornness was the fear that you might think less of me. But I was going to be a lot less without you in my life anyway. So here goes nothing, I thought, as I walked up Broadway toward your street.

I decided to phone from the corner first. I could have walked in with my key, but I wanted to give you a chance to invite me up. At that moment, I needed all the encouragement I could get. No answer. I was about to redial when I spotted you across the avenue, heading west. I recognized the red cashmere coat I had given you for Christmas and that undeniably proud strut. Was she taking a walk? I thought. Going out to meet friends? By the time I'd made it across Broadway myself, you were turning the corner two blocks ahead onto Riverside Drive. Perhaps it was glimpsing the side of your face or a certain angle of your shoulders that gave me the feeling something wasn't right. I started to speed up. I turned the corner and was just about to call out when that door closed behind you in the lobby.

I waited all night.

IT WAS A GRAY and cold morning when I came out of that building and saw you standing there across the Drive, leaning against the promenade wall, your trench coat buttoned to the neck with the collar up. It didn't matter how you got there. All those months I had wondered, and this is how it ends. I was too drained to feel anything — shame, fear — when you finally walked over. Your face was still unreadable. And your voice was matter of fact when you took your hand out of your pocket and slapped the living daylights out of me.

"My mother was a whore. And that's why I don't like being called the son of a bitch."

My eyes were still blurred. My bottom lip had been slammed against my teeth and was starting to bleed. Your fingers were like a vise when they gripped mine as you began dragging me up Riverside Drive to Harlem. We reached the pier at 125th Street. Still crushing my hand, you pointed to a brownstone across the way.

"I found out that's where I was born. She was fifteen years old.

And she worked out of that house. My father was one of her customers."

A deserted, crumbling restaurant stood near the pier. The side windows had been broken, but across the front in peeling letters I could read, Bailey's Cafe. And I could hear the cars moving above us on the overpass, the muddy water hitting against the rocks, the sound of gulls.

"The man who owned this place found me one morning, lying on a stack of newspapers. He called the shelter and they picked me up. I was three months old."

We went past Bailey's Cafe to the edge of the pier. You finally let my hand go, put yours back into your pocket, and stared into the water.

"Later, her body washed up down there. I don't have all the pieces. But there are enough of them to lead me to believe that she was not a bitch."

You then looked me straight in the face.

"The last name I have was given to me at the shelter on Staten Island where I lived until I was eighteen — Wallace P. Andrews. And how do I *feel* about all this?"

You smiled. I guess I could call it a smile.

"I feel that men will often grow up thinking of women in the same way they think of their mothers. You see, when I was growing up, there was no reason for me to neglect her on the days that would have been important: her birthday, anniversary, or the second Sunday in May. I didn't forget to call now and then to ask her how she was doing. I didn't find her demands annoying, or her worries unnecessary. I was the kind of son who didn't refuse to share my friends, my interests, or my hopes for the future with her. Yeah, that's pretty close to the kind of son I was."

I don't know how long I closed my eyes, but when I opened them, I asked you to marry me. Next week, you said, if I didn't mind spending my honeymoon in New Orleans.

◇◇◇

USUALLY, THERE AIN'T much happening here between Candle Walk and the first spring planting. Folks that keep gardens putter around, spreading a little manure, wood ash, and fish waste on their soil. They may sharpen some hoes, scrape the rust off the teeth of their rakes, or do a bit of pruning in their fruit trees. Them that still gig and fish will use the days to repair their nets and haul their boats up on shore to oil the rudders or slap a new coat of paint on the sides. But none of that takes but so long, and even with the shorter days there's a good spell of time to fill between making up a bed and getting back into it at night. Parris and Reema see a lot of their customers in the barber shop and beauty parlor this time of year, while not seeing a lot of business. Folks will wander in and talk about what ain't been brought into the general store for them to buy if they had the money. Will even get into hot arguments about the quality of goods that ain't on the shelves. Small places live on small talk, but sometimes the happenings can be too lean for everybody to get enough fat out of it to chew over. It gets kinda depressing the winters when nobody's bothering to fool around with somebody else's wife or husband, when nobody's wild boy got picked up beyond the bridge on a drunk and disorderly or a wild gal's done got herself in the family way. Even Reverend Hooper gets down in the mouth them winters. All that hell and brimstone in his sermons don't carry the same kinda sparkle when there ain't no likely candidates to feed the fires.

This year is gonna be way different. And the word is speculation. More than talking about what is, folks love to talk about what might be. They got Cocoa Day and the widow Ruby to thank for that. Cocoa went off and got herself married about a month after Candle Walk. Hooked up with a city boy — a big-time railroad man, some say. An engineer and all — owns his own train. Some argue back that an engineer only *runs* a train. But Miss Abigail says — and she should know — that the boy has his own business. What other kinda business would an engineer be into? Into the business of lying, half that's standing by the store answer back. New York City is full of con artists. Muggers, pickpockets, and God knows what else. Why didn't Cocoa come home and get herself a husband, somebody she could trust? Now, if that don't beat the band — come home and get a husband. Who was she gonna marry here? This sorry lot in Willow Springs can't even *spell* train, no less run one. Whatever the boy is into, Mama Day says he's all right. And you know, they don't make enough wool —

even up in New York — to pull anything over her eyes. But Mama Day ain't seen him, has she? Nobody down here's seen him yet. Awful suspicious, you up and marry somebody folks ain't met. Awful smart, if you ask me. Get him first and then let him see the mess you had to grow up around. One look at this place and there wouldna been no wedding bells. But Ruby's bringing plenty of wedding bells here come spring. *Plenty* of everything — mercy, mercy.

Willow Springs owes Ruby a debt of gratitude this winter. Since no one really knows Cocoa's new husband, there's a limit to figuring out what he is or ain't — what did or didn't go on up there in the city. Folks woulda tired of the subject long before spring. But Ruby and Junior Lee now, there was no end to what could be said. And as that wedding approaches, there's something new each week to carry talk along. First of all, Ruby is planning herself a real church wedding. Those are rare in these parts, even for the first time around. Most of the young ones do it simple and quiet like Cocoa did. They'll go beyond the bridge to a South Carolina or Georgia courthouse and take out a license, and then, depending upon their standing in church, Reverend Hooper will marry 'em in his office or they'll go back over the bridge the next week and have the county clerk do it. The wedding dinner is a big thing, though. About six months after they start keeping house, their folks and neighbors will cook up one something of a feast. We wait half a year to make sure it's worth going through the trouble — human nature being what it is and all. No point in barbecuing a whole side of meat, frying tons of fish from The Sound, and using up a barrel of flour making cakes and pies if she's gonna be back home with her mama before the food gets digested good. So if this thing of Cocoa's is going to last that distance, the pots and pans will be out when she brings him down mid-August.

Ruby and Junior Lee is another matter. Their wedding is gonna be BIG — beginning to end (in more ways than one, folks say). The church is to be decked out in flowers, Reema playing the piano, and Reverend Hooper in his Sunday robes. Ruby's ordered Junior Lee a new suit from the Sears catalogue and bought a whole bolt of blue silk cloth for her dress. Talk had it that she needed three bolts of cloth, but that's just being evil. One bolt will surely do it — it's to be a short dress. And Ruby ain't asked folks to cook her a single biscuit for the party she's throwing right after. She's gonna do it all herself: twenty chickens, a whole hog, and fifty pounds of drumfish. But what are the rest of us gonna eat? some ask. Oh, the jokes don't end. There's one for every pound on Ruby, so we're talking about a lot of fun. And yet you couldn't rightly call Ruby fat — she's amazing. Nothing jiggles when she walks or gushes out of her clothes. Whatever she puts into her mouth turns into solid meat and it's distributed even-like on all six feet of her: arms and legs almost thick around as small tree trunks and spreading out from a middle that *is* as wide as the old oak down by Chevy's Pass. Ruby made a bet with Parris years ago that one of her aprons could be tied around that oak tree. She won. And she's gotten bigger since then. Folks done forgot the color of her eyes — they been pressed into tiny slits, but her face's gotten lighter over time 'cause the skin keeps stretching out. Yeah, folks can say all the mean things they want. That them roots she's working may have got Junior Lee to the altar for her, but Ruby being so much older than him, she'll be dead before he finds his way into all of that. Or him having the reputation of being far less than ambitious; he'll tire out on the wedding night just trying to roll up her gown. All that talk aside, that wedding's coming this spring. And Junior Lee is getting more than a woman, he's marrying himself an event.

While things are going on loud like that inside the beauty parlor or in front of the general store, other things are moving along quietly. And they can be the more important. See, we ain't paid too much attention to the change in Bernice Duvall. She's a lot less nervous than she used to be, and she's walking everywhere now. That old green Chevy stays parked in her side yard and she makes it the three miles from the south end to the stores at the bridge junction on foot. She's there once a week to pick up her special order of blackstrap molasses, brown rice, and brewer's yeast. She'll stand a while and exchange the time of day with folks, her packages hoisted up on them hips that are starting to fill out slowly but surely. And if someone asks her about her mother-in-law, she don't get that funny little twitch around her mouth anymore. She'll say real pleasant that she's helping Pearl make her dress for the wedding — Pearl is gonna be Ruby's matron of honor — and things are going along just fine. The only time Bernice will hurry along is when she's got frozen meat in her bag: twice a month the store brings in a box of liver, beef kidneys, and beef heart for her. Nobody asks why she and Ambush is eating them strange things now, and Bernice don't offer the information. But she'll nod her head and agree out loud when for the hundredth time someone says they'll be glad come spring. Her words hold a different ring, though — it's like when the visiting choir sings they'll be glad going on to glory come Judgment Day. Contentment is the last thing folks want around here in the winter, and so Bernice Duvall goes unnoticed as she quietly moves about the business of preparing for her miracle.

Down the road at the Days' there's busy preparation for a miracle that Miranda says has already happened: Cocoa's marriage. She was beginning to think that she'd never live to see the day, and she'd geared herself up to live for a long time. It's still kinda hard to believe that telephone call that came from New Orleans, but she'd spoken to the boy herself and they got the pictures in the mail this month. He had a strong face, and a good strong name — George. He was gonna need all the strength he could get to put up with Baby Girl, Miranda thinks. Just out-and-out aggravating, that's what she could be — demanding to have herself a double-ring quilt as a wedding present. Like all folks got to do this winter is sit around sewing together tiny bits of cloth till their fingers ache. Not a bit of consideration for her arthritis or her grandma's failing eyesight. And she knew they weren't gonna let anyone else help — not for something like this. All the chalking, padding, stretching, and hemming was up to them if it was gonna be done at all. And you couldn't send an old poor-mouth quilt with one double ring, no — from edges to center the patterns had to twine around each other. It would serve her right if it took till next year, and it probably would if they had the sense not to keep at it all day and a good part of the night.

"Well, that's it for me. It's after ten o'clock." Abigail bites off the knotted end of her thread. She sighs and runs her hand along her end of the quilting frame. "It may be taking forever, but it's gonna be some kind of beautiful. You were right, Miranda, using that cambric muslin instead of a regular cotton lining is gonna make this feel like velvet. But it's a pain in the neck to sew — a stitch will slip away before you know it."

"Just gotta keep waxing your needle."

"Next to threading, I think I hate waxing the most."

"I hate the whole mess. This cutting, shaping, measuring. And I told Baby Girl, don't ask me for spit after this."

"But she did finally say she'd settle for a simple pattern."

" 'Cause she ain't got no pride. This'll be passed on to my great-grandnieces and nephews when it's time for them to marry. And since I won't be around to defend myself, I don't want them thinking I was a lazy old somebody who couldn't make a decent double-ring quilt."

"Great-grands." Abigail shakes her head. "It couldna been more than yesterday when I was a bride. And now we're sitting here talking about my great-grandchildren." Abigail's eyes look off in the distance, pride and sadness all mixed up in one.

"No, we're sitting here *planning* your great-grandchildren." Miranda licks her thumb to thread another needle. "You can't count on nothing with these young people today. And knowing my grandniece like I do, if she ain't found herself a saint, it's gonna be a long haul between that honeymoon and her getting me that new teacup with Great-Great Aunt on it."

"Miranda, you're always downing Baby Girl. If this doesn't work out, why it gotta be her fault? We don't know nothing about him."

"He told us all about himself on the phone."

"His name? What he does for a living? And a whole lot of promises anybody can make. Talk is cheap, Miranda."

"I know, that's why I listened real careful to the way he talked. Remember what he said when you told him to take good care of her? He said, 'She has all I have.' "

"Yeah, real pretty. But how many right here in Willow Springs done heard them same words? Junior Lee probably said it to Frances, and you see where Frances is."

"No, Abigail — listen to him good now. The boy ain't said, 'All I have is hers.' We both know that's a lot of nonsense, 'cause nobody would — or could — give away *all* of themselves to somebody else. That person is an out-and-out liar, or if they was of that mind, they wouldn't be nobody worth living with. No, he said — 'She has all I have.' That means sharing. If he got a nickel, she's got a part in it. He got a dream, he's gonna take her along. If he got a life, Abigail, he's saying that life can open itself up for her. You can't ask no more than that from a man."

"Maybe you're right." Abigail stands up and stretches her back. "Like you was right about this muslin. But I'm going to bed now. How much longer you sitting at this?"

"Just a bit more. It's less I'll have to do tomorrow."

"Don't forget to cut off my lights."

"Woman, don't I always cut off your lights?"

"No, 'cause you're getting senile like me."

The old walnut clock in Abigail's living room ticks away as Miranda's silver needle slips through the layers of padded cloth: the curve of each ring is fixed into place by sending the needle down to the bottom and up. Down and up, a stitch at a time. She's almost knee deep in bags of colored rags, sorted together by shades. The rings lay on a solid backing of cotton flannel; from a distance it looks like she's bending over a patch of sand at the bottom of the bluff when it's caught the first rays of a spring moon — an evening cream. The overlapping circles start out as golds on the edge and melt into oranges, reds, blues, greens, and then back to golds for the middle of the quilt. A bit of her daddy's Sunday shirt is matched with Abigail's lace slip, the collar from Hope's graduation dress, the palm of Grace's baptismal gloves. Trunks and boxes from the other place gave up enough for twenty quilts: corduroy from her uncles, broadcloth from her great-uncles. Her needle fastens the satin trim of Peace's receiving blanket to Cocoa's baby jumper to a pocket from her own gardening apron. Golds into oranges into reds into blues . . . She concentrates on the tiny stitches as the clock ticks away. The front of Mother's gingham shirtwaist — it would go right nice into the curve between these two little patches of apricot toweling, but Abigail would have a fit. Maybe she won't remember. And maybe the sun won't come up tomorrow, either. I'll just use a sliver, no longer than the joint of my thumb. Put a little piece of her in here somewhere.

The gingham is almost dry rot and don't cut well, the threads fraying under her scissors. She tries and tries again just for a sliver. Too precious to lose, have to back it with something. Rummaging through the oranges, she digs up a piece of faded homespun, no larger than the palm of her hand and still tight and sturdy. Now, this is real old. Much older than the gingham. Coulda been part of anything, but only a woman would wear this color. The homespun is wrapped over and basted along the edges of the gingham. She can shape the curve she needs now. Extra slow, extra careful with this one: she pushes the needle through, tugs the thread up — two ticks of the clock. Pushes the needle through, tugs the thread down — two ticks of the clock. *She ain't bringing that boy home mid-August.* Miranda feels a chill move through the center of her chest. She doesn't want to know, so she pushes the needle through and tugs the thread down — tugs the thread up. *Or the next August, either.* She tries to put her mind somewhere else, but she only has the homespun, the gingham, and the silver flashing of her needle. *Or the next.* It doesn't help to listen to the clock, 'cause it's only telling her what she knew about the homespun all along. The woman who wore it broke a man's heart. Candle Walk night. What really happened between her great-grandmother and Bascombe Wade? How many — if any — of them seven sons were his? But the last boy to show up in their family was no mystery; he had cherished another woman who could not find peace. Ophelia. It was too late to take it out of the quilt, and it didn't matter no way. Could she take herself out? Could she take out Abigail? Could she take 'em all out and start again? With what? Miranda finishes the curve and runs her hands along the stitching. When it's done right you can't tell where one ring ends and the other begins. It's like they ain't been sewn at all, they grew up out of nowhere. She'd finish off this circle with the apricot toweling, leave the two openings to connect in some of that light red crepe, and call it a night. This quilt was gonna be treated real tender, and it was gonna cover a lot of tenderness up there in New York on them cold winter evenings. But she won't bring that boy home mid-August. Be a long time before Willow Springs sees him.

She turns off the lamps before she leaves for home. She wasn't gonna work on that quilt by herself no more at night. When Abigail stopped, she'd stop. If it took 'em longer, so be it. Some things you don't need to know, especially when you can't do nothing about it. The past was gone, just as gone as it could be. And only God could change the future. That leaves the rest of us with today, and we mess that up enough as it is. Leave things be, let 'em go their natural course. The night air hits her face, it's sharp and chill, but she can feel the earth softening under her feet. Spring's coming. Wild azaleas be blooming soon, the thorn apples and crepe myrtle. Them woods won't look the same. No fertilizer, no pruning — no nothing, and they'll beat her flowers blooming by three weeks. Yes, spring was coming. And would God forgive her for Bernice? But she wasn't changing the natural course of nothing, she couldn't if she tried. Just using what's there. And couldn't be nothing wrong in helping Bernice to believe that there's something more than there is. It's an old house with a big garden, and it done seen its share of pain. And I'm just an old woman who'll be waiting in a rocking chair . . .

The first new moon come spring. She can hear her coming, smell her coming, long before she makes that turn down by the old pine stump. Moving through the bush, guided by the starlight that glints off the two pair of eyes waiting and rocking, both unblinking. One pair cradled low in the lap of the other, soft rumbles vibrating its feathered throat. One pair humming a music born before words as they rock and stroke, forefinger and thumb, gently following the path of feathers, throat, breast, and sides. The right hand stroking, the left hand cupping underneath the tiny egg hole that sucks itself open and closed, open and closed. Two pair of eyes breathing as one when hope rounds that bend. She can taste the fear that hesitates on the edge of the garden walk; it's thick in the air moving before the feet passing by the tube-roses, the camellias, the hanging vines of the dwarf honeysuckle. Feet passing into the other place where flowers can be made to sing and trees to fly. Fear trembling at the bottom of the porch steps, watching the gleaming of two pair of eyes, hearing the creak of wood against wood under the soft rumbling from feathers, the humming begun in eternity. But it's hope that finds a voice: Mama — Mama Day?

The right hand strokes, the left hand reaches out, the palm wet from the cradled egg, gray and warm. Confusion waits a bit too long. The shell dries and grows cold under the hidden moon. One pair of eyes unblinking, one pair frowns and smashes the egg into the porch steps. Silent, she pleads for another chance. But she must wait — and listen. Not to the humming, not to the creak of wood against wood. Naw: the moon inching toward the horizon, the tiny hole sucking itself open and closed, open and closed. The left hand reaches back out. Knowing takes the egg while the shell's still pulsing and wet, breaks it, and eats.

Now, it only takes a nod of the head to move them all inside. Pine chips smoking on the fire blazing in the parlor hearth makes the air steamy and sweet. Every shadow in the unlit room is dancing along the floor and walls. She ain't gotta be told why the dining table is covered in a white sheet and has padded boards nailed upright on one end. She strips down naked, rests her head on the embroidered pillow, and props her feet high up into the scooped top of each board. It'll be easier if she closes eyes. In the morning she can tell herself it was all a dream. And it can't be human hands no way, making her body feel like this.

Nine openings. She breathes through two, hears through two, eats through one, the two below her waist, and two for the life she longs to nurse. Nine openings melting into the uncountable, 'cause the touch is light, light. Spreading each tiny pore on each inch of skin. If she could scream, she would, as the touching begins deeper at the points of her fingertips to expand the pores that let in air, caressing down the bones of each finger joint to the ones that join the palm, the wrist, the lower arms. Her shoulders, sides, and stomach made into something more liquid than water, her breasts and hips flowing up against the pull of the earth. She ain't flesh, she's a center between the thighs spreading wide to take in . . . the touch of feathers. Space to space. Ancient fingers keeping each in line. The uncountable, the unthinkable, is one opening. Pulsing and alive — wet — the egg moves from one space to the other. A rhythm older than woman draws it in and holds it tight.

◆◇◆

SOMETIMES I WOULD wake up and ask myself if it really happened. I'd look over at you on your back, your right arm flung across your forehead, and think, Perhaps she's just here for the night. You'd turn in your sleep, grasp the pillow, and then I'd catch a slight glimmer from the gold band on your left hand. I'd close my eyes and drift off again — sometimes at peace, sometimes not. Sure, there were a lot of doubts. We had plunged into this very quickly. That week in New Orleans flew past as an exhilarating blur while reality came slowly in daily increments: the jarring colors from a second brand of toothpaste on my bathroom sink, stumbling into a wicker plant stand where a space should have been, reaching blindly for a clean shirt to find a

linen blazer in my hands. New smells, new sounds. Not always un-
pleasant, but always strange.

I was living with a stranger, there was no way around that. And
even if we had waited another year, the process of discovery would
have still been slow and arduous. And it meant a whole year in which
I would have postponed the delight of really getting to know you. You
were the first female I had lived with, and that in itself was a challenge.
I'd had no practice with sisters, cousins, or even aunts. I did what I
normally did when a subject was new to me: I bought books. Forget
The Joy of Sex and *The Sensuous Man*, Bruce told me through his six
years of experience. If you're going to be under the same roof with
them, you better learn about their cycles. Of course, I had the rudi-
ments: ovaries, a womb, Fallopian tubes. Those diagrams on Mrs.
Jackson's blackboard were graphic and indelible. And every twenty-
eight days, give or take, the womb released its lining if there wasn't
conception. A period. I thought it an appropriate word, because it was
a short phase. It's arrival had brought relief if a mild inconvenience
when it coincided with a night I wanted to sleep with a girlfriend.
And that's all the thought I'd ever given to it. Men see and don't see
those pastel boxes on the shelves in the drug store or supermarket. It
made you squeamish if you dwelt on the fact that you were constantly
surrounded by dripping blood, and a little frightened, too.

But those books I bought horrified me. It seems it was more than
"a period." Women stayed on an emotional roller coaster: between
being premenstrual, postmenstrual, and menstrual, they were normal
only about seventy-two hours out of each month. That seemed a bit
impossible to me: I'd watch you go about your day and wonder how
you even managed to lift your head off the pillow if you were fighting
that kind of battle with your hormones. Because you were saints, one
female doctor kept harping, and just imagine how much more you'd
excel if you didn't have your nerves getting on your nerves, and men
getting on your nerves. I found the whole philosophy of that particular
book ridiculous. Every time you snapped at me or refused to be reasonable, it wasn't you — it was your estrogen. No, I had met women
who were simply miserable human beings, and this doctor had nothing
to say about personalities. I made sure the next thing I read was written
by a man. It was the same slew of depressing charts with another
ongoing plea for tolerance: you were all, indeed, shrews through no

fault of your own and men should try to be supportive. The inequality in our social system intensified your innate envy of us — the "tampon complex," he called it. The shape of our sexual organs reminded you of the cruel trick biology had played on you. It became clear to me that I was never going to find a totally objective guide to what was going on inside of females, I was on my own. The goal was simple: I wanted to make you happy. And when you were irritable, I thought the easiest way would be to ask if it was something I was doing or that your body was doing: Are you premenstrual today, sweetheart? We got into some awful fights that way. And to be honest, I was hurt by your reaction. How was I going to understand if I didn't ask? No, I found out very quickly that when living with a woman, the shortest distance between two points is by way of China.

Not only your hormones but your minds are incredibly complex. You can manage disruptions and absorb ambivalences much better than men. It never ceased to amaze me, the hours you would spend tracking down a twenty-five-cent overcharge in our checking account. Where does she find the patience? And what was the point? It had nothing to do with practicality: the letter to the credit office or the phone call was going to wipe out the advantage of finding the over-charge. It's the principle, you would say. I was all for principles, but women could expend tremendous energy on twenty-five-cent ones. Unlike some, I didn't call it petty — it was a special complexity. But some things can be so complicated, they deteriorate into the nonsens-ical. My partner had warned me to expect to be awakened in the middle of the night because there was "something on her mind." Sure, it had been sitting there all through dinner and the eleven o'clock news, Bruce laughed, but it's that predawn moon that gets their juices flowing. I didn't worry about that: you slept like a rock as soon as your head hit the pillow — you weren't going to be one of those moonlight thinkers. Unfortunately, it was the sound of running water that set you off. I took long, hot showers in the morning. It was the one luxury I had promised myself when I left the shelter: no more two-minute splashes in tepid water because six other boys are lined up behind you. I didn't sing during my half hours in the shower, but I was content enough to. Some mornings I could hear you puttering around in the bath-room, and before long I knew I was going to feel a cold breeze on my backside as the curtain was pushed open. You'd stand there, leaning against the wall with your arms crossed, and just stare. If I ignore her, she'll go away. I'd duck my head under the nozzle and shampoo my hair again, letting the soap suds run into my ears. But you'd wait me out.

"George, if something happened to me, would you get married again?"

Always something far-fetched like that. And awfully stupid, because how was she expecting an honest answer, being out there within arm's reach of the razor blades, nail files, and Drano while all I had to protect myself was a bar of Lifebuoy?

"That depends, Ophelia. If I was eighty-five, I'd probably call it a day."

"No, I mean right now. If I left for work this very minute and got run over by a truck, how long before you'd get married again?"

"I can't answer that."

"Why?"

"Because there'd be a thousand factors to consider: did the truck just maim you so you lingered for a while, or did it kill you instantly? Then there's the funeral — some ministers talk longer than others. The time I'd need to clean out the closets. The —"

"So you would want to get married again?"

"Well, if the tables were turned, would you?"

"No. I'd never get over *you*."

"Same for me. Never get over you."

"You lying dog."

The trick was to make you laugh, or to get you angry enough to leave me in peace but still avoid any arguments at breakfast. Living with a female: a day-to-day balancing act, and I really enjoyed the challenge. Because the times I got it right, your being different made all the difference in my world.

Could any woman have served? In the beginning I thought about that, and I wondered about Shawn more than I ever admitted to you. As a matter of fact, there was no time I mentioned her. I wasn't that disoriented, even with soap in my ears. And she inevitably came up as one of your water questions. Are you sorry I'm not Shawn? That answer was easy because I'd rehearsed it — Oh, baby, never. Never,

I said, as I drew you into the tub and spent the last fifteen minutes of my shower time with you. You tell the unvarnished truth when it serves: No, I wasn't sorry you weren't Shawn. But could Shawn have been you? There is a spectrum of women and personalities that can make one man happy. I was past the age, and had never been inclined, to believe that there is one special somebody waiting on the horizon. You meant enough for me to give us a chance — that's all. But she had meant something, too. I was with her five years and couldn't make a commitment; I married you after six months. It's only natural that I would wonder.

And I think it's the word *natural* that finally put it to rest. We had been married about three months and we'd talked about your going back to school. You wanted a history degree, and we hardly needed your salary. I couldn't have cared less if you'd quit working after we got back from New Orleans. I wanted to start having children immediately, but you were set on this idea of first getting your degree. I doubt if you remember the particular incident. You had gotten your acceptance letter from NYU and were excited when I came home.

"Ophelia, this looks like goulash."

"Because that's what it is."

"It was your turn to cook."

"I cooked."

"No, *I* cooked pot roast last night. And you took the leftovers, threw tomato sauce on it, and gave it back to me."

"You're right. I was so busy reading through these brochures about the college, the time flew by."

"There's always going to be something for you to read. But fair is fair."

"Okay, I'm sorry."

"So what am I supposed to eat? Not this mess."

"You want some tuna fish?"

"No, I don't want tuna fish."

"Then I'll make you an omelet."

"And kill me off with all that cholesterol? Besides, eggs are breakfast food. Check out the clock, this is dinnertime."

"Well, what spoiled your day?"

"Coming in here and looking at this goulash."

"*Nigger — please.*"

Only you could have put your hands on your hips, narrowed your eyes, and come out with that. It was effortless and real. And above all — no, I should say, beneath it all, we both understood. A small moment, long forgotten in the drama of our lives. And so much of why I was with you, instead of her, hinged on it. No, I didn't marry you because only you could call me a nigger. It's just that you'd never feel the need to explain.

GEORGE, you were always so exacting, and that made you pretty hard to live with. Some things just couldn't be boiled down to a formula that you could shove new elements into and have it all come out nice and neat. The closets, for one. When I was moving from Manhattan to your house on Staten Island, you brought out a slide rule and graph paper — yes, graph paper — to measure the length of my closets and figure out how much of our clothing we would have to store in the basement in order to share the space in your bedroom. And then when your damn diagrams didn't work out, you carried on as if I was purposely trying to sabotage our marriage because I hung up an extra linen blazer. So we just shove one of your shirts over. No, we don't do that because then you don't have the rod space allotted for five days' worth of shirts — and you must always have five pressed shirts ready in that particular corner at the beginning of your week.

It was more than a routine; you operated by rituals. A place for everything and everything in its place. I guess a lot of it came from growing up in an institution, or maybe it was the work you did. You often said that Bruce dreamed up the impossible and you found the nuts and bolts to make it happen. You were not an imaginative man, but you were constant. In my better moments that was comforting to me. With all the odds against us, you could be counted on to hang in there for the long run. But getting along with you day to day was another matter. I understood perfectly why taking your heart medicine was second nature. Every morning after you'd used the toilet, you'd slide over the right door of the vanity, remove one of the digoxin tablets from your bottle, and take it with half a glass of water. Twice a day without thinking: a second bottle at your office and one you always carried with you. I moved the bottle in the vanity once, not to another place in the house, not even to another shelf — I pushed it a fraction away from the right-hand side to put in a flat box of Q-Tips.

I cried half an hour after you stormed out of the house. Yes, I knew how important your medicine was, how important it was for you to be able to find it. The thought of anything happening to you was unbearable. I wasn't upset because you'd left the way you did. I knew you were only going to walk around for a while and then call from the nearest phone booth. You were never able to stay angry with me for very long, even when you were justified. But it was a fraction of an inch, George. That's what I was crying over. There were six rooms in that house, and if I was to be afraid for every small change made, what was I to think about the biggest change of all — me?

I couldn't forget how quickly we'd gotten married. It's as if we didn't dare stop and think. But I was thinking now. And I wanted us to work so badly that I would be tempted to try and squeeze myself up into whatever shape you had calculated would fit into your plans. How long could I do it? The answer scared the hell out of me: I could have done it forever. You start out feeling a little uncomfortable, but then when you look around that's the shape you've grown into. Yeah, I could have worked myself into your life. "She has all I have," you told my grandmother on our honeymoon. But I was determined that *we* were going to have a life that would work. And that's really why I didn't want children right away — they would have confused the issue. I was only twenty-seven and there was time. I knew you didn't agree, and I understood why you wanted to be a father. The irony is that you would have made a good one, but there was us to consider. And if we weren't going to make it, it was better that the "we" be kept to just two.

My resolve about children would weaken from time to time. You would catch yourself refolding the towels on the rack, look at me and laugh: I guess you think I don't want you here. Sometimes, I said, I do. Your face would get very serious: Well, don't ever let me be a big enough fool to find out what that would be like. It was especially difficult when Bernice wrote me that she was finally pregnant. She'd been trying for so long, and I knew Ambush was going to make a great father. There were a lot of ways in which he reminded me of you. And then our wedding present came from home in the same summer. After I unfolded the quilt, all seven square feet of it, we stood there in awe for a moment. You wanted to clear a wall in the living room and hang it up. But it had been made to be used, and I also knew they hadn't gone through that kind of labor just for me. I ran my hands along the multicolored rings. They had sewed for *my* grandchildren to be conceived under this quilt. I looked at you standing beside me — the blue cotton shirt as always, hair cropped short and parted to the left as always. Our grandchildren? Let's see how it fits on the bed, I said.

The next week I kicked myself for not putting in my diaphragm. It was back to business as usual. No, you were definitely not going home with me mid-August. You'd have to meet my grandmother and great-aunt another time. There was Hopewell's apartment complex to oversee and the bidding for your first government contract. You had already taken a vacation in January, remember? And wasn't New Orleans a romantic city? How would I know, I had seen it through fifty thousand people running up and down Bourbon Street screaming, "Go, Eagles. Go, Raiders," flapping green wings on their backs and waving tinfoil swords. And all that nonsense about making sacrifices when you're working for yourself didn't fool me. When January of '82 rolled around, you'd be off to wherever they were playing the Super Bowl. Separate vacations — it looked like that was in the cards for us. And it was one fight I wasn't going to get into our first year. Nor was I going to jump into motherhood. Wait and see and measure: how much would I be asked to give for what I'd be given? And if the difference turned out to be too wide, I didn't want you — or any man — enough to stretch the bodies of my children to fill it.

My friends thought I had given up too much already. Selma came over to Staten Island with the same enthusiasm she'd have for traveling into the Congo bushland. He's got you all the way out here? The negligee she'd brought me from Saks had to cost more than the rent on my old studio. No, I didn't miss the traffic and noise on Broadway. I'd grown up being awakened by the sound of birds and it was nice to have it happening again. Also nice to roll over into a warm spot that someone had left in the bed. And yes, I was quitting work. No, he wasn't forcing me. I was hardly the type to be chained to a stove barefoot and pregnant. I'd be starting school in the fall. And I don't care what Jewel's husband did, it would take a very sick man to put pinholes in my diaphragm. Well, yes, he'd probably expect me to do more housework once I began classes — I was only going twice a week and he worked fourteen-hour days sometimes. No, his schedule didn't give us much time together, but we made the most of it. Separate vacations? It did seem a little odd, and maybe it was a golden opportunity for him to be with someone else. But any woman who'd be willing to fly People's Express and stay in Holiday Inns once a year with a man who only wanted to rant on about football couldn't be much of a threat. Would she be staying for dinner? No, because George didn't like her. She was right, you didn't.

Selma may have been the eternal pessimist, but she voiced the doubts I would have kept buried inside. Hearing them out in the open from her gave me a chance to debate with myself and to realize how easily I won.

◈◈◈

IT'S THE SEASON for butterflies when Cocoa comes home. Some years we get more than others, depending upon the wind and the amount of rain that spring. This year there's so many it's bound to be remembered as the summer when the woods bled gold. You can't walk anywhere near a patch of milkweed or wild clover without sending up a storm of color. The woods are full of laughter as the children chase 'em down — the one a gal catches is the new dress she'll get her next birthday, and counting spots on their wings for a little boy is the number of kisses he's due. Butterflies are a good sign, and this is a good summer. Drumfish and mullets ain't waiting to be hooked, they're jumping into the boats. Crawdaddies and oysters are a dime a hundred and crabs are coming up as big as two hands. Nobody's sick. Everybody's working. Gardens are doing so well it's ridiculous. If it weren't in the nature of some folks to complain, it could be said that every soul in Willow Springs had a reason to be happy.

Lord knows, Miss Abigail is fit to burst. Only twelve months since Cocoa was last home and look how much done happened. She come back a Missus. Didn't bring no Mister, but they don't seem to be getting on too ugly. She's been with him long enough to heat up the stoves for a wedding feast if he had come. Cocoa sits around on the front porch a lot more than she's done before, 'cause her running buddy is in the family way.

And you'd think it was actually a whole litter Bernice was having, how she carries on. The baby ain't due till the first of next year and she's run Dr. Smithfield ragged — that is, the times she ain't running beyond the bridge to the clinic. Taking all kinds of tests for the baby's blood, the baby's weight, the baby's heart. She's even already paid for her hospital room. Won't be no midwives delivering her grandchild, Pearl is crowing, that baby is getting the very best. Once Bernice listened to her and stopped taking all that "bush medicine," see what happened? Word got back to Miranda about what Pearl was saying, but she just hoisted her garden tools on her hip and headed for the other place. And Pearl can't do enough for Bernice now, won't let her feet touch the ground. Them two is thick as fleas — you woulda thought Pearl was the daddy. Miranda told Bernice she could keep on walking and doing everything else she was doing, but now it's Dr. Smithfield says this and Dr. Smithfield says that. There's a lesson in gratitude floating around here somewhere, but it looks like it's gonna be a while before it settles.

But Cocoa makes a nice sight up there on the porch in her pants and halter tops. You wonder why they call them little bitty things "shorts," when they fit so much better on gals with long legs.

"Miss C, you can't find nothing better to do, with your grandma's pole beans doubling over to the ground?" Miranda calls from across the road.

"She told me she had too many in the house already. And besides, I —"

"What's that?" Miranda cups her ears. "You know I'm getting old."

"I said, she told me she had too many in —"

"Don't be shouting like you got no upbringing. Speak to folks proper."

Cocoa takes her own dear time swinging her legs from the railing to cross over to Miranda's trailer.

"Well, now that you off your fanny, you can help me over here."

"That's all you had to say in the first place."

"I can see marriage ain't tamed your mouth none. I'm gonna have to send some hickory sticks to that boy."

Cocoa throws her head back and laughs. "He wouldn't know what to do with them."

"He'll learn."

But Miranda is right pleased by her answer. She done seen and heard a lot to please her in the week that Baby Girl's been home. She don't carry on all sweet and gushy over the boy, 'cause that ain't her style. And too much sweetness and light would make you kinda wonder anyway. Naw, there's just the right glow, like you get from banking a bed of coals before going to sleep on a chilly night. The heat's bound to flare up and flare down, but it's gonna burn steady and long. Abigail might get herself some great-grands out of this yet, allowing for all of this modern-day nonsense about waiting to "build up a working relationship," and using college to "find herself." Marriage brings its own work — you ain't gotta add nothing on to it. And you only go looking for things that've been lost. Baby Girl did have something lost to her, but she weren't gonna find it in no school.

"Ophelia, I got me some gardening to do at the other place. Pick up them baskets."

"What did you call me?"

"Don't stand there with your mouth gaping open, I called you by your name."

"But in my entire life, you've never used that name."

"That ain't true. The day you dropped into my hands, I first used it. Your mama said, 'Call her Ophelia.' And that's what we did. Called you that for a whole week to fix it into place. So you've heard me say it before, but you don't remember."

"You mean, I can't remember."

"I mean just what I said. Pick up them baskets."

The talk is of avoiding the poison sumac, marveling at lightning-struck edges of tree limbs, the blooms on sweet bays, but they're walking through time. Heavy shafts of sunlight form a slanting ladder for butterflies to tip on up among the pine branches as twigs snap under the feet moving in and out of sun-flecked shadows. The shadows erase the lines on the old brown woman's face and shorten the legs of the young pale one. They near the graveyard within the circle of live oaks and move down into time. A bit of hanging moss to cushion each foot and they're among the beginning of the Days.

John-Paul waits to guide them back as they thin out the foxglove at the head of his stone: I had six brothers born before me, five that lived. Matthew, Mark, Luke, Timothy, and James. But I carry the name of the one that didn't make it — John. I was the last boy and the last to marry. Some say I held her too dear. My daddy said it often when I was courting her. Hold back, John-Paul, I can look in that gal's eyes and see she'll never have peace. He passed on before I had the chance to tell him he was right. My daddy's name was Jonah. And there was six brothers born before him. Two come for one: Elijah and Elisha, Joel, Daniel, Joshua, and Amos. All them was born in slavery time, but they lived as free men 'cause their mama willed it so. She became such a legend that black folks, white folks, and even red folks in my time would only whisper the name Sapphira. I can't tell you about their daddy, they carried no surname till my daddy was born. God rested on the seventh day, their mama declared, and she would too. So my daddy was Jonah Day and it's what I got to pass on to you.

No headstone for Jonah Day. He waits under a blanket of morning glory vines tangled among the sweet peas. They know he's there, 'cause they listen: Some of my brothers looked like me and some didn't. But it wasn't for me to ask Mama. In them times it was common to have a blue-eyed child playing next to his dark sister. And any daddies that may have been were gone long before I growed. But I was there for mine. I took pride in all my sons, but my baby boy had my heart. Guess 'cause he came right after the one I lost. So I gave him and his bride the house that Mama gave me. I passed on without seeing his children, but I knew they had to be girls. The seventh son of a seventh son is a special man.

Tears catch in the back of the pale woman's throat as she brushes the dried weeds away from her mother's headstone. Grace Samantha Day: I gave the first and only baby my grandmother's name. Ophelia. I did it out of vengeance. Let this be another one, I told God, who could break a man's heart. Didn't women suffer enough? Eight months heavy with his child and he went off to chase horizons. I hoped he'd find them in hell. If I had known then what I was knowing all along, I woulda named her something else. Sapphira. My grandmother only softly broke a heart. My great-great-grandmother tore one wide open.

The young pale woman and the old brown woman look at each other over those mounds of time. The young hands touch the crumbling limestone as her inner mind remembers. A question from those inner eyes: the two graves that are missing? The breeze coming up from The Sound swirls the answer around her feet: Sapphira left by wind. Ophelia left by water.

As they round the bend by that old pine stump, the brown woman's walking cane becomes a thing of wonder.

Remember this —

A wave over a patch of zinnias and the scarlet petals take flight.

And this —

Winged marigolds follow them into the air.

Listen —

A thump of the stick: morning glories start to sing.

The other place. Butterflies and hummingbirds. And the wisdom to draw them.

Ancient eyes, sad and tired: it's time you knew. An old house with a big garden. And it's seen its share of pain.

It's getting toward dusk when Miranda and Cocoa make it back from the other place with their baskets loaded down. Abigail is glued to the porch rail, and Miranda can see she's none too happy. You'd think I took her off to kill her, from that look on Abigail's face, she thinks. A little gathering of lemon balm and cleaning off some old graves is all we done. But I'll let Baby Girl tell her, she wouldn't believe me no way.

"Nice of y'all to sneak off and let nobody know."

"We wasn't sneaking, Abigail. Didn't you say you'd love to have a mess of fresh kale to mix in with your collards for our dinner tonight?"

Abigail fixes Miranda with a stare. "It's too early for decent kale."

"Not at the other place, Grandma." Cocoa lifts up a full spread. "Look how big they've grown."

Abigail takes the basket. "So that's all y'all be doing — picking greens?"

"Yeah," Cocoa says. "And I wanted to stop by the family plot to clean up a little. Grandma, it's a shame the way you let that place run down."

"I'll be spending plenty of time there soon enough," Abigail says before she goes into the house.

"Sooner than you think if you stay so evil," Miranda calls behind her back.

"I wonder what's bothering her?"

"Nothing, child," Miranda says. "Nothing at all. Now give me that there balm. I'll strip the leaves and start up some cologne to take back with you."

"Mama Day, I still have gallons of lavender water."

"Yeah, but it's good to change up every now and then — keep the man interested. And I'll show you how to take a few fresh leaves and make up a nice female wash. It'll have your insides smelling like lemons." She pauses for a moment. "And it don't taste bad, either."

Cocoa turns two shades deeper. "Oh, so I can put it in his salads?"

Miranda shrugs. "If you wanna waste good lemon balm."

A kinda muggy evening. Another ounce of moisture and the air would turn to fog; the crickets and marsh frogs sound bloated and far off. But the mosquitoes are humming low, so Abigail's got two piles of wood, sprinkled with sweet fern, burning at the foot of the porch to let them sit in peace. Miranda's brought a truce by praising Abigail's potato pies though the crust is still glued to the roof of her mouth. Better to let that afternoon rest. We're like two peas in a pod, but we're two peas still the same.

The Duvalls' old green Chevy pulls up with Ambush driving. They can't make out the other men sitting in the car.

"Evening, Mama Day. Evening, Miss Abigail."

"Evening, Ambush. What brings you here?" Abigail asks.

"Ain't Cocoa told you? Muddy Waters is playing beyond the bridge, and we're all going to hear him."

"All who?" Miranda gets up and peers through the smoke.

"All us." Dr. Buzzard sticks his head out the back window and grins. "Muddy can pick — it's gonna be a hot time in the old town tonight." The rooster feathers on his hat just wiggling. "I even got my buddy to come along."

"Evennning, everryboddy." Junior Lee slurs his words, drunk or sober. He ain't famous for putting too much effort in nothing, least of all his appearance. More the pity, 'cause he could be a handsome man. Honey-colored skin and eyes. But that softness done seeped into his backbone, making him slouch when he could sit, shuffle when he could walk. Ruby keeps his closet full of new clothes since their wedding, but they never hang right on him. Jackets droop on his shoulders, belts can't seem to buckle his pants in place. And them alligator shoes want to melt off his feet.

"Junior Lee, is that you?" Abigail calls out. "You ain't hiding from Ruby is you, slouched down in the car that way?"

"She's my wiiife, not my jaillerr." The men in the car laugh.

"And how is your wife, Ambush?" Miranda puts her hands on her hips. "While you gallivanting to jukes beyond the bridge?"

"She was supposed to come, Mama Day. But she said the night air wouldn't be good for the baby. So she's staying in to watch TV with my mama."

"This time of year, night air and day air is all the same," Miranda says.

"Try telling her that." Ambush shakes his head. "But she don't mind me coming out to have a little fun."

Dr. Buzzard draws his mouth down. "Why you ain't asked me about my wife?"

"Don't start with me, Buzzard." Miranda narrows her eyes. "They couldn't marry you off in a zoo. And a man your age shouldn't be all up under these young people no way. You need to be home praying — tomorrow is Sunday."

"I come along as chaperon for Cocoa."

"Well, she won't be needing your services tonight. She's got a sick headache and she's gonna stay in."

"Is she bad, Mama Day?" Ambush starts to get out the car.

"No, she ain't too bad. Y'all go on and enjoy yourselves."

Abigail's biting down on her bottom lip and frowning as they drive away. She starts patting her left thigh like she does when she gets real nervous.

"I don't wanna be here for these fireworks. You had no call to do that, Miranda."

"If it had only been Ambush and Buzzard, I woulda just sat here and fussed. But Junior Lee was in that car."

"They was only going to listen to music."

"And May Ellen was only digging oysters with him in full daylight. We buried her last month, Abigail."

"You starting up with that again? Ruby ain't did nothing to that child."

"You weren't there, I was."

"You were there to nurse May Ellen. But you saw Ruby poison her, too?"

"I ain't said that."

"Then what are you saying? You, of all people, should know better. This hoodoo mess is just that — mess."

"I know it is." Miranda stares into the smoky fire. "I also know what trouble looks like when I see it. And I ain't in the mood to tangle with Ruby."

"Well, now you're gonna have to face Baby Girl. And my nerves can't take a lot of shouting."

"Then you better stay out here."

Cocoa is sitting on the edge of her bed, strapping on a pair of high-heel sandals. She's got silver barrettes pinned up in her hair to match the silver strings on her halter dress. It's too hot for stockings, so she's shaved and creamed her legs with a little rose glycerine.

"You ain't mentioned at dinner that you were going out," Miranda says, watching her from the doorway.

"Because I didn't want to start this fight too early." She reaches for her other shoe. "I guess Ambush is already out there."

"You think it's proper for a married woman to be sitting up all night, drinking and smoking in jukes with other men?"

"No, I don't. But I grew up with Ambush — he's the closest thing I have to a brother. And neither of us drinks or smokes."

"Buzzard drinks plenty."

"Dr. Buzzard is always drunk. So if I had to stay away from him because of that, I would've stayed away all my life."

"And Junior Lee . . ."

"Junior Lee? I thought you were talking about men. Listen, I'm going out."

"No respect for your own self, I'd think you'd have a little for Bernice — carousing with her husband and she's in the family way."

"Bernice gave me her ticket! And because she's carrying on like she's having fifty babies, my world doesn't have to stop."

"Always been selfish. Me and your grandma see you once a year and you can't spend two minutes with us."

"You're scraping the bottom of the barrel now, Mama Day. Not when I've been around here all week, beating rugs, cleaning out chicken coops. Look at the scratches on my hands from those tomato vines. It's Saturday night and it's time for a little fun."

"Well, your husband got himself a bargain."

Cocoa gets up and snatches her bag off the dresser. "If George was here and he didn't want to go, he wouldn't be acting like you. You're not going to make me feel guilty, so forget it. I'm going to hear Muddy Waters."

Miranda blocks the door. "If you're gonna hear Muddy Waters, you'll have to walk over water to do it — your ride's gone."

The air turns electric between them two. Both set of lips pressed tight as iron lids. Cocoa opens hers first, slow and deadly.

"I'm not going to ask you if you really did that, because you did. You have always been an overbearing and domineering old woman. But I am not a child anymore — do you hear me? I am not a child. I'll pack my things and leave tomorrow. If I have to be treated this way, I'll never set foot on this damn island again until it's time to come to your funeral!"

She flings her bag across the dresser, scattering bottles and combs every which a way. The vase of wildflowers smashes into the mirror, a jagged crack webs out from the corner.

"Better my funeral than yours." Miranda slams the door without another word.

The wood fire outside is burning down as the smoke hangs in the heavy air. It swirls up slowly from the glowing embers and spreads out, grayish fingers blocking out the road before disappearing into the edges of darkness. One moment she wasn't there. One moment she was. The smoke clears on the silent figure, staring up at the porch from the gate. A mountain. Huge and still. But the voice could be a light breeze, whispering from its summit. "Junior Lee left with Ambush. The car stopped down here."

Two small slits catch the fading light from the fire. Seems like a cat's eyes floating in the night.

"They went on, Ruby." Miranda leans forward in the darkness. "Half an hour ago."

"Come on up and sit a spell," Abigail offers.

A whisper. "The car stopped down here."

Miranda leans way back in her chair, crosses her arms over her chest, and heaves a deep sigh. A jealous woman. Creeping through the woods, picking up nightshade and gathering castor beans. Coming to the edge of the other place, the full moon shining on twisted handfuls of snakeroot. May Ellen's twisted body. Ain't no hoodoo anywhere as powerful as hate. Don't make me tangle with you, Ruby, she thinks deep into the smoke. I brought you into this world.

"I ain't looking for trouble," Ruby answers as the smoke blows over her face. "But the car stopped down here."

"Cocoa's in the house," Miranda says. "She's in the house, Ruby."

A long silence. The mountain turns.

Abigail stares at Ruby's back until the night swallows her up. "Now, if that ain't the strangest thing."

Miranda can hardly hear her through the pounding in her head. "I told you, Ruby is a strange woman." She brings her fingers up to massage her temples. But the inside of her head keeps raging. It feels like water and wind.

"You all right, Miranda?"

"Yeah, I'm tired, that's all. And that row with Baby Girl didn't help none. You know that heifer called me overbearing and domineering."

Abigail gets up behind her chair to massage her temples.

"That feels good, Abby. Overbearing and domineering — me."

"She ain't meant it."

"Said she was packing her suitcases tomorrow."

"She ain't meant that, either."

"And wasn't coming back till my funeral."

Abigail's soft laughter melts into the night air. The gentle pressure of her fingers working down into the bone of Miranda's skull. The waters and wind slowly hush.

"Well, if you could manage that by next August, she won't have to explain why she's back home then."

◇◇◇

TIME IS A FUNNY THING. I was always puzzled with the way a single day could stretch itself out to the point of eternity in your mind, all the while years melted down into the fraction of a second. The clocks and calendars we had designed were incredibly crude attempts to order our reality — nearing the close of the twentieth century, and we were still slavishly tied to the cycles of the sun and the moon. All of those numbers were reassuring, but they were hardly real. Reality was the unshaven face in my mirror, the sound of your running water in the coffee pot, and where was the calendar to explain that when I woke up yesterday — yes, yesterday — it was the first time and now it was the fifteen hundredth? We'd invented nothing, had yet to conceive of anything, that could chart the mental passage of time. Looking in that mirror and hearing you in the kitchen, I could truthfully say, I've been with her all my life and I'll be with her for the rest of my life. That instant I could say that, and the next and the next. The life without you resided only in my memory, and the more time we built up, the more distant that memory would become. I understood then how couples lasted forty, fifty years. Get through the eternity of the longest day and you've gotten through them all. And we had made it through with a silent consensus that even our worst days were manageable enough to be endured forever. With that as the bottom line, our constant tug-of-wars went on. It was all about change, wasn't it? Inevitable change. I know I resisted it much more than you to wake up one morning and wonder what all the fuss was about. My house had become our home. And after four years "our" things were starting to outnumber what had been your things and my things.

And slowly we found ourselves wrestling within a whole new set of horizons. Diets. A ceramic mortar and pestle suddenly appeared in the cabinet. And your concoctions of parsley, thyme, basil, sage, and tarragon tasted far better than my regular salt substitutes. But I hated chives — why did you insist upon putting chives in that mixture? A touch of mint gave the same results. I was always a better cook than you, so it was grated parsnips instead of carrots to sweeten tomato sauce. Two egg whites alone cut down my cholesterol much more than adding a whole egg with little difference to the texture of a cake. If I had taken time to think about it, I would have laughed. We'd be squared off at both ends of the kitchen, and since when had I bothered with those things at all? Since you had started growing fresh herbs on the windowsill and in the back yard. Since your letters from Willow Springs, filled with advice about "keeping that boy's heart ticking."

The video cassette recorder. If you used up all the spare tapes on your inane soap operas while you were in class, how was I going to record the games while we were at Selma's for dinner? She insisted on giving these things on Monday nights. You insisted on us going. So keep your hands off the tapes. And since when had I given up football? Since never. But a recorded game once a month or so wouldn't kill me. And neither did spending Thanksgiving with you, since our anniversary always fell around the Super Bowl and you spent it alone. Still only two of us, but we were a family. And Thanksgiving was a family day. I made it very special for us: breakfast in bed for you, the afternoon game in bed for me, and then both of us in bed before we'd get up and cook dinner. We'd talk about the number of children we were going to have one day at the table with us — my figure always higher than yours. Let's trade places, I'd offer. I'll gladly stay home and have four babies if you promise to go out break your back for me. You've got a deal, you'd nod.

But that morning when we left the house you were going to make good on another deal we had made. I had supported you while you got your history degree and so I could decide how to celebrate your graduation. We both knew what I wanted. It was always windy in the middle of the George Washington Bridge. I thought about the first time I'd been up there with you, the look of sheer wonder on the face I could read so well now. The lean body that held no more secrets bent over the railing. I liked that knowing which could only deepen as we went on together. A comfortable form of possessiveness. Only I owned the codes to a certain turn of her head, a slight narrowing of her eyes, the varying textures of her silences. We needed words less and less as time went on. Why, if we had eternity, I thought, looking at all that space above and beneath us, we'd find ourselves in a place where we'd need no words at all.

The day was gorgeous and clear. It seemed that every sailboat in the marina was out there on the water. The game was for you to appear annoyed but you were as excited as I was, because you enjoyed it whenever I did something impulsive. Those times were rare. How would you put it — I was so straight, I squeaked? But a little drama was in order for the occasion. I did wait until we were by ourselves on the bridge walk before I took your diaphragm out of its case.

"George, you're insane, you know that?"

"A deal is a deal."

"Okay, go ahead."

"Should you do it or me?"

"No, I want you to do it. Because later on you'll turn around and say it was my idea, I was always the weird one. I'm just going to stand right here and remember every minute of this so I can tell our kids — in detail."

"That's the point, sweetheart."

I held the diaphragm like a Frisbee and sent it flying over the railing. It spun out for a few feet under its own motion before the wind picked it up and kept it suspended in the air before us.

"Oh, my God, it's not going anywhere. This is so embarrassing."

Suddenly, it began a downward spiral, end over end, spinning past the outstretched wing of a gull, catching the bright glare from the sun before it was lost from our sight. We were laughing so hard, we couldn't have seen it hit the water anyway. There was so much more than laughter in your eyes when you turned to me.

"Have I ever told you . . ." you began.

"Many times," I said.

◇◇◇

LIVING IN A PLACE like Willow Springs, it's sorta easy to forget about time. Guess 'cause the biggest thing it does is to bring about change and nothing much changes here but the seasons. And if we get a warm spring, a slow fall, and a light winter it don't seem like even the seasons change much at all. Yeah, it could easily be one long summer here, with a few less leaves on some days, a few more flowers on others. It's the same folks coming into the general store to pick up their supplies, the same group hitched up on chairs outside of Parris's barbershop, the same heads leaving Reema's all oiled up and curled. The smoke drifting up over the south woods from Dr. Buzzard's still might as well be painted on a picture, it's always there. Like the droning from his beehives out by Chevy's Pass, the pounding of the ocean water against the east bluff, the creaking from the wooden slats on the bridge over The Sound: a still life. Four pictures would just about do it, one for each season, where you'd have to look real close to see a gray hair or so inching around some temples, a little extra roll starting over some belt buckles. But slow, real slow. So slow it's like it's not happening at all. Until it happens. Overnight, some say. Living here you can see how they're right and they're wrong. It's all one night, one day — one season. Time don't crawl and time don't fly; time is still. You do with it what you want: roll it up, stretch it out, or here we just let it lie.

Reminders do come around that it's there, mostly in watching children grow. There's a whole passel in Willow Springs, different ages, shapes, and sizes. Some leave, some stay and add their own brood to replace the faces that eventually gonna fade off into the surrounding oaks and the mist coming up from The Sound. Every time you look, there's a new one born somewhere. Reema's done her part to keep up — she's had close to a dozen till it's hard to get their names straight. Now, Bernice done had only one but it's still the same problem. She loaded that baby down with every name in the book: Charles Somebody Harrison Somebody-Else Duvall. We called him Chick. That's what he looked like, toddling around: little pecan head sitting on a scrawny neck, two bright buttons for eyes, and a feathery mess of hair she couldn't keep slicked down for nothing. He's gonna have Ambush's coloring but her build, kinda narrow and bony. Folks had to stop calling him Chick 'cause Bernice would pitch herself a fit whenever she heard it. But who could remember all that other mess she tied onto the child?

Things simmered down when she traded in that old Chevy for a white convertible. She would have him strapped into his baby chair beside her, two sets of harnesses over his chest, although nobody drives more than twenty miles an hour on the main road. And he'd just be swiveling his tiny neck around, waving at folks. Somebody gave him a red plastic flag and she couldn't pry it from him even in his sleep. So with Bernice giving him them daily airings in that open-top car and him waving that red flag like he was on parade or something, we started calling him Little Caesar, and it's easy to see why that name stuck. You couldn't find a king that's treated better than that child. He's almost four now and his feet hardly touch the ground. Bernice takes him everywhere in that car, even the hundred yards down the bluff to visit his grandma Pearl. And when she brings him to the store, after unstrapping them two sets of harnesses, if there's the slightest bit of mud around, she'll pick him up and carry him. What's the point of him having a dozen pair of shoes when he never gets the soles scuffed? At this age, he's gonna outgrow 'em all within the next six months anyway. But that don't stop Bernice from both buying and sewing enough for Little Caesar to have two changes of clothes each day. And she changes him, too, morning and evening, for them daily rides.

Folks had hoped she'd have another baby to save this one, but it don't look that way. Guess it's gonna be up to Ambush to balance things out. He's proud as punch of his son, but he ain't lost his head. When Little Caesar's with him, the child walks like anybody else, and Ambush has been known to give him a swat or two when he acts up. But never in front of Bernice. You don't breathe too close to that boy with Bernice around. Literally don't breathe. 'Cause he's always been a friendly child — will come up to you and spread them knobby arms, not wanting candy or a dime or so, but for you to pick him up and hug him. And it's hard not to, with them bright eyes and that little pointed head bouncing up and down on his scrawny neck. But Bernice is there in a flash to grab him away — kissing strangers will give him germs. And since when any of us been strangers? Most don't take offense; she waited a long time for that baby. But the older heads fear that trouble is coming. When you raise a god instead of a child, you're bound to be serving him for the rest of your days.

Same thing holds when you marry a god. Not that Junior Lee got anybody up in heaven worrying about losing their job, but you couldn't tell Ruby that. Fact is, you can't tell Ruby nothing lately, and if you a female over seven and under seventy, you better not stop by that porch to yell a good morning. Folks thinking Ruby is close to losing her mind over Junior Lee. What goes around comes around, some say. Didn't she run Frances crazy? Where is all her roots now that Junior Lee won't stay home nights? She done accused every woman in Willow Springs — with the exception of Mama Day — of fooling around with him. Wherever Junior Lee is sneaking, it ain't to a single house in this place. Ain't nobody over seven and under seventy that desperate. No, even the ones who might find it challenging to try to tame a good-looking, no-good man wouldn't come within a mile of Junior Lee. He's driving that Coupe de Ville Ruby bought him beyond the bridge to where some unsuspecting woman ain't heard of the way May Ellen died. Where they ain't had a night's rest broken by them piercing screams echoing from that brick house on the edge of the south woods. Uh, uh, them that believes in roots and them that don't, all know that child died a painful death. And that is fact enough to leave anything Ruby says is hers alone.

Even the men done stopped bothering with Junior Lee. Ruby going on about they setting him up with their sisters and daughters. That's when folks was certain she'd about lost her mind. Any man who'd lose more money than you at a poker table and then be happy to turn right back around and drink you under that same table is the last thing you'd bring home to meet any woman you cared about. Dr. Buzzard is about his only friend, him having neither sister, daughter, nor girl-friend for Ruby to feel threatened by. But Dr. Buzzard says Ruby knows better than to mess with him. He's got a ying for her yang, a do for her don't — and anything else she can come up with. But while he's rattling them buckeyes and black-cat bones hanging around his neck, it ain't lost on the listener that he's speaking awful soft.

But with Little Caesar growing up and Ruby's marriage winding down, it ain't really what you'd call change. It's all happened before and it'll happen again with a different set of faces. So time's doing what it's always done, standing still this summer here in Willow Springs. We might as well be a picture postcard as Dr. Buzzard's blue pickup comes wobbling over the bridge with Cocoa this mid-August. No different this August than the last, even though he's got an extra passenger. We're finally gonna see this new husband, while he ain't gonna see nothing new at all.

◇◇◇

YOU NEVER SAY NEVER. That was good advice Mama Day gave me when I was growing up. But some things you just know are never going to happen — or do you? Mountains flying. Birds on the moon. You giving up the league playoffs to come home with me. Then again, there are degrees to those impossibilities. Since the earth is really a satellite, you could say the mountain ranges are flying through space.

Man's survived on the moon and so could parakeets in specialized environments. And if World War III was looming with the Russians planning to use the site of the Super Bowl as ground zero, you'd probably say, What the hell, for that year at least.

It took a little less than an atom bomb though. I just shut up. Shut completely up, and went about the business of settling into a future with you. My children were going to have a fanatic for a father, and that's all there was to it. You didn't have a preference but I prayed hard for sons, knowing I was going to battle to the death before you'd turn one of my daughters into the neighborhood's wide receiver. Family planning. Each room in the house, the front yard, our very location, had a new point of reference. Our daily routines took on a different edge: this would probably be the last year we'd be reading the newspapers in silence, dropping only one quart of milk into the shopping cart, sleeping in late on the weekends. And even the sex was different: having that goal gave it a deeper excitement and a strange tinge of reverence that wasn't there before. Making a baby. Our bodies could really do this — bring about a miracle? And that feeling of being involved in something special flowed over into the way we looked at each other.

A peace settled into the house that summer, and at the beginning of August I quietly went about preparing for my vacation. No hints. No accusations. I was through with all that nonsense. I don't know why it bothered me so much — Grandma and Mama Day didn't seem to care. As far as they were concerned, you could do no wrong. I didn't think they'd be bought off so easily with a few lousy Mother's Day cards and a call once or twice a year. I wrote them every month, but the sun sure seemed to shine on you. The boy's working hard for you, leave him be. He's there when you go back, ain't he? I would have given anything to see what kind of propaganda you put in those notes on their birthdays. I already knew how large the checks were because I balanced the account. But it had to be more than the money. I guess they knew all along what it took me four years to accept: you leave well enough alone.

So I was minding my own business, playing a game of clipping grocery coupons for Pampers and Enfamil. Just the ones with no expiration dates, to be on the safe side.

"Okay, okay, okay — I can't take the nagging. I'm going home with you next week."

I never looked up. "George, we haven't had a fight in over three months. Is that too much for you?"

"I know when I'm licked. Up to my butt in new construction, a six-figure commission waiting in the balance — count 'em, six — and the Pats going to the playoffs as sure as I'm standing here. But a woman's tongue is a mighty — "

"Because I can give you what you're looking for. I am more than ready to give you exactly what — "

"But I just want to warn you, separate vacations have been the salvation of this marriage."

"My patience has been the salvation of this marriage."

The hand that covered mine was wide and strong. The blunt fingertips darkened by blueprint ink with the thumb permanently flattened from holding a compass, the fine hairs thinning along the knuckles, the veins beginning to push their way through the tightening skin. The hand brought my chin up firmly to make me meet your eyes.

"I think you're right."

No, I was wrong. And as we crossed over the bridge, squeezed into the front of Dr. Buzzard's truck, was that the time to turn everything around? I've asked myself that over and over these years. At what point could we have avoided that summer? At the beginning of that bridge? The beginning of so many others? And when I try, George, when I try to pick a point at which we could have stopped, there is none. I don't think it would have mattered if we had come a year before or a year after. You and I would have been basically the same, and time definitely stands still in Willow Springs. No, any summer we crossed over that bridge would be the summer we crossed over.

MIRANDA is having the kind of day that's best spent in bed. Everything is determined to go haywire and she wishes it could just go on without her. Edgy. Start the morning with your nerves sticking out all over the place and you're bound to be upsetting whatever you touch all day. Them cakes took one look at her evil face and refused to rise. Out-and-out refused, as if it hadn't been enough that the button popped off her best Sunday dress to roll God knows where under all that clutter in the closet, and she spilled the last bit of shoe polish right in the middle of the bathroom floor before finding a big old run in her only pair of stockings. And calling Abigail for anything is to risk having her head handed to her on a platter. The way she been going on across the road all week, you'd think the governor of New York was coming. If she ain't put that rug out on the clothesline and beat it fifty times, she ain't beat it once. Well, that house'll be good and clean when the folks come to view her body, 'cause that's what she's working herself up to.

Miranda yanks the oven door open and eyes the cake pans as if she could will the batter to rise. That's what she gets for trying to be fancy. Stay plain, no pain, Daddy always said. If that advice stood eighty years ago, it stands now, especially looking at this mess that's passing for angel food. She could whip up a peach cobbler with her eyes closed, and that's what she was gonna do. Abigail can be over there with all the shrimp Newburg and crab soufflés she wants, that boy's gonna know they don't eat like that everyday. Everyday? They never eat like that. It's iffy when Abigail bakes chicken, so Lord help them poor little crawdaddies drowning in her cream sauce. And all them rich foods ain't right for him anyway. Baby Girl says he has to watch his heart. It's funny, Miranda thinks, a good-hearted boy with a bad heart.

The hot pan slips out of the dishtowel and burns her on the left wrist. Blast it all to Hades! The cake up-ends, splattering all over the bottom of the stove and cabinets. She brings her wrist up to her mouth to wet the burn as she kicks aside the pan to get to the icebox — it was going into chicken feed anyway. Running an ice cube up and down her wrist, she tries to remember where she put her ointment. Be too much to ask for it to be where it's supposed to be. A whole tinful shoved into that side drawer right after Candle Walk. All she did that night was to rub more blistered fingers and arms than she could count. Some Candle Walks go by without a murmur and others see her using every bit of oak bark, red sumac, and mallow root she could work into a little wax and benne oil. No point in opening the drawer, that tin done probably walked away like everything else this morning, and she weren't about to make up no more. The ice helps to draw the heat and she figures it won't blister. And if it do, it'll just round out the picture for that boy: a beat-up old woman with buttons missing on her dress, runs in her stockings, and a no-'count pair of shoes.

Miranda leans against the sink, crosses her arms over her chest, and takes a deep breath. When absolutely nothing is going right, it means you started out on the wrong foot. So it's gonna be wrong foot after wrong foot unless you go back and straighten it out. This day began all wrong 'cause she's acting like a stranger's coming, and George ain't no stranger. She's never laid eyes on him, but that means less than nothing. She *knew* this boy. Knew him from that first call in New Orleans and the last four years ain't brought no surprises. He's strong willed, dead set in his ways, proper to a fault, as Daddy would say, and he worships the ground Baby Girl walks on — without being about to admit none of it. Yeah, Miranda thinks, picking up her broom, that's exactly who's coming. And since you wouldn't let a dog see this trailer, the state it's in, clean up this mess, go rake your yard, and pick yourself a few peaches for a cobbler.

The chickens that run loose around her trailer come scrambling to her feet when she lets herself out the back door.

"There ain't nothing in this bag for y'all." She pushes 'em away with the rake. "This here is angel food and you're nothing but devils."

They flock behind her to the side bushes as she scatters a few crumbs over their far side near the woods. There's squawking and feathers flying as the chickens scatter through the bushes to reach the crumbs.

"That's right, no messing in my yard today — company's coming. And anybody caught over here after I rake this ground is going straight into the pot."

This was gonna be the last year she'd be bothered with these loose hens — nothing but pets. But old habits die hard. Miranda don't spot her frizzly black hen. Now, where was Clarissa? It ain't like her to miss a free meal. She begins cleaning up the stray leaves and sandy gravel along the side of the trailer, making her way toward the front. Stopping a moment to stretch her back, she glances along the main road. Couldn't be she got run over by a car, Clarissa's never up past them dogwoods. And she's too old to be setting. Might have gone off some place to die — it's about time. Yeah, this was gonna be the last batch for her. She couldn't be spending her last little energy running after loose hens. Miranda hears a scratching and squawking near the front steps. Lord, she done got herself hung up under the trailer.

Anchoring her rake handle in the grass so she can bend down easy, Miranda spies her hen, digging and pulling at something in the ground. "What are you into, Clarissa?" She gets on her knees, shoos the chicken away with the rake, and drags out what looks like a dirty piece of cloth. The hen had ripped the flannel covering, so when Miranda pries it from the end of her rake it falls apart in her hand. The flannel bag was holding about a tablespoon of dirt mixed up with a few white specks of something, little purplish flowers and a dried sprig. Lord have mercy, look at this. She shakes her head as the black hen runs toward the others in the bushes. Frowning behind Clarissa, she wonders if there was anything to them old wives' tales about chickens after all. But who coulda been this stupid? Even Buzzard would know better than to give somebody something to put under her steps, no matter how drunk he was.

Getting up off her knees, she examines the stuff in her hand a little closer. She spits on some of the white grains. They dissolve between her fingers and she licks at them real quick — salt. It don't take but a minute to see that the dried sprig is a piece of dill and the purplish flowers is from verbena. And she'd lay her life that the rest is graveyard dust — not sandy enough to be from the bluffs, no fishy smell for it to be from The Sound, too poor for garden soil. And it ain't been there long, 'cause the flannel woulda rotted more. Matter of fact, this flannel almost looked brand-new. Miranda's about to throw it on the ground so she can rake it up with the rest of her litter when she remembers what verbena's called by some folks: herb of grace. She stands there so quiet at first it would be hard to tell she was breathing. And what better concoction to use if you've singled out the child of Grace?

She lays her rake against the side of the trailer, goes inside to come out with her walking stick and a empty quart basket before she heads north on the main road up to Ruby's. Her clapboard house is sitting back off the right side of the road, flanked by rows of peach and empress plum trees. Ruby is in her regular spot up on the porch in that cane-bottom chair. Miranda stops in front of the gate, leaning there on her hickory cane.

"How do, Ruby."

"How do, Mama Day."

Ruby don't make an offer for her to come into the yard and Miranda don't seem to want to.

"I come for a favor." Miranda shifts her weight on the walking stick, her eyes never leaving the porch. "Your peaches over there is riper than the ones I got at the other place. And I'm making up a cobbler for supper tonight. You mind if I took some of yours." It wasn't a question.

"Plenty there." Ruby nods.

"I'll need plenty," Miranda says. "Cocoa's coming in today and she's bringing her new husband. They'll be four of us for supper instead of three. And with her and him staying two weeks and all, I figure I'd make enough cobbler to last."

Miranda puts the flannel bag on the gate post and she watches Ruby watching it as the breeze draws it into her yard. They both talk to the grayish dust and purple flowers spilling out around the foot of the gate.

"Yeah, with them staying two whole weeks, I'm gonna need plenty."

"Plenty there, Mama Day."

"Glad to know that, Ruby," Miranda says before she turns to go home with her basket empty. " 'Cause if something unexpected happens and we run out, I'll know where to come."

Ruby watches her back until it disappears down the main road but Miranda is concentrating on the tip of her stick as it scrapes against the blacktop. Last thing she needed was this nonsense, with that boy visiting. Folks had to up and show their color with him not understanding their ways. Didn't Ruby know who she was messing with? There was a year's worth of anger here, but she'd bide her time for two weeks. This all boiled down to one thing: it was a fool at work. Fool enough over some man to even think of messing with what was hers, or fool enough to believe that she was too old to do anything about it. Either way, her ninety years done given her more than enough remedies for that. Or had they? The air hangs heavy around her and she's bearing down on the stick real hard. This was funny, funny weather. It's tightened up her bones so she needed this cane for a lousy two-mile walk, but look how dry the blacktop was. Heavy air that stays just above the knees. That don't bode well. She'd have to really concentrate: look and listen. No point in thinking about the time when it would just come to her, that was that time and this is this time. But there was something in the air. And now that heifer up the road would pick this summer, of all summers, to act up. Maybe, she still ain't too big a fool to understand a warning. I don't want to tangle with you, Ruby. And I don't want that boy seeing anything he ain't got no business seeing. But before I'd let you mess with mine, I'd wrap you up in tissue paper and send you straight to hell.

Miranda gets to the patch of dogwoods beside her trailer and leans on the stick, feeling the throbbing moving up her legs into the hip joints. She could go on through the woods to the other place and get herself some fresh peaches or she could use that bag of frozen dewberries in the trailer. While it's true a berry cobbler would be a nice change for him since it ain't no secret Baby Girl can't cook worth a spit, it's also true she'd be settling for second best 'cause her legs are aching. And something tells her to push her way on through this small inconvenience. It ain't gonna be a easy two weeks no way you look at it, so don't start getting used to cutting corners now.

But it's not her legs, it's the heavy air in the woods that finally makes Miranda turn around. It's like the air ain't willing to be breathed: the birds are motionless on the pine branches, the katydids can hardly be heard, and there ain't a butterfly in view. The sound of the twigs breaking under her feet is hollow and the echo can't move up through the haze. Miranda stands still and listens. Funny. There's something funny going on. The graveyard is just up at the turn, but she won't go past it today. Tomorrow maybe or the day after. She heaves a deep sigh. I ain't up to all this, Lord. I'm an old woman. And I'm tired, tired of knowing things I can't do nothing about. Whatever is waiting in here today, I just ain't ready to face.

◇◇◇

IT'S HARD TO KNOW what to expect from a place when you can't find it on the map. Preparing for Willow Springs upset my normal agenda: a few minutes with an atlas always helped me to decide what clothes to pack, whether a raincoat would be in order or not, a light pullover for the evenings. Your insisting that the place was exactly on the border between South Carolina and Georgia wasn't terribly reassuring. What if it was like Seattle? That was the city closest to Alaska and you'd think it would be cold, but that's not taking the mountain shelters and the balmy air currents from Puget Sound into account. And look at Palo Alto, California. If my atlas hadn't forewarned me, I'd have gone up there to the games expecting it to be warm. But where was Willow Springs? Nowhere. At least not on any map I had found. I had even gone out and bought road maps just for South Carolina and Georgia and it was missing from among all those islands dotting the coastline. What county claimed it? Where was the nearest interstate highway, the nearest byroad?

My questions annoyed you because you thought I was working up excuses to stay in New York. I really did want to go, but I wanted to know exactly *where* I was going. In the end I just threw up my hands and depended on you to make the arrangements. We would be flying into Savannah, which was the nearest airport, and a friend would be picking us up. You waited until the plane had landed to tell me that the man who would be waiting for us at the gate was a little strange. And since your "little strange" turned out to be chicken feathers in his hat, a string of white bones around his neck, and a name like Dr. Buzzard, I spent that half hour in his truck with a growing suspicion of your "pretty little island."

My suspicions were confirmed when we drove over that shaky wooden bridge: you had not prepared me for paradise. And to be fair, I realized that there was nothing you could have said that would have made any sense to me. I had to be there and see — no, feel — that I was entering another world. Where even the word *paradise* failed once I crossed over The Sound. Sure, I can describe what I saw: a sleepy little section of wooden storefronts, then sporadic houses of stucco, brick, and clapboard all framed by palmettos, live oaks, and flowering bushes; every now and then a span of marshland, a patch of woods. But how do I describe air that thickens so that it seems as solid as the water, causing colors and sounds and textures to actually float in it? So as that old blue truck crept along, there was no choice but to breathe in lungfuls of oaks dripping with silvery gray moss, the high leaning pines. My nose and mouth were coated with the various shades of greens, browns, and golds in the muddy flatlands. And if someone had asked me about the fragrance from the whisperings of the palmettos, or the distant rush of the surf, I would have said that it all smelled like forever.

With all of that, I was still surprised by the two women waiting on the porch steps of that small yellow bungalow. It's not that I had always associated old age with infirmity, but when you get to be eighty-eight and ninety — and that's what you swore your grandmother and great-aunt were — I was reasonable in expecting wrinkles, sagging skin, some trembling of the limbs. It must have taken me ten minutes to regain my equilibrium. Looking like this, how could these women ever die? It's an awful thought, but it's the first one that came into my mind. I later found out your grandmother had false teeth, but at that point it was easy to believe that she hadn't lost one of her own. She certainly hadn't lost her looks: the thick head of flashing silver hair complemented the olive tones in her smooth face. A few laugh lines around the eyes and mouth, but then I had some around mine. The veins were knotted in the hand that grasped mine — if you ain't ready to call me Grandma, call me Miss Abigail — but the palms were soft and the grip firm. And then there was the little one: I don't know why I thought your Mama Day would be a big, tall woman. From the stories you told about your clashes with her, she had loomed that way in my mind. Hard. Strong. Yes, it definitely showed in the set of her shoulders. But she was barely five feet and could have been snapped in the middle with one good-sized hand. On second thought, I wondered: the dark brown skin stretched tight over those high cheekbones and fine frame glinted like it was covering steel — I'm Mama Day to some, Miss Miranda to others. You decide what I'll be to you. That type of straightforward honesty would cheapen anyone returning less than the same. So I was glad to have finally met them, and said it. But I thought they'd be old, and said that too.

Their laughter had been waiting for me, and as it circled around us, I could finally tell that they were sisters. The heads thrown back in similar angles to let out a matching pitch of flowing sound. Miss Abigail put her hands up on each side of my face — Well, bless your heart, child — and a lump formed in my throat at their gentle pressure. Up until that moment, no woman had ever called me her child. Did they see it in my eyes? The intense envy for all that you had and the gratitude for their being willing to let me belong? I couldn't have summoned up something light to say even if my life depended on it, but Miss Miranda came to my rescue. We're showing off for you today. We done left our age in the house. Without her glasses Abby can't see more than two feet in front of her, and I can't walk more than two without my cane. You winked at me as if to say, George, don't believe a word of it. And as they led me up the porch steps, I thought of something you had actually said when we pulled into the yard: Relax, we're coming home.

THE WHOLE PLACE seemed so different with you there with me. And I was much more nervous than I let on. Regardless of how well you thought you knew me, it was only one part of me. The rest of me — the whole of me — was here. And I wondered how you would take the transformation, beginning with something as basic as my name. Outside of my family, no one else in Willow Springs knew who in the hell Ophelia was. And even if you were a more flexible type of man, it was too late for you to start calling me Cocoa. But it was Cocoa's bedroom that we were going to share, and as I watched Ophelia's husband carefully unpacking his clothes and hanging his shirts on one side of the closet, his underwear stacked into one set of drawers, his toiletries arranged neatly on one side of the dresser, I felt as if we were going to have an illicit affair. I had never slept with a man in my grandmother's house. It was going to be a new experience in an old bed, and the thought of doing something that was sanctioned but not quite right brought on a nervous excitement. As we got the room in order, it actually made us a little awkward with each other.

I saw that room as you must have seen it and each flaw stood out: the slope in the wooden floor leading to the bathroom, the constantly dripping shower head that left a blue-green stain in the base of the tub. There were two doors into the bathroom, the other belonging to my grandmother's room. Unpainted plywood doors with inside hooks for privacy — I had never thought about those hooks before and rarely used them. The crack in the corner of the dresser mirror had spread over the years since my fight with Mama Day. A vase of fresh wildflowers sat in front of the crack, and I smiled remembering that night and Cocoa's temper tantrum. No, my temper was nothing new to you but, try as I might, I became a child again in this house. You respected Ophelia's anger just as she respected yours. How would you react seeing that Cocoa's anger, whether coddled or dismissed, was never taken seriously here? My bond with them was such that even if hate and rage were to tear us totally apart, they knew I was always theirs. And I sensed that knowledge dawning on you from the moment we crossed over the bridge: you were entering a part of my existence that you were powerless in. Your maps were no good here, but you still came, willing to share this with me. And from another perspective, that room was now a place my family couldn't touch. Our presence together transformed it into a world where only Ophelia and George belonged. Placing my combs and brush on the dresser and watching you testing the mattress through the cracked mirror, I could smile. I knew you and I knew that mattress — it would be firm enough for your back. It hit me then that I had absolutely nothing to worry about. I was a very fortunate woman, belonging to you and belonging to them. Ophelia and Cocoa could both live in that house with you. And we'd leave Willow Springs none the worse for the wear.

◈◈◈

MIRANDA BRINGS OVER her berry cobbler a little bit before suppertime and it seems to her that Abigail done tried to give Cocoa and George a wedding feast single-handed. There's hardly no place on that table for the eating plates with all them platters of God-knows-everything. Abigail looks real cross-eyed at the pan in Miranda's hand, saying that she had baked up and frozen some decent cakes, figuring she'd do something poor-mouth like that. And couldn't she at least have managed to wear a Sunday dress to supper? Miranda says there ain't no point in stuffing them to death the first night, it was gonna take the two weeks they'd be here just to finish up the food on that table. And why put on airs? Ain't the boy showed right off that he was real? Stepped straight out of Buzzard's truck and said he thought he was gonna be meeting two old farts. Abigail manages to find space to slap down some knives and forks — he ain't said no such thing, said they looked a lot younger than he thought. Miranda switches the silverware around as noisily as Abigail put 'em down — You're going deaf as well as blind. But once they all sit down to supper, the butter Abigail's got somewhere on that table would melt in their mouths.

Miranda knows her sister loves a lot of fluff and feathers and tonight she lets her have her way. All that bustling to put George at the head of the table — "It's good to have a man in the family again" — and he's pleased as can be while a little bit embarrassed from all her attention. And as her sister does everything but chew his food for him, Miranda thinks it's a pity that Abigail never remarried. She glows when she's got a man to do for. But she better stop doing too much 'cause Baby Girl don't like it a bit. She done rolled her eyes twenty times with all her grandma's goings-on, and remarks that nobody's bothered to fill her plate again. For all they know, she could be eating for two.

"You're so puny, you'll show your first half hour," Miranda says. "I hear happiness is supposed to put flesh on a woman, and I know he can't help but make you happy."

"How do you know so much?"

" 'Cause he ain't followed my advice and taken a hickory stick to you."

Everybody laughs but Cocoa as she kicks her husband under the table. "Don't encourage her."

"I'm not doing anything but enjoying —"

"Here, baby," Abigail says, "can I give you some more greens?"

"Thank-you-Grandma." She says the words as if she's stuck her tongue out at Miranda.

Miranda shakes her head. "A grown woman acting like this. If you can't be the center of attention, you're gonna pout. Spoiled rotten from day one. I don't know how he puts up with you."

"I've got strong arms."

"Two weeks go by quick, George."

"Don't be threatening that boy. Now, tell us, what y'all got planned — for every day except this Friday."

"Why Friday?" Cocoa asks.

" 'Cause me and Abigail thought we'd throw a little party."

"Oh, you mean like the wedding parties Ophelia's told me about?"

"Oh, no, nothing fancy like a wedding feast," Abigail says to him, straightening up and using her best English. "You've been married too long for that. But some of the neighbors are anxious to meet you and a few of our close family friends — the minister, the school principal, and Dr. Smithfield and all. We'd just bake a little something, fix up a bowl of punch . . ."

"Since when have Reverend Hooper and the principal been close friends of ours? And Dr. Smithfield and Mama Day are rarely on speaking terms — he says she steals his patients. The only real close friends we have are Dr. Buzzard and —"

Miranda cuts her off. "Ignorance is a mighty ugly thing to watch in action. It's worse than spite and envy. You bring yourself home once a year in the last eleven years and you're gonna sit there and tell your grandma who we got for friends and who we don't? And besides, nobody was talking to your little yellow tail. If you got better plans for Friday, you can go off and we'll have the party without you. But everybody else is gonna be here so you'll be kinda lonely in them honky-tonks, patting your foot and shaking your . . ."

"Shaking my . . . ?"

"Yeah, shaking whatever will move!"

Cocoa whirls around in her seat, ready for Freddy, as Abigail grabs the hand that's tightening around her water glass. That's her own grandma's good crystal.

"Please, y'all, not the *first* night." Tears spring up into Abigail's eyes. "If you both want to kill me, go ahead. You done shamed me enough to die already."

"Abigail, why you going on so dramatic? We was just having us a conversation."

George done sat there smiling through the whole thing, and he's smart enough not to let nobody catch his eye as he splits open another corn muffin.

"Miss Miranda, Friday sounds good to me if it's good for Ophelia."

"Yeah, it's fine. I'll be able to catch up on what all our old family friends have been doing in the last year besides running moonshine and — "

Abigail gets her prayers answered 'cause there's a loud knocking from outside.

"Miranda, you mind going to see who's at the door?"

"You know it ain't locked. Just call for 'em to come in."

Ruby is in red and fills up the doorway. When she steps inside they can see that Junior Lee is with her and he's carrying a whole bushel basket of peaches. He ain't brought it no farther than from the trunk of his Coupe de Ville, but he drops it down like it weighs a ton and straightens up, such as he can, grinning from ear to ear. She's had him dress up for the visit: a shirt and tie, good suit pants, his alligator shoes.

"How do, everybody," Ruby says.

Miranda leans forward and don't say nothing, head cocked and hands locked under her chin, as the rest of them all greet her. Abigail offers them a sit-down and a bit of supper.

"We ain't staying long," Ruby says, pulling up a chair. "But I thought it would be nice for us to meet Cocoa's new husband."

"It's a pleasure," George says.

"Doubly mine," says Ruby. "And this here is my new husband, Junior Lee."

"Pleasssurre." Junior Lee manages a nod. "Hear you a big railroad man."

"No, I'm an engineer."

"That's what I hear. Ain't never been on the railroad myself, except hopping a few freights."

"No, baby, he's an engineer." Ruby pats Junior Lee's arm.

"I said, that's what I hear. Job must take you all over the country."
George knows when to give up. "Not really. But what do you do?"
"Little as posssibbble."

Junior Lee is about to fall out his chair with laughing, not seeing
that he's the only one in the room to find that funny. He done slumped
all down with his head laid back. "Yeaah, little as posssibbble."

"Don't let him tease you." Ruby done drawn her mouth into a tight,
tight line. "He's looking for work now. Place he was in a few years
ago beyond the bridge closed down."

"It's happening all over the country," George says. "Decent people
just can't find work."

"Other kinds, too." Miranda says.

"So how're you finding us?" Ruby asks George.

"Well, we just got here — or rather, I just got here. But it's a
beautiful island."

"It's a friendly place," Ruby says. "And that's what we stopped by
to tell you. You're one of us, 'cause you married one of us. And Cocoa
is our own."

"Well, I feel like you're family, Miss Ruby," Cocoa says. "You
watched me grow up."

"Indeed I did. And look at us now — we're just two married girls."

"Yeaah, you're girrrls." Junior Lee finds that's even funnier than
before. " 'Cepting one of you got to touch up her hair with shoe polish."

Nobody has the heart to look at Ruby until Cocoa snaps, "Putting
up with you could turn anybody gray," and gives them all a chance
to join in the laughter.

"That's telling him." Ruby smiles. "It's good you ain't lost your
tongue — like some done lost their manners."

"I ain't wanted to come anyway." Junior Lee sulks. "And I got
businesss if you throughhh."

"Just a few more minutes, baby." Ruby pats his arm again, but
Junior Lee snatches it away and gets up.

"If you stay, you're walkinnng home."

"My boy loves to tease," Ruby says. "But we do gotta be going.
Mama Day, them peaches is for you."

"Thank you kindly, Ruby."

"Yes," Ruby says, getting up, "you didn't take hardly enough when you came by this afternoon. And after thinking about it, I didn't wanna give you no reason to make that long hike back up the road again."

"I appreciate it." Miranda nods.

"Ruby, if y'all ain't doing nothing this Friday," Abigail says, "we're having a little get-together for Cocoa and George. I know you don't get out much, but —"

"I'll think on it," Ruby says.

"A little fun? While she's thinking, I'll be here." Junior Lee opens the front door. "And while she's taking twenty minutes to say goodbye, I'm goinng onnn."

The total quiet in the room is broken only for a little while by the gunning of Junior Lee's motor before it creeps on back in.

"We got us a decision to make right now," Miranda says to George. "Either you're company or you're family. 'Cause if you're company, we'll be right polite and wait until you're out of the room to talk about the disaster that done just left here. But if you're family, we'll get to it right away."

"Every man in Willow Springs ain't like Junior Lee," Abigail says.

"No man in Willow Springs is like Junior Lee," Cocoa says.

"Why don't you make that the world and be done with it." Miranda shakes her head. "I can see why she don't go anyplace with him — big or not. But for the life of me, I can't see why she believes any other woman but her would want him."

"How long have they been married?" George asks.

"About as long as we have — four years, right, Mama Day?"

"Give or take," Miranda says.

"Well," George sighs. "It's sort of flattering when a woman is jealous of her husband, if he's worth it or not. I wouldn't mind if my wife was a little jealous of me."

"Not that jealous." Miranda is looking off in space, so she don't notice Abigail trying to catch her eye. But she ain't about to say nothing else.

"What was all that business about you needing peaches?" Abigail asks. "You're loaded down at the other place."

"I know. But then I figured with folks coming over Friday I didn't wanna run out of pies."

"I hope you don't think I'm staying in all week to be baking." Cocoa sucks her teeth.

"I hope you don't think I'd ask you," Miranda says. "It ain't no secret to anybody at this table the way you cook."

"George, you don't have anything to say about that?"

"Yeah — this is really one beautiful island."

◇◇◇

WHO WOULD HAVE THOUGHT that with me growing up in a city, the noise here at night would keep me awake? The sound of silence: the deep droning of marsh frogs, a million crickets pressing in against the window screen, way off the cry of a whippoorwill, farther off the eternal whispering of the surf. I thought, perhaps, it was the strangeness of the bed, but how could any bed be strange with your body moving so predictably in the spaces left by my own? I only needed to nudge a leg under yours and place a hand on your back for you to turn and spoon yourself into my arms, your gentle breathing to be just under my ear. It would be that way anywhere in any bed. The sound of silence: the ticking of the wall clock out there in the sitting room, the steady dripping from the bathroom, the creaking of the floorboards. You would hear none of it, and suddenly I felt intensely alone. If I could have dissolved myself within you at that moment, I would have, and I fought the rising urge for second best. You would have responded, thinking it renewed desire, not fear. Why wake her up for that?

I did something I hadn't done since a child. When you can't sleep and you know there is no one to call down those long corridors, you close your eyes and tell yourself over and over again, I can't find it because it's waiting in my dreams. A slow, rhythmic chant. The "it" could be anything, and I would drift off to sleep, more often than not, to dream of a new bicycle, a good test score — my mother's constantly changing face. But that night I dreamed of you. You were calling me and calling me. And I was swimming across The Sound. I couldn't see you on the other side, but your voice kept getting louder, the water heavier, and the shore farther and farther away. If I just try harder, I thought, but my increased efforts made it all the more impossible. Your cries were desperate now and my strength was giving out. In my struggles I saw Mama Day leaning over the bridge. Her voice came like thunder: No, Get Up And Walk. She's a crazy old woman, I thought as I kept swimming harder toward the receding shore. A wave of despair went over me as I began sinking, knowing I'd never reach you. Get Up And Walk. I was fiercely angry at her for not helping us. With my last bit of strength I pushed my shoulders out of the water to scream in her face, You're a crazy old woman! And I found myself standing up in the middle of The Sound.

I slept through the night and woke up very early the next morning refreshed. For some reason the memory of that dream was not unsettling. And now I could really talk about noise. Those million crickets must have been eaten up by the thousand birds outside our window and a rooster started crowing to be answered by another and another. But to stretch and smell that air — the mixture of salt and topsoil, pine needles and honeysuckle — went into the pit of my stomach and increased my erection. I put my arms behind my head, thinking I'd count to ten and if the tented sheet between my legs was still there, I'd wake you up to admire it along with me. I did, and you turned your back and told me to go to hell. So last night I walked on water for you and this is the thanks I get? You clutched the pillow over your head, murmuring that I should take my twin brother along for the ride.

I decided to get up and take a walk instead. I opted against my regular shower, with your grandmother's bedroom just on the other side of the door. She had really knocked herself out for us, and one look at those pipes told me that they would resist water pressure loudly. You could sleep through an atomic explosion, but I didn't know about her. So it was a quick splashing and my pill before heading outside. It's only seven miles long; I'd be able to cover this place a few times before going home. But New York seemed so far away as I stood on the front porch, surveying the road through a veil of heavy dew splattering from the eaves onto the toe of my sneakers. It looked so fresh and clean, I was almost tempted to stick out my tongue and catch a drop. No one was around to see me — the shades on the silver trailer across the road were still drawn. How would dew taste? God, I was acting like a kid. But something about this place did that to you, it called up old, old memories.

Me and Bernie Sinclair, arguing about how to get better grades, studying in morning air or night air. I liked to do my homework in the early morning before any of the other boys woke up. Breathing in "unused" air, I said, kept your brain cells from being dirtied up by everybody else's carbon dioxide. But he liked "leftover" air — How do you know it ain't Einstein's carbon dioxide you miss breathing into your head? As I began walking south on the shoulder of the road, I had an intense longing to see Bernie again. I wondered how he turned out, the kid with enough rage — and guts — to spit in Mrs. Jackson's face? I remembered that she finally insisted that he go into the carpentry workshop, and my last image of Bernie was his pounding and pounding away at the heads of iron nails.

Unused air or leftover air, back then none of us could even imagine an atmosphere like this. More than pure, it was primal. Some of these trees had to have been here for almost two hundred years, and the saltwater feeding into the marshes dated back to eternity. A lot of this land and open space could be put to good use: nothing parasitic like resorts or vacation condominiums, but experimental stations for solar energy, marine conservation. I could even see small test sites for hydraulic power. It would bring much-needed income to the island, new people. A beating of wings and a high screech as a snow-tipped heron flew up from the marsh grass. I stopped and shook my head — beautiful. But what kind of people? How had that large woman put it last night? You're one of us because you've married one of us. No, even I don't really qualify as their kind. And they'd never give up this land to anyone but. They know that even well-meaning progress and paradise don't go hand in hand. Well, I thought, at least this place is unique or I'd soon be out of a job. If I'd followed Mrs. Jackson's philosophy, I could have straddled both worlds: Don't redesign water systems, she would have said, become a plumber.

When I reached the little L-shaped section of stores in the junction of the road that heads toward the bridge, I saw the blue truck belonging to the man who had picked us up from the airport. I thought he was asleep in the back. He had one blanket rolled up under his head and another pulled over him. As I was about to pass by, he sat up and waved to me.

"Morning, George."

"Good morning, sir."

"I guess you done forgot me. I'm Dr. Buzzard."

How could you forget someone like him. But I felt totally stupid addressing the man that way. He had to have another name.

"No, of course I remember you. And it was awfully nice of you to drive down to Savannah and pick us up yesterday."

"Well, Miss Abigail wouldn't trust just anybody hauling Cocoa around. Naw, when it's something important they all know you can call on Dr. Buzzard."

I simply had to ask. "Is that your real name?"

"Naw, it's what you might call my professional name. Most folks here don't know me by anything else."

"Oh, I see. What line of business are you in?"

"You mean, Mama Day ain't told you? It don't surprise me — we have us a little professional rivalry going on. You see, some folks just can't stand it when other folks' glory leaves 'em spellbound — not that I'm saying anything against your people and all, you being married into them. But Mama Day ain't never appreciated my magnitude. I guess you can't blame her none, it's hard for a woman to have the right frame of mind to encompass something like Dr. Buzzard's work. But you ask anybody else around here about me and it ain't no secret what I can do."

It was still a secret to me, but he seemed so satisfied with his answer, I didn't have the heart to ask him what he had said. I nodded my head and made the appropriate sounds in my throat. He hopped down from the truck, shook out his blankets, and folded them up neatly. A washcloth and toothbrush came from under the driver's seat. He went over to the water spigot by the general store and began cleaning up.

"I see your business must get you up early."

"Naw, I wouldna been up now, but I saw you coming by. Parris don't open up his shop till about ten."

"Oh, you work out of here?"

"Naw, today's the day to get my hair cut. I likes to be the first one in — that way I can make sure he sweeps up that floor real good after me. And I carry every shred of it away." He gave me a slow wink. "In my line you can't be too careful, you know what I mean?"

Clearing my throat got me through again, but I had to change the direction of this conversation. "I'm up early myself, just taking in the lay of the land."

"You ain't gotta walk, I'll be glad to show you around."

"No, I really enjoy it. I do a lot of walking at home."

"In New York City — with all them cutthroats? You'd never catch me walking up there."

"It's really not as dangerous as people think. You have your good and bad everywhere."

"Don't I know it. This place was wide open before I hit here. And look at it now — that hellish element don't raise their heads."

I wondered if perhaps he could be in some form of law enforcement. But he couldn't be kept terribly busy. People here didn't even see the need to lock their doors at night.

"It seems like a very peaceful place."

"Looks is deceiving."

"I suppose you're right. But I'm sure they're glad to have you here."

"Some is, some ain't. Now, Reverend Hooper, he's always preaching against me. But that don't make no never mind. Been here before he came and I'll be here after he's gone."

"I don't see why you shouldn't."

"You know, I like you. You got a lot of understanding for a city boy. You play poker?"

"I've done my share."

"Well, why don't you come on around some night. This time of year, there's always a friendly little game over by me."

"You have a house here?"

Obviously, I couldn't hide the surprise in my voice. He looked at the toothbrush in his hands and threw back his head and laughed. "Yeah, I got a home. And it sits on the seventy acres my uncle left me. I was the only boy child. See, my sisters and cousins, them, they married on off beyond the bridge." The morning light was growing stronger, playing off the thousand tiny lines in his burnished skin. His head was turned to the road leading to the bridge in a way that said his mind was traveling miles beyond it. He ran a callused hand over his gray stubble of a beard. "I got married too. But some folks can live here and some can't. And with seventy acres and a house . . . Somebody had to keep it." He seemed to remember that I was there — "Did I tell you I was in vaudeville?"

"No."

"Yeah. Never made it over to New York, but Detroit, Baltimore, Kansas City — Rainbow Dan with the dancing hands. Dan not being my real name, mind you. But I could do with my hands what some folks couldn't do with their feet. Still can — with a bit of inspiration in me. You drink, city boy?"

"No, I —"

"Just as well, living over there with them Day women. But I do brew a bit — it's another one of my sidelines. That and my hives. I keep myself busy here."

"I'm sure you do."

"Yeah, come on over to the south woods where I make camp. We'll play us a little cards."

"Oh, we're not playing in your home?"

"Naw, I stay away from there." He rinsed off his toothbrush before wrapping his washcloth tightly around it. The battered felt hat with the red feathers was placed firmly on his head after he had rearranged his necklace of bones. Eyes are a funny thing: they squint up exactly the same when we're ready to laugh or cry. " 'Cause if I was in it," he said — and now I knew he was going to smile — "there wouldn't be nobody out here to miss it."

IT WAS WELL into late morning by the time you returned up the road with a bunch of wilted daisies in your hand. I'd been sitting on the porch railing for over two hours and my immense relief at seeing that silly bouncing stride of yours told me how panicky I had been. Obviously, I hadn't really convinced myself when I convinced Grandma not to worry about your absence at breakfast. He's a grown man and where can he possibly get lost in Willow Springs? She quickly brought up the cypress swamp and the patches of quicksand in the east woods. But he's also a cautious man, and his first time out he'd stay on the main roads. And no, I wouldn't go out hunting you down. When you were ready, you'd come back.

Under the pretext of wanting some sun, I spent the morning outside wondering about where you were, finally getting angry at myself for not going along with you. But you had gotten up so early — I wished I could remember how early — I knew my brain hadn't cleared. And hadn't you woken me up to talk about — it couldn't be — a tree grow-

ing in the bed? That made absolutely no sense and neither did your
drowning in the cypress swamp. Hadn't I dreamed it, though? No, I
had dreamed that you were swimming in The Sound. It all came back
then and it was very disturbing. I was standing over here calling to
you — I was in some kind of trouble — but you were swimming in
the other direction. The louder I called from here, the faster you tried
to reach my voice on the opposite side. You were starting to falter,
and if I kept it up you would drown out there, so I clamped my mouth
shut with my voice pushing inside my chest until it felt I would
explode. And there I was, trying to hold my screams inside of me,
hoping you could make it back to shore, to wake up in a cold sweat
and find myself alone in that bed. There was the weirdest sensation
that everything about you had been a dream. It was only a fleeting
second, but it was still long enough to start my heart pounding.

So where in the hell were you? I was out there for an hour when
Junior Lee drove by, calling out his window, "Legggs, legggs," with
that stupid grin on his face. I started to wave him down and ask if
he'd seen you down by the junction, but I wasn't desperate enough
at that time to try getting any sense out of him. At the end of another
hour I would have tackled Junior Lee or any village idiot to get some
information. And as it crawled on into the third hour and you came
bouncing up the road, I knew we were going to have our first fight
on southern soil. You knew it too, which explained the flowers.

"I bet you were wondering where I was."

"I bet I didn't give a damn."

"Well, you lose." You tried to kiss me and I jerked my head away.

"Don't touch me."

"You see, that's what you said this morning. And now you're angry
because I went out to walk my frustration off."

"Why don't you stop lying, George."

"I'm not. I woke you up for a little attention and —"

"You woke me up to talk some nonsense about a tree growing in
the bedroom."

"It was a *redwood* — right there beside you."

"Ohhh, light dawns. Well, I could have saved you all that frustration
if you had mentioned something a bit smaller in scale, like a —"

"Don't say it."

"You'd deserve it if I did."

"I see you were a lot more worried than I thought. I'm sorry."

"I told you, I wasn't worried."

"You've been sitting out here a long time."

"How would you know?"

"The marks on the back of your thighs."

"I had my legs up on the railing to get a tan. And I want you to know that while you were gallivanting all over the place, a lot of people were passing by and admiring what you'd left here at home."

"Like who?"

"Junior Lee, for one."

I didn't mind your laughing, but it didn't have to go on so long. "For a minute I thought you were trying to make me jealous. And sometimes when you were down here alone, I did wonder. But not anymore."

"Junior Lee isn't the only man in Willow Springs."

"Yeah, I know. I've been talking to the others down at the barber-shop."

"Well, at least that explains where you were."

"And it also explains why you were hanging over this railing waiting for me so desperately."

"I told you —"

"I found out there are a lot of Saints fans in this town."

"Who are the Saints?"

"Anyway, did you know that Dr. Buzzard's real name is Rainbow Simpson?"

It was amazing how much you had managed to find out about people I thought I had known all my life. But then I had never spent any time among the men in the barbershop. It was a place to be passed if I was going to the general store or on my way to having my own hair done. Any news about their lives came to me secondhand or even thirdhand, filtered through their daughters or wives, sometimes bits and pieces from Grandma and Mama Day. No, I didn't know that Parris had gotten his name from fighting in France during World War II with the Ninety-second Infantry Division, that Winky Browne had batted against Satchel Paige in the bush leagues, or that Dr. Buzzard was once married to a dancer on the vaudeville circuit. You never pried, so they must have volunteered the information — some of it showing off for you, a lot of it simply because they knew you'd be interested. And you had been, enough to spend an entire morning with them. How much could I kick? It was your vacation too, and you were always most at ease with a group of men. You were one of the few men I knew who had absolutely no female friends or business associates. It wasn't difficult to figure out why, but it suddenly struck me that the three of us here were the only women in your life. Still, did you have to get bored with our company so soon?

I thought it was hysterical that you'd been suckered into a poker game with Dr. Buzzard. Since they only played for nickels and dimes, the most you were going to lose was six or seven dollars. At tops, you'd be out ten if he could also talk you into buying one of his "gambling hands," but that wasn't your speed. You'd been with the man all morning and couldn't figure out what he did for a living. I told you to go ask Grandma. After all, he was one of their close family friends. She almost fell over in the dishpan when you brought up the "professional rivalry" between him and Mama Day. Her advice, after much hemming and hawing, was for you to go get it straight from the horse's mouth. I didn't want to follow you to her trailer because I'd be blamed for putting you up to it.

It turned out I was still blamed when she came blazing over later that day. What did she want from me, anyway? I couldn't tell you where to walk and who to talk to. They didn't know how stubborn you were. The kiss of death was for me to tell you not to do something. You were going to come to your own conclusions about what you saw and heard in Willow Springs. But she was furious that he'd mentioned her in the same breath with himself. She wasn't in Buzzard's line of business at all. Buzzard was a con artist, bootlegger. Buzzard was a shiftless, no-good, slew-footed, twisted-mouthed, slimy-backed . . . Oh, the adjectives went on and on. I was sure she'd have enough of them to last until he came by the house that Friday night. That is, if I didn't see him first to ward him off.

◇◇◇

IT AIN'T BEEN LONG since Miranda got home and the sun is already riding the top of the pine trees. The peaches Ruby brought her last night is sitting in the middle of the floor, but she weren't about to start cutting 'em up before she got herself a cup of tea and a long hot bath. And she knows her hens is almost fit to be tied, the morning passing without them getting fresh feed and water, but there weren't no phone where she was so Abigail or Baby Girl coulda come over and taken care of it for her. No, weren't nothing where she was but a house full of — she didn't know what kind of people, letting that baby suffer that way. Someone addle-brained as Reema shouldna had child the first, and for that child to go on and have children was a sin before God. Leave 'em where they are if you can't take care of 'em. If you ain't got sense enough to marry nothing but a pitiful specimen of a man like Reema's oldest gal, Carmen Rae, did. Taking the money her mama ekes out from pressing hair, and instead of buying milk and diapers she puts gas in his car. Giving him six babies to keep raggedy and underfed down there in that shack. Wading in filth up to their ankles. Soap and water wouldn't put nobody out of more than fifty cents — nobody. And push come to shove, you could get away with just the water. Try as she might, she couldn't understand these women who balked at killing a baby before it got here and then living so they're sure to kill it after.

She almost started not to go. It was way late and she'd had a full day, finally settling down into a good sleep when Carmen Rae came banging on her door. Could she give her a little medicine to work the worms out her baby? He was fretting something awful and going into fits. Miranda guessed that all them children coulda used a good worming with a dose of warm castor oil and jimson. But when Carmen Rae told her that he was running a fever and his eyes were bloodshot, she knew it couldn't wait till morning. Sounded like that baby had the croup, and Lord knows how long it been going on.

It's just what she expected: the flushed face, his little chest heaving as the air whistles through his clogged throat. Every now and then he goes into a spasm of coughing that almost makes him strangle on his own spit. And when he is able to catch his breath again, he starts to whimper since he can't work up a good cry.

Miranda throws out the pot of onion water Carmen Rae had been trying to make him sip, hoping he would pass the worms. She has to clench her hands to keep from shaking Carmen Rae when she tells her she's been using that onion water for three days — the woman wasn't really after hurting her own baby, she just didn't understand. Carmen Rae is told to pick him up and pet him while Miranda scours the kitchen down. No, she'd do it herself because the baby was used to his mama. She scrapes off the caked grease from inside the pots, and while boiling them down in two changes of water, she scalds the countertops before opening her canvas pouch and laying her dried herbs out on them. She don't use much: all together it's only a teaspoon of senna pods, coltsfoot, horehound, white cherry bark, and black cohosh set to steep into the third change of water. She weighs them out by touch — some the roots, some the leaves, some the whole plant.

She's gonna need that charcoal brazier for the rest they gotta do. He's gotta have special vapors to breathe in to help him on his way. Is there a spare room in the house away from the other children? Carmen Rae shows her the pantry, and after Miranda cleans out the cobwebs and dusts down the empty shelves, she makes up a pallet for the baby and sets another pot boiling in there on the hot charcoals. Putting in another bit of horehound leaves, she takes the baby from Carmen Rae, getting a feel of his weight before she measures out the Indian tobacco for the makeshift steamer in the pantry. She's unde-cided about the amount — this is powerful stuff. The baby's misery calls for more, his body weight for less. She'll just have to sit up in there with him herself to see how it goes.

Hour by hour, the baby cradled in her arms, she gets him to sip a tablespoon of the mixture from the kitchen stove as she watches his fretful sleep through the steamy air in the pantry. At least he's sleeping now; his breathing's still rattled but even. He cries only when she wakes him to sip the mixture and each hour he gets louder. Good — if they're lucky, he'll be screaming at the top of his lungs by morning. Between being sent out to bring in more charcoal and water, Carmen Rae gets read the riot act: A sow takes better care of her young. And don't be sitting there whining about a no-good daddy — if he ain't never here, it means he ain't stopped you from cleaning this house. And he ain't the cause of you stuffing this child with white bread and sugar lard to keep him quiet while you're watching them soap operas. That's right, cry, you oughta cry. And while you at it, use them tears to water the truck garden you're gonna start growing with a dollar's worth of seeds and a little work. Chickens will eat anything you won't eat — even their own mess — and give you eggs for breakfast to boot. God don't like ugly, but He must have found something worth saving in her 'cause the child was gonna make it.

And he's a pretty thing, Miranda thinks, pulling her shoes off in her trailer. Skin like a blackbird's wings, and when his throat would let him squall he almost broke her eardrums — that showed spunk. He was angry as all get-out for that inconvenience and didn't mind letting the world know it. Reminded her a bit of Baby Girl when her body said she was too puny to live. She'd have to go back over there again tonight, so she'd better get herself a nap — she wasn't gonna trust nobody with that Indian tobacco. But Carmen Rae could make it through the day with them simple instructions she left her: Just keep him warm and start building back up his strength with a lot of fruit juices and some oatmeal broth. Ain't gotta be no fancy fruits, there's wild grapevines and cherry trees in that ravine below the house, and this time of year peaches and plums is to be had for the asking. Still, she'd have to bring over some seeds and a couple of setting hens to start her out in getting them children on a proper diet. That is, if my hens are even talking to me. She laughs. I done kept 'em hungry all morning. Now, who do I feed first, me or them?

She's outside running water into their trough when she spies George crossing the road. Could be Abigail done sent him over to look for her. When you get to be their age and nobody answers the phone, it pays to worry. She likes the way that boy walks, kinda free and bouncy. And he holds his head up high. A man should have starch in him, especially a colored man. There's too much out there to mow him down permanent if he ain't got the where-with-all to spring back. But he done made out real well — his own business and all. She didn't rightly understand what he did, all that talk last night about keeping peas on a knife with honey, but it was bringing in enough for him and Baby Girl to be planning on buying a bigger house for the family they was finally gonna start. He kinda hesitates when the chickens outside the coop start flocking around his feet.

"Don't worry about them," Miranda calls. "Them miserable beggars think you're there to feed 'em. Just come on in here, but make sure you close the gate."

He don't seem any more comfortable inside the fence, tiptoeing around the pullets who're scrambling over each other to get to their mash. And George looks about to break and run when her old brown rooster lets out a mighty crow, flying up in the air, a flurry of feathers and spurs, 'cause he's being pushed away from the choicest spot.

Miranda lays back her head and laughs. "Come on, they ain't gonna hurt you."

"You sure have a lot of them," George says, braving the distance between the fence and her.

"And you're used to seeing a lot of them. But in your neck of the woods they're all wrapped up neat under cellophane."

"I think I like them better that way."

"Well, you best never watch me wring one of their necks. It'll probably turn you into one of them vegetarians."

"So you eat most of these?"

"Them in here. Them out there is something else again. Abigail send you looking for me?"

"No, I just wanted to come over and say hello."

"That's right nice of you. I figured she was wondering 'cause she couldn't get me on the phone this morning, I was out nursing a sick baby."

"Oh, I knew you were a midwife. So you nurse, too?"

"When need be."

"That's really wonderful — natural remedies are really in now. We have centers opening up all over the place in New York."

"Well, they always been 'in' down here. When doctors is scarce, folks ain't got much else."

George's face lights up. "*That* explains his name. I —"

"Whose name?"

"Dr. Buzzard's. I ran into him down by the barbershop."

"You walked all the way to the bridge junction?"

"That was nothing — I like to walk. You know, he's a pretty interesting man."

"He can be. And if you caught him before eight o'clock, he wasn't drunk."

"Oh, it was well before eight. And he invited me to play poker with him."

"Make sure you don't lose too much."

"I'm hoping not to lose at all."

Miranda smiles to herself as she turns the water spigot off.

"But at first I couldn't figure out what he did for a living until you just —"

"He don't do crow's squat for a living. So you ain't gotta worry about that."

"Well, he did say there was a little professional rivalry between you two." George smiles. "And I guess everyone feels that no one else can do their job as well as —"

"He said *what?*"

Both George and the chickens back away from the thunder in Miranda's voice as she straightens up to face him with a storm brewing in her eyes.

"Run that by me one more time. He said *what?*"

"Look, Miss Miranda, if I had thought it would cause any trouble, I never would have mentioned it. These little friendly rivalries go on in any profession. The important thing is that you're both serving the community."

"Serving the community! How're you serving some community from the bottom of a liquor jug? You know what he gives folks when they got an ache in their left side? Moonshine and honey. And for an ache in their *right* side? Honey and moonshine. That is, when he's not selling 'em worthless bags of —"

Miranda snaps her mouth shut. This boy don't really know her and he sure don't know Buzzard. Ain't been here a day and he gotta pick up with the worst Willow Springs had to offer. She warned Abigail not to have Buzzard go meet 'em at the airport. No telling what he's had time to fill this child's head with. Professional rivalry. She'd profession his rivalry as soon as she got her hands on him. And where was Baby Girl while he was out rubbing elbows with hoodoo doctors? Sleeping on her fanny, no doubt. But no point in flaring up and scaring this boy half to death.

"Let's just leave that be for now," she says.

"I'm sorry, I didn't mean to upset you."

"Naw, I ain't upset, it's just my way. But I see you like to get up early."

"Yeah, I always have."

"Well, you sure married the wrong woman. My niece can sleep through a hurricane, even if you put the bed outside. Always been an early riser myself. It's right nice around here in the mornings when the air is still unused."

He laughed. "It's amazing — I used to say that as a child."

"It's the best time in the world to fish, too. You do much of that?"

"No, but my business partner is a great fisherman. Trout."

"That's freshwater. But you can pull some beauties up here with our saltwater. Let's get us a few poles and go out one morning. We can have 'em cleaned and fried before Cocoa and Abigail gets up. Honey, you ain't lived until you had hot drumfish with grits and buttered biscuits for breakfast."

"Sounds good to me."

◇◇◇

I NEVER REALIZED you were paying me such a high compliment whenever you said I reminded you of Ambush Duvall. There was something so steady and genuinely kind about the man. We were about the same age, but he appeared older than me, perhaps because he was married almost three times as long. But after a while I began to feel that it was due to his infinite patience. He had to have it in order to put up with the temperamental nature of the weather and his farm crops, and he certainly needed a good measure of it with Bernice. She was a nice enough woman, but nervous, nervous, nervous. We were sitting in that living room for only half an hour and she had hopped up twenty times — to take Charlie's thumb out of his mouth, to retrieve Charlie's stuffed bear from the empty fireplace, to help Charlie pry the top off of his Erector set, to gather the loose pieces that rolled under the sofa. Between all that — her fiddling with parts of her clothing, her coffee cup, the fabric on the sofa — for you to turn and say so casually that motherhood had calmed Bernice down a lot; I couldn't imagine his life with her before that kid was born.

There was only one time when she became still — totally still. I asked Ambush if Miss Miranda had delivered his son. He said no, but he had wanted her to. Mama Day had been very helpful to them when they were trying to have the baby. Obviously, Bernice had not wanted

Miss Miranda as midwife, but there was no spoken reply from her, and I couldn't read her stillness. The strangest thing of all was that Ambush couldn't read it either. The confusion was there in the glance he gave her — a little hurt, perhaps — that however adamant that past refusal, it was built on something she'd never shared with him.

But it was clear he adored his wife — a lid for every pot, someone once said. And if we could make it just as long as they had, we'd be in good shape. Except that I expected us to have three children by the time we were married eleven years — a compromise on my part, magnanimity on yours — and they were going to be much better trained. I didn't believe in abuse, but a child definitely needed more discipline than this one got. Every time he screamed no and called his mother stupid, she laughed, you raised an eyebrow, and Mrs. Jackson turned over in her grave. A small cloud would pass over Ambush's eyes but he sat through it, talking nonchalantly with us. I was ready to lynch that kid after the third episode, but it took Ambush until about the twelfth to turn his head, barely raising his voice to stop a tantrum midstream — "Little Caesar, go to your room." He looked at his mother, but she had already looked at her husband, and whatever their private codes of body language, she knew he had had enough; and above all, the kid knew that they'd all reached a point where she couldn't save him if his father got up from that chair.

He was awfully cute, though, dragging his bear out of the room by the leg as though they'd both been condemned to life without parole. He got to the door and stood there, pouting and staring at his father, waiting for him to begin the motion that would swing him out of his chair so he could knock him back down in the way only a child could — "I have to kiss Aunt Cocoa goodbye." Our silent laughter came from knowing exactly what he'd done and that he'd succeeded. Even his father was rooting for him a bit. There was a quiver in the pit of my stomach, watching you take him into your arms. So that's how it will look — "Now, say goodbye to Uncle George" — and this is how it will feel.

"Let that be your last goodbye, Little Caesar." Ambush could keep the smile from his lips, but not from his eyes.

Bernice wasn't really complaining about the child's name — "Ambush, if you keep calling him that, he ain't never gonna know who he's supposed to be."

"Well, I've been answering to Ambush all my life and I know my name is Charles. And I bet you can't even remember Cocoa's real name."

She couldn't, so you helped her out. "It's Ophelia."

"Anyway, Cocoa is a pretty name. But these know-nothings in Willow Springs just gave my baby that pet name out of spite."

"It wasn't spite, Bernice. A pet name is just that."

"I think a mama should have a say about what she wants done to her baby — and his name is Charles."

"But don't you call him Charlie?" Ambush teased.

"It's a lot better than Little Caesar."

"And that's a lot better than Chick," he said. "Remember how put out you were when folks was doing that?"

She seemed angry about it still, wincing at the mention of it, her fingers beginning to pleat at the slipcover. "I ain't talking about this no more. My own mama never gave me no outside name but the one I was born with — Bernice. And your mama didn't either, did she, George?"

"No," I said. "She didn't."

"I bet you're glad."

"When I think about what I could have been left with, I guess I am."

"Tom-Tom, Rickshaw, Sue Bee — all that silliness."

"Aw, Bernice, lighten up," you said. "I'd rather have older people tag him than the kids at school — they can be really cruel. Remember? You were Needle Legs and I was Lulu the Leper."

"I think the strangest one I've heard to date," I said, "is Dr. Buzzard."

"Oh, you've met him?" Ambush smiled.

"You know Dr. Buzzard always picks me up at the airport. And he and George have become fast friends."

"I wouldn't go that far."

"Aren't you playing poker with him tomorrow night?"

"I'd go along myself," Ambush said. "But I don't have the money to lose this month."

"Why is everyone always saying that? Is he that good a player?"

"No, he cheats."

"You're kidding me. I heard at least three other guys at the barbershop agree to play."

"Yeah, but they all know he cheats."

"But then why —" You all burst out laughing at the look on my face.

"We go because it's fun," Ambush said.

"There's no fun when someone cheats."

"Sure, it is. It ain't like he does it now and then, he does it every hand. So the challenge is how much you can get away with not losing. It about amounts to the same thing."

Walking with Ambush through his fields was to watch the hand of a virtuoso stroke the instrument of his craft. An absentminded handful of soil worked between his fingers as the endless rows melted into the blurred outlines of the horizon. The weight, the texture, the smell, telling him of possibilities I couldn't begin to understand. In the fading light it could have been his own skin flaking off gently into the ground. Four hundred and twenty acres.

"It's all going to my son." He handed me a tomato, heavy and blood red. "But if I have my way, he won't be a farmer. Unless by the time he's grown up, they find a scale to pay you for what really goes into one of these."

The tomato broke between my teeth like warm flesh; the juices running down my chin were pure sugar. "Not a chance," I said.

"I know, and that's why he's going on to college. Let him sit up somewhere in a shirt and tie. He can build golf courses and swimming pools here for all I care. As long as he keeps the land, that's what matters. But he's gonna be tall like his mama's side of the family, so it'll probably be basketball courts."

"You know, I hadn't thought about who our kids will be like. I guess her looks and my brains, I'll be happy."

"Better not let Cocoa hear you say that."

"I'm just saying she's an attractive woman."

"But do they ever figure things that way? You been married long enough to know better than that. Look at Bernice, carrying on in there. But you try to tell her a Charlie Duvall won't be fit for nothing but designing ladies' panties while a Caesar Duvall is gonna be welcome into many of 'em, and she won't get the point."

"Ambush, I needed to hear this years ago. No wonder I kept striking out with a name like George."

"Well, you could borrow mine."

"It's too late now."

"Know what you mean." It was a deep, deep sigh. "But, man, there was a time . . ."

YOU WERE GOING to talk about my breasts. We dropped Little Caesar at his grandmother's. Had dinner with Bernice and Ambush. Listened to old rock 'n' roll songs at my favorite club. Walked back to the house from the bridge road so we could hold hands and exchange the teenage memories that the music resurrected. The first broken hearts: a doe-eyed, caramel princess in ninth grade algebra for you, an ebony god with winged feet on the basketball court for me. A long, long kiss by that burnt patch of pines in which I tried so hard to repay you for every moment when I should have spoken but didn't, when I spoke unnecessarily. We climbed the steps to the darkened house and quietly closed our bedroom door on an evening that was full and complete. But you were going to talk about my breasts.

Bernice had guaranteed that. It was an innocent question, cushioned way back in the evening, part of an ongoing struggle between her and Ambush. She was arguing for the child's name, but the issue was control. You offered her a possible ally and my stomach took a nose dive as soon as the words were out of her mouth: "My own mama never gave me no outside name but the one I was born with. And your mama didn't either, did she, George?" I regretted having never told her the whole truth. But how could I reach cab drivers, store-keepers, news commentators, a dozen waitresses — all of whom were likely, through casual remarks, to freeze the muscles in the lower part of your jaw? Put that cold light in your eyes. When I finally made the connection, it was in the realm just beneath thought. To have thought it would be too ugly and so how to speak about the unthinkable? We held this secret between us that we couldn't even reveal to ourselves. I knew after one of those incidents there was nothing to do but wait.

You had to hurt me — just a little. It might be a playful jab, short of cutting to the bone. A crushing comment, its vindictiveness well out of place in a light argument. A matter-of-fact observation, bringing up an insecurity I had shared at some previous time: They *are* beginning to sag a bit — it's to be expected at your age. That purple birthmark near the nipple does look like a scar.

So as I undressed for bed I waited. No, I wasn't going to linger in the bathroom, hoping you'd fall asleep. And yes, I slept in the nude — there would be no difference tonight. I would have given anything to call back Bernice's words, but just let's get this over with. You were sitting up in bed with your back against the headboard, staring out of the window. There was no moon; I couldn't see your face once I cut off the bathroom light. Everything was pitch black, but I knew that room like the back of my hand. The mattress gave under my weight as I lay down, trying not to touch you. To give you any reason. Your face stayed turned and it was barely a whisper: I'd like you to nurse our children. I said nothing as I waited. The silence grew longer and longer. The silence stayed. You slipped under the covers, cradled your head between my breasts, and we never spoke about the tears.

◇◇◇

MIRANDA wakes up earlier than usual. Feeling mighty good this morning, mighty good. The liniment she rubbed her legs down with last night got 'em spry enough to join in the front line of them kicking girls at Radio City. If anything would take her to New York, that would. She liked the holiday commercials with them all decked out in their spangles and feathers, sending their heels almost up to their heads. Sitting up on the edge of the bed, she stretches her feet out in front of her and grins. All they need is me up there with these knobby legs — it wouldn't be a matter of the manager giving folks back the price of admission, he'd have to find a way to keep himself from getting lynched. She gives her thighs a healthy slap. Well, you ain't good enough for Radio City but you does all right here. They had carried her to Carmen Rae's yesterday with a whole sackful of peaches on her back and she liked what she found there. Her little blackbird was doing fine — that's what they oughta call him, with that pretty skin, Blackbird. And with a spirit like his that boy was sure to fly. It was encouraging that Carmen Rae had managed to keep that kitchen passably clean for two whole days — not encouraging enough to eat any of the sweet potato pudding Carmen Rae had baked special for her, but the signs were good. And these old legs were gonna carry her out fishing this morning. That is, if the other signs were right.

Standing up and stretching, she listens to her bones go off like a series of firecrackers as they pop into their joints. They get louder each year. She sighs. And I guess I want 'em to get louder still, since I ain't ready for 'em to quit. And it was about that, being ready to lay down and die. Sure, the body could get sick and put you down long before you wanted, but everybody held on until they had absolutely had enough. Sometimes the pain just got too much for the mind, the struggling got too much, the being tired of being tired. But in the end — the very end — you do *give up* the ghost, it ain't taken away. She had it all planned for herself: something nice and simple. A warm flannel gown with ruffles on the sleeves. Propped up in bed with extra pillows at her back. Her windows wide open to let in whatever season of air it was. And Baby Girl's children bringing her in little sips of soup, cups of tea, and heaping dishes of pistachio ice cream. She couldn't with all certainty put Baby Girl in the middle of that picture, but the children she'd get from that boy, having only half of his heart, would be there for their old auntie.

I know I ain't giving her credit. Miranda laughs. She done mellowed plenty since this marriage. Soft around the edges without getting too soft at the center. You fear that sometimes for women, that they would just fold up and melt away. She'd seen it happen so much in her time, too much for her to head on into it without thinking. Yes, that one time when she was way, way young. But after that, looking at all the beating, the badgering, the shriveling away from a lack of true touching was enough to give her pause. Not that she mighta hooked up with one of those. And not that any man — even if he tried — coulda ever soaked up the best in her. But who needed to wake up each morning cussing the day just to be sure you still had your voice? A woman shouldn't have to fight her man to be what she was; he should be fighting that battle for her. It weren't so in her time, though, and from what these young women tell her, it's rare to find it now. So a lot of 'em is waking up like me, except they're waking up young and alone.

The day is just about to break when she leaves her trailer with her fishing poles and a can of bait. The wind's blowing right — not too heavy and straight from the west. But look at those crazy chickens, roosting with their heads turned east so the wind is ruffling their tail feathers — you'd think a storm was coming. Not today, with the sky dawning like it is — naw, that horizon was shouting fair weather. Couple that with a new moon to bring in high-tide water for that little bay off by the ocean caves, the fish would be pleading for a hook today. But she couldn't see dragging George all the way over there through the east woods. The Sound would make fair enough catches, and she had to keep in mind where he was from. With nothing to look at all his life but goldfish and canned tuna, he'd be more than thrilled with them puny two pounders taking a nap in The Sound. She ain't waited on Abigail's porch for five minutes when he comes out, clean shaven and smelling only a mite less fresh than the day. His blue plaid shirt is starched and the creases in his jeans are sharp enough to cut butter. Sleep still hangs around his smile, but it always takes longer to leave the young since they get into it deeper. This is a boy who wakes up smiling, she thinks, and it's nice to know that Baby Girl has a little something to do with it.

"Good morning, Miss Miranda. I thought I was going to come over and surprise you."

"Not a chance of that. I guess they both still sleeping in there."

"God, yes — Ophelia is out cold."

"We coulda left at noon and found her that way. Well, now I know for *sure* you ain't much of a fisherman."

"Huh?"

"There ain't a serious fisherman on this island who would speak to any old woman before he casts. Bad luck."

"I've always made my own luck." A good firm laugh with maybe just a hint of bitterness. "Always."

"That ain't a foolish policy. One I leans toward myself. But if the tides was against us, we'd have to be frying both good and bad luck for breakfast."

"Not necessarily. With the proper engineering, reels can be designed to work well in high and low tides."

"Maybe so. But they ain't designed fish like that."

She sees he's not gonna argue no more, although he don't agree with a word she says. Polite. He thinks he's talking to a doddering old woman, and if he had just thought it, she was willing to let it be. His undoing comes when it slips over to give a kinda oily coating to his voice.

"I'm sure they haven't, Miss Miranda. I guess we should be on our way. Where's your walking stick?"

"Where it belongs — in the house. I'm feeling more than good this morning."

"No, I don't think you should take any chances. It's a pretty long hike to The Sound."

"Ya know, I think you're right." If he notices the narrowing of her eyes, he don't know what it means. "Run on over to the trailer and get my stick. We'll head out to the ocean instead — through the east woods."

They walk east into the sunrise, Miranda taking the lead. She don't know these woods as well as the ones in back of her house, but none are too strange to her. She coulda easily taken him the opposite way hopping on one leg, through that smaller set toward The Sound. But there were more lessons to be learned in these. They were a bit wilder, stray creepers to tangle up his foot and let him stumble, a sight more hilly so he'd get a little winded, patches of waist-high bulrush for him to wade through. She'd keep him from the real danger: stinging nettles, poison sumac, or the suck mud that could break an ankle. This here was just to be a little spanking.

He takes it like a man, though, and she's gotta admire the set of his top lip as he wipes the sweat off it quietly with the back of his hand. Never calling out when he skids to his knees on a wet clump of decaying toadstools. She stops every now and then to point out nesting cat birds or the rare glimpse of a red fox, so he can catch his breath. These here woods were terrible, she tells him, when her daddy was a boy. Weren't nothing to see whole families of copperheads coiled around them low branches, and that little bit of slimy mud coating his suede sneakers and the hem of his pants is all that's left of a tidal marsh that used to creep up to the edge of these trees. Most of the alligators disappeared with the marsh. Did he know that gators could sing? Sure enough. Naw, they don't sound nothing like that — it's a wild turkey if anything. And you couldn't hear the few in the cypress swamp from all the way over here. Watch out for the leaves on those palmettos, they can cut like a razor. Step smart over these cockleburs, they'll eat through the leg of them jeans. Too late! Well, just pick 'em out, but put a little spit on your fingers. Naw, that ain't nothing but a rotten pine log — she told him before the gators disappeared with the marsh. Long way? Maybe it just seems so. See, they nearing the clearing at Chevy's Pass — means the ocean bluff's not far away.

When they reach the clearing, she needs a good second wind herself since she's kinda double-stepped him for about four miles. Chevy's Pass is a right pretty place. Open and flat with the ocean breeze almost always whispering through the hanging moss on a big ancient oak, sitting right in its middle. With the wind in any direction, you can smell the saltwater, but when it's coming from the east you can taste it. Not a real heavy taste, sorta like you ran your tongue over your lips and touched a few dried tears. Just near where the woods sparse out is the lime tombstone of Bascombe Wade. Facing due east and still standing erect, it's footed with the rich green vines of wild ginger.

George kinda crumbles down under the live oak, his sweat-soaked back propped against its trunk. He says he can see why a cemetery would sit up there, but it's a wonder there aren't more graves. Miranda throws back her head and laughs. She's remained standing, leaning on her walking cane. Naw, that's the only one, she tells him, and there's a story behind that. Bascombe Wade used to have the whole island before he deeded it over to his slaves. Said he fell under the spell of a woman he owned — only in body, not in mind. Naw, nobody knows her name. But she got away from him and headed over here toward the east bluff on her way back to Africa. And she made that trip — some say in body, others in mind. But the point is that he lost her. He kept a vigil up here at Chevy's Pass — he's keeping it still. And when the wind is right in the trees, you can hear him calling and calling the name that nobody knows. Yeah, she had children — Miranda motions that it's time to go — she had seven sons.

She watches George bend down and clear away the ginger vines so he can read the inscription on the stone. The early sunlight filtering through the edge of the woods forms barlike patterns on his back. It's a good strong back, belonging to a good strong man. She fights back the urge that comes up in her to snatch him away from there. But it's harder to fight not seeing the way them heart-shaped ginger leaves twine around his knuckles, as if they were pulling him in closer to listen, willing to hold him there until he does. Ain't *nothing* he needs to hear around here — the sharpness of her voice surprises him when she tells him to come on. She places a hand gently on his forearm, saying there's a bit of pain in her leg. So stay by her side in case she stumbles, and she's sure glad now he made her bring that cane.

Miranda talks without letting up — through the fishing at the sea cove and on the journey back. She talks until they clear the east woods, until her voice is almost hoarse. Now, sea life, birds, and wood creatures, they got ways just like people. 'Cepting they live in the sky, the earth, the tides. So who better to ask about their home? You just gotta watch 'em long enough to find out what's going on. She tells him what part of that forest she uses in the fall, summer, or spring. Differences in leaves of trees, barks of trees, roots. The tonics she makes up, the poultices, the healing teas. There's something in here for everything, she tells him, if a body knows what they're doing. Finding a rare growth of wild foxglove, she rips 'em up. Children might wander in here and there's a reason it's called dead men's bells. But in her hands she could make the same medicine he uses for his heart. She tells him about the foxglove leaves needing two years' growth and picking before the plant flowers. About the drying, layering, measuring, and watching. She talks what she knows, not what she's afraid to remember. So the ginger vines on that tombstone whisper in vain under all her chatter. And she don't say nothing about them, and least of all, Candle Walk.

She figures she ain't gotta worry about George heading back in that direction again. He's so tired his knees are wobbling by the time they get home. And them suede sneakers are sure messed up for good. It's only a little past ten with them hauling in enough drumfish and mullet for Cocoa and Abigail to fry until next year. They can clean 'em too, she says — we went out and got 'em. Cocoa ain't none too happy when she sees the condition her husband's in. Where he ain't muddy, he's sweaty; where he ain't sweaty, he's scratched. He just about makes it to the bedroom, saying wake him up for breakfast. And he's sound asleep on top of the covers before she can pull off his shoes and socks.

"The east woods? Mama Day, you didn't."

"Mama Day, you didn't what? We took us a little stroll and got in some fishing. I don't hear him complaining like you."

"Because he's knocked out, poor thing."

"Aw, hush up. He's not a baby. He made it back in better shape than I did — I even had to take my walking cane."

"You should be ashamed of yourself. You know about his heart."

"Yeah, and mine's been beating more than half a century before he was born. A hike that don't kill me, won't kill him. He's in there resting them city legs, that's all. You wear him out more in that bed at night than I wore him out."

"You're one fresh old lady."

"And you better clean my fish."

◇◇◇

I WAS SHOWING a pair of nines with an ace kicker, and twenty cards out with no one else showing higher than kings and not a possible straight in sight. I called and raised, got a five in the last deal, which didn't worry me too much with my ace in the hole — that's right, the proverbial ace in the hole — and he still beat me. My pair of aces and nines went down to Dr. Buzzard's full house. And that's when I was *sure* he was cheating. Even if we forgot the odds for that hand (they had been running six to one for me; fourteen to one for him), it was pretty hard to believe that an entire game could render one player three of a kind or better through the last twelve hands. But no one else was having problems believing it; they had gotten to his campsite talking that way.

He had said around eight, but I was the first to arrive. There was an open fire going and lanterns had been hung in the trees so the top of an oak stump we'd be using for a table was well lighted. Most folks sit on the ground or pull up a rock, he said, but he had borrowed a special canvas chair for me. I appreciated that because my thighs and legs were still sore from following Miss Miranda, but the south woods were a playground, considering what I'd been through that morning. Here I only had to follow his instructions and stay on a well-worn path that led me straight to his campfire and still. And since I wasn't a drinking man, he said, there was a six-pack he had cooling down in the stream. Budweiser. He shrugged his shoulders. Nothing but grown-up Kool-Aid, but he wouldn't feel right not having a little something for all his guests.

"You got my nachos?" Parris, the barber, was the first to arrive, his bald head gleaming under the kerosene lanterns. Keeping it shaved off was good for business, he had told me a few days before.

"Yeah, I got your damn nachos." Dr. Buzzard grinned.

"And I got your number tonight." Parris jingled a bulging pocket full of change. "I ain't losing more than two dollars if I'm losing a dime."

"Buy one of my gambling hands and you'll cut your losses even more."

"Nigger, I don't need your gambling hands. You're talking to a man who's played with the best in the Ninety-second Division. We had colored boys there from Miss-is-sip who could make a card cry."

Parris asked me how much I was planning to lose. And when I told him that actually I was planning to *win*, he and Dr. Buzzard found that very funny. Parris took his place, leaning back against the trunk of an old palmetto — facing east was good for his luck — while Dr. Buzzard brought him his bag of nacho chips and poured him a paper cupful of clear liquid from an earthen jug.

"In honor of the city boy, y'all getting my best stuff tonight — no second run of mash here."

"I'll remember that and take pity when you're howling about only two dollars from me."

Junior Lee was next to arrive, accompanied by a man who was introduced to me as Rickshaw. I had already met Junior Lee when he came to your grandmother's with his wife. He wouldn't be much competition — "I don't care how much I looose, I'm rolling in moneeey toniiight" — a good poker player needed sharpness if anything. This man was so soft, he was eerie. The one with him was a bit different, dark skinned and tall but eager, much too eager for a nickel-and-dime game. Did I know Reema — she ran the ladies' beauty parlor? No, I didn't. Well, he was husband to Reema's oldest gal. Dr. Buzzard asked Rickshaw how Carmen Rae was doing — heard their baby was down with the croup. Rickshaw said yeah, it was pretty terrible for a while. He was doing better now, thanks to Mama Day. It was a good thing she never took no payment, he wouldn't have as much to spare tonight. And he hated leaving a game early.

It was totally amazing: each in his own way expected to lose. Rickshaw was the only one who wanted to buy a "gambling hand." Dr. Buzzard said he'd sell him one for only a dollar tonight. He might need medicine for his baby. Rickshaw said he'd rather pay full price — he didn't want no half-assed gambling hand. Dr. Buzzard said no, it would be a good one — live frog and all. I was told the chamois bag had lodestone, sugar, black pepper, and cayenne in it. It definitely had a frog, because the thing kept croaking while we played. All of it was beyond ridiculous to me. The man, Rickshaw, was actually happy with his little red bag since he'd lost only a dollar fifty by the sixth hand. He was normally a much worse player, he confided to me, but look at how he knew to fold even showing a queen high on a possible pair before the third deal. The whole night was boiling down to that: how quickly do you fold — give up the dream — a battle between yourself and the possibility of the ever elusive royal flush. A straight flush, maybe. It was *never* a question of you against the man with rooster feathers in his hat, jumping up to refill cups, bringing in new bags of nachos, padding Rickshaw's seat with his sleeping blanket — and probably hiding jacks between his thighs. Parris finally took a pot with four of a kind. You should have seen the jubilation.

But I had gotten awfully angry by the twelfth hand. Stud poker was my game — with my experience, there was no way for me to come out less than even and I had lost more than anyone so far. I had learned to play at Columbia in a mathematics course dealing with game theory. I came out of that course with an A and a solid grounding in analyzing problems of conflict by abstracting common strategic features from an infinite number of conflict situations. And once you had distilled those handfuls of strategic features, you devised methods that could give you what is called "a most favorable result." The dozens of matrix charts I had labored over in graduate school proved that, all things being equal, there *is* a payoff matrix within the axis of maximizing a minimum result and minimizing a maximum result. In short, if Dr. Buzzard wasn't palming jacks between his thighs, stacking the deck, or marking the cards — whatever he was doing — I wouldn't have lost consistently for twelve hands and been out five dollars and twenty cents. I had played and bet in absolute proportion to the odds.

But I had learned something else in that math course: the study of game theory includes learning the principle of "extensive form" — a branching diagram in which at each juncture a player has several options to continue a course of play. The bizarre type of poker we were playing fit right into that. The pure strategy I'd been using wouldn't work to my advantage against him; I needed to introduce the formulas for behavior strategy. I had to discover exactly how he was cheating in each hand and then weigh those variables out to my advantage. In a way, the other guys were doing that, but to minimize their losses. I was going to win.

It took a little while. If my first show card wasn't the highest, I'd call whatever the bet was and always fold after the second deal — once even with three of a kind — to sit there and watch. I soon found out the cards were definitely marked, but that could only help Dr. Buzzard when he was the dealer. It was too shadowy for him to see the nick he had made in the left corner of the aces on our hole cards when someone else dealt them out. I asked him for another beer, although I'd barely touched the first one, and while he went down to the stream, I made a pretense of idly toying with the cards and nicked all the deuces in their left-hand corners. This cut his advantage in half at least, and more than that until he figured out what had happened. With Dr. Buzzard dealing, I played the next round through and Junior Lee won with two pairs — one pair was my deuces.

The next pot went to Parris, holding only a king high, the next to me with a pair of jacks. When Rickshaw took the next with three aces, a pall began to fall over our circle. They all looked toward Dr. Buzzard, extremely puzzled.

"Well, what is happening heeere?" Junior Lee let out a low whistle.

"Beats me." Dr. Buzzard shrugged. "Y'all wanna change the cards?"

"We better do something," Parris said. "This mess is becoming a mess."

Dr. Buzzard snapped the rubber bands off a new deck. He extracted the two jokers — and a seven of hearts. I had him now. I adjusted the odds for a fifty-one-card game with no seven of hearts in any hand but his. And with stud poker always showing four cards, it wasn't too hard to see when that seven could possibly help him and hurt me.

Slowly, I broke even and then began to win. Now all eyes were on me — and were they, I thought with amazement, suspicious? Afraid? Yes, a bit of each. The joking ended completely then. No one talking to or kissing their cards. No joy when Rickshaw came up with a full house. He raked in the pot to his corner as if the coins were dirty. The crackling of the dying fire and the shuffling of the cards were the only things punctuating our silence. The calling went on by rote, everyone folding early in the next hand except for me and Dr. Buzzard.

The others became so still they could easily have not been there. Just myself and the old man with deep lines of concentration added to the others in his forehead, a slight quiver in his tightened bottom lip. But I was paying more attention to his hands, waiting for him to exchange his hole card with the hidden seven of hearts. His fingers were long and delicate, the palms callused with hardened ridges along each joint. Dancing hands. You could imagine them supporting his lean body in a handstand, moving to music. But they were sweating now, little flickers of moisture staying on the surface of the coins he fed into the pot. I called and raised him after my third card was dealt. The aces were running in my favor again. With the third deal I was showing two of them and had an eight of clubs in the hole. Dr. Buzzard was showing only a deuce, a six, and a jack high, but all were hearts. With his hidden card that meant the possibility of a definite flush; with his real hole card that could be anything from a lower pair than mine to a legitimate flush if it was a heart. The fourth cards were dealt: a deuce of clubs for me, a ten of *diamonds* for him. Gone. Gone. Gone. I called and raised — big. Rickshaw let out a long expulsion of air, Junior Lee started to hum, and Parris leaned forward in a fervent whisper, running his palm over his shaved head. "What ya got working there, Buzz? What ya got working?"

But his eyes never left mine as he called that bet. Their clear brown caught the reflection from the hanging lanterns and they were actually pitying me. I had to blink and look at our cards again just to be sure: No, any way he cut it, I was winning. But my throat was dry until he dealt out the last cards with those long delicate fingers. A ten of hearts for him, an eight of spades for me. He was showing a pair of tens against my aces. But we were up to three calls and a raise — three. And each time I kept doubting what was in front of my face, even doubting the eight of clubs in the hole that gave me *two* pair. No, there was absolutely nothing he could have in the hole, legitimate or otherwise, to win this hand. My mind knew it, but somehow the message hadn't reached my gut because the fourth time he met my bet the strain was enough to make me fold. My voice cracked as I called and raised the fifth time — all of three dollars and fifty cents on the table and my hands were shaking. If he called and raised me again — well, damn it, maybe he's palmed two cards (as unrealistic as that could be) and I'll just fold with my aces and eights. Then he smiled — a brilliant, brilliant smile. Slow, even, and gleaming it spread over his face. He made a motion toward his money as if he were going to see my bet, and with that same shade of pity in his eyes, he flipped over his hole card — the king of hearts. I sat there staring at it stupidly, wondering why he didn't pick up the pot. Then with a wave of disappointment I realized he had not won.

But that's not why I came home drunk. It was the clapping. Dr. Buzzard started it off, his callused palms meeting each other with the rhythm of dirge as he looked straight into the eyes of the other men. His lone clapping echoed loudly into the night, persistent and slow. One by one, they joined in. At first it was for me. The small sip of beer did nothing to dissolve the lump in my throat. Neither did the next or the next. So I drained the can. And then the rhythm of their clapping shifted slightly and this time it was for him. Dr. Buzzard took off his feathered hat and the necklace of bones. He emptied his overall pockets of crumpled tissues, bits of stone, a rabbit's foot. The clapping continued between the deep baritone of Parris's voice:

> Take my hand, Precious Lord.

He slipped out of his sneakers and with a huge grunt he was swaying upside-down on his hands.

> Lead me on. Let me stand.
> I am tired. I am weak. I am worn.

Each syllable was beat off in time with their hands while his raised small clouds of dust on the ground —

> Through the dark. Through the night.
> Lead me on to the light.

I didn't understand the rhythm and I refused to spoil it by attempting to join in. Perhaps if I had known that I only had to listen to the pulse of my blood —

> Take my hand, Precious Lord
> And lead me home.

How long could he stay that way? His palms and muscled forearms balancing his body so that through the shadows his feet seemed to stretch up to the stars. I wanted it to go on forever —

> When my way grows drear
> Precious Lord, linger near.
> When my life is almost gone
> By the river I will stand.
> Guide my feet, hold my hand.
> Take my hand, Precious Lord
> And lead me home.

I wanted his feet anchored up there in the sky. The clear liquor in the paper cup that was pushed toward me burned every part of my body it touched. But it didn't touch as deeply as the rhythm being pounded into my ears.

> Sometimes stumbling
> Sometimes falling
> Sometimes alone . . .

After the first cupful it stopped burning entirely. And through my watery eyes his body *was* stretching up into the stars — they outlined and illuminated the soles of his feet.

> Take my hand, Precious Lord
> And lead me home.

I said I fell asleep, you said I passed out. But when I woke up, I was holding on to the post of your grandmother's fence for dear life. It seemed the logical thing to do: her front yard had been replaced by a huge cavern and I needed to get to the three of you sitting up there on the porch without falling in. My pockets were loaded down with change and I was afraid that the weight of the coins would throw me off balance and straight down into that gaping hole. I was aware that I was a little tipsy, but if I held on long enough to get my direction around that cavern, I could make it up to the porch with a modicum of dignity. I didn't want your grandmother and Miss Miranda thinking that you'd married a drunk. I just hadn't tasted beer in over seventeen years and I'd never tasted moonshine before. So I was just going to hang on there, both arms wrapped around the fence post, and think my way through this.

"Honey, ain't you coming up on the porch?" Miss Abigail asked me.

"No, there's money in my pockets."

My answer was reasonable and I had concentrated carefully to avoid slurring my words, but after a moment of stillness, soft laughter encircled me before three pairs of even softer arms were guiding me up the steps.

TWICE in less than twenty-four hours you ended up sprawled out on the bed with me having to undress you, and it was getting to be a bit much. That mess Dr. Buzzard brewed up was known to take paint off a wall — it had to be almost two hundred proof *after* he cut it down. What could have possessed you? Trying to be macho, no doubt. But you woke up after your wild drinking spree feeling a lot better than you deserved to. You had Mama Day to thank for that: she said just force two aspirin and a pint of water down your throat and you wouldn't have a hangover in the morning. Personally, I wanted you to suffer, especially when you got up arrogant and lying through your teeth about the condition you'd been in. Yes, I was always exaggerating and downright spiteful because you had gone out and had a little fun alone without clinging to my side. And, oh, now, you weren't going to humor me by having tea and dry toast for breakfast. You felt fine this morning because there had been absolutely nothing wrong with you last night. You insisted on pancakes and I *soaked* them with butter. You didn't stay arrogant long, did you. I didn't even bother repeating myself about your stomach muscles being paralyzed — you couldn't have heard me anyway with your head buried in the toilet.

I could have told you then, the vacation was over. Grandma and

Mama Day had decided that there'd be no more free time for you, kid. But you wouldn't have believed me because they never said a word as they sat at that kitchen table chatting away with you retching in the background. But I knew them: idle hands are the devil's workshop, and you had come home reeking with his brew. There was a soul in that bathroom to be saved with hard work. They were going to demand practically every minute of your day while you would think you were volunteering your butt off. When she puts her mind to it, no one can beat a southern woman at manipulating a man. And these women had been around long enough to take it to the level of art.

They were much too skilled to honey, sweetheart, or sugar you into anything. On the contrary, you would be told to run off, to rest, to leave them alone with their work. But context would be their master stroke and versatility their finishing touch. So Grandma starts out talking about her age. This will probably be the last year she'd fool with that garden. Her appetite is hardly what it used to be — why worry about growing beans? More there than she'll ever use and even too many to give away. A long, long sigh. She'll just go on up to the store and buy a few old frozen packages of something. She's a lot better off than them other old people she reads about in the newspapers having to eat cat food. You see, then she totally drops that subject. Goes on to something else, and finally with another long, long sigh, she says that since these beans are already growing, she'll go through the last hurrah and get out there and tie them up. To grab at her back when she stands up would be a bit too much, so she just shuffles slowly toward the rear porch. And, of course, you volunteer. That's gentle pity.

Mama Day jumps in by the afternoon and uses fierce pride. She waits until she spies you on the porch before dragging that heavy rag rug out to the clothesline. She lets it trail along the ground, stopping several times to hoist it up in her arms. That gives you the time to get across the road with an offer of help that's flatly and emphatically refused as she struggles unsuccessfully — much too unsuccessfully — to swing it over the line. You get begrudging thanks for insisting that you do it and finally several pointers on the most effective way to beat out the dust. But she'll keep you supplied with lemonade for your dry throat — at least she ain't too old and decrepit to squeeze a few lemons. They exchange tactics on the second day and by the third, none are needed. You've been allowed to overhear the quiet whispers about how marvelous you are, to witness glimpses of melting awe at the strength of your back, your arms. Yeah, they could lie back now, your ego would take over.

I guess if I'd really taken those lessons to heart, we could have gotten along better. They had you under their heels and you were purring. But I found treating a grown man like a five-year-old a little nauseating. If they had just come out and said, We want you to help around the house, you would have. As a matter of fact, you would have done it for the remainder of your vacation and not have resented it. That was more my style: Hey, look, keep your tail here and help me. But like I said, they were artists. And they wove the illusion that you were doing more than helping, you were in charge. You wanted to do all those chores. You even thought of things to be done that hadn't crossed their minds. The *fact* that you weren't in charge had absolutely nothing to do with the results: Grandma's roof got painted, the garden got weeded, Mama Day's rugs were spotless. And you were too tired to go anywhere. If you only knew, I thought, watching you laughing and talking with them on the porch at night. Grandma shelling boiled peanuts for you, Mama Day rubbing liniment into your sore shoulders. And maybe you did know, but it was what you believed that counted.

THE WEST WOODS were a real pleasure to walk through. The ground was flat and dry with a well-worn path shaded by pine trees for a good distance in before you came upon sporadic patches of live oaks. You told me the names of the other trees that seemed to spring up just for the opportunity to provide a burst of color among all the dark greens and browns: magnolia, yellow jasmine, wisteria. None of these flowering trees had been in the other woods in such abundance. This place was more like a wild garden — and a garden with a water view. As I looked to the right through spots where the trees had thinned, I could glimpse bluish strips of The Sound. A little farther on and we can see it fully, you said. There was a short cut through the family plot. I didn't understand why we had to put moss in our shoes before entering the graveyard.

"It's a tradition," you said.

"But what does it mean?"

"I don't know — it's just something we've always done."

"Well, what would happen if I didn't?"

"Why be a pain in the butt, George? Nothing would happen if you didn't. But it shows respect."

"I was just asking — every tradition has some kind of background to it."

"Then ask Mama Day, she'd probably know."

An odd custom. But then I was entering the oddest graveyard I had ever seen. The tombstones — some granite, some limestone — were of varying heights with no dates and only one name. You explained that they were all Days so there was no need for a surname. But what, as in your case, if a woman married? You live a Day and you die a Day. Early women's lib, I said with a smile. A bit more than that, you answered. You showed me how they were grouped by generations: the seven brothers and then the seven before them. The sizes of the headstones represented the missing dates — but only in relationship to each other. There was a Peace who died younger than another Peace and so her stone was smaller. There was your mother's stone — Grace — and she had obviously died younger than her sister Hope. Mama Day, you said, would have the tallest stone. She'd already lived longer than any Day before her. The closeness of all this awed me — people who could be this self-contained. Who had redefined time. No, totally disregarded it. But it couldn't be the custom in the whole place. I remembered the tombstone at Chevy's Pass and mentioned it to you. Bascombe Wade's stone had been marked 1788–1823. Who exactly was he? And I got the same legend. The unnamed slave woman. The deeds to Willow Springs. The vigil by the ocean bluff. Except that you told me that woman had been your grandmother's great-grandmother. But it was odd again the way you said it — she was the great, great, grand, Mother — as if you were listing the attributes of a goddess. The whole thing was so intriguing, I wondered if that woman had lived at all. Places like this island were ripe for myths, but if she had really existed, there must be some record. Maybe in Bascombe Wade's papers: deeds of sale for his slaves. Where had his home been on this island? Did he have a family? Who erected his tombstone?

I stopped asking you questions you couldn't answer, because it was irritating you. I didn't know why, but I could guess. You were always very sensitive about your complexion, going out of your way to stress that you were a black woman if someone was about to mistake you for a Spaniard or Creole. It was certainly one I could never make. We only had to get into an argument for me to be reminded — your fists balled up on your hips, you drawing blood with your never-ending mouth — you were, in spirit at least, as black as they come. No, you could have easily descended from that slave woman who talked a man out of a whole island. But you hated to think about the fact that you might also be carrying a bit of him. What difference did it make? All of us carried strains of God-knows-what from God-knows-where except the American Indian. And if they were traced back far enough, there were strains of Asian blood in them. I thought it was unique that you had a heritage intact and solid enough to be able to walk over the same ground that your grandfather did, to be leading me toward the very house where your great-grandfather was born. Even your shame was a privilege few of us had. We could only look at our skin tones and guess. At least you knew.

The open slope just outside the circle of oaks surrounding your family plot provided a view of just a thin curve of the powder blue water in The Sound. Lying on that grassy slope with its tangled patches of wildflowers, I wondered how you ever brought yourself to leave a place like this. And you actually *owned* this land.

"No, I don't own it. Our children own it."

"But we don't have any children."

"Well, once you stop falling out unconscious at night, we will. And then it's theirs. Some kind of crazy clause in our deed. It's always owned two generations down. That's to keep any Day from selling it."

"But you're two generations down."

"Yeah, but once I was born it automatically flipped over to them."

"And what if you don't ever have any children?"

"A likely possibility, the way you've been acting lately."

"Come on, I'm serious."

"Well, I guess it reverts back to the original owner."

"How? The original owner is dead. Isn't that his tombstone at Chevy's Pass?"

"I don't know, George. Maybe to his original family over in Europe. Who cares?"

"Well, you should. And if you don't, I do. This is all too beautiful to let go."

"If Mama Day had to come back from her grave, this land isn't going anywhere — believe me."

"I don't want to go anywhere either. I could see myself staying here forever."

"Well, help yourself. Sure, it's nice in the summer. But the other nine months of the year, there is absolutely nothing going on here."

"Ambush Duvall manages — he farms."

"Oh, I can just see you farming. Ambush isn't playing, he works hard."

"I've worked hard all my life."

"You've *thought* hard all your life. A successful farm takes backbreaking work. Look at the condition you're in just from weeding a few rows of beans."

"So you wouldn't stay here with me?"

"No. You would not chain me down here while you played at growing tomatoes and corn. And this whole conversation is stupid anyway, because you have no intention of staying here and becoming a farmer."

"It's not a stupid conversation. The point is that you said you wouldn't stay with me."

"Not in Willow Springs."

"Well, that's good to know, Ophelia."

"George, I said 'till death do us part,' not starvation."

"I wouldn't let you starve."

"No, I'd have all those half-assed ears of corn you're dreaming of growing. Boiled corn. Fried corn. Cornbread. Succotash — if we could afford a can of lima beans. No thanks."

"So if I'd been a painter or a musician — or a farmer — you never would have looked at me. Not enough security."

"Why are we talking about this? You were not a painter or a trumpet player. You were you. And I married *you*."

"I'd still be me if I stayed here. And so what if I had a dream? You wouldn't be there for me."

"Okay, George. This is what you want to hear: anywhere in the world you go and anything you want to do, I'm game. I'll freeze myself, starve myself, wear Salvation Army clothes to be by your side. I'll steal for you, lie for you, crawl on my hands and knees beside you. Because a good woman always follows her man."

"Let's just drop it, Ophelia."

"Yes, let's."

"But I'm going to remember what you said."

"Please do."

It was so hard to tell with you. On one level I believed that if offered an ultimatum, you would be there if I chose to go scrambling after some sort of impossible dream. And I was hardly the man to do that: the steadiness and certainty of my work, of my marriage, was really all I wanted. And if we are defined by the limits of our desires, then the man you met was one for whom an impossible dream was un-thinkable. I was putting you into an unfair position: I might as well have asked, I know you married me as a human, but what if I turned into a frog tomorrow? Would it be over? Basically, you were saying it would be. Realistically, you were right. But in the midst of a setting that was so unreal — the water, the flowers, the trees — I had an intense urge for you to offer reassurance that there were no limits to how far we would go for each other.

I wasn't going to get it that day. You were in a mood. And I guess that old adage was true: you keep 'em laid and you keep 'em happy. But I had just been too tired the last few days. There was so much to be done around that place and those poor old ladies couldn't handle the heavier work. Your grandmother's foundation needed cementing, the east end of her garden had to be plowed under, Miss Miranda's chicken coop could use a good coat of whitewash after it was cleaned out. I dreaded the thought of the last task. I didn't want to admit that I was a little afraid of live chickens, but what to do when you see her dragging gallons of disinfectant by herself? She had promised to fence them off so I could work in peace. Yeah, if I ran from roosters, how could I be a farmer? But there was more to do in Willow Springs than farm. I could fish, open some sort of store at the bridge junction, or just sell Bruce my half of the business and write textbooks while we raised a family. It wouldn't cost much to live down here. We could heat our home with solar energy — it had to stay warm more than six months out of the year. And all of this beauty to make up for what you were giving up. A nice dream. I leaned over and whispered in your ear.

"Let's play Adam and Eve."

"You know, George, I'll be so damned glad to get you back to New York. You've just about lost your mind down here. I hardly know you anymore."

"Never pleased — and this time you're the one with no imagination. We have a chance to sneak up among these trees and take advantage of paradise, and you're sitting there with your knees locked."

"You really don't know this place. But just go on and roll around in those woods with your clothes off, and the first red ant that bites your behind will tell you all about paradise."

I laughed but you only smiled, and with effort at that.

"What's wrong, Ophelia?"

"I don't know, I . . ." Your fingers pulled and pulled at the grass. "Why is it taking me so long to get pregnant?"

"We've only been trying for three months."

"Maybe we've waited too long. And now I'm too old."

"Thirty-two? And I'm just thirty-five. Baby, we average only thirty-three and a half years old. And next year, we'll average only thirty-four and a half. The year after that . . ."

"I get the point, George."

"I don't think you do — there's no rush."

"I just feel like there is. I don't know, maybe . . ."

"Hey, look. We can scratch the fig leaves, but from now on we'll just work overtime. I've put in worse hours doing much less pleasant things."

"But it should be natural."

"What won't be natural? I could jump your bones twice as much as you let me anyway."

"There you go, lying again. I never refuse you."

"In the mornings?"

"Six A.M., George!"

"You see, that's the problem. We've just got one of those kids waiting to come here at dawn. And you're going to have to accommodate it. And if the first one's a girl, we'll call her Dawn. Let's do that with all our kids. Dawn, Midnight, Shower — Oops. It'll be an easy way to educate them about sex. Just explain their names to them."

I finally got you to laugh, but your eyes remained sad as they looked out over The Sound.

"You know, you can be a very sweet man."

"I try."

YES, GEORGE, you tried hard. But it would have been too much to ask for you to understand those whispers as we passed through my family plot. As soon as I put the moss in my shoes, I could hear them all in the wind as it moved through the trees and stirred up dust along the ground. That's what upset me so the day we first sat right here, looking at the water. A beautiful day like this. I knew I wasn't the best of wives, but I gave it my personal best and you — or any man — would have to accept that or nothing at all. And I was lucky enough to have found someone who often accepted much less than the best from me. So how — I wanted to scream at all those silent whispers — how would I break his heart? Instead of screaming at them, and having you think I'd lost my mind, I snapped at you. And you probably thought I was in one of my uglier moods. Well, it was the lesser of two evils.

No, you didn't know this place. And you didn't know my people. I was sorry I had brought you — on that walk, to Willow Springs period. And if what they said held any truth, then I was sorry I had married you. But I'd never allow myself to think that, so I told myself it had all been a figment of my imagination. I was simply annoyed because you were being dreamy and hypothetical. You'd last in Willow Springs about as long as a blizzard lasted. Or would you? Could there be just an outside, outside chance that you would insist on staying down here? Stranger things had happened — they had just happened when we passed through the family plot. And if you really insisted, after all the fuming, battles, and hysterics, *really* insisted, what would I do? Why, I'd resent that you'd put me in a position like that, that you'd demand something of me that you knew I absolutely did not want. Yes, I might even hate you for it. And I would stay. But we'd be trampling on dangerous ground: to be unable to live without some-one is one thing, to be forced to prove it continually is something else again. No, it was all a dream for a lazy summer afternoon. Our marriage was safe within a catch-22: knowing I cared enough to go beyond the limits for you, you'd have to care enough not to ask me.

So what could those voices possibly mean? The voices I told myself I hadn't heard in the graveyard and did not hear when we got to the other place. The house where my grandmother was born and her father before her. The stories about my great-grandfather, John-Paul, were legion and just as fanciful as the ones about what Mama Day could do out there in that garden. Sure, when a child I was delighted with the game of following Mama Day around her garden, looking under bushes and in tree hollows for the family of mockingbirds her daddy carved so lifelike one day they just took off and set up housekeeping on their own. John-Paul's wooden roses and lilies sprouted buds and his magnolia leaves dripped dew. But his oldest daughter did him one better: her trees sang and her flowers took flight.

Wonderful stories that fed a child's imagination through her eyes and ears. I saw those same flying petals now as our legs brushed a patch of zinnias and startled a group of scarlet butterflies. It was exactly what you said, an old house with a big garden. The oldest house in Willow Springs. The only house with three stories and a full verandah, a second floor balcony, sloping dormers, and bay windows. Too old to have been built by even my great-grandfather, but he played on those verandah steps and later he climbed them with his new bride, Ophelia. What had Grandma said about her mother: an unhappy woman who never recovered from the loss of her youngest child? But Mama Day, in her no-nonsense fashion, had gone right to the bone: crazy as a bedbug and she died without peace. Yes, just an old house with a rocking chair on the porch. A hand-carved rocking chair that was moving ever so slightly in the breeze from The Sound, its rounded slats creaking relentlessly against the wooden planks. Why couldn't you hear it? Over and over: *you'll break his heart*. You wanted to sit in the rocking chair and play southern gentleman with me on your lap. I wanted us to get out of there; I couldn't stand it anymore.

THERE WAS NOTHING to stop that house from sitting right in the beginning of the nineteenth century except a fresh coat of paint. White paint, of course, because it had originally belonged to Bascombe Wade.

Or he had originally lived in it; it actually belonged to the garden engulfing it on four sides and there was little difference between that garden and the woods that stopped at the front gate. It was an old house *and* it was an old garden: a garden designed by a woman. A subtle arrangement of human hands had peach trees and pecan trees flowing into flowering bushes flowing into low patches of herbs; the same herbs you grew in our kitchen window flourished in abundance outside the door that led into the pantry of that house. And then there were so many strange plants I didn't recognize and you couldn't help me with; the refrain was familiar by now — ask Mama Day. It was her garden and the iron kettles near the huge fireplace I saw through the windows were for her medicines. Those dried bundles of herbs over the mantel may have been hers, but they hung on hooks that were rusted and ancient. Miss Miranda was not the first to use them.

It was an odd place for a plantation owner to have a home, isolated in the woods like that, but odd had been the word for that day. Your behavior, the graveyard, the facts that were as clear as your complexion while you ignored the evident — you'd inherited his house. No, you'd inherited *their* house. The other place. Had he built it so he could come out here and be with her? Sit on that verandah and watch her pruning roses that grew as large as my fist, snipping sprigs of mint for his tea? It was a nice image but it didn't feel that way. The place felt uneasy in spite of the gentle breezes coming from The Sound. That house had known a lot of pain. And more than what you talked about: your great-grandmother, Ophelia, losing her baby daughter at the bottom of a well; closing herself off from her husband and her children. Your grandmother hating the place so much she hadn't set foot there in over fifty years. No, there was something more, and something deeper than the old historical line about slave women and their white masters. A slave hadn't lived in this house. And without a slave, there could be no master. What had Miss Miranda said — he had claim to her body, but not her mind? Yes, that house resonated *loss*. A lack of peace. And both had begged for peace. What caused those two people to tear each other apart in this old house with a big garden?

But, God, it was a lovely place. Why not move out here for the last week of our vacation — a sort of second honeymoon. We could wake up and see what those morning glories entwined around the pillars would look like in full bloom. There was an ancient bed on the second floor, a mahogany headboard ten feet high, and we could call the girl Mahogany — Mahogany Andrews. Let's bring ourselves into the house and erase a little of the sadness. Your grandmother would have a fit, you said, a natural fit. The other place wasn't a joke to her. I wasn't trying to turn it into a joke; I felt we had something to give — maybe something we owed — to those other couples who tried but didn't make it. I was that sure about us; we could defy history. Obviously, I was not the first young man to stand on that verandah and feel that way.

◇◇◇

DEATH. Miranda feels death all around her. A bowl in her lap and her hands coated with peach juice, she can't shake it off. She frowns real, real deep, picking up another peach and peeling away the skin without hardly touching the flesh underneath. The slippery ease of it disturbs her until her knife hits the hard core as she whacks the fruit into slices. It ain't like the death she been planning for Buzzard for the last two days. First lying about her to that boy and then dropping him off like a sack of potatoes in the front yard drunk as a skunk. Naw, all them fancy tortures she was visualizing to get back at Buzzard would probably only amount to her letting all the air out of his tires or sneaking over to the south woods and throwing potash into his still. This here was real death. But whose? It didn't have to be a who — it could be a what.

Why, she was feeling the way she felt just before they got a sudden fall. Overnight the air turning cool and frost killing tomatoes on the vine. Leaves dropping like rain from the trees. She was feeling change. Naw, it didn't have to be a who — but it could be. It could be I'm getting beyond old, she thinks, stirring cinnamon, vanilla, and sugar into her peaches. Could be I'm getting to be Old's mama. It seems like it in her bones when she stands up to heat the stove. That liniment works a shorter and shorter time with the years. Her bones are talking today. But something else was telling her something and if it just got a little louder, she was willing to listen. She measures out the flour for her pie crusts, throws in a pinch of salt, quickly starts working in her shortening. But she always sprinkles her ice water and seeing it dripping from her fingers into the bowl, everything stops. Her head turns to the salt shaker, she picks it up again on the slant, and her eyes widen as the clumped-up crystals start falling slowly over each other. Like them forgotten nickelodeons, the pictures move backward and it all falls into place.

From the dripping water to the clumped-up salt to the white foam washing up on shore at the east side of the island. And so much in between. Them waves had been coming in — just a bit too fast. After ninety years the natural motion shoulda been in her blood, but she had been talking, hadn't she? Talking and fishing. Talking and walking. She walks back over it all now: them high high hills the crawfish built up around the mouths of their burrows; the kingfishers and bank swallows nesting way way up from the water; bush rabbits — she walks past a dozen of them hollows if she walks past one, and all of them is deep deep into the ground. And right there at Chevy's Pass, Buzzard's bees are clustered close close to the door of their hives. Yes, it was high high, way way, and deep deep. This was gonna be a big big storm. Miranda goes to the back door of her trailer — wind steady from the southeast and not a cloud in the sky, Oh, Lord. She shakes her head, looking at George out back, whitewashing the sides of her chicken coop. There's more of it on him than on them walls, but he's going at it full of steam. A waste of effort; the thing might not be standing by the end of the week.

She apologizes to her chickens, calling them foolish for standing with their backs to the wind for days, when she was the real fool. What had she told that boy? You just gotta watch all these creatures long enough to find out what's going on in the elements where they live. Well, she had looked without seeing, listened without hearing. Ain't her rag rugs been warping and the chairs been creaking? Ain't she been listening to crickets trying to tear their legs off for nights on end? Listening without hearing. But she knew what she'd hear now: crows, hawks, ducks, and geese making a mighty racket for no *earthly* reason; 'cause the reason was coming in from the southeast, pushing clear skies before it. And storms like that are born in hell.

The last one blew the bridge down back in 1920 when she was younger than Baby Girl. She was living at the other place with John-Paul then and The Sound almost reached their back steps, saltwater gouging out the soil, killing their garden and leaving hordes of dead fish piled up along the trunks of the fruit trees. That is, the trees that were still standing. Nothing much was standing out there after that storm. She claimed that garden back, inch by inch, handful of soil by handful of soil. If it happens again, Miranda sighs, I ain't got another sixty years. She finishes rolling out her pie crusts and has 'em in the oven before she rings up Abigail.

"You there, Sister?"

"Uh, huh."

"A storm's coming."

"Ya know, I been feeling something for days."

"This here is an 18 & 23er."

It's a sharp intake of breath — "Lord have mercy."

Miranda remembers that Abigail was carrying Peace when the last one hit. Her husband was caught beyond the bridge, and Abigail came to wait out the storm with Miranda and her daddy in the other place. Behind them shutters in the darkened house, John-Paul whittled while Abigail sat in Mother's rocker, her hands resting high up on her stomach as Miranda fed the parlor fire and heard the garden die. What was Daddy whittling that day? A toy for his first grandbaby? Whatever, it was lost and so was Peace. And it was the last time Abigail set foot in the other place.

"Are you sure, Miranda?"

"The signs don't lie, Abigail. At least, not these signs."

"It may not hit us head-on."

"It may not. But it's best to be prepared."

"Oh, no — and with the children here. And their party tomorrow night."

"Watch the sky, it ain't coming before tomorrow. But it's coming soon."

"What have I done to deserve this trouble?"

"Abigail, stop your foolishness. All God got in mind is to send *you* a hurricane? It ain't got nothing to do with us, we just bystanders on this earth. Sometimes I think we was only a second thought — and a poor second thought at that."

"Well, the Scriptures do say it: man was the last thing the Lord made."

"He shoulda quit while He was ahead."

"I ain't listening to this blasphemy today, Miranda. Not with a storm on the horizon. And don't come sitting over in my house, 'cause I don't want it blown down."

"So you'd leave me over here in this flimsy old trailer?"

"It'll be a fitting punishment for you."

Miranda has her peach pies cooling on the countertops and table when she goes out back to see how George is coming with the chicken coop. He's got himself a job, 'cause her hen house is larger than some garages in Willow Springs. The long-handled brush he's using can reach up to the roof, but until he got the knack of shaking out the excess and covering a section with small strokes he splattered white-wash all up his arms and across his face. It's a good thing she found a pair of her daddy's old overalls for him — he woulda made a mess of them city clothes. He actually looks like he's having fun, John-Paul's overalls belted around his middle, him working away white as a ghost. Her coop looks fine, too. She ain't got the heart to tell him right now that it might all be in vain.

Miranda looks up at the sky. Clear. Clear as a bell. But the chickens pinned up in wire cages is making an awful racket. She gotta get them out of there soon or they'll start eating each other alive. She don't know why folks believe chickens are cowardly. She's seen two of 'em stand toe to toe and peck each other to death. And you couldn't get her to go near a brooder's nest for nothing in the world, unless she was after losing an eye or a plug out of her hand. She even had an old hen once that would attack a rooster — a young rooster, spurs and all. Naw, that boy had the right idea being a little wary. If you don't know their ways, it's best to give 'em their distance.

"You appear to be a man who could stand a big hunk of peach pie with a tall glass of iced coffee."

"It sounds like heaven, but I want to finish this first."

"You ain't gotta worry about the back. Nobody sees it facing the woods."

"No, when you do a job, you do it right. It's not going to take me much longer."

Miranda just nods but she likes his answer. It scares her sometimes how much she likes this boy. She hopes Baby Girl knows what she's got. It would be a crying shame for them to go the way of so many of these young people nowadays. Just letting things crumble apart, 'cause everybody wants to be right in a world where there ain't no right or wrong to be found. My side. He don't listen to my side. She don't listen to my side. Just like that chicken coop, everything got four sides: his side, her side, an outside, and an inside. All of it is the truth. But that takes a lot of work and young folks ain't about working hard no more. When getting at the truth starts to hurt, it's easier to turn away. Yeah, you go on and paint the back of my coop so them live oaks can witness what you made of.

◈◈◈

OUR WORST FIGHT EVER. And it was all your fault. I had told you a thousand times — not once, not a dozen — a thousand: if you don't really want my honest opinion (about your hair, clothes, shade of eyeshadow, or the latest fashions for Pygmy women) *don't* ask me for it. And you kept pushing, didn't you? You always looked good to me, no matter what you wore. But that answer wouldn't satisfy you that night, and it's not as if we were dressing to petition the pope. It was a simple gathering of people you'd known all your life. I was going to be the one under scrutiny, and it had taken me only twenty minutes to ensure that they wouldn't think you'd married a slob. I was a little nervous to begin with and your constant complaining about the humidity caking up your powder and curling your hair only put me more on edge. Who was coming to this party? An old boyfriend or something? Yes, the halter top was fine with the strings shortened, the strings long, tied into a bow, tied into a knot — untied. I came up behind you at the mirror and kissed the neck I was fighting the urge to strangle. You had used lavender water for so many years, your perspiration carried its scent without your wearing any. But that night they were in full bloom as I ran my thumbs from your chin to collarbone to relax the taut muscles under your soft skin. It helped you but now my groin muscles were tightening, and the second time I brushed my lips across your neck was for me. Just leave the top off altogether, I said as my fingertips stroked your stomach, and we just won't tell anyone. I got an elbow right in the ribs.

"You're not being a help, George. Everything's a joke to you. And stop wrinkling my blouse."

"Okay, okay. No hands — see?"

"Is my make-up all right?"

"It's fine."

"No, really."

"Really, it's fine. I like that eyeshadow on you."

"But you hate the foundation?"

"No, I don't hate the foundation."

"So why didn't you mention the foundation?"

"You didn't ask me about it."

"I asked you about my make-up — that's eyeshadow, lipstick, foundation, blush — all of it."

"Ophelia, that is great eyeshadow, great lipstick, great blush. There will be a hundred women here tonight who would kill for your eyelashes, since you never need mascara. And I don't hate your foundation."

"I guess you think I'm stupid — or deaf. Not hating something isn't the same as liking it. You purposely did not say that you liked this foundation."

"Guilty as charged."

"And?"

"Well, sweetheart, why do you always buy make-up that's too dark for you?"

"This is not too dark for me."

"Okay."

"But you think it is, don't you?"

"To be honest, yes."

"Well, who asked you?"

I had been married long enough to shut up when a conversation reached this point, there was nowhere to go from here but down into a brawl. And it was not the time or place. I didn't remember what I mumbled under my breath, but I knew what I was thinking: if you wanted to smear that muddy stuff on your face with a bare back and arms so you looked like a Tootsie Pop, it was your business. These were your friends, not mine. It took two to tango and I was determined to let the music play on and sit this one out. But you had been married long enough as well to know how to push the right buttons to get me started.

◇◇◇

THE VOICES behind the closed bedroom door been rising and falling, rising and falling, for a good twenty minutes. Every now and then Miranda and Abigail will catch a word that don't make no sense to them, but it means something inside 'cause it sets off a fresh slew of shouting. Mascara. Shawn. Pumpernickel bread. Them kids might as well be fighting in Arabic. Miranda realizes there's a whole world in there that she ain't got nothing to do with. Abigail spreads the lace tablecloth and wrings her hands, sets out the punch bowl and wrings her hands, while Miranda keeps on slicing up peach pie as calmly as if she was at a church supper. The first crash catches her off guard so she jumps a little, the next string of words flying through that door meaning about the same in any language. Right behind it comes another crash with a chair getting turned over, but she still won't let Abigail barge into that room. Somebody wants help, they'll call for it. And he ain't in there killing your baby. If anybody's doing the killing, it's her.

The quiet that follows worries Abigail more than the noise before a door gets slammed and water starts running in the bathroom. She's near about in tears when Cocoa finally comes into the living room, a little flushed and out of breath, but none the worse for wear. Miranda's interpretation of events seems a bit closer to the truth when Cocoa asks her what George could do to stop a cut on his head from bleeding. How big a cut, Miranda wants to know. Not big enough, Cocoa tells her.

◇◇◇

OUR WORST FIGHT EVER. And it was all your fault. You knew how nervous I was about that night and not a bit of sympathy. That's because you never remembered anything important I told you. No one in Willow Springs thought that anyone would ever want to marry me and half of them were coming just to be sure that you were real. It had taken four years to get you down here, and each time I came home alone it was the same doubt in their eyes. Who could possibly want the leper? It was awful growing up, looking the way I did, on an island of soft brown girls, or burnished ebony girls with their flashing teeth against that deep satin skin. Girls who could summon all the beauty of midnight by standing, arms akimbo, in the full sun. It was torture competing with girls like that. And if some brave soul wanted to take me out, they would tell him that I had some rare disease that was catching. It would have been worse if I hadn't been a Day. Everyone respected my family name, and Mama Day let it be known that anyone calling me anything that she didn't call me would have to tangle with her. If they wanted to see a leper, she had ways to show them a real leper when they woke up one morning. I was treated very differently beyond the bridge — my physical features were an asset at times. But I was always distrustful of the black men who fawned over me. What was there about me that I should be so highly prized? Sure, I had grown up enough to accept myself, and no, I was hardly an ugly woman. But there had to be something a little twisted within them to think of me as a true beauty.

I know my old school friends were shocked to find out that you were successful, so it meant that you probably drooled on your shirt front or had such a godawful personality that you couldn't get any other woman but me. I couldn't wait for them to meet you so I could gloat. And I was going to be dressed for the part. Eat your hearts out — and he's all mine. I couldn't believe that you would sit there and watch me get ready for a whole hour before deciding that you wanted to fool around. Where were you when I came out of the shower without my hair done and my make-up on? And then to get back at me you refused to tell me what you knew I needed so desperately to hear. Of course that foundation wasn't the right shade, but couldn't you lie? I had to be perfect that evening and I was shattered. But it wasn't the time or place for an argument, I was going to ignore you until you made that snide remark about me looking like a Tootsie Pop. Loud — you practically shouted it all the way across the room.

"I think you'd be the last authority on make-up for me, since you spent all your time running around with white women before I rescued you."

"It was *a* woman named Shawn who happened to be white. A difference with a huge distinction."

"Look, George, what you wanted was what you wanted. And what you got was what you got. It's that simple. I know I'm not your ideal —"

"And neither was she."

"Yeah, right."

"Right!"

"So what was your ideal, George?"

"I'm not getting into this with you."

"No, I really want to know. Have I disappointed you that badly?"

"Ophelia, you haven't disappointed me at all. Only a fool would spend his life looking for some dream woman. The right woman is the one you can live with, not the one in your head. The one in my head was sheer fantasy. I used to have images of someone who was deep, deep brown . . ."

"Oh, deep brown?"

"Yeah, an even brown all over — her lips and everything. With smoky eyes. Crazy, huh? And she'd be dimpled and curved, so that every place you touched there was a roundness that was warm and she — "

"A woman? You were fantasizing about humping a loaf of pumpernickel bread. That's beyond sick, George. That's sicker than running after white girls."

"Don't you ever ask me anything again, okay? I was trying to be serious. And when you say I don't talk to you, this is why. You're hopeless. You can take the ignorant and turn it into the sublime."

"Oh, now I'm stupid?"

"No, true stupidity is genetic. Your ignorance is a deliberate choice."

"Well, I'm sure all your white women weren't ignorant."

"A woman — Shawn. Shawn!"

"That's right, tell the whole house. Go open the window so they can hear you up in Canada, since you want the world to know that you haven't forgotten her name!"

"And little else about her."

"Of course not — your precious redhead with freckles. If I hear that redhead-freckled shit once more, I'll throw up. She sure messed with your mind — to be proud of going out with Howdy Doody in drag!"

"I'm not proud of it — and I'm not ashamed, although you keep trying, don't you. Well, it just won't work. That was a good time in my life."

"After that dream, I must be a poor second best."

"Yeah, a living nightmare. I hope that finally makes you feel dark enough, so you can just stop this garbage."

"Attacking me doesn't change the fact that you have your values all screwed up."

"And you're the one painting yourself with tar? Don't you preach to me about values until you learn to accept what you are and wipe that crap off your face."

"Get out of here and leave me alone."

"Baking yourself in the sun all the time — you're headed straight for skin cancer."

"I said leave me alone! Go on out there and wait for all your ideal women to show up — the place will be crawling with them. And if you strike out here, when you get back to New York, you can fuck the other kind you like until you're dizzy."

"Any kind that knows what she is would be an improvement."

"You can kiss my . . ."

"That would be an improvement too."

"Better yet — go kiss something on Shawn. She's the one who made you so goddamned happy."

"Being with a real woman would make any man happy."

"She wasn't woman enough to hold you!"

"Or a bitch enough to keep reminding me!"

I swear to you, that vase materialized out of nowhere into my hand . . .

◇◇◇

CARS ARE PARKED all along the roadbed and jammed into Abigail's front yard. This being a word-of-mouth invitation, anybody with a mouth to wrap around some peach pie shows up. Bernice and Ambush get there with the first group and she's still double-strapping Little Caesar into that convertible, even though he's riding next to his Grandma Pearl. Most folks are in what you'd call their middling clothes: a little fancier than everyday since it ain't every day you get invited to meet a visitor from New York City, and a little less than Sunday wear, him hardly being the angel Gabriel.

Folks who woulda been standing around talking about two things end up talking about three. The weather is first off when they come into the house with them bulletins being on the radio and TV all day.

A tropical storm is heading toward Florida, due to hit by tomorrow morning. Might peter out before it gets to Willow Springs, and then again it might not. A little rain would be welcome, a lot of rain a nuisance, and more than that — well, it's to be fretted over when the time comes. Just keep listening to them bulletins. You better listen to the crows, Miranda says. When it gets so they start screaming, the wind's gonna come in screaming too. The older heads, like her, remember 1920 and each got a story to tell. How whole trees come up by the roots, a Model T sent a mile down the road, the bridge exploding like it been fused with dynamite. The telling of the old stories gets better than the forecasting of the new storm and just about as fanciful. Pearl was hardly born and she got one about a house being set, furniture in place and all, right smack on the roof of another house. To some that sound more like a tornado than a hurricane; to Miranda it's pure nonsense, since she was twenty-five that year. Nonsense or not, Pearl says, if something that big again is heading this way, her God will protect her. Miranda hopes He tells her to get her butt away from low ground — she done built that house too close to the water.

George gets asked a dozen times if hurricanes come his way. Rarely, he tells them in that clipped, proper way of his. Still the city can see some pretty bad storms. It don't matter what answer he gives as long as they can get him to themselves for a few minutes, since he's the second thing folks come to talk about. They been waiting years for this opportunity. It don't pass notice that him and Cocoa manages to always be on different sides of the room, while it's Abigail or Miranda who's left to introduce him to folks. Polite as all get-out, he don't fill the picture most had in their minds: taller for some, shorter for others; broader, narrower. And nobody expected to see that big old bandage over the left side of his head, which gives them the third thing to talk about. How did it happen? In one of them Central Park muggings? No, he tells them, he was out walking and ran into a tree branch.

"What was her name?" Parris asks him, grinning.

"Huh?"

"Your tree branch? I once ran into one by the name of Louise. And got a missing tooth to prove it."

Someone else ran into a Bernadette who dislocated his right jaw. A

Hester who was partial to splitting lips. A Tina Marie who bit a plug from his arm when he was out sleepwalking at night.

"Yeah, you gotta watch them tree branches." Ambush puts his arm around George's shoulder. "Especially the ones we grow here in Willow Springs."

"And Junior Lee done run into whole ruby-colored *tree trunks*, ain't you, Junior Lee?" Parris asks.

"Neeever," Junior slurs.

"Ain't no tree branch ever gonna get me, either." Dr. Buzzard hitches up his pants. "Unless it wants to get chopped down."

"Buzzard, you can just be quiet," Miranda says. "You in this house by my good graces, 'cause I don't feel like showing out in front of real company. But I got a reckoning with you."

"Now, Mama Day, everybody's standing around having a little fun and you gotta bring up ancient history. I was just about to tell you I ain't tasted pie this fine since Hector was a pup."

"Well, you better eat your fill. 'Cause it's the last you or Hector is getting from me."

Miranda takes the empty punch bowl into the kitchen to refill it. For the occasion she's adding fresh pineapple to her secret recipe and the party's going real well, 'cause the riffraff she didn't want no way left early when they found out Buzzard wasn't gonna spike the punch. And she had to admit he was on his good behavior for her; he knew not to press his luck. She was almost decided against not letting the air out of his tires. Miranda looks up while she's stirring in the raspberry syrup, and Bernice is in the kitchen door holding Little Caesar. His shorts, knee socks, and shirt are light blue and match her dress. She sews that way for all of them, but Ambush refuses to wear pastel dress clothes — we ain't triplets, he says, we're his parents. Bernice is standing there like she don't know whether to come or go, hitching up Little Caesar on her narrow hips.

She ain't visited proper with Miranda since the baby was born. In church or at the bridge junction, she might swap a few words with her if they happen to meet but she seldom lingers. Miranda's never acted no different, admiring the baby when she gets a chance and passing on a hint or two about his milk, his teething, his potty training. If Bernice appeared nervous when Miranda was near him, it was the same with anybody near him. But Miranda knows she probably wouldn't be there tonight if Ambush hadn't made her come for Cocoa and George. Whatever was going on in that child's head, she'd have to work it out for herself.

"Ain't he getting too big for that?" Miranda concentrates on measuring in more syrup, "You gotta watch your spine."

"But when I let him down, he runs all over the place. I don't want him getting into nothing."

"Then you just make him stay by your side."

"Easier said than done, Mama Day."

"Yeah, raising a child ain't easy."

The talking just outside the kitchen makes the silence inside seem heavier while Bernice shifts her weight from one leg to the other, watching Miranda, who is right comfortable stirring her punch and tasting it for sweetness. Little Caesar starts whining and reaching out to the table.

"You want a little?" Miranda says, and the child nods. "You got a tongue — ask for it."

"Give me some juice."

"That ain't how nothing is gotten in this house. Mama Day, may I have some juice, please."

"Please."

"Now, that's nice. Come on here and get it. But you gotta walk like the big boy you are."

Bernice puts him down and he takes his little knobby-kneed self over to Miranda. He eyes her kinda suspicious while drinking his punch, two hands grasping the cup tight. Finishing it up real quick, he holds the cup up to Miranda with a big grin on his face. And he starts looking puzzled when she don't take it from him.

"Let me tell you something about please," Miranda says, taking his hand. "It ain't happy in the world all by itself. It gets real lonely without its twin brother — thank you."

"Thank you, Mama Day!" He's so happy with himself that he lets the cup drop. Bernice cries out and runs over, scaring him more than the cup that's rolling on the floor. Little Caesar glances up at Miranda. "Oooh, look what I did, please." He's out the kitchen before Bernice can catch him, and Miranda laughs.

"You got a smart one there."

"I'm telling you, he's a trial." Bernice smiles, picking up the glass cup. She turns it round and round in them thin fingers of hers, watching the rainbows reflected off its edges. Her face is serious when she finally meets Miranda's eyes. "I never thanked you for my son."

"And you were right," Miranda says, taking the cup and giving her hand a gentle squeeze. "I ain't in the business of miracles, so I wasn't the one to thank."

There's only a scattering of folks left around now, what Miranda calls the second-class riffraff. The first-class took off when there wasn't any liquor and these others will wait till you throw 'em out just for the heck of it. That might not happen before next Tuesday from the looks of Abigail. She's running around dishing up pie and refilling glasses. Poor thing, Miranda thinks, she'll keep at it until she drops. Another half hour and she'll shoo their butts out of there. It may not be my house, but that's my sister. Looking around for the rest of her family, she finds Cocoa is still on one side of the room and George on the other, listening to Dr. Buzzard tell him and Junior Lee about the time he scared off them twelve haints in the south woods. That story is close to making Buzzard a legend in his own right.

Miranda motions for Cocoa to come over and sit down next to her. "Folks is thinking it's mighty peculiar, you and your husband ain't passed a single word all night."

Cocoa lets out a sigh and there's no fight in her voice. "I don't care what people are thinking. I wouldn't even be here if you and Grandma hadn't gone to so much trouble. And believe me, he's not worth it."

"Whatever it is, it ain't so bad it can't be patched up. I done seen him watching you two or three times when your back was turned, and he looked about as unhappy as you're sounding. Why don't you go over to him and make nice? Save the rest of the evening."

"After the things he called me, *I* should be the one to talk to him? He should live so long."

"You done called other people awful things, right in that very room. Called somebody an overbearing, domineering old woman, and that somebody didn't stop talking to you for the rest of your life. If my memory serves, that somebody came to you the next day and said she was willing to let bygones be bygones . . ."

"*If* I was ready to apologize for being a selfish, ungrateful heifer. Yes, I remember, Mama Day."

"The point is that if you care about someone enough, you give 'em a chance to take back the things they may have said in anger. And you oughta make the first move.'"

"Yeah, always the woman."

" 'Cause we got more going for us than them. A good woman is worth two good men any day when she puts her mind to it. So the little bit we gotta give up, we don't miss half as much."

Dr. Buzzard done just about roped and tied that last haint for George and Junior Lee when he sees Cocoa coming across the room. He leans over and tells George confidential-like that he got a cure for pruning them wild tree branches in his back yard, and since they was friends, he'd give it to him at a discount. George just shakes his head. Then how about a tradeoff? His tree pruning kit for George helping him get better mileage out of his still, him being an inventor and all. Junior Lee tells Buzzard he's out of his head, this here is a railroad man. George is trying to explain to them what he really does for a living when Cocoa puts her hand on his arm.

"Would you like some more punch, George?"

"No."

He turns his back to her and when she asks if maybe he'd want another piece of pie, he ignores her and keeps on talking. He takes off his tie clip and when he's demonstrating how marvelous them little indentations is, Cocoa agrees with him. He stops talking, flat out, waits for her to finish, and then never looking at her, picks up where he left off as if she wasn't there. There's fire in Cocoa's eyes, but since she got her lips pressed tight, it don't come out of her mouth and the red is left to flare up in her cheeks.

She ain't in the mood to talk to nobody now, so she goes out to the back porch. There's a sliver of a moon, kinda blurry through the hazy sky. Sitting on the steps, arms wrapped around her knees, she looks off in the distance at the east woods. After a while she can make out the dark of the trees from the dark of the horizon from the dark of the hilly ground. And if she breathes real soft, there's just a whisper of the ocean washing up on the far bluff. The dampness of the night sneaks up on her, but the longer she sits out there, the harder it is to get up and go back into the lighted house. She hears the screen door open and Junior Lee comes out and sits down beside her.

"If you was my wiiife, I wouldn't treat you that way."

Since Junior Lee ain't big on hints, he figures she don't answer because she wants to give him all the space he needs to talk.

"Yeah," he goes on, "if you was my wiiife, I'd keep you real happy."

There's more silence and it gives him more encouragement. He moves a little closer to her and Cocoa turns her head to him slowly. Her voice is awful quiet. "I'm going to tell you something, Junior Lee. And I want you to listen good. Right now, I'm angry. And since you're not the reason I'm angry, I'm giving you a chance to get away from me. There's no reason for you to be caught in the middle of something that's none of your business."

"But, honey, I want to maaake it my business."

"No, you don't."

"For a sweet thing like you, I'd do annythinng."

It's a deep, deep sigh for Cocoa. A sigh that says she's tired of fighting, tired of cussing — and much too tired to explain the obvious to the likes of Junior Lee. Whatever he takes her sigh to mean, it ain't that. And before she knows it, he's reached up and yanked the bow loose from her halter top. Cocoa holds her blouse up with one hand, brings the other around to swing at him and knocks her wrist on the porch railing. She don't hit it bad, but it gives her a reason she's been needing to cry. She jumps up and runs into the house. Junior Lee is set to run the other way and finds himself staring straight at Ruby.

"Baby," he says to the mountain, "she tricked me out here."

◇◇◇

I TRIED TO IMAGINE what could ever get me to possibly talk to you again after forcing me to meet a whole roomful of strangers, looking like an idiot. And since you'd always said I was not an imaginative man, I came up with nothing. I wouldn't talk to you in Willow Springs, I wouldn't talk to you on the plane home, I wouldn't talk to you back up in New York — I'd never talk to you again. The thought of such a silent future depressed me during breakfast, not your own silence, which I welcomed since I wasn't going to talk to you anyway. I was thinking about my children's college commencement and how strained the whole event would be for them and us. A big leap, indeed, with you sleeping in the room with your grandmother, but I'd had the whole night to worry about the effect on their toilet training, puberty, and choice of mates. What if my daughter married a moron because she grew up thinking that monosyllables were a natural form of communication? She deserved better than that, and so did any son of mine who would never argue back to a football referee. For their sake, I might relent and talk to you once they were old enough to know the difference.

But that morning there was absolutely no need. I didn't even have to look at you with your grandmother keeping up a constant flow of chatter about how nice the party was and how nice So-and-So looked and how nice So-and-So had filled out and how nice it was that everything was nice. I agreed with her about the people I could remember and asked questions about those I didn't. I liked Miss Abigail and was trying to make that breakfast as easy for her as possible. She was a genuinely soft woman — a touch high-strung, but with very fine sensibilities that filled her home with lace and chintz. And she obviously believed that vases were meant to hold wildflowers. The best thing I could have done for her was to leave early. I checked and there were no planes scheduled because of the hurricane warnings. I could have taken a train, but that was precluded by an impossible discussion of the whereabouts of my credit cards and extra money given to you for safe-keeping. I didn't know what your plans were for the day; I had promised to help brace down Miss Miranda's trailer and tighten your grandmother's shutters. I assumed that you were staying in Willow Springs; I knew I had to stay. So it appeared that we were to prepare ourselves for a storm.

◇◇◇

THE ROCKING CHAIR is put inside the parlor along with the potted plants that was on the verandah. The upstairs shutters are bolted, the screen door on the pantry is roped tight. Nothing left to do but for Miranda to take a final walk amidst her garden. She stoops to pull off a wilted leaf hereabouts, grab a handful of weeds there or so — like it's really gonna matter. She's just walking to remember in case nothing's left after tonight. They can storm-warn all they want, hurricane-watch till they're silly — she didn't have to stand by for no further bulletins. The only news that mattered started coming in a week ago; the final warnings she needed was in them snake trails she had to cross to get to the other place. Them diamondbacks and copperheads was always the last to smarten up. No, next to last; after the snakes came all them meters and graphs down at the Hurricane Center.

Miranda shakes her head and takes a final look around her garden before she turns her face to the sky. Gray. The color you'd get from blending a bridal dress and a funeral veil. A netted sheet of clouds is spreading up slowly from the southern horizon. Sorta like a web that she knows will get wider and thicker — and much much lower. Maybe not this time, Miranda thinks, but one time a wind's gonna come and blow this old house down. That's when it's soaked up about as much sorrow as it can and ain't nothing left for it to do but rot in little pieces at the bottom of The Sound. Lord, she's getting morbid. Well, it's the weather and the early grieving for the loss that's bound to come to all her work.

And she had built that garden back exactly the way it was, though it woulda made more sense to have the pecan trees behind the peach trees, so the taller branches wouldna blocked off the southern light. And she wasn't as partial to morning glories as she was to the deeper-colored wisteria, but it was to be morning glory vines that twined themselves on the pillars of the verandah. She'd known that without thinking like she'd known that kitchen garden must have a patch of pepper grass. She didn't cook with it, didn't use it in her medicines. But somebody had. And it wasn't Mother — Mother hardly cooked at all. And later she didn't eat much. Later she didn't do nothing but sit in that rocker, twisting on pieces of . . . Too much sorrow. Miranda sighs. Much too much. And I was too young to give you peace. Even Abigail tried and failed. No, this wasn't your garden.

That spreading cloud net from the south is just about over the main road as Ruby brings out a little stool to her front porch. She arranges her tiny ceramic jars on the table beside her chair and sits to watch for Cocoa. The jars are still hot from sitting in the boiling water on her stove, and she lays out her pile of colored string beside them. She's got a new brush and comb in case Cocoa forgets her own, but seeing her off a distance she knows she won't have to use 'em. She's coming with a canvas bag on her shoulders, dressed in one of them halter tops and shorts she likes so much. A long-legged stride that Ruby watches intently as the webbed clouds move on northward to cover Willow Springs.

◇◇◇

I HAD BEEN MAKING a list of what would have to happen before I'd ever speak to you again: a cold day in hell, a heat wave in Siberia, a blue moon (I scratched out a red sun — I'd seen plenty of those here), a winter Olympics in Antarctica, the Super Bowl in Havana, your left ear rotting off followed by your big right toe followed by your middle finger (either hand) followed by . . . — when one of Carmen Rae's children brought me that note from Miss Ruby. She had such tiny handwriting for a large woman, it was almost too small to read. *I'm sorry I married a fool. Come see me.* I could definitely identify with her problem. But as disgusting as Junior Lee was, I could forgive him easier than I could forgive you for treating me the way you did. At least he was a slime out in the dark — you were one in front of everybody. *I* was called a bitch, *I* was shoved over a chair, and still I'm the one who tried making up for you to ignore *me* like a piece of junk? Mister, you don't know how lucky you were that two old ladies stood between you and disaster.

I planned to visit Miss Ruby after I went shopping for fabric with Bernice. She had brought Little Caesar and he kept pulling off his shoulder straps when it took her almost twenty minutes to harness him to the car seat, making absolutely no sense with her driving less than twenty miles an hour. The hurricane she was worrying about so much would be here and gone by the time we got to the bridge junction. It seemed she couldn't talk and drive at the same time. She kept putting on her brakes to turn and look at me, her eyes widening at my story.

"Well, ain't that nothing? He calls you filthy names, knocks you over a chair, and then hits you in the head with a vase. You'd never guess it by the looks of him — all quiet and sweet."

"No, I hit him with the vase."

"Well, I don't blame you — him knocking you over a chair like that."

"No, Bernice. First I swung at him with the vase, *then* he pushed me. And the chair was behind me."

"Well, ain't that nothing? Like you supposed to stand by and hear yourself called them filthy names. A bitch — ain't it awful?"

"*And* a living nightmare."

"A living nightmare — ain't it awful? I'm telling you, Cocoa, these men are something else. And the quiet ones are the ones you gotta watch. Sneaky, you know what I mean? Still water runs deep. Folks always telling me what a saint Ambush is. But they don't know the half of it — he's got his ways. Not that I've ever been beat up like you."

"And you saw how he acted at the party."

"I sure did. Just as cool and collected, grinning and laughing with folks like there wasn't a thing wrong with him having that big bandage plastered on his head. When he shoulda been shamed to his shoes and your feelings hurt like that. Carrying on as if you weren't even there. Ain't that nothing?"

It certainly was. And I decided I wouldn't speak to you again even if they held the Super Bowl in Havana. Why, you would have to get down on your knees and crawl back. And then by the time we had finished shopping, I was starting to get really depressed because you would never crawl — so how were we going to get out of this mess? Life used to be so simple, on that same road I was taking up to Miss Ruby's. A lost notebook. A scraped elbow. Finding a double-dutch partner. Those were my biggest worries. And comfort came so easily with a good report card or being chosen captain in volleyball. Sitting on that little stool and letting her braid my hair brought that comfort back, the day she saved me from a spanking by removing the evidence that I'd been playing down in the ravine. Stickier problems had taken the place of cockleburs, but her huge legs were a fortress I could hide between and her voice was soothing.

I was brought close to tears when she apologized for Junior Lee. Here was a woman who had done nothing and she was asking me to forgive her. He was a dog, she said, an out-and-out dog. And she'd let him run loose too long. You had to watch your menfolk when they were weak like him, given to all kinds of temptation. And these young girls nowadays, she said, don't have a bit of shame. Will go around flinging themselves in front of men who ain't got the good sense to turn away. Yeah, Junior Lee was a trial to her — and it's time she was judge and jury. A soft hypnotic voice with firm fingers massaging that warm solution into my scalp. It's gonna make this pretty hair of yours prettier — she kept rubbing and rubbing — and these braids, she'd make sure these braids would hold good. Young girls like these braids nowadays, and it ain't nothing new. They was twisting up hair with twine from before she was my age. Pick a color, she told me. I let her choose, I didn't care, it was so wonderful not having any decisions to make.

Twenty years melted away under her fingers as she sectioned and braided my hair. She'd comb, pull, and loop, giving me the loose strands caught in the teeth of the comb. A gentle nudge and I knew to bend my head, turn it to the left or right. Tight braids. So tight they pinched my scalp up along the temples and nape. Always tight braids to last for two or three days of school. And my palm coming up for the loose strands of hair. A ball of hair in my hands to be burned when we were through. A bird will take it and make a nest — you'll have headaches all your life. All unspoken and by rote. I felt a void when she was done. A thank you meant hearing my own voice, older and deeper; a walk back home to pass you on a ladder fixing shutters; a need to pretend that your stony face didn't matter.

◈◈◈

RUBY USES the white twine. White goes with any color dress, she tells Cocoa. She moves her hands along the temples to get the shape of the head before making the first part. A straight part down the middle, north to south. The teeth of the comb dig in just short of hurting as she scratches the scalp showing through the parted hair before she dips her fingers into the round jar and massages the warm solution down its length. The second big part crosses the first, going east to west, and this time she dips her fingers into the square jar, massaging hard. North to south, east to west, round to square. The braids start forming, tiny and crisscrossed under her flying fingers. They drop like a fan on top of Cocoa's shoulders as Ruby knots the white thread on each end.

Done, Ruby tells her, and Cocoa asks for a mirror. There ain't none inside worth using, but go on home and see how pretty it is. She cleans out the comb one final time and gives Cocoa a match to burn up her loose hair. Before she goes Cocoa leans down and kisses Ruby on the cheek. Ruby is still smiling as she watches Cocoa head back down the road. She caps her jars and presses the lids on tight. She then brushes a few strands from her lap into her hand and puts them in her pocket.

◇◇◇

YOUR HAIR was gorgeous. The braids were like the ones I'd seen on prints of African women with those colored beads draped over their necks and crossed under high, tilted breasts. You should really wear it like that all the time. I wanted to follow you in the house and tell you, but that's sort of hard to do when you're not talking to someone. This whole state of affairs was less than twenty-four hours old and it was becoming extremely inconvenient, but where was the out? I was getting a throbbing headache; I finished what I had to do and took a walk to sort things out in my mind. The day was perfect for my mood, bleak and awful. I needed the east woods — rough going so I could feel the muscles pulling in the back of my thighs and work up a sweat, my heart beating close to its limit. If I got mauled by an alligator, she'd be sorry enough to apologize. Or if I had a heart attack, that would fix her. That sort of thinking was getting me nowhere, it was as childish as the behavior that had gotten us into all of this to begin with.

But I was right, damn it. That's what was so infuriating. And why should I be the one to back down? I felt better when I finally made the climb up to Chevy's Pass. That large oak tree was rustling loudly in the wind. Its Spanish moss reminded me of old-fashioned feather boas the way it was swaying in those branches. There I go, thinking about women again, and there was a time when I didn't have my whole world complicated with them. A wonderful time. Just dozens of boys. Clean fights. Straight talk. Order. You did what you were supposed to and left it at that. No tantrums. No nonsense. And your hard work was appreciated. Just look at that poor slob buried there — he gave her a whole island, and she still cut out on him.

The ocean was going crazy. The waves would come crashing in, spraying foam halfway up the bluff, before rolling under like a clawed hand, gouging out pebbles and sand to drag away from the shoreline. Another and another. Tireless fury that somehow I found soothing to watch. Standing there for a while, I realized how varied gray could be: the horizon, the sky, the clouds, the water, the foam. It was ghostly off in the distance, smoky overhead, with cinders in the waves spraying up liquid ash, droplets that left salt stains on my shoes. Behind the clouds even the sun had become a smashed pearly gray. I knew it had to be the sun, although it could have been any shape up there. Oval. Square. The whole landscape was blended in gray but each feature was distinct.

My breath felt that color too, a heaviness that wanted to push itself out of my chest. There had to have been some days like this, I thought, when he stood here and waited for her. I turned to head toward home with the sky becoming increasingly darker and the surf churning at my back. Bascombe Wade's tombstone was barely visible in the clearing as the oak branches swished even louder in the building wind. *Waste. Waste.* Yes, I looked at his monument; those leaves could easily be crying that. But legend or no, for you that wasn't her name.

◇◇◇

SOMEWHERE behind the clouds the sun sets and the quarter moon rises. And folks are doing the things that normally come with the evening: the suppers are cooked and eaten, the babies put to bed, but this night it's with the static from radios and the blue glow of the televisions. Hurricane watch. They evacuating beyond the bridge, the Red Cross is putting up shelters, the National Guard is called into Savannah to stop the looting that might come after. Picture after picture of boarded-up stores, deserted marinas, and interviews with mayors, out-talking each other about who's bound to have the worst disaster area and how much emergency aid they been promised from Washington.

Things is always been done different in Willow Springs. First off, it ain't never crossed nobody's mind to leave. Them sitting close to the water just get back a little more, though nobody's been fool enough to build right up to the edge. Ain't been a bad hurricane in most living memories but that's the last memory to count. It's a place always been hit by storms, leaving a lick and a promise, so houses just don't get built near the water like fields don't get planted. A promise is as good as your word here, and you learn to live like every rain is gonna be the big one. Second off, there ain't no mayor, governor, or the like. If anything gets blown down, it's understood everybody will get together and put it back up. In 1920, Miranda says, they had to redo parts of the bridge. Sure couldn't depend upon South Carolina or Georgia, since they don't collect our taxes. It's like we don't exist for them, and near about midnight when that Hurricane Watch becomes a Wait, they stop existing for us. Them televisions and radios get turned off so folks can sit in the quiet, a respectful silence, for the coming of the force.

Abigail is reading her Bible in the light from the burning fire that Miranda feeds with pieces of kindling. It gives her hands something to do with the waiting; she's tired of sitting, tired of pacing near the shuttered windows. Miranda can't get rid of the heaviness way down in her center, holding there for a reason she can't put her finger on. It ain't Cocoa in one room, and George in another, after that miserable supper with him picking at his food and her real listless, refusing to eat at all. Both suffering from heart trouble and both of 'em stubborn to beat the band. But that's to be left alone; the same passion that flared up to start all this mess can be depended upon to burn it away. And it ain't them winds building up outside; she done felt that pressure for days now and it's got a texture all its own. Naw, this was other trouble. And she'd just have to wait it out. Too much else going on around her to call up what it might be.

The old walnut clock ticks on behind the soft murmuring of Abigail's voice, while far off and low the real winds come in. It starts on the shores of Africa, a simple breeze among the palms and cassavas, before it's carried off, tied up with thousands like it, on a strong wave heading due west. A world of water, heaving and rolling, weeks of water, and all them breezes die but one. *I cried unto God with my voice, even unto God with my voice.* Restless and disturbed, no land in front of it, no land in back, it draws up the ocean vapor and rains fall like tears. Constant rains. But it lives on to meet the curve of the equator, where it swallows up the heat waiting in the blackness of them nights. A roar goes up and it starts to spin: moving counterclockwise against the march of time, it rips through the sugar canes in Jamaica, stripping juices from their heart, shedding red buds from royal poincianas as it spins up in the heat. Over the broken sugar cane fields — hot rains fall. But it's spinning wider, spinning higher, groaning as it bounces off the curve of the earth to head due north. *Thou holdest mine eyes waking; I am so troubled that I cannot speak. I have considered the days of old, the years of ancient times.* A center grows within the fury of the spinning winds. A still eye. Warm. Calm. It dries a line of clothes in Alabama. It rocks a cradle in Georgia. *I call to remembrance my song in the night. I commune with mine own heart* — A buried calm with the awesome power of its face turned to Willow Springs. It hits the southeast corner of the bluff, raising a fist of water to smash into them high rocks. It screams through Chevy's Pass. *And my spirit made diligent search* — the oak tree holds. *I will meditate also of all thy work, and talk of thy doings* — the tombstone of Bascombe Wade trembles but holds. The rest is destruction.

Miranda hears it in her soul. The tall pines in the south woods go. The cypress in the east woods go. The magnolias and jasmines in the west woods go. A low moan as it spares the other place. But then a deep heaving, a pounding of wind and rains against wood. A giving. A slow and tortured giving before a summons to The Sound to rise up and swallow the shattered fragments of the bridge. *The waters saw thee, O God, the waters saw thee; they were afraid. The depths also were troubled. The clouds poured out water. The skies sent out a sound. Thine arrows also went abroad. The voice of thy thunder was in the heaven. The lightnings lightened the world. The earth trembled and shook.* Miranda goes over to her sister, and gently she closes Abigail's Bible. Their gnarled hands rest for a moment on the worn leather binding. Abigail puts the Bible away and sits beside Miranda to listen to the heaving, screaming winds.

Willow Springs is a barrier island, and unlike beyond the bridge, it ain't a matter of calling them winds by a first name, like you'd do a pet dog or cat, so what they're capable of won't be so frightening — a prank or something that nature, having nothing better to do, just decided to play: one time a female, one time a male. But Abigail and Miranda is sitting side by side, listening to the very first cries from the heaving and moaning outside that darkened and shuttered house. Feeling the very earth split open as the waters come gushing down — all to the end of birthing a void. Naw, them winds will come, rest, and leave screaming — *Thy way is in the sea, and thy path in the great waters, and thy footsteps are not known* — while prayers go up in Willow Springs to be spared from what could only be the workings of Woman. And She has no name.

◇◇◇

I SAT ALONE in our room and was moved beyond fear as the very walls of the house wanted to give way. When I was just out of school I worked with a team of engineers in redesigning a nozzle for a nuclear steam turbine generator. I was more of a blueprint filer than anything else, but your first real job is exciting. It was an awesome machine: the size of a railroad train, a tandem-compound, six-flow generator with blade rotations of eighteen hundred revolutions per minute. Its capacity was over a million kilowatts. And when it ran — in theory — lighting up every home in New York, a feeling radiated through the pit of my stomach as if its nerve endings were connected to each of those ten million light bulbs. That was power. But the winds coming around the corners of that house was God.

I hadn't thought about God much before then. Declaring myself an atheist would have taken more conviction than I had one way or the other. I was more of a comfortable amnesiac. When things were under control — and I lived my life so that was usually the case — there was no need to think about having to deal with some presence that might be governing what was beyond my own abilities. I had no delusions of grandeur, wanting to stir up the world. I asked only to be left alone to seek happiness where I could find it, and since I sought it only within the limitations of my daily existence, I was normally a satisfied man. Every now and then when a day went haywire and I felt overwhelmed by unforeseen barriers to some goal I'd set for myself, I might take a deep breath and say, God help me, really meaning, Let the best in me help me. There wasn't a moment when I actually believed those appeals were going beyond me to a force that would first hear, secondly care, and thirdly bend down to insert influence on the matter. No, I saw the Bible as a literary masterpiece, but literature all the same; and Christianity owed its rules and regulations to politics more than anything else, while filling its pews with uncertainty and fear. Substitute the Torah, the Koran, the Bhagavad-Gita, a synagogue, a mosque, a temple, for all of the above and the formula still worked perfectly. All of the bloodletting and chaos, the devotion and beauty, martyrdom, and even charity could be reduced to a simple formula of politics and fear. But the winds coming around the corner of that tiny house on that tiny island was God.

And I was even smaller than them. Trivial. Every thought, ambition, or worry diminished as it became my being against the being on the other side of two inches of wood. Fear never entered the picture: at first an exhilaration of the possibility of having the barrier broken and, for one brief moment, to be taken over by raw power. Pure power. What a magnificent ending to an insignificant existence. But remaining untouched with the relentless winds keeping on and on, the growing and pervasive realization of my insignificance caused a lump in my throat. You yearn for company then, any company, to have some minor evidence of your worth reflected back at you. I got up to go and sit in the living room with your family and found myself walking through the connecting bathroom doors to watch you sleeping.

I stood in the doorway and envied your oblivion. No thoughts of loneliness, the cosmos, and human frailty. When you woke up the sun would probably be shining. You'd reach up with that funny little stretch of yours, a small frown across your forehead, before getting your bearings. One last turn to grab the pillow, a sigh, and then you'd swing your legs over the side of the bed. I wanted to see you wake up that way for the rest of my life; you wanted it too. And we both knew it. So what had all the fuss been about? With the winds howling and beating against the house, I remembered but I found it hard to care. I had to face another irreducible formula: as little as it was, it was going to be you and me. And when you woke up tomorrow, it should be where you belonged. You were heavy because it was dead weight and I had to turn sideways to clear the space between the sink and tub. I finally got you into our room, a bit out of breath, and you had never stirred. My niece could sleep through a hurricane, Miss Miranda had said. I smiled to think how prophetic she'd been.

I WAS HAVING that terrible dream again with you nearly drowning in The Sound and me trying to keep from calling out so you could make it back safely to shore. Only this time I didn't succeed. Through my clenched lips I could hear the screams echoing out over the water. They seemed to go on forever, churning up the waves you were struggling in until I couldn't see anything at all with the water hitting me in the face and blurring my vision. But where was the screaming coming from? My mouth was closed — so afraid I was sick to my stomach — but my mouth was closed. I couldn't see, but I knew you had gone under. And suddenly there was such a feeling of peace because that's when I told myself, This has to be a dream. He would never leave me. I was waking up with that same peacefulness because my legs were tangled into someone else's, and as I turned over to snuggle closer with my head buried into that shoulder, it hit me that something was wrong. I tried to force myself fully awake — Grandma didn't have hair on her chest.

"George, how did I get in here?"

"You mean, you don't remember?"

"No."

The room looked strange behind the closed shutters, a grayish light filtering over everything. My clothes were folded in the chair the way I normally put them. But I couldn't have gone to sleep in here, could I? Nothing was clear and there was a dull throbbing in my head; it felt as if I had a hangover. It seemed to take you forever to yawn and stretch. You put your arms around me and I didn't know if I should let them stay there or not.

"Ophelia, it was so touching."

"What?"

"Why, the way we made up. You came in here in the middle of the night. Started right over there by the door on your hands and knees — I was worried that you might get splinters . . ."

"George —"

"But you said no, let you do it your way. All along the floor, begging me over and over —"

"I'm getting out of here, George." But I was gripped so tightly I couldn't move.

"And I thought, why not let bygones be bygones. She was only asking me to forgive her for marrying a fool. So that's how you got in here. Whether you stay or not is your own business."

I was very very sleepy. That gray light seemed to be pressing down on my eyelids. I buried my head into your shoulder again and moved my fingers through the hair on your chest. You brushed the braids gently away from my face, but our motions were all underwater and the sleep was quickly overtaking me. When I wake up, I remember saying, remind me to tell you about the fool that *you* married.

◇◇◇

SHE'S WALKING under cloudy skies through her garden, ankle deep in leaves and broken branches. But crumbling a fistful of earth and then licking at her fingers, she knows there's reason for hope. It's all right, you took six peach trees and my big pecan, but at least there's no salt. The roof was a small price to pay for the unspoiled topsoil. Getting that back would only take money, and at this stage of the game she had more money than time. But she'd have to get workers from beyond the bridge — once there was a bridge — 'cause nobody in Willow Springs would come out to the other place. Folks do get the strangest notions. They oughta see it now, porch steps sunk in, a big gap over the balcony. That pecan tree musta taken out the roof, but the branches ain't smashed no windows on its way down.

The rest of the garden is sure enough gone, but it was August anyway. She'd salvage what she could and just turn the rest under, fallen birds and all. Let it lay through the rest of the year and start again next spring. Her throat tightens up at the rush of gratitude that there would be a spring. And if it hadna been, she didn't know what she'd do. Well, ain't no cause to carry on about ifs and hadna beens, what *is* is enough work to see her through the end of the month and into September. She's thinking she might move out here till it's done — save that walking twice a day, let Abigail have a fit or no. Wouldn't be no telephones no way till long after the bridge was up. These little telephones we got is the least of their worries over there. Folks done without telephones for longer than they've had 'em, without lights or gas to boot. Spoiled. That's all it's about — can't live without this, can't live without that. You can live without anything you weren't born with, and you can make it through on even half of that. Naw, she'd just get her a tarpaulin to nail up under that hole so she wouldn't be rained out of there — looks of the sky more was coming — and she'd sit here snug as a bug till her garden was laid by.

She runs her hands along the fallen trunk of the pecan tree. Why, there was enough wood right here to give her light and warmth through most of the winter if need be. She wasn't much on swinging an ax, but she'd bring George out here before they headed home. Use that young back of his before Baby Girl wore him out, now that it seems like they've made up. She knew that bedding arrangement with Abigail wasn't gonna last too long — she'd slept with her sister, and Abigail kicks you in the side. If it hada been up to her, Baby Girl wouldna been allowed in there the first night. You make your bed hard, you just roll over the more often, Daddy always said.

Old as she was, she still missed her daddy sometimes. Miranda runs her fingers in the ridges of the tree trunk. Skin color close to this, and in later years them skillful hands knotted and hard just so. And now her hands was the same, knotted and hard, but ain't half as skillful. John-Paul could carve flowers that looked more real than the ones she grew. Under the grayish light her skin seems to dissolve into the fallen tree, her palm spreading out wide as the trunk, her fingers twisting out in a dozen directions, branching off into green and rippling fingernails. She tries to pull her hand away, only to send the huge fingers and nails rippling and moving in the air. She cries out startled, pulling so fiercely she scrapes her knuckles before realizing her thumb is stuck under a branch. With a pounding heart she nurses the sore knuckle in her mouth, the stinging taste of blood on her tongue. Slowly, she looks from the fallen tree out to the garden gate and shakes her head, no. She takes a step back as she removes her bleeding hand from her mouth, her eyes never leaving the gate. But she can still taste her coming. From the south and past the bridge junction. No. But she's driving steady and heading north. Her legs don't want to support her no more; she sits on the verandah steps amidst the torn morning glory vines with her hands dropped still into her lap. Her shoulders are slumped. A light rain is beginning to mist in her hair. But she sits, staring at the empty garden gate.

◈◈◈

THE MAIN ROAD looked as if it had been through a war — branches and leaves strewn everywhere — and in a way it had. I expected the sun to be shining, thought really that we deserved to have it shine after a night like that. Wasn't that the way in those Victorian novels? A wild tempest, flaming passions, and then the calm of a gorgeous sunrise. Well, we were hardly going according to the script. The tempest had come in on cue, but you were still sleeping and I got tired of lying there waiting for you to wake up in a burst of flaming passion. And then the news that the bridge was gone — how were we ever going to get home? All of your grandmother's reassurances that it would be repaired in a few days did not reassure me. A week in Willow Springs was enough to understand that words spoken here operated on a different plane through a whole morass of history and circumstances that I was not privy to. A few days could mean anything, and I had to return to work. No phone lines, so there was no question of calling. And on the transistor, there wasn't a single mention of Willow Springs among the areas hit. It might as well not exist, and so there would be no Coast Guard coming to the rescue. It was incredible. What if there were casualties, a need for medical assistance? We take care of our own, your grandmother told me, and for her that finished the matter. But I began helping her clean up the front yard with the growing — and uncomfortable — realization that I was marooned on an island in the middle of the twentieth century. At least, I thought it was the twentieth century until I saw Bernice Duvall drive up to that silver trailer.

◇◇◇

FOLKS IS SURE to disagree for years about what caused the death of Little Caesar. A drowning in them gullies dug out by the storm. Live wires hanging from the electric poles. There's no eyewitnesses to the condition of his body as his mama drives him up the main road — some things you just can't watch. Nobody was there but everybody heard the door open up on that white convertible. Ambush sits in his living room chair, staring straight ahead at nothing, while Bernice glances up at the clouds and goes back into the house for his red rain hat and slicker. Little Caesar slumps over in the front seat, his head bent and arms slack at his side. She braces his neck to fit on the hat and works the sleeves of the raincoat up his arms, and she's careful to buckle all them straps tight around him before she gets in and starts the motor. No telephones left but the news goes before her, Bernice and Little Caesar is in that white convertible heading north on the main road.

Some things go beyond curiosity. Some things you just can't watch. Nobody turns from picking up loose shingles, dragging broken tree branches out of their front yards, as the white convertible moves on past, heading north on the main road. She drives slow like she always does, slower 'cause the surface is slippery from wet leaves and debris. If too big a limb blocks the way completely, she brakes and sits there quietly until someone runs out and drags it away, never once glancing over their shoulders at the woman and her child in the car. Never once looking after her as she drives on past. The group at the bridge junction keeps on talking about it being a fair storm: the shacks blown down that shoulda been, the old leaning fences that needed replacing anyway, the screen doors hanging by a thread to begin with. Some is short-tempered about the bridge; they ain't getting to work today and there's crops to be taken over. No use thinking about the few boats that was, boathouse and dock is sitting at the bottom of The Sound. Out of the corner of their eyes, the white convertible moves on past without interrupting a word. After a while even the motor ain't heard as she heads on north up the main road to that silver trailer.

◈◈◈

IT WOULD HAVE BEEN DIFFERENT if I hadn't met Bernice Duvall. But I had sat in her home, a split-level ranch with central air conditioning. Her husband had plans for building on his stereo system and ordering a new diesel tractor. They had a high school yearbook, wedding pictures, and a tuition account for their son. I had talked to that couple about the advantages of municipal bonds over no-load mutual funds for that very account. She had brought me a linen napkin and served me coffee. She was tall and thin, brown skinned, with flecks of amber in her eyes. And she was lifting her dead child, dressed in a raincoat, out of her convertible.

It was one of those moments when your mind simply freezes to protect itself from the devastation of a thousand contradictions, which freezes your body as well. If this was reality, it meant I was insane, and I couldn't be — and she couldn't be, because I had met that woman. I turned to your grandmother for confirmation of my sanity in her spoken words, in her eyes, perhaps. But she glanced across the road and silently returned to raking her yard. Bernice was carrying the child upright into the woods, her arms around his back and her shoulders cradling his head. No, this was the stuff of dreams. I spoke because I needed to hear the reality of my own voice, although my question was as insane as the answer I received: "She's going to the other place."

◇◇◇

THE MISTING is turning to rain as she sits outside on the verandah steps and waits. A morning rain, it's warmed by the clouded sun just tipping up toward the top of the pines. It's an old face that waits in the rain. A tired face. Deep hollows suck under the creviced eyes, fine lines running from the chapped lips down around the grizzled chin. A face broken down with the weight of knowing what's coming through the woods and that there ain't no need to pray. No words to form the plea in her heart if there was another place to send it. Old hands grasp the walking stick, hands knotted with veins and splattered with warm rain. She rises from the verandah steps to walk the path running through her crippled garden. She stands at the gate and waits.

She comes through the woods. Her flesh in her arms. Climbing over fallen trees that ain't there. Wading through mud holes that ain't there. Slipping and cutting her knee on rocks that ain't there. She's holding the only thing that is. The sun keeps moving up to another branch of the pines. The rains come down.

She stops her at the opening to the garden. And they stand. Grasping her carved stick, she holds her head erect as the water wets her gray hair and runs down her face. The clouded sun reaches the top of the pines. The rain is soaking through the cotton dress, outlining her withered breasts and corded thighs, matting the cloth into her back. They still stand. Water streams from the end of her chin, the end of her gnarled fingers; water flows in rivulets down her legs and into her shoes as the clouded sun begins its slow descent behind the other place. The rains stop. The evening winds come. It's a crescent moon. A chill night. A clear sunrise. And the orioles take to wing, the bruised morning glories open. With the red rays filtering again through the bottom of the pines, she finally stretches out her hand to touch the broken face of the other woman. Go home, Bernice. Go home and bury your child.

◇◇◇

AT FIRST it felt as if I had a virus: the achiness in my head, the fever. I couldn't seem to keep my eyes open, and when I forced myself to sit up in bed everything kept swimming in front of me through this crazy gray light. What time was it? How long had I slept? My throat was sandpaper and I needed to get to the toilet, but the floorboards were wavering up and down — it would have been easier to think of walking on water. I wasn't the type to panic. I couldn't be in that house alone, and if I was, it wouldn't be for very long. I leaned against the headboard, closed my eyes tight, took a deep breath, and forced them back open again. That awful light was still everywhere but the floor had stopped moving. Making it into the bathroom, a few feet away, left my legs weak and trembling. I pushed open the connecting door to Grandma's room. It was empty. I called out; my voice sounded as if it was coming through a tunnel. The effort of getting back into the bed broke me out into a cold sweat. When I wake up again, I thought, George or someone will be here.

I was woken up instead, a firm hand shaking my shoulders, and two faces floating above me. By squinting I could finally focus you in with Grandma behind you. Your mouths were opening and closing, but there was a long lapse between your lips forming a word and its reaching me, like I was in the middle of a badly dubbed movie. And to make it worse, there was a lapse between my hearing a word, being able to comprehend its meaning, and then having it bring on any type of response. A whirl of confusing echoes — visual, emotional, verbal. You told me Little Caesar had died, and I answered no, I didn't feel like getting up, it taking that long for me to understand the previous sentences. And by the time I understood that something had happened to Bernice's child and started to cry, I could hear your voices echoing over and over — What's wrong with you? What's wrong with you? I tried to say that nothing was wrong, I only had the flu, I was just feeling so very sorry for Ambush and Bernice. It was easier to fall back into unconsciousness.

YOU WERE SICK and I was totally helpless. It was a feeling that I hated even though your grandmother said that it seemed as if you'd only caught a virus. *Seemed as if* wasn't good enough for me. I didn't like your paleness, those splotches of red around your temples, and the constant sleeping. I wanted to get you to a doctor, or at least call one about your symptoms, so we'd know what to do. But I saw a side of Miss Abigail I didn't know existed, the no-nonsense, clinical efficiency with which she went about boiling something she called boneset tea and straining fresh chicken broth. You'd wake up and drink the liquids only to doze back off again. My protestations for a better — and, of course, impossible — solution fell on deaf ears, and she gave me the same look I'd gotten out in the front yard when Bernice pulled up in that convertible. Bernice's car sat there all through the day, and when the rain began to pour I went out and put up the top. It was frustrating sitting behind that steering wheel, trying to reconcile the sanity that would slip car keys over a visor to the insanity of carrying dead children into the woods without so much as a word from anyone, and not being able to throw you into the back and just drive us the hell away from there.

I tried to get a hold of myself. I was nervous, that's all. I wasn't used to your being ill, outside of a cold or an abscessed tooth. My own disability I always took in stride, knowing exactly what to do if I'd overtaxed myself and my heartbeat was fluctuating. But the thought of something serious being wrong with you was another matter — I couldn't control what was going on inside your body. Still, there was no need to jump from my anxiety over my own helplessness to imagining weird, unnatural rituals behind those dogwoods. There was some rational explanation for what I had seen, another custom that I wasn't privy to. This was, after all, the place that you really called home. And why not? Your grandmother was doing everything for you that anyone would do if they couldn't reach a doctor. And it's not as if they didn't have a doctor. He lived beyond the bridge, and I had met him at the party. An ordinary-looking man in a room full of ordinary-looking people. People who knew and greeted him. No, they used doctors here. And they had televisions, radios, air conditioners. Tuition accounts for their sons. They were just . . . I looked through the veil of rain into those woods with my hands resting on Bernice's steering wheel and sighed.

I WAS A LITTLE GIRL again and it was so nice. My head cradled in Grandma's soft bosom, her hands stroking my forehead as she coaxed me to take small sips of that awfully bitter tea. I liked it when she was there to promise me a new dress or a set of real silk ribbons if I'd take just one more swallow, while Mama Day would have promised me a spanking if I didn't open my locked mouth. Are you feeling better, baby? Yes, call me baby again. You'll be the one to make the gray light disappear. To protect me from that strange man peering over your shoulder. He reached out to touch me and I shrank away. I begged her to make him leave me alone. She's out of her head. No, I was inside of my head and it hurt, God, how it hurt. The echoes had gone away. Now each word was a tight, tight pinpoint bursting in my brain. I needed silence. I put my fingers up to her lips to keep her from talking and I felt tears.

◇◇◇

MIRANDA doesn't feel she'll ever get warm again. And, wrapped up in blankets, she sure don't ever want to move from in front of that parlor fire. She's spent the day dozing off and on in that rocking chair, getting up only to heat another brick for her feet or to pour herself another cup of chamomile tea. Sitting inside the shuttered house, watching the kettle steaming in the fireplace, is comforting. More comfort than she deserves. You play with people's lives and it backfires on you. As another wave of grief passes over her, she clutches her teacup and tries to rock it back into an ebb. More crushing, just a bit more crushing than that baby's death, is the belief that his mama came to her with. There'll be no redemption for that. She ain't gotta worry about going on to hell. Hell was right now. Daddy always said that folks misread the Bible. Couldn't be no punishment worse than having to live here on earth, he said.

Naw, she knew about hell. In this very room, in this very rocking chair — and once before, in another like it — she'd seen all the hell on earth there could be. Miranda throws another log onto the fire and it sputters up, blazing blues and oranges, sparks flying at her face. She sinks back into the rocker with a sigh. Yeah, blaze on up, and if you tried to blaze on out I wouldn't stop you. Maybe my sister was right, this old place needs to burn down. But something deep inside of her won't let her truly believe that. A house is a house, ain't it? Wood and plaster and brick. It's the people that brings the sorrow. Or the hope. That same man told her that she had a little more than others to give. You have a gift, Little Mama. But who asked her for it? Who made her God?

Miranda rocks and thinks of the things she can make grow. The joy she got from any kind of life. Can't nothing be wrong in bringing on life, knowing how to get under, around, and beside nature to give it a slight push. Most folks just don't know what can be done with a little will and their own hands. But she ain't never, Lord, she ain't never tried to get *over* nature. Hadn't she seen enough in this very house to know that that couldn't be? John-Paul woulda moved the earth for his wife, but with all of them lifelike carvings, he couldn't give her Peace. And Abigail, trying to form with her flesh what Daddy couldn't form from wood, still didn't get Peace to live again. There is things you can do and things you can't, Miranda thinks, looking into the fire. *And there's more sorrow coming.* The rocker stops. No point in asking where the last thought came from. No point in trying to tell herself it ain't so. She could now tell herself whatever she wanted. She could fling herself into that fire. But nothing could stop that front door from opening and them footsteps moving toward the parlor.

"The Baby Girl is sick, Little Mama."

Miranda don't look at her sister in the parlor door, she keeps staring into the fire. It's a huge hearth, 'cause it's an old house. She grew up seeing them rusted hooks empty over the mantel, but when the time came she knew what they were for. They hold her dried bundles of rosemary, thyme, woodruff, and linden flowers. Her chamomile and verbena. She makes her medicine from those and many others layered in clay jars inside the pantry. But Abigail wouldn't set foot in the other place for that. So Miranda is staring past her dried herbs, past the birth of Hope and Grace, past the mother who ended her life in The Sound, on to the Mother who began the Days. She sees one woman leave by wind. Another leave by water. She smells the blood from the broken hearts of the men who they cursed for not letting them go. She reaches up and touches her own tears. Miranda lets them fall; she wouldn't have the strength for them later. She finally turns her face to her sister, the weight on her soul reflected in the eyes that meet hers. "It's gonna take a man to bring her peace" — and all they had was that boy.

◇◇◇

I HAD WALKED to the bridge at least six times that day. If there was a boat or even a raft, I would have taken it alone to get you help. I stood at the edge of the shore, with the broken planks and bloated fish floating in The Sound, and actually thought about swimming across. Quite a feat, since I couldn't swim a stroke, but the memory of that glassy look in your eyes caused me to shudder. Didn't people get something called brain fever? It had to be, for you not to recognize me. Why hadn't I studied medicine instead of a subject as useless as engineering science? What good was all that math and logic now?

I tried to remember that I was angry and frustrated with myself, not at the people working on the bridge. I had volunteered, hoping to use what little knowledge I had to help them speed it up. But no matter how I reasoned, they would not melt more than a gallon of tar at a time. They were working between cloud bursts, they told me. Why tar more wood than would dry properly in a short period? But they could have put tarpaulins over it if a rain came, and then with enough melted pitch, you could have two crews — one on each end — laying down boards toward each other. And I could calculate it for them, making a diagram, to ensure them that the boards wouldn't gap. But no, that wasn't the way things were done here. Parris would only trust his overseeing each board that was laid down, and with two crews, he couldn't do that. See, this bridge had to last till the next big blow. Two-hour lunch breaks, half-hour quarrels over which plank end should go down first — I gave up. Swimming across didn't seem quite as impossible anymore.

◇◇◇

MIRANDA brews her sister a strong cup of chamomile tea to help her rest. It's pitiful, that slump in Abigail's shoulders and the dark circles under her eyes. She musta tried everything in her power before she was forced to come out to the other place. The heavy trembling of Abigail's hands as she brings the cup to her lips is enough alone to make Miranda kill Ruby. She ain't had to go in that bedroom and see them red splotches around Cocoa's temples. To bend down and sniff the scalp between the parts of her hair. Yes, that sow had hoped she'd discover the nightshade and think that's all it was. And hoped she'd spend her time untwisting them threads and washing the poison out of her hair. And then maybe she'd spend even more time thinking of ways to poison her in return. Ruby knows there were so many things she could choose from. She ain't had to step a foot into the woods; she could reach down in any flower garden. Buttercups. Oleanders. Hyacinths. And who don't have azaleas in Willow Springs? Morning glories, even? While Abigail sips her tea, Miranda goes to the kitchen window and looks out over the ravished garden. Rhubarb leaves. Cherry bark. Plums. She could take apple seeds and kill her. But all that would take time. And Ruby had hoped to buy herself just that.

Miranda puts Abigail to bed. Just take a short nap, she tells her. She'd see over Baby Girl until she woke up. When Abigail's breathing is deep and regular, Miranda goes on into the other bedroom. Cocoa is stirring uneasy in her sleep, them braids flung every which a way across the pillow. Miranda lifts them up in her hand, watching the little red welts that are beginning on her neck and spreading down to her shoulders. She runs her fingertips over one and it causes her to shiver. She ain't really understood what it meant till now — that killing's too good for somebody. Naw, death is peace. Ruby deserved burning in that hell which don't exist. Taking the shears out of her pocket, she begins cutting off each braid. They fall, curled up like worms on the pillow around Cocoa's face. Miranda has to keep her stomach from heaving at the sight of them. She cuts each off close to the head, and with that done she takes the shears and snips carefully through the plaits woven next to the scalp. The white strings pop out, looking even more like worms. Maggots, really. She's gotta force herself to go on until each plait is loosened.

Well, you a frizzly chicken now, she thinks as she combs the spare threads out of the hair that's left. There's a half tub of warm water waiting as she leads Cocoa staggering and mumbling into the bathroom. She spreads a charcoal paste on her head, leaving her slouched drowsy in the water, her head thrown back over the rim of the tub. Miranda balls up the sheets and pillowcases around the shredded hair and burns the lot in the back yard. When the fire's going good, she throws in the wooden comb she used. Only three of them left from what her daddy had carved, and Abigail owned the other two. She shakes her head as her comb goes up in smoke.

The warm water spraying from the shower on Cocoa's bent head brings her out of her sleep struggling. Stay still now, Miranda tells her as she massages more of the grayish paste into her scalp, this needs to be soaked in for a while. Them red welts is coming up between her shoulder blades, but Miranda's got to ignore 'em as she rinses the paste from Cocoa's hair. That's out of her hands and she's doing the only thing she can. Towel her down good, wrap her in flannel 'cause it's soft and warm, and get her to sit up at the kitchen table to take something nourishing, even with her nodding off again. She's been almost two days on nothing but boneset tea and chicken broth. But God bless Abigail for helping to clean out her system. Now them charcoal grains done drawn up what's left of the poison in her scalp. But the rest — well, the rest was just about out of her hands.

She don't think Cocoa is gonna remember sitting at that table, having oat gruel and bone marrow spooned into her mouth. But she ain't gotta remember for it to do her some good, and it's just as well, 'cause she'd resist her if she saw how awful it looked. It's like feeding her when she was a baby, propping up her chin, prying open her lips with the tip of the spoon. But it was a grown woman's body leaning over the table, and for a brief moment Miranda allows herself to wish that it wasn't so, that she'd never left to go beyond the bridge and still belonged only to them. She had fought for her life when she was theirs and she could fight for it again, give up her own if need be. But what ain't so, just ain't so. Baby Girl done tied up her mind and her flesh with George, and above all, Ruby knew it. But Ruby don't know me, Miranda thinks, she *can't* know me or she wouldna done this.

◇◇◇

DURING our lunch break — or dinner rest, as they called it — I came to check on you. I was relieved to see that Miss Miranda was finally back at the house. She wasn't a doctor, but perhaps with all of her experience, she could do something for you that your grandmother hadn't. It seemed that she had. She told me that you had taken solid food and there would be an improvement in a day or so. You'd stop sleeping so much and it wouldn't hurt your head when people talked to you. And yes, you would definitely recognize me again. But all around the edges of her carefully chosen words was the sense that she was holding something back. It worried me and I wanted to go in and see you, sleeping or not. But Miss Miranda told me to sit down for a minute. Don't be shocked when you see Cocoa, I've cut off her hair. Of course I asked why, and I was answered with a riddle. You have a choice, she said to me. I can tell you the truth, which you won't believe, or I can invent a lie, which you would. Which would you rather have? What a crazy old woman. All of these people, with their convoluted reasoning, were starting to wear on me. As sick as you were, how dare she play these types of games? What I want, I said, getting up from that table, is some way to get my wife out of this godforsaken place as soon as I can. Surprisingly, neither my anger nor my answer disturbed her.

◇◇◇

MIRANDA is sitting on the edge of Abigail's bed when she stirs awake.

"You there, Sister?"

"Uh, huh."

She lays a hand on her shoulder, telling her to rest easy, George is back and he's with Cocoa now. Miranda is twirling her walking stick between her knees, watching the carved snakes wind themselves down into the floor and up into her hands.

"Remember this stick, Abby? Us teasing Daddy, and him saying, 'Just live on'?"

Abigail don't give an answer, 'cause she knows none is needed.

"Daddy was right about some things," Miranda continues, her eyes never leaving the cane, "and wrong about others. He was wrong about you, Abby. Him saying you'd never have my strength. But having a sharp tongue and a fiery temper ain't always the same thing as having strength. I done seen you hold up under many things — when you lost Peace and when we almost lost Baby Girl. I was right proud of you, having the presence of mind to give her a fitting crib name — a name that helped to hold her here."

"What are you trying to say, Miranda?"

"You're gonna need that presence of mind again, Abby." Miranda stops twirling her walking stick and frowns down at Abigail. "I got rid of the nightshade Ruby put in her hair. Her vision will be clearing and she'll stop all the sleeping in a little bit. But I can't get rid of all she done to her."

The sound from Abigail is a fluttering of smothered birds as a deep trembling starts around her mouth and chin.

"We ain't got no more time for tears, Abigail." Miranda's voice is harsh. "And you gonna have to see her through this, 'cause I can't be here."

"How bad is it gonna be?"

"How bad is hate, Abigail? How strong is hate? It can destroy more people quicker than anything else."

"But I believe there's a power greater than hate."

"Yes, and that's what we gotta depend on — that and George."

"That boy is from beyond the bridge, Miranda." Abigail's voice is bitter. "We ain't even got his kind of words to tell him what's going on."

"Some things can be known without words."

"With or without, how is he gonna fight something he ain't a part of?"

"He's a part of *her*, Abigail. And that's the part that Ruby done fixed to take it out of our hands."

"George ain't never gonna believe this, Miranda. Go to him with some mess like this, and he'd be sure we were senile."

"That's right. So we gotta wait for him to feel the need to come to us. I'll have to stay out at the other place. And when he's ready, head him in my direction."

"That boy'll never make it, Miranda."

"Don't sell him too short too early. He'd do anything in the world for her."

"I know that. But we ain't talking about this world, are we?"

"No," Miranda says, "we ain't talking about this world at all."

◇◇◇

WE WERE at it again only for about an hour when they stopped working, almost in mass. But no one had given a signal, that I understood at least. "It's time to go to the standing forth." I followed them through the fields in back of the stores at the bridge junction to a little wooden church — and what they meant was a funeral. No flowers. No music. People were coming from all directions, each dressed apparently in whatever they were wearing when they knew the time had come. The men who had been working on the bridge in dirty overalls with tar under their fingernails. Miss Reema in her blue smock from the beauty parlor. One woman with her hair shampooed and a towel around her head. One had on a house coat and fuzzy slippers. Even Bernice and Ambush weren't in special clothes, but black wasn't needed to set them apart.

We filed into the pews, facing the simple pine coffin set up in the front. The minister was there, but he had little to say. When the rustling and moving had quieted, he cleared his throat and said, Charles Kyle Duvall, 1981 to 1985. Who is ready to stand forth? He sat back down and for a while there was silence. And then Miss Reema got up and walked to the front of the church and stood looking down at the closed coffin: When I first saw you, she began, you were wearing a green bunting, being carried in your mama's arms. You had a little fuzzy patch of hair on your head and your mouth was open to let out a squall. I guess you were hungry. And when I see you again, she said, you'll be sitting at my dining table, having been invited to dinner with the rest of my brood. It went on like that, person after person. Dry eyed and matter of fact. The minister calling out, Who is ready to stand forth? Someone had seen him in a stroller and would see him again in his own car. If they first saw him walking, they would see him running. Dr. Buzzard got up and had first seen him sucking away on a pacifier, and when he saw him again he'd be more than ready for a handful of his special ginger candy. Always addressing the coffin, and sometimes acting as if they expected an answer back. You liked

my toy whistles, didn't you? the owner of the general store asked him.
Well, when I see you again, you'll be buying my silver earrings for a
sweetheart of yours.

Why did I get the feeling that this meeting wasn't meant to take
place inside of any building? The church, the presence of the minister,
were concessions, and obviously the only ones they were going to
make to a Christian ritual that should have called for a sermon, music,
tears — the belief in an earthly finality for the child's life. His parents
weren't even crying and I could have cut Ambush's grief with a knife.
He was the next to rise: You were bunching up your fists, angry and
small. And I thought I had a fighter on my hands. A golden glove
champ, maybe. And when I see you again, you'll be fighting for the
place you deserve among other great men. Surely, Bernice couldn't
take part in this. The woman had gone out of her mind when that
child died. But she also stood up, trembling. Her voice could barely
be heard. And she turned to the coffin with an air — could it be? —
of apology: When I first saw you, you were so very glad to be alive —
new and declaring it to everyone. And when I see you again, you'll
be forgiving of your old mama, who didn't remember for a moment
that you were still here.

And that was it. It took only two men to carry the coffin because
it was so small. It was laid into the open grave that was waiting behind
the church and covered up. They began to disperse as calmly as they
came. I stood there immobile by the fresh grave, trying to sort out
the meaning of all this in my mind. Dr. Buzzard's callused hand applied
gentle pressure to my arm. Come on, he said, we got us a bridge to
build.

◈◈◈

First she's to head north. Ruby sees her coming up the main road
and goes inside and bolts her door shut. Yeah, run inside and lock your
door, Miranda thinks, that's just where I want you. She stands at the
gate and calls her name — Are you in there, Ruby? Well, maybe she
don't hear her. She'll get a little closer. She stands at the foot of the
porch and calls her name. Are you in there, Ruby? She grips the top
of that hickory stick as she gives her one more chance. Loud. Are you

in there, Ruby? Well, three times is all that she's required. That'll be her defense at Judgment: Lord, I called out three times. She don't say another word as she brings that cane shoulder level and slams it into the left side of the house. The wood on wood sounds like thunder. The silvery powder is thrown into the bushes. She strikes the house in the back. Powder. She strikes it on the left. Powder. She brings the cane over her head and strikes it so hard against the front door, the window panes rattle. Miranda stands there, out of breath, with little beads of sweat on her temples. There's a long thin crack in her walking cane, running down the back of one snake and cutting through the head of another. She examines it close to make sure it'll still hold her weight, and then she turns around to head south on the main road. The door don't open when she leaves, and the winds don't stir the circle of silvery powder.

They're near to calling it quits on the bridge for the day. Some don't like the looks of the storm clouds building up. Could be nothing but a light shower, and then again you don't know. The hurricane's still got folks edgy, but it ain't uncommon to have rains come and go for a few days after something like that. The matter gets settled when Miranda shows up. She tells 'em that if she was them, she wouldn't want to be caught near water in a few hours, them's the type of clouds that hold lightning. There's still a bit of disagreement, some being anxious to get on with the work. A word to the wise is sufficient, she says under the roll of far-off thunder, but a whole dictionary wouldn't help some fools. They start clearing up and getting ready for home.

She's on her way east toward Chevy's Pass, taking a short cut along the far edge of the south woods. Them east woods is almost impassable without half the trees blown down, and those patches of suck mud done probably turned into pools. She spies who she was hoping to meet in the distance. Dr. Buzzard is shoring up his leaning beehives.

"I shoulda figured you'd be hiding here from any real work," Miranda says.

"Naw, now you got me wrong again. I was down there earlier, but they had so much help I come on back here a little after the standing forth. I ain't seen you at the church, though."

"I woulda liked to have been there, but Cocoa is right sick and I was with her."

"Anything serious?"

"Yeah, I think it is." She watches Dr. Buzzard real careful. "Matter of fact, I know it's serious."

"Well, she got herself the best doctor in Willow Springs."

"We both know there are some things a doctor can't do."

Miranda don't try to fill the silence that follows as Dr. Buzzard putters around his hives. "You know," he finally says, "it was the most amazing thing. That storm took out my still, but it left these hives."

"It should be a lesson to you."

"I'm thinking of taking it as one," he says. "The children would be right disappointed if I ain't had no sweets come Candle Walk. Little Cocoa is fond of my ginger candy."

"She is at that," Miranda says.

Dr. Buzzard straightens up and puts his hands in his overall pockets with a frown. "How serious?" he asks.

"Serious enough for you to tell George what I'm sure Junior Lee has already told you."

"I figured he was lying."

"He wasn't," Miranda says.

"I just didn't figure Ruby was crazy enough to mess with what was yours."

"I got a good twenty years on you, Buzzard. And I done seen people crazy enough to do a lot of things. And she done also messed with what's his. Tell him what you know."

Dr. Buzzard shakes his head. "But that's a city boy, Mama Day."

"Tell him."

"He ain't gonna believe it, so to what end?"

"To the end that, at least, he's gonna know what he ain't believing."

West is the last direction and Miranda feels as if she's not gonna make it. As she passes her trailer, her body cries out for her to go inside and rest — no sleep last night, covering a good part of the island today — but once she sits back down, she won't be able to get up again for a long, long time. Which is worse, the dull stabbing pain from her spine to leg muscles or the grinding sound that the bones give out with each step she takes? She puts her mind at the end of her journey, tasting the hot vegetable soup, smelling the liniment for her thighs and legs, feeling the soft flannel they'll be wrapped in and the mattress on the old mahogany bed she's gonna fall into. Yes, fall straight in and sleep away the coming sunrise and the one after that. Keeping her mind there gets her through the few chores left around her trailer.

She ain't fool enough to think that she could outrun Cicero and get him into her sack, but the day that she couldn't outsmart a rooster was the day for her to give it all up. And she weren't about to leave him and that other rooster there together. Cicero would mount that coop fence in no time without the proper watching. She throws down just one or two crumbs for the outside chickens, so they'd have something to squabble over as she gets one of her wire cages from inside the coop fence. Y'all will catch it now, she tells the ones inside the fence, 'cause Abigail will be feeding you — the party's over. Taking the cage to the side of her trailer and spreading a thick layer of crumbs in the bottom, she stands back and lets 'em peck and shuffle each other to get inside. Cicero, being younger and stronger, makes it past the hens, even past Clarissa, who's the weakest but the smartest. Imagine, Clarissa survived that hurricane — look like her and that hen is gonna live forever. With Cicero busy defending the opening to the cage from the other chickens, she snaps the door shut. He starts setting up an awful racket, banging against the wires, and when he's gotten himself into a frenzy, she opens the door for him to run right into her sack.

It's only a matter of getting to the other place with the sack held off some to avoid his beak and spurs. That little ache in her left arm is nothing compared to the ones in her legs. And she pushes herself a little, 'cause the thunder's starting up good and she sees the rain ain't far off. She frees him inside the garden and he's right indignant about it all. Go on now, she tells him, have yourself a holiday among all these ruined vegetables by yourself.

Miranda climbs the verandah steps and enters the front door of the other place. She closes it securely behind her. The lightning is flashing in the clouds. She's asleep when the clouds get lower and the lightning nears the earth. It dances around that silver trailer, but it hits mostly along the edge of the forests, scarring a pine or two. It hits the bridge, though, taking out the new tarred boards and a day's worth of work. It hits Ruby's twice, and the second time the house explodes.

◈◈◈

IT WAS LIKE coming out of a deep sleep that had lasted for three days. Remembering myself ever leaving that bed or talking to anyone held the texture of a dream. And still you were pressing me for answers to some of the things that had happened. I didn't know why Mama Day had cut off all my hair and then secluded herself out at the other place. Until I could talk to her, I'd take it in stride. When we got back to New York, I'd have the ends trimmed evenly and get it marcelled in body waves — a sort of 1920s style that you saw in old photographs of those swanky women when Harlem was in its heyday. And that would mean all new clothes, of course, which I expected you to shell out for. I couldn't get you to smile with me. I was so glad that the sun was finally out to stay and I could see my surroundings in its true colors: yellows, blues, greens, and browns. My head felt free and light, but to listen to you, there was a hidden agenda brewing between Grandma and Mama Day. My God, these were the women who raised me — I would trust them with my life, and so whatever Mama Day had done, it was for a good reason. But you refused to share my optimism — why was I still so weak? Well, I couldn't expect anything else since I hadn't been up in a long time. A little sunlight and short walks around the house would straighten me out. And you were worrying me more than those red welts on my body.

You were edgy and short-tempered in a way I hadn't known before. Finishing the bridge. Finishing the bridge. A constant obsession when you left in the morning, came back for lunch, and returned again in the evening. No one was working fast enough, no one was working long enough. Between that and your eternal hovering over me, I was ready to pull out what little hair I had left. You were working yourself into a terrible state — and for what? The bridge was going to take only a few more days, and I was coming along fine — really. I didn't dare tell you anything else. But if you hadn't come up with that crazy scheme about rowing a leaky boat across The Sound, I might have told you about those hallucinations when I looked in the mirror.

*

PAR FOR THE COURSE. That's how I figured it when the lightning storm cracked and singed five feet of the new planking on the bridge. A day's work gone, then half a day to take it up, another day to put it back down, so we were guaranteed to stay here an extra thirty-six hours. Thirty-six hours. And I had just as many reasons to leave as soon as I could — each of them with your name on it. The needless complications were driving me up a wall. When you have a job to do, you do it. You don't stand around, discoursing on the obvious. The lightning destroyed the new planking — period. But, oh, no, there was something *strange* about this lightning. It struck twice in the same place. Theoretically, it is possible, but not probable, for lightning to strike twice in exactly the same place. The first exchange of electrical charges between the ground and the clouds, which in a sense is a strike, causes the negative-charge center up in the clouds to short-circuit and nullify itself. So it would take another exchange of negative electrons from higher in that same cloud to the same positively charged spot on the earth to have lightning strike twice. That's rare. Unless, of course, in a scientific experiment someone purposely electrifies the ground with materials that hold both negative and positive charges to increase the potential of having a target hit. No one was running around with that kind of knowledge in Willow Springs, and it was highly improbable that it would happen naturally. Others were there, thinking it unnatural as well, but for very different reasons. This was a deliberate and definite sign, since it had happened to Miss Ruby's house. It seemed that she'd had a host of sins, going back several years, so the destruction of everything she owned and the burns on her body was her getting her due. And the *time* that was wasted, examining those planks to determine if they had been struck twice also. I dreaded to think that if they found such evidence, they'd stop working altogether — it being a sign to them that the bridge should stay like it was.

I was deciding I didn't even need the whole thing finished. Just let it get rebuilt far enough toward the other half for me to take a running jump over the gap, and I could make it back to the real world and charter a boat, or demand that the Coast Guard come over and get us. What happened later that afternoon, I would call providence. A rowboat washed up on the shore among all the loose planking and debris. Sections of fishing boats and even parts of the former boathouse had been washing up for days, but this one was practically intact. The rear seat had been ripped out and the stem was split in places, but the bottom was in fair shape, the oarlocks loose but workable. I could buy spare oars, wood putty, and waterproofing in the general store. Of course, they all thought I was crazy. Why take a chance in a boat like that when in no time at all the bridge was gonna be rebuilt? Yes, I thought, *no time* at all.

IT STARTED with my thinking that the crack had just distorted the bedroom mirror. Over the years it had spread from the far corner where the vase chipped it up toward the middle. I had been meaning to replace Grandma's mirror, since it was my temper that did it. I decided I'd get a whole new bedroom set, but from my own money, not yours. A temp job for a few months should pay for it, and I'd just have it shipped down here without asking her, because she'd say no, if she knew. I had only wanted to fix myself up a bit; a little powder and blush to cover the paleness, since you were both worried about me, each in your own way. You were just pointblank ridiculous with a thousand questions, while she sang spirituals all morning. When Grandma started going to the Cross and waiting by the Jordan and then on to six choruses of "No Ways Tired," I didn't care how much she came out to the front porch and smiled at me. She was deeply troubled — justified or not — about something. I was thankful that those awful welts weren't on my face and could be covered up with a caftan; a touch of make-up would take care of the rest until I was truly better. And I was beginning to feel stronger, my vision was clear, so the welts must be an allergic reaction to the virus that had been in me.

I put a dab of powdered rouge on the brush, and when I stroked upward on my cheekbone my flesh gummed on the brush bristles and got pushed up like molten caramel. I brought the brush back down and the image frowning at me had a gouged cheek with the extra flesh pushed up and dangling under the right ear. I moved over; the image moved and remained the same. Bringing my fingers up to my cheek, I felt it intact and curved while the fingers in the mirror were probing a gross disfigurement. Had that crack splintered the mercury in the back of the mirror? Ignoring that side of my face, I dabbed more powder on the brush, stroked even firmer on the left side — and gouged a deeper hole. The flesh from both cheeks was now hanging in strings under my ears, and moving my head caused them to wiggle like hooked worms. I stepped away from the mirrored image with my hands on my cheeks. There was nothing wrong with my face. But I couldn't stand to see myself clutching that stringy flesh in front of me.

The mirror over the bathroom sink showed me the exact same thing. I turned my back and leaned against the sink. My fingers moving up and down my face — the face I knew I had. All right, so I was hallucinating. Now, what to do about it? Nothing. Just wait for it to go away. It's just another side effect of the virus. But it was getting harder to put everything on the flu. Grandma was in the kitchen and I just had to ask her, trying to keep my voice as even as possible. Is there anything wrong with my face? I panicked for that instant when she tilted her head and frowned at me. And if she hadn't spoken up, I might have fallen apart. Well, honey, you ain't got your make-up on right. You gotta blend them two red lines into your cheeks better. She frowned even deeper when I laughed — a bit too shrill. Cocoa, is there something the matter with you? No, nothing at all. I was just trying a new technique, I said. I guess it didn't work, huh? Well, don't depend on me, she answered. I ain't up on them new styles.

I didn't want to look at myself again, so I bent low under the bathroom mirror to wash the blush off my face. I dried it without looking as well. But feeling it fresh and whole, I thought I'd chance one more glance. I couldn't help myself — I screamed. My eyes, lips, chin, forehead, and ears had been smeared everywhere, mashed in and wrinkled, with some gouged places still holding the imprints from my fingers and the terrycloth. Of course, she came running, and my second instinct would have been to lie. But she got into the bathroom too quickly, and when I told her what was happening, she took me in her arms and soothed me, told me what I needed desperately to hear — it was all in my mind. And it wasn't until much later, after she'd made me lie down and I heard those spirituals again, that I remembered that not once had she expressed surprise.

Grandma covered all the mirrors in the house. It was both comfortable and discomforting to see them that way. At least I could move around without fear. But why wasn't I hallucinating now about my hands or legs or stomach? It was the same vision that took them in as well as the image in the mirror. I couldn't remember, and I wasn't going to test whether the rest of my body had also been distorted in those mirrors. I would just sit on the porch where it was warm and pleasant to watch an incredibly lovely sunset. Hours after the incident, it didn't seem as horrible anymore. And one day it would give us all something to laugh about. You were certainly a comical sight, coming up the road in those whitewash-speckled overalls that now had streaks of tar on the knees and cuffs. Where was the man who even insisted on dry cleaning his jeans?

When you greeted me with the news that you were going to repair some leaky-ass boat and row across The Sound, I stopped thinking about a way to explain the incident with the mirrors and concerned myself with a closer reflection of true danger — the earnestness on your face. George, you didn't even swim. Not that swimming would have helped once you got caught in one of those undertows. There was a notorious undercurrent in the middle of The Sound known as the Devil's Shoestring, and it had drowned experienced fishermen. Didn't they tell him that at the bridge?

I pretended to listen to you carefully laying out your plans while I was forming a strategy of my own. Being stuck with a stubborn man, I had learned not to waste time with reasonable arguments when your mind was made up about something. You would agree with everything I said, especially now since you thought I wasn't well, and then go out and do exactly what you wanted to anyway. But I was so very fortunate that you'd also had experience with a stubborn woman. The tone of voice I used was the one that normally came after your flattery, sarcasm, or raging — depending upon how badly you wanted something — had all been to no avail. You called it my go-drop-dead tone. I called it end-of-discussion. But I had to jump straight into it: There is nothing wrong with me that can't wait a few more days. Now, you can row over to the other shore if you'd like and bring back all the chartered boats you want. But when I pack my bags and leave this house, I'm going across that *bridge*. It was then time for me to lean back in a posture that, like my voice, was devoid of all expression save finality. For your lips to get pressed into that tight line as I was thrown a stony glare. And then for you to stomp past me and slam whatever door was available. This time it happened to be Grandma's screen door — and it was a sweet sound.

◇◇◇

THE OILCLOTH Miranda tacked up under the hole in the roof collected a pool of water before it broke loose. Half done is always worse than undone, she thinks, looking at the rusty stain spreading down the bedroom wall. But she had just been too tired to be stretching up and nailing a heavy tarpaulin in that cramped corner of the attic. She'd have to do it the right way now, although all that sunshine makes it sorta like locking the barn after the cows are gone. She's of a mind to just leave it be. When the roofers came from beyond the bridge, she'd just get 'em to paint the bedroom as well. All these rooms could use a fresh coat of paint and a nice varnish on these oak floors. It was really a lovely old house with the walnut moldings and engraved wain-scoting, them high arched ceilings and bay windows. And there were good times in this house, and it's the good times she's gotta call up, or there weren't no reason to come here. All that Baby Girl is was made by the people who walked these oak floors, sat and dreamed out on that balcony. It couldna all been like her and Abigail's life, growing up with a mother who died trying to find peace. She musta been so out of her head that she thought The Sound was the bottom of that well. She woulda still ended it all with water, 'cause if Daddy hadn't nailed that well shut they woulda eventually found her at the bottom of it. But the way it was, she wasn't to be found at all — until Grace brought her back with Ophelia. Unyielding, unforgiving Grace. That beautiful baby girl to live for, and she chose to wither away in hate.

Miranda stops herself. No, these ain't the memories she needs. Think of others. But, Lord, it's so hard 'cause she was so young when Peace died. She calls up one springtime when her head didn't reach the top step of the verandah. Was Abigail born then? Miranda can't see her sister, but she is being lifted up into a soft bosom that holds the fragrance of lemon verbena to be brought upstairs into this very room. And there *is* laughter — a lighter and a deeper laughter. She can't see her daddy either, but he musta been there 'cause she feels the rush of

air as she's taken and lifted high, high, up toward the ceiling to see —
what? Why, a butterfly. A blue and silver butterfly. *Make the baby one,
John-Paul, and we'll hang it around her neck.* Was that really said by her
mother, or did she just wish it? There was so little that was ever sane
coming from her mouth to hold on to.

Thinking about the ceilings is what finally leads her toward the
attic — another storm and the water might cave 'em in. She climbs
the suspension ladder with the proper equipment this time, a thick
rubber matting and a bag of ten-penny nails. It's hardly more than a
crawl space up there, but being short she can stoop over and make
her way through. Her back scrapes along the damp and moldy rafters,
but it's either that or make her way on them rain-soaked boards on
her hands and knees, and if the splinters didn't get her, the rheumatism
surely would. The wet dust has an awful smell, a cross between dried
phlegm and sour dirt. Thank goodness there was nothing up here for
her to step over. All their trunks and old junk boxes were always kept
out in the shed.

There's a memory of being in there with Abigail, peering through
the slitted window down into the front garden. But that's a memory
she don't want to have. It meant that they were hiding from something — voices, most likely, and voices that held no joy. None of her
personal memories that would include Abigail held much joy. No
wonder she avoids this place like the plague. No, think of other things.
But there's nothing to call up in this space — they wouldna brought
her up here as a baby. She's pushing and nailing the matting up into
a small corner when she spies the ledger. Black leather binding, long
and narrow, bent almost in two from being jammed into the point of
the roof. That had to be hidden there on purpose. Miranda tries to
wedge it out and the cover practically falls apart in her hands. The
pages are swollen and discolored from years of dampness. She couldn't
read it in this light anyway, even if the ink wasn't all run together.
Finishing up what she has to do, she takes the book with her, holding
it to her chest with one hand and climbing down the ladder with the
other. She knows, in the way that she knows things, that her daddy
hid it there. But why not just burn it?

In the bright light of the bedroom, there's nothing to be read in it.
Too old. Too long gone. She finds a slip of paper in the back that tells

her just how old. *Tuesday, 3rd Day August*, then a 1 and half of what must be an 8, with the rest of the date faded away. *Sold to Mister Bascombe Wade of Willow Springs, one negress answering to the name Sa . . .* Water damage done removed the remainder of that line with the yellowish and blackened stains spreading down and taking out most of the others as well: *Law . . . knowledge . . . witness . . . inflicted . . . nurse.* It's all she can pick out until she gets to the bottom for the final words: *Conditions . . . tender . . . kind.*

She's staring at the name and trying to guess. Sarah, Sabrina, Sally, Sadie, Sadonna — what? A loss that she can't describe sweeps over her — a missing key to an unknown door somewhere in that house. The door to help Baby Girl. She thinks. Samantha, Sarena, Salinda — them old-fashioned names. Sandra Bell? Sapphron? She'd once met a woman long ago called Saville. She runs them through over and over until her head aches. The paper, itself, means nothing to Miranda. All Willow Springs knows that this woman was nobody's slave. But what was her name? And what had been written here so that John-Paul hid it away? Law. Knowledge. Witness. Inflicted. Nurse. Conditions. Tender. Kind.

Miranda goes out to the balcony to take in deep breaths of fresh air. She gazes east through the top of the trees, letting her mind clear itself with the endless blue sky. She closes her eyes and runs her fingers over the crumbling paper, and all she sees is a vast gray wall. She tries again and fails. She scolds herself for not knowing better: a gift is something that's given, not demanded. Miranda begins scrubbing floors and thinking, Samarinda. Washing out cabinets and thinking, Savannah. Clearing fireplace ashes and thinking, Sage Marie. Making her supper, she throws a few crumbs of cornbread to her rooster, can you tell me, Cicero? The dishes get dried until they shine — Samora? Over and over until she goes to bed to get down on her stiffened knees and pray to the Father and Son as she'd been taught. But she falls asleep, murmuring the names of women. And in her dreams she finally meets Sapphira.

❖❖❖

IT WASN'T QUITE a full moon, but it was extremely bright coming into the bedroom and it spilled across your body, highlighting even the tiniest hairs on your chest. Your right arm was thrown across your face as if protecting yourself from its rays. I'd been lying there for hours, and I wondered why it didn't wake you up since you were a much lighter sleeper than me. Then I thought about how tired you'd looked that evening, a resigned tired that came from being confused and unsure, and it made my heart ache. Could it be I wasn't as careful at the table as I thought? Trying to hide the fact that I wasn't looking straight into a plate, my water glass, the curve of a spoon. Perhaps you wondered why even the clock face was covered. But I would rather have you confused than risking your life in the middle of The Sound. I didn't want to lose you, I didn't even want to think about losing you. The bridge would be finished in a few more days — you just weren't bred with the type of patience found in Willow Springs. Time, for its own sake, was never a major factor here. The crops, the weather, the seasons — they all controlled behavior much more than your elaborate digital watch.

I took it off the night stand to peer at the time: 2:14 A.M. If I pressed a certain button, I'd get the readings for the large cities all over the world — even Beijing, you were once so proud of telling me. But it was the same moon they saw in China, wasn't it? Just the other side of the moon. It was bathing the floor in patches of luminescent cream that eventually washed up along the dresser to the bottom edge of the mirror. I lay there staring at that mirror for a long time. When the moonlight had cut it in two with a jagged diagonal line, I quietly got up and removed the sheet. My heart was pounding, but I was more determined than afraid. Whatever I saw, I saw. And if it was a monster reflected back at me, I was still going to stand there and face it. Hallucinations are simply not real. The mirror could take in my head down to the top of my stomach. I, the mirror, and my reflection were all bathed in that brilliant cream. My face was no longer distorted; in fact, along with my neck, breasts, arms, and midriff, it was perfectly smooth. Where were the welts? Right there on my arms, shoulders, and chest when I looked down my body, but nowhere to be found when I took in my mirrored reflection. So the mirror was never to be trusted. Trust only your natural eyesight. Only what you literally see is real.

And I saw that the fine welts spread over my body had changed in color and texture. They were like clear water blisters, softened and jelled. I held my arm up in the moonlight and touched one. It started to move. A pulsing motion as if it was breathing. And then ever so slowly, it began to sink under my skin and disappear. I grabbed the edge of the dresser to keep myself from trembling as my stomach started to heave. With my left hand braced against the dresser, I touched another welt. The same thing happened, but I did not scream. Not with you there behind me, not with those watery welts pulsing like a living heart before slowly sinking under the surface of my skin.

I WASN'T ASLEEP. The room was too bright, and the mattress kept shifting slightly. It wouldn't have bothered most people, but I was normally a light sleeper — and times like this, I could hardly sleep at all — so each turn you made would momentarily jar me awake. I didn't roll over and ask you what was wrong, because you would have lied. Just like your grandmother was lying about a special cleaning polish under the covered mirrors. Why, I didn't know. And there was more than that going on which was being kept from me. I was supposed to look at those dark circles under your eyes and those awful welts on your body and believe that you were well? That you would think me so stupid angered me. What scared me was that you might know it was some terrible illness; and if that was, indeed, the case, why weren't you sharing it with me?

It must be something very serious to keep you awake like that. I watched you get up and uncover the mirror. And you just stood there, staring at yourself — thinking what? You'd bring one arm up to your face and then another, turning them over slowly. Your body suddenly went rigid, and it stayed rigid when you got back into bed. You lay on your stomach with the pillow crushed between your fists and just shook. One of the hardest things in my life was not to reach over and hold you in my arms when you started crying. But you were trying to muffle the sound, so my comfort was not what you wanted. I didn't know what you wanted, or what you even needed, but I knew what I was going to do. It was an issue of priorities. I'm getting up at daybreak, I thought, and I'm going to repair that boat. I'm going to put the oars into the oarlocks and begin to row across The Sound. That much I can do for her. And at the point in time when I can feel those oars between my hands, whether I make it or not won't be the issue. And if the boat begins to sink — I looked at my hands lit up by the moonlight — I'll place them in the water and start to swim. Yes, I would *begin* to swim. And at that point in time, finishing would not be the issue.

◈◈◈

MIRANDA opens door upon door upon door. Door upon door upon door. She asks each door the same thing: Tell me your name. And her answer is to have it swing open so she's facing another. She feels the weight of her years with each question, the heaviness of each ache, each sorrow, she had learned to step over in order to get the strength to go on. They all build up on her shoulders, bending her back and buckling her legs, until she's forced to open yet more doors with nothing put pure will. 'Cause her fingers done gave out long before, cramped and trembling; her arm stopped obeying her to lift itself up in its joint a hundred doors ago. And when she feels that even her will done run out, that she just can't turn another knob — to reach out and do it — she finds herself in a vast space of glowing light.

Daughter. The word comes to cradle what has gone past weariness. She can't really hear it 'cause she's got no ears, or call out 'cause she's got no mouth. There's only the sense of being. Daughter. Flooding through like fine streams of hot, liquid sugar to fill the spaces where there was never no arms to hold her up, no shoulders for her to lay her head down and cry on, no body to ever turn to for answers. Miranda. Sister. Little Mama. Mama Day. Melting, melting away under the sweet flood waters pouring down to lay bare a place she ain't known existed: Daughter. And she opens the mouth that ain't there to suckle at the full breasts, deep greedy swallows of a thickness like cream, seeping from the corners of her lips, spilling onto her chin. Full. Full and warm to rest between the mounds of softness, to feel the beating of a calm and steady heart. She sleeps within her sleep. To wake from one is to be given back ears as the steady heart tells her — look past the pain; to wake from the other is to stare up at the ceiling from the mahogany bed and to know that she must go out and uncover the well where Peace died.

Sitting off forgotten in the far edge of the garden, it's covered with almost a hundred years' worth of rotted moss and tangled creepers that done come up and died over and over to form a rich bed for the deep green patches of ground holly circling its base. A few scattered runners of wild ginger done taken root among the holly, them double pairs of heart-shaped leaves twining themselves up along the hewn stones toward the mouth of the well. The mortar is crumbling, the stones worn smooth by the weather and time, but the wooden lid is still bolted tight. Miranda has to lean on the crowbar to undo the first set of rusted spikes that John-Paul pounded and cemented into the holes he drilled by hand. She's thankful he ain't thought to cement the whole thing over, it woulda taken her a sledgehammer then. The work that took him days, takes her hours, each spike coming loose with the determination it was put in with. A tearing, scraping sound as the metal threads give way, splintering the wood and dusting her arms with dry flecks of cement. Using the loosened board ends for leverage makes the second set easier, the third easier still, until the lid flies off, tumbling end over end, ripping and bruising the slender ginger vines as it crashes to the ground.

Miranda's pulse is racing for a good many reasons as she grasps the edge of the well and peers down. A bottomless pit. Foul air hits her in the face, but she holds on waiting for it to clear. Then, taking a deep breath, she looks down again, squinting her eyes to try and find the surface of the water. It's slimy and covered with floating pools of fungus when she finally makes it out. There ain't much chance of seeing through to the bottom, of even seeing her face, 'cause the sunlight is swallowed long before it reaches that far. *Look past the pain.* But there ain't nothing down there and this looking is straining her eyes. Something she's not doing right. Refusing to let go of the edge, Miranda closes her eyes and stands there, her feet tangled in the ground holly, her stomach pressed against the heart-shaped ginger. And when it comes, it comes with a force that almost knocks her on her knees. She wants to run from all that screaming. Echoing shrill and high, piercing her ears. But with her eyes clamped shut, she looks at the sounds. A woman in apricot homespun: Let me go with peace. And a young body falling, falling toward the glint of silver coins in the crystal clear water. A woman in a gingham shirtwaist: Let me go with Peace. Circles and circles of screaming. Once, twice, three times peace was lost at that well. How was she ever gonna look past this kind of pain?

And then she opens her eyes on her own hands. Hands that look like John-Paul's. Hands that would not let the woman in gingham go with Peace. Before him, other hands that would not let the woman in apricot homespun go with peace. No, *could* not let her go. In all this time, she ain't never really thought about what it musta done to him. Or him either. It had to tear him up inside, knowing he was willing to give her anything in the world but that. And maybe he shoulda, 'cause he lost her anyway. But she wasn't sent out here for that — the losing was the pain of her childhood, the losing was Candle Walk, and looking past the losing was to feel for the man who built this house and the one who nailed this well shut. It was to feel the hope in them that the work of their hands could wipe away all that had gone before. Those men *believed* — in the power of themselves, in what they were feeling.

And now there is that boy. Miranda looks down at her hands again. In all her years she could count on half of her fingers folks she'd met with a will like his. He believes in himself — deep within himself — 'cause he ain't never had a choice. And he keeps it protected down in his center, but she needs that belief buried in George. Of his own accord he has to *hand* it over to her. She needs his hand in hers — his very hand — so she can connect it up with all the believing that had gone before. A single moment was all she asked, even a fingertip to touch hers here at the other place. So together they could be the bridge for Baby Girl to walk over. Yes, in his very hands he already held the missing piece she'd come looking for.

Miranda fights back a heavy inner trembling. She needed George — but George did not need her. The Days were all rooted to the other place, but that boy had his own place within him. And she sees there's a way he could do it alone, he has the will deep inside to bring Baby Girl peace all by himself — but, no, she won't even think on that. Her head was already filled with too much sorrow, too much loss. No, she'd think on some way to get him to trust her, by holding her hand she could guide him safely through that extra mile where the others had stumbled. But a mile was a lot to travel when even one step becomes too much on a road you ain't ready to take.

*

I COULD SEE the flames and smoke as soon as I passed the stores at the bridge junction. A handful of people had already started working with three large vats of tar being melted over the open fires — and they were feeding the flames with the chopped remnants of my boat. In the early light, they all looked like specters behind the wavering air from the bubbling tar. They ignored me while measuring and cutting planks, sorting through piles of nails. I finally understood the phrase blind fury. A dozen trees felled by the hurricane and they used that boat. Deliberately used it. I stood there with my fists clenched, the blood pounding in my head. Where to strike out first?

"The weather's cleared, George, so we'll be speeding things up."

I was too angry to even look at Dr. Buzzard. He took me off to one side, but I didn't want to hear anything about their plans. I could have smashed each one of those fools, and I wanted nothing more than to get the hell off of that island. It was like he read my mind.

"Your way," he said gently, "woulda been suicide. Our way, that same boat is certain to get you over."

"When? Next month? I don't have that much time."

"Boy, you got more time than you think."

"I'm sick and tired of being called a boy — and of being treated like one. If it was going to be suicide, it's my damn life. You had no right to do this."

"It's your life, but it wasn't your boat. And I guess folks figured they had a right to do with their property what they wanted. But then you got some rights in this matter too. You got the right to hear why even if you had gotten across, it wouldna done you or Cocoa a bit of good."

What do you do when someone starts telling you something that you just cannot believe? You can walk away. You can stand there and challenge him. Or in my case, you can fight the urge to laugh if it wasn't so pathetic: the grizzled old man with his hat of rooster feathers and his necklace of bones, shifting his feet and clearing his throat as he struggled to provide me with the minute details. I had stopped listening after the first incident about some woman named Frances who Junior Lee used to live with, because I was thinking that since my one hope for deliverance from the acute madness of this place — a madness exemplified by his story — was in front of me, going up in smoke, I would do the only thing left for me to do: help work on that bridge. Snakeroot. Powdered ashes. Loose hair. Chicken blood. I would work until I dropped to get you out of there. It seemed as if he was finally finished, and I thanked him for telling me all of that, anxious to get away from him and start. He put his hand on my forearm.

"I told Mama Day that this wouldn't do no good. I'm really sorry, George."

"Not half as sorry as I am."

"Naw, I'm doubly sorry. 'Cause I know how serious this thing is that you can't believe."

THE MOST difficult thing of all was not being able to depend upon the mirrors. That morning I looked at myself in different types of light throughout the house. What I couldn't see, I touched with the tips of my fingers. It was no illusion that the welts had left the surface of my skin — it was smooth. And George, it was no illusion that they had begun to crawl within my body. I didn't need a mirror to feel the slight itching as they curled and stretched themselves, multiplying as they burrowed deeper into my flesh. I'm trying to remember when I felt that I was slipping beyond help. It wasn't with the realization that they were spreading so rapidly because they were actually feeding on me, the putrid odor of decaying matter that I could taste on my tongue and smell with every breath I took. Or my urine coming thick and brown with little flecks of the lining from my bladder left on the toilet tissue.

No, I think it was when I managed to walk into the kitchen with Grandma's back to me at the sink. It seemed she had never let that water stop running or her voice give out from the countless choruses of "No Ways Tired." She had a lovely voice, a clear soprano, which was becoming hoarse and cracked. But glancing over her shoulder at me dropping into the chair, she never stopped singing as she came over and cradled my head to her chest, stroking my hair before gently lifting my chin. Reflected off the clear brown of her irises, I finally saw my face in a mirror that could never lie — the sunken cheeks, the deep black circles under my eyes — flooded with a pity so intense it would have been cheapened by tears.

*

WHEN I LEFT at dawn you were sleeping, and when I returned late that evening, you were asleep again, but I was relieved to see that the welts had disappeared. I was filthy and my swollen knuckles were caked with tar, so I tried to bend over to kiss you lightly on the side of the forehead without touching you, and there was the most awful smell. At first I thought it was coming from my own body, but it was worse than sweat. A kind of rotting sweetness that hangs in the air when you pass a pile of garbage on a hot day. I frowned and put my hand on your forehead in spite of the tar. No high fever, just barely warm. You murmured and turned over fully on your back, your arms spread out, so I could see your entire face. She couldn't have looked like that this morning. I turned up the kerosene lamp. Yes, it was still the face of a cadaver. It had always been long and thin, but you seemed to have lost five pounds in the course of a day. Your cheekbones pressing hard against the sunken flesh that was turning a sickly pale, the purplish black circles blending almost perfectly with your closed eyelashes. My throat tightened at the thickness and beauty of those lashes, the one remaining feature that I could recognize.

Your grandmother had been at that sink when I left at dawn and she was still at that sink. And it was the same song:

> Oh, I don't feel no ways tired.
> I've come too far from where I started from.
> Nobody told me that the road would be easy — no, no
> I don't believe He brought me this far —
> I won't believe He brought me this far —
> I can't believe He brought me this far to leave me.

Only this time her words were sending up piercing echoes within me because I had been saying that to myself all day: How could I believe?

There was one place setting at the table. Baked chicken tonight, she said before turning back to the sink to continue draining the water from a pot of fresh beets. I waited for her to say something else — surely, a comment about your appearance — but she went back to softly murmuring those verses. I sensed a waiting on her part as well. A waiting tinged with a subtle edge of disappointment that stung. I was doing everything I could.

"They burned my boat," I spit out.

"Because they like you."

"Then they must hate your granddaughter — I was going to get her some help."

She didn't answer as she turned on the faucet to rinse away the splattered red stains in her sink. Then she picked up the paring knife and began to skin the warm beets. The juice ran over her fingers like blood.

"It's the *only* way I could help," I said.

She nodded as she took my plate and began to slice the beets onto it. How did she think I could eat? Getting angry at her for that was easier than facing the reason why I was really angry.

"And she needs help badly," I continued sharply. "Have you seen her?"

"I don't have to see her," Miss Abigail said. She took an eternity to wipe her hands on that dishtowel, leaving long red smears running against the grain of the terrycloth as she cleaned each finger, concentrating so hard I was sure she'd forgotten I was there. It was only a whisper. "But have you seen her?"

What little strength I had was draining away. I fought the urge to simply lay my head down on my folded arms and never leave that table. The Formica was cool to the touch and firm, the edges shiny and clean. Just let my aching shoulders follow the pull of gravity to slowly keel over on that surface and pillow my head in my arms as I stretched out my cramping leg muscles. Did she realize what effort it took for me to open my mouth instead to ask her, "What can I do?" And surely, she must have realized that when she answered, "Please, George, go to the other place," that the road I took south to work on the night shift at the bridge was a much longer walk.

I WOKE UP to an empty bedroom bathed in moonlight and the ever-present sound of running water accompanying my grandmother's voice. Where was George? Could he still be working on the bridge? The stench was horrible in that bed and it coated my tongue so heavily that the little saliva I had was bitter when I swallowed. It was reaching a point where I couldn't stand it anymore. There is a limit to how

long you can feel your insides being gnawed away without beginning
to lose your mind. And I had been fighting to remain sane, for your
sake as well as my own. But they were multiplying up toward my
throat, and once I saw that I was spitting out worms, it would surely
take me over the edge. If I was going to die, I didn't want it to happen
while I was ranting and raving.

For a moment there was total silence in the house. Silence except
for the tiny gnawing, like the scraping of rough cloth, inside of me.
My God, was I alone? Without the sound of the water, their chewing
magnified in my ears, and yes, they were moving faster. I opened my
mouth to scream and the first beginnings of a high-pitched note was
taken up by Grandma's voice as she came into the room:

> No, I don't feel no ways tired.
> I've come too far from where I started from.

She sat on the bed, gathered me in her arms, and with the flat of her
hand, she began to stroke — my back, my arms, my chest. A heavily
veined and wrinkled hand with soft palms pressing firmly up and down
my skin:

> Nobody told me that the road would be easy — no, no
> I don't believe He brought me this far to leave me.

When her hand passed over a place where they were burrowing, they
would remain still until she went on to another part of my body. And
by the time they had built up momentum again, she was back there
stroking.

> I don't believe He brought me this far —
> I won't believe He brought me this far —
> I can't believe He brought me this far to leave me.

Her one hand against so many of them. If only there was a way to
bring me this kind of peace forever. The last thing I remember was
her leaning over to whisper, Don't worry, I won't sleep.

I HAD a lot of time to think that night, surrounded by smoking kerosene
lamps that seemed almost unnecessary with the moon being so bright.
I took the job of stirring the tar, because I was too bleary-eyed to have

seen how to align the boards and hit a nail properly. My efforts would have only slowed up the work, and they were determined that the bridge was to be built right, built to last, or not at all, so that there would be no space for them to consider its destruction by the last hurricane or the next to come as evidence of any failure on their part — a weak brace, a loose nail — while the forces beyond their control were just that. It was slow progress, but it was progress, and watching them as my hands moved by rote, stroking the sides, stroking the bottom of the boiling vat, I thought of how I had lived beyond the bridge. I mean, all of my life.

George Andrews. A smattering of applause as my name was called in the elementary school assembly — him? Yes, George Andrews with his government-issued shoes and ill-fitting shirt, the kid nobody wanted, as he came up the aisle, marching proudly to the beating of his own heart thundering long after all had stopped clapping, because that somber, reed-thin woman sitting in the audience had taught him that it was the only music worth marching to. And a faulty heart at that. A dozen missteps and countless mistakes, but I could never say that it was from a lack of trying. There were times when I tried too hard, pushing myself with the knowledge that I was all I had. And now you were all I had, and with you needing me, I had to hold on to what was real.

That paddle stayed in my hands all night, and by dawn my fingers and arms were so numb I couldn't feel them. But there were ten more feet added on to the bridge — that was real. And the sun coming up to bring in the outlines of the other shore — that was also real. When the others had left for home, I sat down and rested my head on my knees, waiting for the day shift to start up again. Just a few more hours with them, I told myself, and then I'd go home as well. I must have dozed off; I never heard the others beginning to work or Dr. Buzzard sitting down beside me. He uncapped a Thermos and poured me a cupful of something that smelled rich and sweet.

"Don't worry, ain't nothing in it but the ginger toddy."

He kept his head turned toward the sunrise as I sipped at the hot liquid, feeling it bring some measure of life back into my body. Another cupful calmed the gnawing in my stomach. I hadn't realized how hungry I was.

"I used to sell that stuff," he said, "when I was dancing on the vaudeville circuit. Passed it off as a 'miracle elixir' — ya know, to help men with their problems in bed. A tablespoon of grated ginger and some honey with a splash of whiskey. And folks believed it, too, came back for more, telling me how much good it had done 'em." He picked at a loose thread on a knee patch of his overalls before finally turning his head toward me to continue. "Ya see, I've always been an old fraud."

He was so close I could see the age in the yellowing roots of his grizzled beard, the knotted veins in his neck surrounded by bones — black-cat bones, he'd told me once — that were dry and splintered. "Yeah, out about every ten, nine would come back and say it done 'em good. And that nine would spread the news about me, which brought in nine more. So I never thought about that other one — the single one who it ain't worked for — till I got older. Really, not till I talked to you yesterday."

I gave him back his Thermos and started to get up. Whatever this man was leading up to, I didn't need to hear it. If it wouldn't help me to keep standing over that vat of tar, what good would it do?

"Ya see, I had given him something that he just couldn't believe in — and him disbelieving, whether I'd offered him a miracle or not, guaranteed it to fail."

"Look, Dr. Buzzard, now, I've heard you out again, but I've got work to do. And if you're worried about us, you can stop. We're going to be fine because I believe in myself."

"That's where folks start, boy — not where they finish up. Yes, I said *boy*. 'Cause a man would have grown enough to know that really believing in himself means that he ain't gotta be afraid to admit there's some things he just can't do alone. Ain't nobody asking you to believe in what Ruby done to Cocoa — but can you, at least, believe that you ain't the only one who'd give their life to help her? Can you believe that, George?"

I didn't say anything as I stood there, staring down at him. I had to press my fists into the pockets of those overalls to keep my arms from trembling, I was so tired.

" 'Cause if you can bring yourself to believe just that little bit, the walk you'll take to the other place won't be near as long as the walk back over to that vat of tar."

He was wrong. It was a long walk as I stumbled through the west woods, trying to step over fallen trees and around huge sections of gouged earth. The stagnant water in those gullies held thousands of mosquito larvae that were buzzing into life as the rising sun warmed them. Another hot and miserable day. My eyes were grainy, and I wasn't sure if I was moving in the right direction. Nothing looked familiar — occasional glimpses of The Sound appearing blood red under the sunrise, the magnolias and jasmines twisted and stripped clean of their flowers — until I came to the pine stump that was just around the bend from where I knew I would find the old house with a large garden.

◇◇◇

SHE SITS out on the verandah all night, her hands never ceasing the oiling and rubbing of John-Paul's walking cane and Bascombe Wade's ledger. Miranda has a whole can of linseed oil out in the shed, but she's using a concoction she made up herself that evening: a handful of poplar buds steeped in heated alcohol. What she's got is a bit too sticky for her liking, but it's gonna have to do. Balm of Gilead is best when it's left to sit for a few weeks before being strained down into an ointment. A smidgen of balm, then the chamois cloth flat against her open palm as she presses and strokes her hand along the length of the cane resting on her lap. With working careful, a patch at a time, she gets the hickory of that walking cane gleaming under the light from the nearly full moon. The leather covering on the ledger is too full of scars and scratches to shine proper, but it gets softened and smoothed under the stroking of Miranda's hand.

When she finishes with one, she places it on the verandah railing directly under the moonlight and takes the other up to start all over again. The light moves and she moves, never allowing the book or cane to stay in the shadows. All night she strokes, and follows the path of the moon. She stops at the first breaking of dawn when her rooster stands near the garden fence and begins to crow. Her hands waxy and slick from the balm of Gilead, Miranda leans back in the rocker with them folded on her lap.

She's still sitting that way when George comes through the gate.

He's limping a bit, the hem of them tar-streaked overalls dragging in the mud. Her heart goes out to him, so young and so confused about why he's there. She can feel it in the pit of her stomach — he came but he don't believe. And it was the end of the road for them all, so there ain't a thing she can do but go on and give him the answers to questions he won't know how to ask, and hope he understands enough to trust her. She waits for him to get up to the foot of the verandah but she don't wait for him to open his mouth.

"I want you to hear me out. Baby Girl is the closest thing I have to calling a child my own. And I did say Baby Girl, 'cause she's the last of the womenfolk come into the Days that I will live to see. There ain't a mama who coulda felt more pain or pride for her when she was coming up — do you understand? But it's more than my blood flows in her and more hands that can lay claim to her than these."

When she holds 'em out to him they're trembling, the fingers gnarled and coated with flecks of balm.

"I can do more things with these hands than most folks dream of — no less believe — but this time they ain't no good alone. I had to stay in this place and reach back to the beginning for us to find the chains to pull her out of this here trouble. Now, I got all that in this hand but it ain't gonna be complete unless I can reach out with the other hand and take yours. You see, she done bound more than her flesh up with you. And since she's suffering from something more than the flesh, I can't do a thing without you."

He's been leaning forward and listening to her careful with a frown on his brow that deepens when she finishes. "I still don't see what you want me to do."

" 'Cause I ain't told you yet. First, I was hoping for you to understand that much."

"Well, you're talking in a lot of metaphors. But what it boils down to is that I can be of some use to you, and I came here for that. So, please, what is it, Miss Miranda?"

It's only in her eyes that Miranda is slowly shaking her head. Metaphors. Like what they used in poetry and stuff. The stuff folks dreamed up when they was making a fantasy, while what she was talking about was *real*. As real as them young hands in front of her.

"Come here, George," she says. And as he mounts the steps she takes up the ledger and the walking cane. She puts them in his hands and folds hers over his. She presses them for a moment: strong and firm. Yes, these are the hands that could do it, but would he trust her enough to follow?

"There are two ways anybody can go when they come to certain roads in life — ain't about a right way or a wrong way — just two ways. And here we getting down to my way or yours. Now, I got a way for us to help Baby Girl. And I'm hoping it's the one you'll use."

She curls her fingers tighter around his that's holding the ledger and walking cane. "Mine ain't gonna be too hard — really. Back at my coop, there's an old red hen that's setting her last batch of eggs. You can't mistake her 'cause she's the biggest one in there and the tips of her feathers is almost blood red. She's crammed her nest into the northwest corner of the coop. You gotta take this book and cane in there with you, search good in the back of her nest, and come straight back here with whatever you find."

Miranda feels his body go rigid, but she won't let him pull back and she rushes to get through. "Now, I'm warning you, she's gonna be evil so watch out for your eyes. But, please, bring me straight back *whatever* you find — and then we can all rest. You look like you could use a lot of it, son."

When he finally snatches his hands from hers, the ledger and cane fall into her lap. It's hard to read what's on his face — he done turned it to stone.

"I can't believe you're saying this — this is your way?"

"It's the only one I got."

"Then I'll find my own."

"I pray to God you don't."

"And I came to you for help —"

"I'm giving it to you."

"All that walking for *this* — this mumbo-jumbo?"

"I spoke plain and I spoke slow. I'll even repeat it if you want. There's an old red hen that's setting her last batch of eggs —"

"Stop it!"

He looks like he wants to strike Miranda and she is willing to take the blows if it would do any good — let him beat her to a pulp if it would get him to that hen house and back to her with those very hands.

"You're a crazy old woman!"

"Yes, I'm a crazy old woman."

"And I was a fool to come here!"

"Yes, you were a fool to come here."

"There's nothing you can give her!"

"There's nothing *I* can give her."

The stone don't crack, but his eyes are made of softer material and his voice becomes softer still as he makes his way back down those steps.

"It's cruel of you to play these games, when it's your own niece that's sick."

"No," Miranda says, "my niece is dying."

She watches him leave, barely able to keep himself from stumbling off the brick walkway running through her garden, his feet dragging through the broken honeysuckle vines and bruised roses. He never looks back as he passes through the wooden gate, and she never stops caressing the smoothed surface of that ledger and cane. George disappears around the bend as her rooster keeps crowing toward the rising sun.

◇◇◇

I HATED that old woman. And I hated myself even more for the weakness that had taken me into those back woods. A total waste — of time and energy, both of which I had so little. I could have been at the house sleeping, and I needed to sleep badly. I was getting light-headed, with thousands of pinpoints burning throughout my body. Each time I had to climb over a fallen tree, I fought the urge to just curl up among its branches and sink into unconsciousness. The heat didn't help, either. My back and shirt front were soaked when I finally made it to the main road. That yellow bungalow looked like an oasis. Just a few hours of rest and then I could get back to the bridge.

Around the edge of the house I could see your grandmother in the far end of the yard, and she was throwing sheets and pillowcases into a trash fire. I didn't care why; the only thing that mattered was seeing you and getting some sleep. I had a moment of panic when I found our room empty, the bed stripped, and the window wide open. It took a while for my heart to stop pounding even after I realized that the shower was running. Of course, she was in there. I took off my filthy overalls and sweat-stained underwear. I would join her. How long since we'd done something normal like bathing together — or even laughing together? It seemed an eternity. And that's how long your screaming seemed to echo.

THE WARM WATER felt good on my head and shoulders, even though I was so weak I had to kneel in the tub. Wherever the beaded spray touched me and ran down, the gnawing inside would quiet. The running water stopped them from eating at me, like the stroking from my grandmother's hands. It was a welcome revelation because I had only gotten in there to try and wash away the putrid smell that had permeated the air in the bedroom and turned the bed covers gray and slick. I didn't want you to find me in that condition. But I could still taste the rot inside of me. I opened my mouth to let the water spray in. Rinsing and spitting it out was to leave a yellowish slime around the drain, and rinsing again was to begin to feel the real texture of my tongue. I tried to drink, but I gagged. That was all right — staying under the water was enough.

I gripped the side of the tub and raised myself to my feet in order to get closer to the spray — yes, let it pour down over me — and to feel this calm inside. Could it actually be killing them? Turning my face upward, I moved it from side to side so the water could spray into my ears and nose. I soaked my hair, bent my neck, and raised my arms up to let the clear streams falling from the shower head cascade over my body. You see, they were the same color as the water. And it took me a while to notice that the spray from the nozzle was thickening and that there was a difference in the weight of the long watery beads clinging to my flesh. Before I knew it, they were pouring down over me and crawling into every opening of my body — some even pushing their way in through the corners of my lips. Screaming only allowed more of them to slide down my throat.

*

THEY WERE the hollow eyes of a lunatic. I don't know how I got you out of that tub into the bedroom, fighting and ranting the way you were. It took my entire body to pin you down on the bed with my elbows jammed into your upper arms and my hands locked around your face, forcing you to listen as I said over and over that it was only water. Pressed under my chest, your heart was beating as wildly as mine, the muscle spasms in your throat rippling the flesh as if it were alive. Your fingernails were digging into my back, but I kept you locked down in that position until your eyes began to focus and the spasms subsided into a gentle trembling. I stroked your wet hair and showed you my hands — You see, baby? It's only water. I ran my fingers along your jutting shoulder blades, collecting the tiny droplets to hold in front of your face. I did the same for your arms, before trailing my fingers over your sunken midriff, the insides of your emaciated thighs — all to show you that it was water.

Your muscles began to relax and you brought your hands around to cradle my face. The trust in your eyes crushed me. I couldn't attain my ultimate desire to get inside and change places with you, but I tried the best I could. You fell asleep almost immediately afterward, your arms still clutching my back. For a long time I didn't move as I rested with my body inside of yours, feeling your steady heartbeat against my erratic one. I managed to leave without waking you and went into the bathroom to turn off the shower. As I put up the toilet seat, I thought it was a drop of semen on the end of my penis, but after I urinated it was still there. I used the thumb and forefinger to pry off the clear jellied substance and bring it nearer to my eyes. I looked at it from several angles until I was certain that I held a live worm. I smashed it between my fingers. It left a yellowish smear with the odor of rotting garbage.

I stood at the bedside, looking down at your wasted body as you mumbled in your sleep and made abortive clawing gestures toward your throat, your stomach. Everything blurred in front of me. My eyelids stung as if they were being washed in hot, molten metal. A fluid metal that burned as it rolled down my cheeks into the corners of my mouth. I put my hands up to my face, it was only water.

◇◇◇

SHE MEETS him at the gate of the garden to save him as many steps as she can. Without a word, she hands over the ledger and walking cane. But she tries to tell him with her eyes how hard she knew the journey was. Harder, 'cause he'd been beaten down to believe. And it was gonna be harder still, 'cause he was taking her way. It ain't a proud man in front of her — his pride wasn't needed — but it wrenches her inside that he'll be traveling without it. Wrenches her inside that the other way — his way — is to lose him. So she tries to say what little strength she has is his. That she'll stand by that gate with her hands outstretched to grasp his when he brings 'em. She don't say none of that. She don't even watch as he slowly takes that bend away from the other place. She done already turned her face to the sky that's well beyond the tip of the pines. Hot. Vacant. It ain't a prayer. And it ain't a plea. Whatever Your name is, help him.

◇◇◇

THE LAST MILE. I didn't bother to swat the mosquitoes and gnats biting me or to wipe the sweat off my face. The air was so heavy I had to pant through my open mouth, and whenever a gnat flew in, I'd spit it out and keep going. To stop for anything — a cut and muddy knee, a cramp in my side — would be to think about what I was doing; and I couldn't afford that. The cane and ledger had to be gripped tightly because they were covered with a smooth wax that melted in the heat, coating my palms. But at least I could put my weight on the cane, so it helped me to keep moving even with the bruised knee.

I slipped again trying to climb over a fallen palmetto, and twisting to avoid cutting myself on its sharp leaves, I lost my balance totally — the cane flying in one direction, the book in the other — and I ended up sprawled out on the ground. Trying to get up with only one good knee was almost impossible, I had to crawl toward the cane and use it for leverage. But where was the book? Surrounded by gnats and with the perspiration stinging my eyes, I couldn't see it among the bushes. That indecision would have opened the door to thought, and thought was certain to stop me. A breeze came out of nowhere. A strong breeze that cooled my skin and rustled the oak branches, sending the hanging moss swaying back and forth. I heard a fluttering to my left. The ledger was wedged between two rocks, the pages turning in the wind. That breeze stayed at my back until I entered the chicken coop.

The stench was overpowering. I couldn't breathe in that raw manure without wanting to gag. I rushed back out into the fresh air, but with nothing in my stomach, I brought up only a mild aftertaste of ginger and honey. The second attempt was better. I took shallow breaths, which helped me to bear the smell. The light was so dim, how would I be able to find a red hen? There was only row after row of yellow eyes, glinting at me from all sides. *The northwest corner of the coop.* North would be to my right, west straight in front of me. It was the only nest in that corner, a low pine box filled with straw. The huge red hen seemed to be in a trance; she sat there immobile until I came within two feet of her. The feathers around her neck began to swell as she emitted a deep throaty hiss, followed by a garbled set of short sounds, her throat vibrating. Her eyes never left me, and when I came within another foot, she struck.

She flew at my legs. I pushed her aside, and tried to reach behind the nest. Too low — I would have to get farther down. A sharp pain seared through my ankle where she was ripping through the denim with her beak. Kicking backward, I heard a high shriek, and the whole place exploded in rumbles and cackling. Quickly falling down on my bruised knees, gritting my teeth against the pain that radiated through my temples, I wedged my hands behind the nest. A blur of red feathers, she sank her claws into my wrist and a beak like rapid gunfire began tearing at my left hand. I ripped my skin trying to get her claws out of me before flinging her on her back. I turned the whole nest over, eggs bursting and splattering into the straw. Another shriek. She came at the side of my face. I raised my right hand to protect my eyes; blood spurted from a pierced vein. I threw her again and hurriedly dug at the loose straw and manure in the corner. Nothing. There was nothing there — except for my gouged and bleeding hands. Bring me straight back whatever you find.

But there was nothing to bring her. *Bring me straight back whatever you find.* Could it be that she wanted nothing but my hands? Another blur of red feathers. The hen flew up, her claws sank into my shoulder blades, cutting my shirt into bloody strips as her weight carried her sunken claws ripping down through my back. I tried grabbing her from behind — my right hand, my left hand. Both hands attacked with her beak and spurting fresh blood. In desperation I threw her off. And when the hen came at me this time, I took up the walking cane and smashed her in the skull. I brought it down again and again. I went through that coop like a madman, slamming the cane into feathery bodies, wooden posts, straw nests — it was all the same. The air was choked with feathers. The noise was deafening. The cane broke, I grabbed up the ledger and kept going until I got a stitch in my side. That finally made me stop. I looked at it all and began to laugh. A tight, airless laughter that got no further than my chest as I sank into the middle of the floor. My forehead bowed to my raised knees, my torn hands grasped in front of me — I laughed. When I could breathe again, I threw my head back and the laughter finally came with sound. There was nothing that old woman could do with a pair of empty hands. I was sitting in a chicken coop, covered with feathers, straw, manure, and blood. And why? I looked around me again and kept laughing until it started to hurt. Why? I brought both palms up, the bruised fingers clenched inward. All of this wasted effort when these were *my* hands, and there was no way I was going to let you go.

I managed to get up from the floor. There was a dull throbbing behind my breastbone that steadily worsened as I made it outside into the sunlight and looked past the silver trailer to your grandmother's house. It was barely fifty yards, but at the time I didn't know that I was dying. I thought I had sprained a muscle when I lost my head inside. Now my mind was perfectly clear: I was to get over to that house, because I was not going to let you go. When I reached the dogwoods on the west side of the road, the throbbing was beginning to turn into an iron vise in the middle of my chest. I put one foot on the paved road and glassy needles splintered throughout my brain. The house was wavering in front of my eyes. The road felt like water under my buckling knees. It was impossible to cross over, make it up those porch steps, and into our room. I did it. But I was too cramped to even unbend my body on the bed beside you.

The worst thing about the blinding pain that finally hit me was the sudden fear that it might mean the end. That's why I gripped your shoulder so tightly. But I want to tell you something about my real death that day. I didn't feel anything after my heart burst. As my bleeding hand slid gently down your arm, there was total peace.

◇◈◇

MIRANDA KNOWS she got no more reason to stand at that gate. He went and did it his way, so he ain't coming back. The morning presses on and she finds herself with a lot to do. In the pantry she rolls up bundles of dried herbs into clean strips of cloth. Now that Baby Girl was going to live, she had to be nursed back to health. And Miranda makes sure to bottle up plenty of tonic for a sedative. She scrapes the pot clean that held the balsam, rinses it, and hangs it up to dry. She closes the shutters upstairs, makes the bed, and sweeps the floor. Ashes get taken out of the fireplace, the kitchen sink and stove gets scoured. She drags the rocker inside from the verandah and finally shuts the front door. Catching Cicero takes a while, but she manages to get him into his sack.

The walk through the woods is longer than usual, since she ain't got her cane and the hickory limb she stripped keeps bending. Back at her trailer, she's got windows to open, a pool of water to mop up from the ice melting in her freezer, and fresh mash to be given to her chickens. After all is done, she goes inside the coop to look around at the bloody straw, the smashed eggs, and scattered bodies. Now, she has the time to cry.

◇◈◇

I THOUGHT my world had come to an end. And I wasn't really wrong — one of my worlds had. But being so young, I didn't understand that every hour we keep living is building material for a new world, of some sort. I wasn't ready to believe that a further existence would be worth anything without you. There was just too much pain in it. Yes, I thought often about suicide and once made the mistake of voicing it. I had never seen Mama Day so furious — never. George, there was actually hatred in her eyes. There ain't no pain — no pain — that you could be having worse than what that boy went through for your life. And you would throw it back in his face, heifer?

It took me almost three months before I was well enough to leave Willow Springs. Three months in which I had to be told that certain things had happened — your business partner coming down from New York, the will that requested a cremation — it all passed in one continual fog. The season changed into what they called a slow fall, which meant there was little difference between late November and August. The weather would remain just like summer until suddenly frost hit. And it was a long journey by train, because Mama Day refused to fly. Coming out of Penn Station, I was shocked to see how gray and dirty everything was. A cold rain was swirling piles of trash into the gratings of overflowing sewers with grimy mud splattering my open-toe sandals and stockings. The smell of wet cardboard as the makeshift huts put up by homeless men and women dissolved in the rain. And the ceaseless noise: impatient car horns, swearing bus drivers, a dozen hawkers of cheap umbrellas and plastic hats. This couldn't be the same city I had seen with you.

I would rather have had Grandma with me to close up the house; at least she would have realized how draining it was to walk back into those rooms on Staten Island — I wanted to drop on that sofa and stay there, perhaps forever. But Mama Day, arms akimbo, put me right to work — A house that's been sitting for three months needs a good cleaning. And it was the oddest feeling, as if we'd just left that morning. My bathrobe was still in a pile on the floor, a few hairs in the sink from when you had shaved, there was even a sprinkling of coffee grounds on the kitchen counter. Straightening it all up, I knew you had to be coming back in that evening. Instinctively, I reached out to stop her from moving your slippers near the bed — No, George will get angry. He likes his things just so — until I *heard* the thought. In silence, I let her move them. And in the silence of our room that night, it wasn't hard to return to the belief that you would still be coming back. I always slept alone that time of year — wasn't this the playoff season? But when I got no long-distance call in the morning to tell me what some team I never cared about had scored, I became suspicious of the order in our house. Could it be possible that you weren't going to open that mail stacked so neatly on the table? After all, I was reading my half and paying the overdue bills. And the thank-you notes I was sending out for all those sympathy cards — well, I had the better handwriting. But those official-looking letters from your accountant, lawyer, and insurance company addressed to Mrs. George Andrews — a name I rarely answered to. Maybe it was just a typographical error; they would just have to sit there for you to handle.

When it finally hit, it hit hard. And it took something as simple as a brochure from the Wallace P. Andrews Shelter for Boys — a friendly reminder that your annual contribution hadn't been received for that year. You see, this was one check that you wrote out yourself and nothing made it late. If Grandma had been there, she would have held me when I broke down and cried. Mama Day only said that for a long time there would be something to bring on tears aplenty; but she was saving her comfort for the day when I had stopped crying for myself and would have that one final cry — for you. God, I thought her cruel. How could my grief be about anything but you?

It took me years to know what she meant. I certainly didn't know as we packed up your things, and any crazy object would set me off: a spare button, a box of drafting pencils, a worn envelope with errands scratched on it — you name it. And the ones I thought would hurt — our wedding quilt, the calfskin and gold-leafed copy of *King Lear* I bought for one of your birthdays, your collection of football programs — all got crated up without a whimper. Then there were the things I couldn't touch at all: the medicine cabinet, for one, and dozens of photographs, which Mama Day sorted through and kept for herself. No, I didn't want to see any of them. I didn't want anything from that house but my clothes and a few personal belongings. The wedding ring I wore was enough from you to keep.

We were going to be loaded down coming back to Willow Springs anyway. Mama Day had cashed in the touring tickets I bought her and took the ferry over to do her own sightseeing — can you imagine? With all I had to worry about, there she was, wandering through the streets alone, dragging in shopping bags full of junk souvenirs from Woolworth's. Plastic ashtrays shaped like footprints, Mario Cuomo dolls, drinking cups from the hollowed-out head of the Statue of Liberty, "Hug Me — I'm Jewish" T-shirts. She said she'd give them away along with her ginger cookies for Candle Walk. I tried to tell her that what she saw in midtown was not New York, when she jumped in to tell me that the man who owned that little coffee and sandwich shop squeezed in between all them high risers — just offa Broadway or thereabouts — why, it had been in his family for three generations. And she had written down the recipe for his mama's homemade sausage. And surely I remembered that there woman we passed last week, sitting near the railroad station, the one with the red umbrella — she used to be an opera singer. And down in all them tattered bags she had a picture of herself shaking hands with the head of Carnegie Hall. Told her all about the place — Lincoln Center, too — so it was one stop she didn't have to bother to make. No, she'd seen plenty of New York right in midtown to last her. Any city is the people, ain't it? And she finally realized how I'd found somebody like you: New York was full of right nice folks.

I didn't have the heart to bring up the drugs and twelve-year-old prostitutes in Times Square, the dark subway corridors where she could have gotten her throat cut for the spare change in her pocketbook, the filthy shelters that made her opera singer prefer the rainy streets. But I should have known that Mama Day had taken all of that into account as well. I'm sorry to say that I couldn't stay up in New York — and I say it each time, don't I — but I know how much that city meant to you. And because it meant so much, it was a constant reminder that you weren't with me. It was a relief to leave for good.

◇◇◇

ANOTHER Candle Walk. This one's gonna be a bit sparse, there being more than our share of troubles this year, what with the hurricane and losing crops, some even losing their jobs beyond the bridge. And it ain't ever easy watching the young pass on, the life that Little Caesar never started or Cocoa's husband finished. Still, it ain't about chalking up 1985, just jotting it down in a ledger to be tallied with the times before and the times after. We figure it'll all even out in the end. And to get on to the end means going through this Candle Walk night. Rainy and drizzly, a fog creeping in from the marsh that's just downright cold. More sniffling and coughing than talk and laughter out on the main road — but folks is on the main road, if it's only with kerosene lamps, flashlights, here and there a sparkler.

Most everybody stops by Miss Abigail's to leave a little something for Cocoa, been a long while since she been home for the holiday.

Looking kinda drawn and tired, but she's out on the porch with a candle in her hand. Rainy or clear, the Days always use candles and they always walk a stretch of the road, at least to the bridge junction. Inside the house Miranda and Abigail are gathering up their gifts and umbrellas. Miranda done taken red ribbon and tied little packets of ginger cookies around them souvenirs she brought back from the city. Folks lucky enough to get one will be sure to prize 'em. It ain't often you're able to display a genuine product from a place like New York. She's got a nice paperweight for Bernice and Ambush; when you shake it up snowflakes fall all over the Empire State Building. And when you stand on top of that building, she tells Abigail, you kinda see the world the way God must see it — everything's able to be cupped into the palm of your hand. Them big cities should have big buildings, with all that plenty around them — it gives folks a chance to keep things in perspective. Too much plenty for some, Miranda says, and not enough for others. Did she tell her about that street that's got nothing but rows and rows of movie houses? She done told Abigail a dozen times, but now she lets her know that she actually went into one.

"Them sinful places?"

"It ain't all that way, Abigail. In some of 'em they show the same kind of movies that they do in the theater beyond the bridge. And with the others, no one's begging you to go in. It wasn't their fault I thought something called *The Milkman and the Old Maid* was gonna be an innocent picture. I figured, what could an old spinster like me be doing? Well, Lord, she used that sour cream for everything under the sun."

"I can imagine."

"No, you can't. I sat through the darn thing twice just to be sure I could believe my own eyes."

"Miranda, are you always gonna be wicked? Let's get on out here for Candle Walk. Baby Girl is waiting." Sighing, she gathers up the rest of her gifts and looks at the door like she can't bring herself to start.

"She's gonna make it, Abigail."

"I wasn't just thinking about tonight."

"But tonight is all any of us got."

It's the three of them under two umbrellas with Cocoa in the middle as they take the stretch toward the bridge junction. Bunched together, so it's hard to say who's holding who up when one stumbles in the fog. But it's Cocoa who keeps the matches dry in her coat pocket to relight the candles that the cold wind keeps blowing out. Not much talk between 'em, and the echoes of "Lead on with light" from the passing figures in the dense night get a muffled return behind their raised coat collars.

"I want to go back," Cocoa says, hands trembling from a little more than the chill as she stops to relight the candles.

"Then we'll all go back," Miranda says.

"No, don't let me spoil your fun."

"Ain't none here to spoil on a night like this," Abigail says. "We'll go make up a pot of ginger toddy to warm folks without as much sense as we got."

"It's called Candle Walk," Miranda says, "so we done got a candle and we done walked. Tradition is fine, but you gotta know when to stop being a fool."

"You don't have to do this for me . . ."

"Unless your name is rheumatism, we ain't doing it for you."

When they get to the house, Miranda tells 'em to go on in, she'll be there shortly, it's something she wants from her trailer. Only Abigail notices that she keeps her candle with her, and when she looks over her shoulder, Miranda and the umbrella done disappeared through the trees at the mouth of the west woods. Abigail starts to call out — this year she had it in her heart to go with her — but the mist closes quickly over her sister's back.

The candle don't light nothing but Miranda's face as she makes her way by touch to the circle of oaks surrounding the family plot. She reaches up for just a tad of damp moss to put in her shoes. And then she makes her way by smell toward the wind coming off The Sound to pass them graves and get to a little rise where the water is visible on clear days. George done made it possible for all her Candle Walks to end right here from now on; the other place holds no more secrets that's left for her to find. The rest will lay in the hands of the Baby Girl — once she learns how to listen. But she's grieving for herself too much now to hear, 'cause she thinks that boy done left her. He's gone, but he ain't left her. Naw, another one who broke his heart 'cause he couldn't let her go. So she's gotta get past the grieving for what she lost, to go on to the grieving for what was lost, before the child of Grace lives up to her name.

Miranda holds her candle in the direction of the waters that carry his ashes: I can tell you now about this here night. You done opened that memory for us. My daddy said that his daddy said when he was young, Candle Walk was different still. It weren't about no candles, was about a light that burned in a man's heart. And folks would go out and look up at the stars — they figured his spirit had to be there, it was the highest place they knew. And what took him that high was his belief in right, while what buried him in the ground was the lingering taste of ginger from the lips of a woman. He had freed 'em all but her, 'cause, see, she'd never been a slave. And what she gave of her own will, she took away. I can't tell you her name, 'cause it was never opened to me. That's a door for the child of Grace to walk through. And how many, if any, of them seven sons were his? Well, that's also left for her to find. And you'll help her, won't you? she says to George. One day she'll hear you, like you're hearing me. And there'll be another time — that I won't be here for — when she'll learn about the beginning of the Days. But she's gotta go away to come back to that kind of knowledge. And I came to tell you not to worry: whatever roads take her from here, they'll always lead her back to you.

◇◇◇

You're never free from such a loss. It sits permanently in your middle, but it gets less weighty as time goes on and becomes endurable. So there were days I wasn't even aware that it was there until it might highlight or deepen my understanding of some moment in the life I was still privileged to be living. I found it one of those twisted ironies that the New England Patriots did get to the Super Bowl that season. I watched the game to celebrate for you, finally understanding that the outcome wouldn't have meant as much as the event.

I couldn't hide in Willow Springs forever. But I knew New York was out of the question. It was easier in Charleston: we'd never been there together, and I drew strength from moving in the midst of familiar ground. Enough strength to build around — and on — that vacant center in me. You left it so I'd never have to work, but I did. And I didn't have to reach out again, but after three years, I did. And he's really a decent guy. I think you would like him. Mama Day even likes him. A good second-best, she said. And she's not wrong, any man would have to come in second to you. There were some mistakes I didn't repeat. I allowed myself to see him for exactly what he was — no chance of being the best, but he's all that he can be. You wouldn't have asked any more of him than that. And he's never said a word about my coming here to see you, or even about my naming the youngest boy after you. But you know me — it wouldn't matter a damn if he did. I have two fine sons, George, and that was the least I could do to thank you for them.

And I worry sometimes because the youngest one is just like me. A quick temper and so flip at the mouth — I've had to backhand him a few times. And stubborn. I guess you'd call it poetic justice that I'm getting from your namesake a good measure of what you had to put up with. But he's a smart kid and more sensitive than his brother, who's the quieter one. When little George was hardly five years old, he asked me about his name. I told him that I had been married once before his father, to another special man. And he wanted to know if he'd been given your name because he looked like you. I told the poor kid no, he would have to go through life looking like his mother. That inevitably led to questions about what you did look like. And since we were in a shopping mall, I glanced around to find someone to point out to him. And it struck me — and I mean, struck me — that there was nothing about you that would have stood out in a crowd. And getting no answer, like any child, he kept pressing. Well, were you chocolate-skinned like his daddy? Or tall like his schoolteacher, Mr. Benjamin? Did you have big muscles? What color were your eyes? I was so confused, I told him that I would show him your picture when we got home.

I searched everywhere. There were none, George. And what I thought had become a light, airy space turned into an abyss opening up within me. All the painful adjustment during those eleven years had been for my life without you — the emphasis on my loss, my life — while a missing photograph shifted it over to a loss that was more than me, more than even you. I remembered that Mama Day had kept our photographs, and I simply phoned her to send me one of your pictures. Little George was curious about it, I said. And when she hesitated, saying she wasn't sure where she'd put them after all this time, that eternal emptiness yawned in front of me. My voice steadily rose. Couldn't she just look? Couldn't she just try? And to think of *what* was lost brought on the final tears. They were, as she had warned me, the most bitter. And with all I had built around me, I felt that I was in danger of being swallowed up inside the pain of the growing awareness that *it* was no more.

She listened patiently as I cried — no reasoning to anything I was saying — about how desperately I needed a picture of you. Not for myself, I had to show my son. And she still listened as I went on to accuse her of being neglectful of my things — I had trusted her. And if my grandmother were still alive, this wouldn't have happened. I didn't have anything, now that my grandmother was gone. Grandma always took care of my things. Oh, I went on and on — bitter tears. All the more so because they had been holding eleven years to come out. And when I was through, her voice was quiet and gentle. Cocoa, if the child wants to know what George looked like, the easiest thing to do is to tell him. And remember, children need the simple truth.

So after washing my face and making myself a cup of mint tea, I called my son inside. I put him on my lap and told him that he was named after a man who looked just like love. He frowned for a moment, tucking in his bottom lip in that peculiar way he has, and said, That's all? I couldn't trust myself to do anything but nod. Well, he loved the center of marshmallows, and he loved it when his daddy took him up high on the Ferris wheel, and when it got to be summer, he loved the way the water and sand felt between his toes — did you look like that? Yes, I told him, all of that.

Would you believe it — I'll be forty-seven next year. And I still don't have a photograph of you. It's a lot better this way, because you change as I change. And each time I go back over what happened, there's some new development, some forgotten corner that puts you in a slightly different light. I guess one of the reasons I've been here so much is that I felt if we kept retracing our steps, we'd find out exactly what brought us to this slope near The Sound. But when I see you again, our versions will be different still. All of that would have been too complicated to tell a child. Mama Day was right — give him the simple truth. And it's the one truth about you that I hold on to. Because what really happened to us, George? You see, that's what I mean — there are just too many sides to the whole story.

◇◆◇

SOME THINGS stay the same. August is August. The hot wind blowing through the palmettos coulda been coming in 1899 when she remembers her first taste of the sweet juices from an icy slice of honeydew. The quivering green slivers melt in a mouth that's a hundred years older, while the pleasure is fresh and new. The last time you're doing something — knowing you're doing it for the last — makes it even more alive than the first. It's her last slice of honeydew on any August twenty-first in that silver trailer, so she enjoys it slow. She lets the juices linger in the corner of her mouth before taking the paper napkin to wipe 'em away — her last time for doing that. It's with a deep satisfaction that she finally gets down to the rind. She don't scrape till the flesh becomes bitter, leave a little of the sweetness. She's had more than her share of enough.

Some things change. Taking up her walking stick, she hobbles out to the front yard and looks over at the yellow bungalow. No need to cross that road anymore, so she turns her face up into the warm air — You there, Sister? — to listen for the rustling of the trees. There's never a day so still that at least one leaf ain't moving. The circle of oaks is as far as she can make it, and it's abiding comfort that she can make it that far. She stops by a grave, here and there, to move aside a stray weed with the tip of her cane. She's always liked things neat, and when she's tied up the twentieth century, she'll take a little peek into the other side — for pure devilment and curiosity — and then leave for a rest that she deserves.

And some things are yet to be. She always finds her in the same place, sitting on the rise over The Sound. It's a slender body, but the hair is streaked with gray. And when she turns around, there are fine lines marking off the character of her face — the firm mouth, high cheekbones, and clear brown eyes. It's a face that's been given the meaning of peace. A face ready to go in search of answers, so at last there ain't no need for words as they lock eyes over the distance. Under a sky so blue it's stopped being sky, one is closer to the circle of oaks than the other. But both can hear clearly that on the east side of the island and on the west side, the waters were still.

N

W   E

S

T
H
E

SOUTH CAROLINA

GEORGIA

FRAMPTON